About the author

John Spencer has had much multicultural experience due to marriage, teaching, travel and years of living in the Philippines and other parts of Asia, has taught English in Australian high schools and overseas, has taught elementary school, has driven taxis in Sydney and on the Gold Coast, and has personally visited and researched the U.S. and U.K. locations featured in the novel. His formal education includes an honors degree in Philosophy and majors in English Literature and History along with a Dip.Ed.

His published work has included article-length pieces of fiction and non-fiction. Much of the non-fiction has been travel and business related (including a considerable amount in David Koch financial publications). His work has been published in Australia, the Philippines, Zimbabwe and the U.S.

As well as this first novel, *Brownout - 666 or the real meaning of the swastika*, John has written a book about the worst kind of grief, the loss of a child. This nonfiction work is titled, *Waiting for a Miracle - Life in the Dead Zone*. He has also produced a book of essays of a political, lifestyle and social nature about the current state of the world. It is titled, *From Brexit to Brazil via Hong Kong, China Russia and the USA*.

BROWNOUT

666

THE COMPELLING INSIDE STORY OF A MISGUIDED LIFE IN THE SEX AND DRUGS TRADE

Chapter One

An uncanny tone pierced the stifling tropical air. A brilliant flash tore the firmament asunder. Then, amidst the blasted debris, a deafening cacophony arose. The sudden arrival of a rocket-propelled grenade was all too apparent. Chilling screams and the acrid smell of burning flesh accompanied the shattering of glass. Smoke billowed from the second-floor balcony of the Intercontinental while a line of tanks cautiously surveyed the scene from the Paseo de Roxas. Swirling overhead in elongated circles WW II vintage warplanes, known as Tora Toras, were bombing Malacanuang Palace. The December sunshine competed with flashes of artillery fire while rebel soldiers took key installations, one after the other.

It was the second day of the coup against the yellow lady, Cory Aquino, who in 1989 was at the zenith of her power and folly. The wish of death had been palpably hanging over this otherwise idyllic paradise for a good many years. From high on verdant hills the fortresses of the privileged and wealthy gazed nonchalantly on the slums of the others below. Priests in their pulpits preached brotherly love, countless unwanted babies made their way into the world, the armies of beggars looked as hopeless as ever and virtually anything could be bought, or arranged, for a price. Yes, for the Philippines, it was almost business-as-usual.

Somehow rising to his feet in the blinding dust, the thirty-something, six-foot tall and slightly muscular Rick Daly strode over the detritus of the balcony and slipped inside the body of the building. He was too dazed to speak. He merely nodded in an inane fashion at every movement or gesture directed his way. After fifty meters or so an immovable obstacle made its existence known. The bar, surprisingly, still boasted intact bottles of whiskey along with surrogate promises. Habit or shock caused Rick to grab the first full bottle and pour a generous portion down his throat.

"Medics!" screamed the officer as the uniformed throng burst up the stairs. Amidst the confusion an arm emblazoned with the Red Cross insignia vainly attempted to relieve Rick of his bottle. "Where I come from people get killed for taking a man's drink but nobody gives a fuck who runs the country!"

"Puting tao" (white person), the medic mumbled and moved on. Unhurt, Rick made his way out of the scene of chaos and into a bar down the road.

It was another world, although not one with which Rick was entirely unfamiliar. Day was night, a sexual rock beat assaulted the ears and flashes of electronic light broke the darkness. Rick was back home. On the dimly lit stage a dozen nubile princesses gyrated. Flashy smiles, breasts itching to burst out of their skimpy bikini tops and curvaceous thighs all seemed to scream, "Pick me!" Rick's curly blond hair and azure eyes were a veritable magnet. No sooner had the war-zone survivor ordered a beer and plonked his ass on a stool than one of the brazen hussies catapulted off the stage, landed somehow on the next seat and with her hand stroking his left leg, gazed into his eyes and insisted on announcing her presence.

"Hi, I'm Maybellene. What's your name?" Rick answered but before the word had even reached her ears another salvo was fired. "Where you come from? You are very handsome."

"Australia, sort of," he replied while checking that his wallet was still there. This girl, having a semblance of decency, grabbed his left hand and pushed it deep into the fluff hiding below the edge of her bikini panty before asking for a lady's' drink. Rick considered that 150 pisos was a reasonable sacrifice for a bit of quiet. Besides, the hot body climbing all over him matched his cold beer nicely. "Why are you girls still here?" he mumbled. "Aren't you worried about being killed in all this fighting?"

Maybellene smiled, adjusting her bikini top to show its occupants to best possible advantage.

"The wars of the rich people don't really interest us. For the poor, surviving each day is a victory. Without money I don't have a life. So I must dance."

The continuing explosions were at least three kilometers away so Rick figured she had a point. He cut short Maybellene's life history by buying her another lady's drink, having heard enough of the tragedy of her family: aunt in hospital, father murdered while driving a taxi, sister afflicted with a rare and incurable illness. Her hands then promptly took over from where her mouth had left off. The remaining dancers worked even harder on the stage to the strains of Madonna's 'Like a Virgin.' In a desperate attempt to impress the three customers, bras were lowered and panties tugged to expose prize assets.

By nightfall on the second day the coup was going very well. Elite rebel brigades had taken some TV and radio stations with hardly a shot fired while entire companies of government troops had surrendered to their brothers. Cigarette vendors plied their wares to the passing jeepneys, beggars cried poor and shop girls reported for work. Those in the piso economy, if even slightly removed from immediate danger, saw the struggle as being above and entirely separate from them.

After the bombing of Malacanuang, Cory Aquino emerged from under her bed screaming. "Where are my soldiers? How dare these upstarts disturb our lives and our duty? Where are the Americans?"

"Your Excellency," replied her adjutant, "we are doing the best we can and may I remind you that you yourself demanded not two months ago that the Americans stay out of Filipino affairs." The yellow lady minced her way to her desk, looking decidedly pale.

The warm flesh of Maybellene and a large handle of cold San Miguel kept Rick focused on more earthy matters. Escapism, maybe but it was a very pleasant removal from the dull ache of daily life. The disco lights of The Box Office pulsated for all they were worth, the beat increased in intensity and the girls on show gyrated even harder. Filipinas generally have good breasts, flattish noses and shapely thighs while their butts are less generous than many. Cupping his companion's now exposed left breast in one hand and nurturing his beer in the other Rick's mind began to wander.

Beer, girls and most of the good things in life have similarities but subtle differences around this globe, he thought. Savoring differences is one of life's great joys. Rio, Manila and Bangkok might all be sexy slums but no matter how drunk or debauched you are you always know which one you are in at the time.

Some ten years before Rick had been holidaying in Bangkok. The coffee shop in the Grace Hotel was all it had been cracked up to be; a vast darkish space broken by a dance floor, scattered tables and hundreds of Thai girls who seemed to almost swirl in formation and swoop at every opportunity. A trim waitress showed Rick to a table. "Singha beer or Mekong whisky? Mekong is cheaper."

"That's a turnaround," he mumbled. "Give us a bottle of Mekong and some cola to go with it please." Fifty baht later and the killer spirit, guaranteed to be less than one month old, arrived. He had only a minute or so to notice that the guys were not circling and eyeballing a static selection of womanhood, as was usually the case in Western bars. The male customers seemed decidedly nonchalant.

A couple of quick drinks and he was getting the feel of the joint. "Excuse me Sir, may I join you?" A pair of dark almond eyes gazed earnestly into his. The eyes belonged to a very stunning and slender lass of around eighteen. Prok Porntit announced herself in a soft manner that, if it did not exactly belie, didn't do justice to her character. "Certainly, please sit down," came Rick's perfunctory answer hiding his natural joy at being approached by one of the most lovely women he had ever seen. It's difficult to be polite in a sexually charged, hunting zone but in the face of such beauty it occurred naturally.

"Is this your first time in Bangkok?" the smiling Prok inquired in surprisingly good English. "Yes," answered Rick, "I'm on holiday and have been cruising around the region. I arrived by train from Singapore this morning." He was determinedly avoiding the "Do you come here often?" line when the girl started talking about herself. "I'm a student at the university and I come here sometimes to mix with foreigners and practice my English. Most of these girls around you are hunting girls trying to support poor families. Once one of them has cornered you no-one else would dare talk to you for fear of trouble."

"Interesting euphemism," Rick pondered, "especially for such determined young ladies of the evening."

"My father's a very successful businessman," Prok stated proudly. "I'm lucky. For me this disco world is just for fun. My family is very modern and I can do as I like." A deliciously wicked thought germinated in Rick's mind but he didn't let it show. Her smooth-colored skin and shoulder-length raven hair offset the girl's gleaming teeth nicely. "What kind of work do you do?"

"I'm a high-school teacher. It's a living, just," Rick mumbled.

"Teaching is a highly respected profession. You must know a lot," his companion mouthed softly. "Not where I come from," frowned Rick. "It's sort of like being a policeman without a gun, surrounded by criminals."

"May I share your Mekong and Coke?" Prok inquired as she began pouring. "What country are you from?"

"It's a long story," replied the mesmerized schoolteacher. "I was born in the States but my father was in the army and we spent eight years in England before ultimately settling in Sydney, Australia."

"What subject do you teach?" asked the girl. When Rick told her that he taught English her face lit up.

There is something about the Grace. The atmosphere could best be described as 'instant falling in love.' Rick felt it, a little in his heart perhaps but certainly in his loins. In a Sydney pub or disco he could only dream about getting to grips with a girl as lovely as this. When reality exceeds your wildest dreams there are no words to describe the joy. Without even noticing the docks, one's ship has come in. The smoke polluted confines of this meeting point have generated such ecstatic feelings in many thousands of Western hearts over the years.

As the night wore on and the beat became louder Prok's allure seemed more urgent. On the dance floor she held Rick tight and he could feel her energy seeking him out. The tenderest of sighs and the teasing touch of gentle fingers spoke their secrets. The Grace never closes but does experience the natural ebb and flow of humanity. An internal chime of three in the morning tends to see great numbers depart to their beds, alone in some cases but more often than not, in pairs.

Summoning the courage, both natural and Mekong-fueled, Rick looked at his watch and thence into Prok's eyes. "It's getting late. Where would you like to go now?"

"With you!" Eighteen or not, the girl exuded a look approaching bewilderment.

"My hotel is only a three star," stammered Rick, feeling rather stupid, "but let's go."

A grinning taxi driver dropped them at the high gates of The Surayami and sped off in a cloud of poisonous fumes. Out of nervousness Rick immediately turned on the TV after opening his door. An attractive girl, a little less alluring than his prize, was advertising the prowess of a laundry detergent, designed for hand washing, that would not only save money but wouldn't damage the hands of the servants too much.

Hitting the power button on the television and killing its raucous chatter Prok turned to face Rick and removed her shirt. An expression of amazement and admiration flashed across Rick's face. The disposal of her bra revealed very full, ripe breasts for such a young Asian girl. When she discarded her blue jeans her body was only clothed in beige, bikini briefs. The ceiling fan seemed, for a second, to beat louder in the incessant heat.

Prok kissed the vacationing schoolteacher hard on the mouth, at the same time stripping him of his pedestrian clothing. Gently dragging Rick on to the bed she began to kiss random parts of his body. When Rick removed her panties he was faced with half a dozen black hairs guarding a pink gold mine. With Rick's onslaught the mine began leaching moisture and as the bodies intertwined, the laundry maid's worst nightmares were realized. Prok's finger nails razed Rick's back as his hands pressed deep into her firm buttocks. Several times in the early morning that tight Thai pussy experienced a happy Western invasion. It was difficult for such sustained lust to break for lunch but normalcy is part of life.

Over a seafood-platter of prawns, oysters and particularly dead lobsters Rick and Prok acted like newlyweds. The illustrious Mr. Daly still had two weeks of holidays left and he cold bloodedly calculated that these would be better spent with this goddess than in hunting for other offerings. "Prok, if you would like to and your family don't mind, how about coming with me to Pattaya for a fortnight?" Rick's question was answered in the affirmative and it was arranged. A less than elegant bus ride saw the couple arrive in the land of sea and good times.

With the assistance of the Thai girl at his side, Rick found a surprisingly cheap guesthouse not more than two hundred meters from the shore. For a lad from the suburbs of Sydney it was total nirvana – a honeymoon without the downside of getting married. The hot tropical sun oversaw their commerce with peddlers while the soft blue waves cooled their bodies at play. The thatched roof of their cottage with its methodical ceiling fan witnessed countless couplings as the bodies formed, broke and formed again. Just as tiring as teaching but a damn sight more pleasant, Rick pondered while rolling over in his sleep.

One afternoon, after a quick dip in the sea, the 'newlyweds' were lying on their bed, the ceiling fan keeping time. Prok hadn't been secretive about her past. In her fourth year of high school she had been sold the sausage-inspired promise of a good-looking fellow student. After that, with a cooler head, she chose her lovers with more discretion. In the tepid heat of the late afternoon she found the desire to inquire further about her darling's life.

"Have you had many girlfriends?" the naked Thai girl ventured, hoping not to disturb even the fan. "Nothing to speak of," answered Rick, wishing to defuse this sort of conversation. His rolling over and snorts failed in their attempt. "You must have had a girlfriend in high school or college!" stated Prok, her proud breasts leaning over her subject.

"I can do better than that! I had a very cute girlfriend in elementary school called Janine. We were both five and it was going swimmingly until she peed her pants and the teacher made her walk round the yard holding her dress up at lunch time. The humiliation just killed it! Later when I was eight and all the other boys went through the girl hating stage, I was the most popular boy in school with up to forty girlfriends who would follow me round. My favourite was Kerry Howell, despite her freckles and her being two years my senior. I actually got to hold her hand once."

"Cut the crap!" echoed the repartee in superb English. "What girlfriends did you sleep with? – You know, penetrate, fuck!" Foreigners tend to use English swear words like they have a 'use by' date and the luscious Prok was no exception. Rick tried fake snoring again but within thirty seconds a vicious pinch on his backside alerted him to its failure. "You really want the sad story of the death of my illusions about love do you? It'll take a while and I would like a coffee."

Rather than scratching him, Prok amazingly complied. The kettle was on the boil and for a few seconds it seemed that all was right with the world. The coffee materialized. "Well! What girls have you slept with?" Rick coughed and suggested a shot of Mekong in his coffee. Why are women always like this? The thought fleeted across his mind before he grudgingly admitted that he knew the answer. There is some bad karma about being male and we will always be made to pay for it.

As he sipped his hypo coffee and tried to drift away a violent pinch on his family jewels brought him to attention. When all else fails, there is nothing like the truth. If she doesn't like it too much she'll just piss off.

"You really want to hear the saga of my sex life, then?" Rick murmured, hoping to be met with a negative silence. Given that Thai girls are renowned for their jealousy this was an extremely vain hope. "Start talking!" A gorgeous naked Thai girl could turn into a vicious interrogator in the twinkling of an eye. Hoping for the best Mr. Daly reverted his memory to when he was just seventeen.

"It was my first year of university and I was struck by the vision of the most beautiful girl I had ever seen; blonde hair, blue eyes, medium height, slim figure and with the greatest pair of legs imaginable. Her name was Brenda and she was one of those born-again Christian types. The cruelty was intense. In my mid-year English exam who should be seated at the next table but this goddess. I think she got an A but I failed and had to re-sit the exam at the end of the year. Amazingly I passed it but the next several years were haunted by this highly sexual and flesh-perfect version of the ultimate Christian girl. Every time she passed me in a corridor or on the campus lawn, or entered a room I died inside. My heart demanded to scream out, 'I love you!' but my social insecurity prevented this from actually occurring."

"You got to screw this girl, didn't you?" Prok's jealousy ventured. "I wish," replied Rick. "I think she liked me in a way but I was never old or big enough for what she needed. I asked her out to the motorcycle races once and I had never heard such a polite laugh of refusal." Actually sounding a little sympathetic, the still very naked Miss Porntit thrust her breasts forward and inquired further. "You never made it with this chick?" A look made of tears accompanied Rick's answer. "Just when I had given up I happened to be talking to Brenda on one of the university balconies. We were both studying

Shakespearian Tragedies and one of the relevant productions was happening in our city. When the goddess asked if I was going to see it, I deferred an answer. Any red-blooded man would have begged her to accompany him but I just said, 'Maybe.' Even now that answer haunts me. What might have been if I'd been able to show more courage?"

"You little virgin!" Prok jumped on Rick again, licking him all over. He'd just about thought he'd gotten away with it when she ceased her sensual kissing. "God! That's your first broken heart but nothing happened! Get real. I just want to know!"

"Ok. Ok. I'll cut to the chase. There was this really tall girl, nice and intelligent but guys seemed to ignore her. She was a perfect height for me and gave me some sort of a look when I talked to her about studies and all that. Louise was a stunning well-proportioned blonde, just a couple of inches shorter than me. However she was in second year while I was only a freshman and I just didn't dare suggest anything. Seven years later I even passed her on the street and when we nodded recognition I still failed to act."

Prok, quite impatient by this time grabbed Rick's slumbering member and tweaked it with a vengeance. "When did you get your first fuck? Never mind the missed chances, odd fingerings and heartaches!" Was she a student of sex after all? Rick pondered in between spasms of terror.

"Some seventeen years ago when I was barely eighteen I got lucky, quite by chance you know."

"What do you mean, by chance?" Prok's gaze caused Rick to wish that, for once, he were lying alone. "Well, I was trying to sell a motorcycle that I had. I'd put up ads all-round the campus. The only reply I received was from this one girl. First she was all over the bike then she was all over me. What more can I say?"

"Details," squawked Prok. "Describe what happened."

"She played sort of hard to get at first. I remember tugging at her nightie and her challenging me as to my intentions. I tossed a coin and laughed, 'Heads I get the nightie and tails I get you.' The coin miraculously landed 'tails, the nightie was discarded and I began to lose my virginity. When pubic hair touched pubic hair and nothing happened I was introduced to the technicalities of making love. 'You'll have to push,' instructed my more experienced and redheaded sex companion. Push I did and some minutes later I was sure that I had finally discarded every teenage boy's curse."

Prok's breasts seemed to enlarge and her nipples distend. "I knew you were no innocent but you've had lots of girls. Who was your second?" Rick, rapidly growing tired of this, described his conquest of, or seduction by, a couple more females who attended his college. "You are certainly a shy one. I'm surprised you ever made it to the Grace," the girl ventured, flexing her buttocks as she bent to kiss Rick on the neck. "I never really thought about it much," came the retort. "I was so unpopular in school that I was lucky if I was picked for the Z grade baseball or football team. I guess that I just grew out of it, a bit."

Happily, at this point, Prok abandoned her questioning and, rubbing her gently furred pubic mound against Rick's appendage, aroused another round of passion from her subject. Sunset saw the pair dining in true romantic style at a palm-studded, open-air restaurant on the edge of the sea. They passed on the local disco and evening merged into night. Once again they fell asleep in each other's arms.

The following day was particularly magical and memorable. Prok had woken first and taken a stroll along the seashore. She returned clutching a handful of incandescent shells. By the time Rick rubbed his blurry eyes he was presented with a simple but charming necklace. The two lovers spent the next hours singing in the sea, playing hide and seek in the palms and gazing into each other's eyes. Forget nirvana, Rick thought to himself, this'll do me.

That evening, after dinner, they decided to sample Pattaya's nightlife. The first few bars were of the girlie variety and didn't impress his Thai nymph. When they arrived at the 'Thai Heaven,' a Western style disco favored by foreigners and party-going locals alike, Prok warmed up. On the dance floor she worked her body into a sweat as the fast beat played and during the slower numbers clung to her man as ivy does to a wall.

At 4 a.m. the schoolteacher and his exotic companion returned to their bungalow. Both were rather inebriated by this time and foregoing the usual 'honeymoon' indulgences, fell fast asleep. The sun was already full in the sky when Rick regained consciousness. He sat bolt upright. Next to him where the shapely brown princess should have been, was an empty space. A bad feeling welled up in his gut. "Prok, darling. Where are you?" Only the geckoes clicking as they chased mosquitoes along the walls broke the silence. As his gaze reached the far corner of the room Rick realized that all Prok's belongings were gone! The door to their room was still locked and there was no sign of any intrusion.

His heart sank. The explanation was as obvious as it was cruel. He'd been deserted. To add insult to injury, Rick discovered that he'd been robbed. His wallet was gone, his emergency cash supply that had been tucked into a money belt and all of his travelers' checks.

As Rick flew out from Sukumpang Airport he was a chastened and wiser man. A damaged heart and injured wallet ensured that this was one vacation he would never forget. "What did you do in Thailand, Sir?" a particularly attractive Year 11 girl demanded in only the second class of his time back in the knowledge factory. "Buddhist temples and great experiences such as the Floating Market kept me pretty busy," smiled the teacher. A low level of sniggering in the class suggested that he was not entirely believed.

The sound of close by gunshots awoke Rick from his delusional sojourn. Maybellene grabbed him in the crotch hard. "The bar is going to close because of trouble," she indicated. "Quick, give me 800 pisos to pay my bar fine so we can go!"

"What's this bar fine then? – some kind of girlie tax on foreigners?"

"How long have you been in Manila, two minutes?" shrieked the girl? "If you want me to go with you money has to be paid to the owners of the bar." Rick had, in fact, been in Manila only three days, but although the lingo was different the financial meaning was the same. A very fast handover of colored paper saw Maybellene, now fully clothed, and Rick emerge onto the street.

"I don't think my hotel is currently an option," muttered Rick pointing to the smoke rising in the distance. "All right, we'll go to my place," answered the girl in a hurry, "although it's a slum compared with where you are accustomed to staying." In the minute or so while the two of them were standing on the pavement they had managed to catch the attention of a group of shabbily dressed young men. "Hey Joe! Malaki otin and maraming peira. Ang puta ni sayu ay sobra pungit! Fuck you Joe!" Rick didn't understand the references to having a big dick and a lot of money or the fact that the girl he was with was assumed to be a prostitute, and an ugly one at that. However the 'Fuck you Joe' phrase did provoke a reaction. Before he had time to even think about it however Maybellene finalized their escape.

She quickly hailed a passing jeepney and the pair clambered on.

"What were those guys saying?" he asked. "They were certainly angry about something but why did they call me Joe?" A schoolgirl sitting opposite them failed to stifle a serious giggle. Maybellene thought that she had better educate this simple foreigner.

"A cultural given of this country says that all white people are Americans and are very rich. You can explain all you like that you might be neither but nobody wants to listen." A few more sniggers from the schoolgirl and polite amusement from the other passengers saw the entire subject descend into silence. After what seemed an eternity and four pisos, they alighted at what appeared to Rick to be little more than a renovated rubbish dump.

The jeepney had been forced to take a more circuitous route than usual in order to avoid being caught up in the fighting. A journey of less than an hour had taken closer to two. However long the ride was, it wasn't sufficient to bridge the gap between Rick's expectations and what he found. Maybellene took him by the hand and led him past open sewers, an abundance of scattered rubbish, and crowds of young folk with dubious intentions along a muddy pathway through the brick-a-brack of life in all its gory color. If the girl hadn't been good looking the very smell of the surroundings would have caused Rick to turn tail and run. This was not exactly the playground of the good life.

They traversed a long plank over an expansive and putrid puddle, ascended a couple of steps and entered into a two-room wooden shanty. The small anteroom that greeted them served as a meagre cooking area and mini lounge. It was almost sunset and a slanting flicker of light pointed to the room at the back with its small wooden bed and bedraggled mosquito net.

Maybellene gestured to Rick to sit down in one of two rattan chairs and poured two glasses of rum and cola. Perched on a bare table in the sparsely furnished space was a tiny transistor radio. "Although I don't care much about it," she said, "You might want to hear some news of the coup." Her guest turned the device on and began to flip stations.

"This is New Philippines radio announcing the successful takeover of large portions of the capital along with many provincial centers. Our brothers and sisters are rallying to our cause." Rick found another station with a different slant. "Radio 3BQ Manila, the voice of the nation, reports that the serious disturbance begun by a small band of renegade soldiers is rapidly being contained. We expect the unrest to be swiftly resolved." The broadcast then went dead leaving only the sound of crackling.

The skyline in two directions, the nearest being about fifteen kilometers away, offered a surreal setting of the sun with the usual red and gold being augmented by the smoky black of unresolved strife.

"I hope the new government is a little more friendly to foreigners," laughed Rick. Maybellene then cooked some rice and served it with dried fish. It wasn't the tastiest meal he had ever enjoyed but he wasn't going to say anything.

After the dinner, the bargirl took Rick by the hand and led him into the second room with its little wooden bed and mosquito net. She didn't speak. She just slipped out of her blue floral dress and discarded a rather worn brassiere. Her white panties offset her dusky skin and she looked every inch the temptress. Rick quickly disrobed and embraced her, kissing her full on the mouth. She pulled him onto the hard bed and slipped her cotton briefs down her legs and gently dropped them on the floor. Her badge of womanhood sported a modest amount of thick black hair that formed an almost perfect triangle. Maybellene's slender body was taut and muscular, the product of countless hours of dancing. With only a modicum of preliminary teasing she pushed Rick onto his back, took hold of his erect appendage and guided it into her moist hole.

Their lovemaking seemed to last for hours until, out of a sated and pleasurable exhaustion they both slipped into unconsciousness. By this time an ominous full moon had made its appearance in the blackened sky. Less than twenty kilometers away a rebel-armored column had surrounded the

Channel 4 television station. A supporting infantry unit was throwing small arms fire at the second floor of the administration building.

A white flag waved violently from one of the windows and the shooting stopped. "We wish to surrender!" a voice urgently shouted over a megaphone. Within ten minutes an entire company of loyal troops had filed out of the building and entrusted themselves to their rebellious comrades.

While the prisoners and their new comrades were fraternizing Captain Enrico Vere spoke rapidly into his radio. "Colonel Honasan, we've taken the TV station with no casualties as the other side surrendered without a fight. What should we do with the prisoners?" Honasan, from his mobile headquarters, snapped back, "Use your brains man! Quickly interview each of them and then integrate their entire unit with our forces. Obviously, if they didn't fight, they agree with our cause."

"Yes Sir." Captain Vere's detachment was a hundred stronger within the hour.

In some parts of the capital resistance was somewhat more spirited and soldiers died on both sides. Yet very few of the military men, or the general population for that matter, had any great love for President Cory. Her glory days when the so-called 'People Power' revolution swept her to power over the 3,000 abandoned pairs of shoes belonging to Imelda Marcos were long over. This woman, who came from one of the richest and hence presumably most corrupt families in the entire country, claimed a false humility when she took office.

"I am but a humble housewife," she'd said. "I will try to learn the art of governance in order to help the Filipino people." While it is true that the new president kept some priests busy with her regular confessions and constant need for reassurance she was hardly a normal housewife. Notwithstanding the fact that her husband had been dead some three years by the time of the People Power revolution she had never washed a dish in her entire life. Very seldom does a mere housewife lay claim to a hundred personal servants and thousands of hectares of lands, in addition to an abundance of the green stuff.

As dawn emerged on the third day Colonel 'Gringo' Honasan was feeling emboldened and confident. The yellow lady, in contrast, was demonstrating an alternating habit for prayer and bursts of abuse at her staff for failing the Filipino people in their hour of need. As advance rebel units came within ten kilometers of her palace her converse with God included reference to the Americans and their airfield at Clark. Gone were all nationalistic thoughts demanding their absence from Philippine politics. Cory, although not a great fan of telephones, spent more than two hours on the instrument.

"General Ramos, what can we do now?"

"Mrs. Aquino, our forces are assuming defensive positions around the remaining key strategic points and all we have to do is hold. As you should know, if a coup attempt does not entirely succeed within a matter of days it swiftly dies a natural death."

"It's looking like we will be overrun within another day or so," the pale lady replied. "I'm not too worried," smiled General Ramos. "We have one more ace to play yet!"

Maybellene awoke before Rick. The unbridled noise of her three-year-old son Filippe caused her to raise her head. "Putang inay mo! Get back to bed now!" The irony of calling her son's mother a prostitute was lost on her. Her temporary lover left the Land of Nod when he smelled the stench of sardines and rice. "Breakfast!" The dance-floor contortionist fancied herself an ideal cook and homemaker. Grudgingly, her lover of the previous night performed the necessary social rites of passage forcing the offered victuals down his throat.

"Thanks for the food, you're a talented girl Maybellene." Rick chewed with that slow, deadly munch of one undergoing a great ordeal. "You spoke in the bar of your family but you live alone. Where are they?"

"In the province," answered the girl. "I'm from Quezon, about 150 kilometers south of here. It's considered a dangerous area you know. After the death of my father I came to Manila to work as a maid so I could send money home but a maid's salary couldn't even support me properly, let alone my family." On seeing Filippe Rick inquired as to his care when Maybellene was working. "He goes to a neighbor's house," she said. "Knowing I was here she must have let him in during the early morning."

Rick continued his reluctant chewing, not wanting to get further into the subject "Why did you come to Manila? You don't look like a tourist."

"I'm on my way to Cebu to set up a business; furniture manufacture and export. The opportunities there are very promising." The girl laughed. So many of her customers had spoken of grandiose plans and ideas. "What did you do in Australia?" she inquired. "I was a high school teacher until a few years ago and since then I have had several jobs, including security and being a salesman."

"Sounds to me like a step down on the ladder," Maybellene commented. "You didn't like teaching?" Rick mumbled a few comments about it not being brilliant for his health and promptly changed the subject.

His instant paramour politely offered him a coffee to wash down his breakfast and served it to him on the ramshackle excuse for a porch. To his surprise, the obnoxious youths gathered around were not paying any attention to him. They were all staring at the sky. A Tora Tora fighter had just completed a bombing run on Malacanuang and was climbing into the soft clouds. The explosion was as brilliant as it was loud. The Tora Tora had been vaporized. A sonic boom echoed over the enthralled onlookers below and the silver flash of an F16 flying at low level seared across the sky. The Americans had intervened.

When Rick had finished his coffee, Maybellene announced that she was going to do some shopping before reporting to work. As a gesture of politeness, she gave him her address scrawled on a scrap of paper and escorted him to the road. He hailed a taxi and, after checking with the driver, proceeded back to the Intercontinental.

The damage was still highly visible but the hotel appeared to be operating almost normally. Rick took his key, went to his room to shower and change and re-emerged on the lobby level to take his customary place at one of the bars.

"Bourbon and Coke please." The bartender was relatively quick to oblige since Rick was the only customer. "What on earth is with this country?" Rick simply couldn't help himself. "It's like a volcanic landscape," replied the bartender as he placed his customer's drink before him. "Every now and then there is an eruption, some excitement and minor changes in the layout of the place. However, nothing ever really changes here. The cultural mores and some of the perversities in this country are more intransigent than logic itself. Why do you think so many Filipinos will sell their souls to get out of the joint?"

"I understand that Marcos was stealing the place blind and that Cory is some kind of super rich idiot but isn't Gringo Honasan's coup designed to make fundamental and positive changes? Could I have another bourbon and Coke?"

The drink materialized along with some more expert opinion. "Sure, the rebels have a good point about the way this country is going from bad to worse. Nevertheless the main reason Colonel Honasan has resorted to this coup like the failed one in '87 is because he was passed over when Cory took power. After being moderately instrumental in the propulsion of Mrs. Aquino into the presidency during the People Power thing Gringo was really pissed off when he didn't receive any reward. Our tradition of utang na loob (moral debt) dictated that he should have been promoted. All the other leaders who sided with the yellow lady were offered good government jobs and promotions."

"Don't people believe in their causes and goals?" inquired Rick between sips.

The bartender enlightened him further. "All business and politics is personal in the Philippines. Revolutions and the most extreme social upheavals are never really about replacing undesirable conditions with better ones or bad ideas with improvements. They are, in essence, about replacing one bunch of feeders at the public trough with another. Whether we are talking about a barangay or local government election, presidential poll or an actual civil war the primary motivations are always the same. Besides, running for office is such a dangerous exercise here, the successful candidates probably feel they've earned the right to steal."

The clock behind the bar showed 3:45 p.m. when a newsflash came over the radio. The bartender turned up the volume. "Loyal troops have, in the past hour, retaken two television stations and pushed the rebel forces onto the defensive. Her Excellency President Aquino will now make an address."

"Filipino citizens, your armed forces have courageously and unfailingly resisted the coup attempt by some rogue elements. Many of the rebels have returned to their barracks and surrendered. The remainder have been surrounded in two locations in the capital. It is only a matter of time before order is fully restored. Our democracy remains safe."

"I notice that she didn't mention the Americans," commented Rick. "Early this morning I witnessed an F 16 shoot down a rebel propeller fighter. It must have been an American plane as the Philippine military doesn't have any contemporary jets."

"What do you expect?" came the reply from across the counter. "Even Cory is enough of a politician to avoid making the mistake of giving any credit to a not-so-popular foreign power."

If he was concerned about the prospects for his business plans Rick didn't show it. After dining in the lobby coffee shop he took a short stroll around the streets adjoining the hotel. Gunfire could still be heard in the distance so he didn't venture far.

People were simply going about their daily business. A barbershop's rotating pole advertised more than just haircuts, a group of office workers were drinking beer in an outdoor café and jeepneys were passing up and down with their polyglot cargoes of schoolgirls, laborers on their way home and housewives with parcels. As he was about to turn back to the Intercontinental Rick spotted an absolutely stunning girl making her way down the opposite pavement. She must have been around twenty years old, was tall for a Filipina and possessed long black hair framing her smooth olive face. This specter of loveliness walked with the assurance of the knowingly beautiful. Her crisp and starched white uniform dazzled in the late-afternoon light and highlighted the natural tan of her skin. Everything about her was in perfect order. In short, she was dressed up like a pox doctor's clerk. Suddenly, she stopped, turned her head to one side and spat comprehensively into the street. The tiny putrescent puddle contrasted strongly with the studied aplomb of its all-too-recent owner, suggesting all manner of disease and decay.

By lunch time the next day the coup was over. Many of the officers and men involved were now in custody and rebel forces in various provincial capitals had surrendered without a shot fired. The ringleader, Gringo Honasan had seemingly melted into the ether. Rick was now able to continue his journey to Cebu.

Chapter Two

"We would like to congratulate one of our longest serving signalmen on his forty years of loyal and steadfast service and wish him all the best on his retirement." Christopher Daly stepped forward and took his place on the dais next to the General Manager of Trackfast's Chicago division. He graciously accepted the traditional gold watch and certificate of service, dated 29th July 1986. "We must apologize for the lack of the usual cake. There was some sort of mix-up in the order and it wasn't delivered."

"Cake is fattening anyway," laughed Christopher. "How are you going to spend your days away from the track?" asked the manager as he slapped Christopher on the back. "Going on a world trip or just taking it easy and doing the odd bit of fishing?"

"I haven't really thought about it Sir?" answered the new retiree. "I can't afford a world trip and I don't like fishing. I suppose I'll finally be able to get the garden into the shape I've wanted for many years."

As the fifteen-minute celebration wound up Christopher looked at his new watch. The time was correct. There were of course no share certificates or other parting gestures of financial worth. Such niceties were reserved for much bigger fish than him.

A big jovial man known as the Spiker for his habit of making dangerous comments caught up with Christopher as the gathering flowed toward the exit. "You'll have time to spend with your family now. You'll be so busy you won't miss the railroad too much." Christopher looked wistful. "Apart from my children and one nephew in Australia I don't have any family to speak of."

"Too bad. Too bad," mumbled the Spiker, "But I'm sure you'll enjoy the extra time with the kids."

"For sure," said Christopher axing this conversation.

During the train journey back to his house in the suburbs Christopher experienced feelings he hadn't known before. An emptiness and uncertainty overwhelmed him. He had worked hard all his life to build a future but the future that faced him appeared rather drab. In his youth he had confidence in his country and in his company but this had slowly decomposed. Christopher felt cheated without knowing why.

There were certainly those worse off than he. His mind wandered back to the day that his friend and immediate superior in the company had been dismissed. Hans Werttenburger, the chief signal officer for Christopher's section, was a man who earned the respect of all those around him. Christopher had known him for the best part of twenty years and the two were buddies as well as workmates. It was almost twenty years to the day that Hans had summoned the entire team to his office to announce what was a complete shock.

"Men, I'm sorry to announce that I have been sacked and will no longer be working here as of 5p.m. today."

"What the …?" interjected Christopher and some others.

"Senior management claim that I delivered an unsatisfactory safety audit, but that is a lie! They deliberately removed an important section so that my work would appear incompetent."

"Why would they do that?" blurted out one of the younger team members.

Hans looked bemused for a second before answering. "A friend in head office told me that a major shareholder in the company, one Isaac Hoffman, had pushed the board to get rid of me. All of you know that during the war I fought in the German army. Apparently Hoffman had somehow or other discovered that I didn't serve in the Wehrmarcht as I had claimed when I joined Trackfast in the fifties. It was in the SS that I served. However, after a long period as a prisoner of war of the British I was released and was not charged with any war crimes. Needless to say, I am not very happy about being fired like this."

"What will you do? Where will you go?" asked a very concerned Christopher. "No ideas at all mate!" At the end of the working day the team took Hans to a bar for a farewell drink. Although he promised he would keep in touch none of them ever saw Werttenburger again.

As the endless cavern of Union Station merged into a sky scape of industrial towers punctuated by glimpses of the river to the right and then gave way to that of car yards and nondescript apartment blocks, separated by the occasional patch of green, Christopher's reminiscence continued. The negativity he was touching seemed to suggest the end of the line. It had only been ten years ago he had met and married the love of his life. From the day he'd paid a traffic ticket in city hall and gazed into the eyes of a short but well-proportioned blonde girl, Samantha had been a constant part of his existence. They'd married in the fall of '76 and Christopher's being had been exponentially enriched. With the birth of Rebecca the next year, a son whom they christened 'George William' two years following and a bubbly bundle of joy called Elizabeth in 1980, life was rich and happy if not perfect.

Then the troubles began. Samantha was only thirty-one when she quit her job at the city hall to become a responsible mother. She had been happy enough in her new role and certainly loved her husband with all her heart. The arrival of the second child saw her busier than ever but she seemed enough content. The baby of the family, Elizabeth, naturally became a prime attachment for Christopher. 'Last in, best dressed,' the old adage describes the arrival of offspring. The signalman would often whistle as he left the house for work. A loving family was the reason one could rejoice in the daily labor despite a rather mundane occupation. Work might set you free but only if you have a worthwhile reason to perform it.

The children screamed and fought more upon their father's return from work. The evening meals became increasingly more dull and ordinary. Sometimes the dinner wasn't ready and Christopher had been forced to knock up scrambled eggs and the like to feed his brood. He should have seen it coming but he was a simple God-fearing man who worked hard, obeyed the commandments and believed life would work out for the best accordingly. Samantha did her best to hide the darkness that was slowly encroaching upon her being and smothering her spiritual fire. Christopher could just barely sense that something was fundamentally wrong but he didn't have the inner strength to actually broach the subject in conversation.

I should have realized what was happening, I should have seen it coming, he accused himself over and over again as the train sped into the suburbs with tall olive-colored trees vying for prominence with row upon row of neat symmetrical homes and patches of bushland.

Should have or not, he simply didn't. The particular day in the spring of 1984 when he returned home was in no way unusual. That was until he opened the garage door and heard the engine of Samantha's Volkswagen idling. "What in Tarnation!" At that instant his eyes focused on the rubber hose from the exhaust to the driver's-side window. Slumped over the steering wheel was his beloved wife.

"Death by suicide," had been the coronial finding. How Christopher had been able to race inside, check on the children, call an ambulance and his friend Susan, he had never understood.

Susan, who had worked with his wife, the ambulance and the police all arrived within forty minutes of Christopher's awful discovery. The signalman was given two day's bereavement leave and then a fortnight's leave without pay. With the help of the Social Security, he acquired subsidized child minding and was able to return to work. It was in a way, a blessing to be back on the tracks. He felt cowardly when he cried at night and silently hoped that the children hadn't heard.

The last two years had been increasingly difficult as Christopher juggled work with a sole-parent's role and vainly searched for some hint of inner meaning. Yet he had managed. In fact, he had felt a damned sight better then than he was feeling now as he hurtled towards home and retirement. He was henceforth confined to performing a mum and dad's role with the body and spirit of a grandfather. The huge expanse of cemetery linking four suburbs did nothing to cheer his spirits.

The wheels ground to a halt at his station and Christopher mechanically alighted, dawdled across the car park and found his vehicle. The three-mile drive home was uneventful and as he entered his driveway he smiled. Gardening. Even the weeds don't look healthy. The car was duly parked in the garage of death as always and he ventured inside his last refuge, a modest timber structure on Enterprise Street. Precisely at 7 p.m., as usual, the day-care-center bus dropped off his three children. This was to be the last time, as Christopher would no longer work. He was too listless to cook and ordered pizza. The children were more than happy with that particular outcome. After they were asleep Christopher felt even more restless. He had never been much of a drinker but new times demanded new measures. The new measure in question was a bottle of bourbon that had hitherto been languishing on the shelf for ten years.

Three months had passed before Christopher received the first phone call from Ulysses Grant Elementary School. "Mr. Daly, It's Marcus Sheen here, the principal from Ulysses Grant Elementary. I'm afraid there have been some behavioral problems concerning George and I'd be grateful if you could come down to the school at your earliest convenience."

"Certainly, Mr. Sheen. I can make it this afternoon if you like."

"I'll expect you then around two o'clock," the principal courteously stated and rung off, leaving Christopher wondering what heinous crime his son had committed and wondering if their troubled lives could get any worse.

At precisely 1:45 Christopher's battered blue and cream '69 Chevy saloon rolled by the stately Methodist Church with its American flag triumphantly fluttering in the breeze. Passing the church was an unnecessary detour but he felt that it might bring him luck.

God, country and a proud heritage, he mused flicking some loose strands of grey hair from a visage that had been distinguished, if not actually handsome, in his youth. If only the past could guarantee the future. What could George have possibly done that warranted such an urgent trip? He was always a boisterous child and perhaps a tad aggressive but he'd always fitted in.

Outside the principal's office a 50's-style clock with its round dial and stark black numbers showed one fifty-seven. Its neighbor, an elegant calendar of the city's landmarks, trumpeted the day as being the 27 May 1986. The oak-paneled door serenely opened and a tall man in his late forties, who could have passed for a Wall Street banker, emerged.

"Mr. Daly, it's a pleasure to meet you finally. Please come in." Christopher touched the doorframe ever so briefly. Stepping through the doorway, to Christopher, it was as if the last thirty years had never happened. The handshake was firm if not entirely sincere. A robust, if not solid, desk divided the home chair from that of the visitor. Tucked away neatly in a corner was an ancient Bakelite wireless and facing it across the shiny surface stood the upper portion of a jukebox that James Dean might have once played. Noticing Christopher's quizzical expression Marcus spoke. "It's all in working order, actually; the product of many years of collecting and restoration. Not really such a strange hobby when you think about it. Why is it all here rather than at home you might wonder? Doesn't it make sense to keep the things we love in the place we spend most of our time?"

Mesmerized by such a time warp, which was only broken by dark and somber photographs from a much earlier period gazing down on the scene from the walnut-lined walls, Christopher had momentarily forgotten why he had come. Marcus's voice startled him. "I had better get to the point of my request for your visit at such short notice." The principal's steely blue eyes seemed to sharpen their focus. "Although we haven't had the pleasure of your attendance at any of our P and C meetings or parent-teacher nights I fully understand the very difficult circumstances you have been under for the last couple of years or so. To lose your wife that way; I can only sympathize. It is with great regret that our first meeting is necessitated by the present serious circumstances."

"What has George done?" interrupted Christopher.

"It is a particularly serious matter," intoned Mr. Sheen, "and although the police haven't so far been called in it is likely that they soon will be. In recent months there have been some tensions between a number of our Hispanic students and a particular group of our African Americans. George was concerned in a fracas this morning that led to the brief hospitalization of a black boy in the second grade. It seems that other students had suspected this boy of stealing some particular item. They hadn't consulted any teacher or school official in this matter. They simply beat the boy almost senseless. To cut a long story short, after the injured boy was hospitalized, we interviewed all the children involved and were led to search your son's locker. We had expected to find some money or private treasure that was in dispute. What we were actually confronted with was much worse."

"Yes?" interjected Christopher in a faltering voice. "Amphetamines; only a very small quantity but nonetheless amphetamines."

"What? Drugs in my son's locker! George is barely eight years old! I can't believe it."

"You can see why I called you down in such a hurry then?" purred Mr. Sheen. "George denies any knowledge of how the contraband arrived in his locker but I'm afraid he is not being entirely truthful. I would be very grateful if you could do as much as possible to sort this matter out at home and then perhaps we can put a stop to a potential disaster. I do not wish to call George here at present."

As a visibly shaken Christopher drove home, Elgin's historic buildings took on a hint of corruption. Even the churches appeared sinister. At 3:20, he was back at the school to collect George, Rebecca and Elizabeth at the end of the school day.

"Well," he stammered as the children climbed into the back of the Chevy. "They made me put the stuff in my locker," sobbed the boy.

"Who made you?" Christopher's voice was stern and somber.

"This gang at school. These boys follow a kid called Jesse and after they beat up the black boy and stole his stuff, they ordered me to put it in my locker."

"What do you mean ordered?" shouted the father.

"They were going to beat me up real bad if I didn't," cried George, the tears flowing down his cheeks like rain.

"Is that God's truth?" queried Christopher.

"Yes Dad."

"He told me about it just before he was called to the office," chirped Elizabeth before she turned her attention to the doll she was holding.

"Well, no matter what happens with these bad kids you just keep away from them. We'll say no more about this."

Rebecca said nothing throughout this exchange, her long blonde hair effectively hiding most of her face.

After dinner, with the children asleep or at least in bed, Christopher poured himself a bourbon on the rocks and turned on the TV. The late news described a buoyant economy for the nation and an optimistic future. Stocks were up, consumer sales through the roof and America was striding ahead with its rightful position in the world. Why couldn't the nation have some dreadful disaster, he was unable to prevent himself from thinking. Good news and sunshine is merely depressing for those on the other side of the fence.

It would be an outright lie to say that Christopher was enjoying his retirement. Boredom, barely enough money to get by and a permeating sense of futility don't add up to an exhilarating existence. He would have liked some part-time work to fill his days, but mature would-be workers receive about the same interest from employers as an ugly girl on Prom night.

The next month went by quietly, almost pleasantly. One weekend saw the family enjoying the summer days in Elgin's largest park. A frolicking group of ducks caught Elizabeth's attention. "Dad, can we buy some bread and feed the ducks with it?" begged the youngest child. "Of course, Petal," Christopher replied before directing the group to exit the park. Ten minutes later, bread in hand they were back.

"We didn't really need that extra exercise just to feed those stupid birds," Rebecca remarked sullenly.

"Why can't we go to an amusement park with rides and side shows instead of all this boring nature crap," interjected George.

"Mind your language and try to enjoy what we have," rebuked their father. His budget didn't run to commercial, whiz-bang entertainment anyway. "Besides if children are not able to appreciate Nature's beauty and revel in it, who can?"

Summer was just at the turn to fall when Christopher was again invited to one of Mr. Sheen's special briefings. "I really don't think George is voluntarily involved in any trouble here Mr. Sheen," he asserted. "There were some thefts from some students' lockers and allegations by a number of pupils that George and his elder sister were behind it."

"Rebecca! She's a very quiet girl," exclaimed Christopher.

"Yes, too quiet," was the reply. "As we don't have any hard evidence there isn't much else the school can do. However, I'm giving you notice that if there are any more serious incidents involving any of your children, I will move to expel all three of them."

"Isn't that somewhat of an overreaction?" challenged their father.

"Not when you're trying to educate a large number of students and keep them from importing the outside society's massive problems," Marcus flatly stated.

"I do what I can to keep all three of my children on the straight and narrow and I don't believe they are the cause of any problems in the school," Christopher aired in a voice of defiance. "Now, if that is all, I shall bid you good day."

As Christopher strode out of the office with its time warp, the principal's secretary entered bearing a cup of coffee.

"I could smell whiskey on him, you know." Mrs. Martese possessed the air of confidence owned by middle-aged women who are always right.

"Yes, I'm afraid the father of that brood is a classic case of White Trash syndrome, although that particular phrase is more at home a thousand miles south of here." Marcus caught himself and stopped. "Mind you, the youngest child, Elizabeth, is a model student and a really sweet girl."

"The exception proves the rule." Mrs. Martese swept out of the office with the same alacrity as she had arrived.

Christopher resolved to keep as low a profile as possible with the school authorities. The twice-yearly reports described Rebecca as a withdrawn, sometimes sullen child, George as a possible future danger to society and Elizabeth as a model student. No more major incidents occurred and life seemed to settle into a dull normalcy. The years rolled on and the two elder children now attended Ellis Middle School. Only Elizabeth remained in the elementary school with its James Dean era principal and Elizabeth seemed to fit in perfectly well.

By the spring of 1989 the retired signalman began to think that he was safe from further harassment and misfortunes. He used some of his excess time to correspond with his few friends and even wrote to his nephew in Australia. Although he hadn't laid eyes on Rick since he was a small child the two now struck up a regular exchange of letters.

"Dear Uncle Chris, I have an opportunity to set up a furniture export business in the Philippines," one such missive began. "This bloke I know from my student days has just returned from there and is convinced there is a real opportunity. I will need to live there for quite a while and work hard but I don't need to put up more than ten grand in capital."

Christopher was happy that his brother's only child seemed to have a positive direction.

◇◇◇◇◇◇◇◇◇

"Christopher, are you there?" The question accompanied by a persistent knocking, announced the arrival of Susan, his late wife's friend.

"Hi Susan. What a pleasant surprise. Come in."

"I was in the neighborhood and I thought I'd see how you and the kids are faring. It must be nearly a year since I've seen you." The hands on the ancient clock in Christopher's kitchen marked the hour as 8 pm. Coffee, a catch-up conversation and a small fuss over how much his offspring had grown consumed ninety minutes. By that time Susan excused herself and swept back into the night. Rebecca, George and Elizabeth went to their nightly rest and Christopher watched a little television. Life was calm if not wonderful.

Through the lounge-room shutters on a modest timber bungalow across the street, Dacey Beaver surveyed the darkened Daly home with keen eyes. A slender woman in her middle fifties with auburn hair and a somewhat shriveled countenance, Dacey prided herself on being the lynch pin in the security and health of her immediate neighborhood. Not much escaped her notice, be it matters of import or sheer trivia.

A week or so later, early one evening there was an unfamiliar knock on the door. Upon opening that wooden bastion Christopher noticed two young women clutching colored pamphlets.

"We hope we haven't called at an inconvenient time but we would like to discuss the role of God in your life." When it came to knowledge of the practices of the Jehovah's Witnesses and such like, Christopher was a total virgin.

"Please come in. I can offer you tea or coffee." Jessica sat in one of Christopher's modest and dilapidated chairs. Her brunette accomplice preferred to stand; Hannah, though in her late thirties, possessed a sleek figure and a seemingly unconscious sexual allure.

"Without God where are you?" Hannah ventured before Christopher had the time to provide the promised tea.

"Probably not much worse off than I am now," he perfunctorily replied.

"You see, it is because mankind has defied the directives of Jehovah (Yahweh if we want to become really technical), that all of the ills we are now facing have occurred. Surely you remember that life was better when you were a boy?"

"If you say so," replied a patient and lonely man.

By the time the ladies were served more tea and some scones the subject had drilled down into bedrock ideology.

"You quote that 144,000 people out of a population of several billion are to be saved. Surely there are a lot more than 144,000 good people? There are even several million devout and sincere Christians."

Jessica leaned forward, her breasts desperately attempting to break free of the tight bodice that restrained them.

"Mr. Daly, we don't know really how good people are. Only Jehovah can decide that. I've heard all the scientific criticisms about the damned including the one about how Cain found a wife and the other one about God making a mistake. It doesn't matter."

A rather tired host, poured more tea and raised his voice slightly. "I'm a God fearing man who has placed his trust in Providence all his life but with not too much to show for it I might add, yet the ideas you are preaching to me seem entirely illogical and weird."

Hannah who had remained standing for well over an hour, wiggled her hips in a manner if falling short of holy, was certainly successful on a sexual basis however unintended that may have been.

"I hope we have been of some assistance Mr. Daly and I'm sorry that so far we have been unable to agree. It seems that we are arguing from different types of logic."

"As far as I'm concerned there is only one type of logic, two-value (true and false) came a depressed and disconsolate reply." The two young spiritually-laden women bade their farewells and promised to return at a later date. They then vanished into an increasingly darkening sky.

God forbid, Jehovah! As if the holy rollers on television weren't enough; just another pestilence crawling around door-to-door. Christopher vowed that if they hadn't been so attractive he wouldn't have let them in let alone allowed them to invite themselves back. Yet back they came the following Tuesday. "If only the weather, the stock market or even the horses, and Christopher didn't gamble, were as reliable." The second visit was much shorter than the first. Telepathically Jessica seemed to think that Christopher was constantly gazing at her breasts although they belonged to Jehovah and even Hannah, who seldom sat down and always remained alert felt certain that not only wasn't he listening to the message but was staring at her pubic regions. A child's voice broke the moment.

"Daddy, I know why the Jehovah's Witness people come round." Rebecca was standing there in her nightie. "They get some kind of frequent flyer points for each person who signs on."

Christopher laughed. "It's something like that, sweetheart, maybe souls on the wing." The child was replaced in her bed.

It is hard to imagine JW's actually breeding as their membership seems to grow only by conversion and Christopher was sorry that the only way he could make new friends was by listening to the chatter of madness. There were no more visits by that particular sect to his door. The next knock on it was much more authoritative.

"Mr. Daly."

"Yes."

"We are from the Child Welfare Department." A tallish gentleman in his thirties introduced himself as John while his forty-ish female companion identified herself as Janice. "May we come in as our business will take some minutes?" asserted Janice.

"I'm not sure if this is a very good time," replied the startled householder.

"That would be a great pity since it is a matter of urgency and one that concerns your children," remarked the gentleman.

"My children are fine. Like all kids they've experienced their problems but for the last few months or so they haven't put a foot wrong."

"The matter of concern isn't anything your children have done I might add," Janice coldly asserted, "yet it is serious enough that you would be making a grave mistake if you were to turn us away at this moment."

Reluctantly Christopher opened the door of his refuge to yet another scourge. Once inside the rather dusty lounge room Janice spied a chair in the corner with a framed picture of Christopher's late wife occupying the seat. Carefully removing it and placing it on the floor she sat down. John merely parked himself on the settee.

"What's going on?" cried Rebecca as she switched off the TV.

"People are here from the government to check up on your school performance," the father stated. "Please go to your rooms so we can talk." All three children dutifully disappeared. Christopher offered the intruders a drink, which they politely refused and then poured himself a bourbon. "We've got to support American industries," he commented as he sat down facing the next onslaught of cruel Fate.

The woman was the first to speak. "Mr. Daly, I'll come right to the point. There have been reports that prostitutes have been regularly visiting your house at all hours and placing your children in moral danger."

"You've got to be joking!" cried Christopher, outraged. In fact he hadn't been with a woman since his wife died.

Lending support to the government assault the male, John, spoke up. "Women have been seen coming and going from these premises and it would be naïve to consider them as anything other than prostitutes. I can't imagine the effect this would have on your children although I am, of course, sorry about the tragic circumstances surrounding the loss of your wife."

At this point, Janice, who may have been considered an attractive woman if it weren't for her attitude, interrupted her colleague. "You very mature men think you can get away with anything and simply don't care about your responsibilities or the effect on others. Think about it! Your own children!"

"I beg your pardon, this is utter nonsense. I get very few callers of either sex and the ones I've had came here for perfectly genuine reasons." Christopher forced himself to remain polite despite a stirring of anger in his entire frame.

"I'm sorry Mr. Daly, you obviously don't appreciate the gravity of the situation." Janice's authority rose to the occasion nicely.

"I'm not to going to sit in my own house and listen to this outrageous crap," Christopher pronounced as he stood to his full height in a gesture that suggested the government people had better leave.

"Who fabricated these ridiculous lies against me? I have a right to know so that I can defend myself and my children."

"I'm sorry, Mr. Daly, we are not at liberty to tell you that," asserted the male in a subdued bureaucratic voice. At that, the gentleman and his redheaded cohort promptly arose and left.

Every month somebody would knock on the door and demand admittance claiming official concern about the children's welfare. Gradually Christopher was losing patience. Didn't he deserve a bit of peace and quiet in his retirement? He'd had his share of tragedy, he'd paid his dues and had a God-given right to be left alone. On the last attempted visit, he'd simply lost patience and uttered the worst oath he could muster as he slammed the door in the faces of the interlopers.

One Tuesday morning when the kids were at school Christopher answered the door. "I'm sorry I'm very busy right now and the Lord literally flows through this house so I must bid you good day."

A determined foot prevented its closure. "We've got good news for you, so if you don't mind." The woman, called Marge, was a decidedly ugly version of femininity in its last gasp but nonetheless persisted in her own version of self-importance.

"Marjory from the Child Welfare. I'm sure you don't mind." The sidestep that she performed on Christopher would have done a much younger and more athletic woman proud.

Making herself as comfortable as possible in the house of a failed human she beamed the glad tidings. "I'm sorry to burst in on you like this, Mr. Daly but I'm sure you'll be relieved to know that the charges alleged against you have been dismissed for lack of evidence."

"I'm not really sure I care any more," said Christopher as he pointedly placed a half-full bottle of bourbon on the table. "Want a drink lady? We have tea or coffee if you want."

"Mr. Daly," Marge stood up and prepared to leave. "I repeat, the allegations about nefarious women of the night visiting your premises have been found to have no basis. Nonetheless two of your three children have been performing poorly at school so it is our intention to provide you with any assistance that you may need to do right by your offspring."

"Piss off!" There being only so many infractions of personal space and liberty that a being can withstand, the retreating Child Welfare officer was lucky to escape with only two whiskey stains on her blouse.

The seasons waxed and waned. Rebecca and George received undesirable school reports while the youngest kept Christopher's hopes alive. I can really understand those literary cretins that described retirement as God's waiting room, Christopher thought to himself as he cleaned the house one day. It's a hard thing to wish oneself dead but if it hadn't been for his responsibilities to his brood who knows what tragic accident may have saved the American health system money?

With the passage of time however Christopher forgot his misfortunes and actually began living. On Mondays he went bowling and on Thursdays he attended painting class. Michelangelo he was not but two or three of his creations were good enough to hang up. One winter, as the snow blanketed Elgin and most of the area, Christopher actually forgot to feel depressed. The best day was the Saturday when he brought all three children to a frozen lake and produced pairs of skates. Their laughter and foolishness somehow brought the old man back to life.

Painting class was a positive joy and bowling was a social event to eagerly anticipate. Rebecca and George were actually making progress in their grades. Best of all, it had been several months since the government had intruded on Christopher's existence. Praise the Lord, the misfits from the Child Welfare had finally given up. No visits from the eager helpers was the sort of blessing that Christopher prayed for at Thanksgiving. To have his prayer answered was all he could ever have wanted. He knew that if he followed the Lord's way and worked hard it would all come out in the end. Even Moses got a break eventually.

One Wednesday, just as the family were about to leave for school, Rebecca decided to check the mailbox. Usually, even such of the more interesting chores were beyond her but, on an impulse, she made the small effort. "Dad, it's a letter from Elizabeth's school!" An instinctive cringe of fear caused her shoulder-length hair to block her face as she handed over the envelope. Christopher ripped it open, praying to God, that there was no more trouble being brewed by his progeny.

Dear Mr. Daly, It is with great pride and satisfaction that we inform you that your daughter Elizabeth has won the Science prize for her grade and invite your family to our end-of-year awards evening. Elizabeth's project on the importance of frogs to our environment was the most impressive from all those received from her grade. The Awards evening is to be held on the 2nd of June 1990 and we look forward to your attendance.

Unused to positive messages from any authority, educational or otherwise, Christopher joyously exclaimed, as he bundled the three children into the car, "Of course we'll all go. Elizabeth, I'm so proud of you." Two almost audible sighs escaped from the lungs of her siblings. On returning home Christopher found himself singing as he finally attended to the weeding of his front lawn. The sun shone brighter that day and the song of the birds was louder and more melodious. After a tough life it appeared that he was going to be spared the commonplace tragedy that customarily holds hands with age.

A week after receiving the letter, a natural high still hovered in the air over the Daly home. George washed the dishes that evening without being asked and Rebecca smiled and cuddled her younger sister. Retirement often means living your life rather vicariously, Christopher philosophized, and how better to comply than through the successes of your children?

The ensuing days rolled by, the children were allowed ice cream for dessert and the song of crickets suggested a natural harmony. "I haven't got a thing to wear," cried Rebecca two days before Monday's ceremony. George was spotted polishing his shoes. Instead of watching TV after the family dinner Elizabeth disappeared into her room to read.

"Why are you studying so much now?" inquired her dad when he came in with her cocoa.

"I'm beginning work on my next project," came the earnest reply.

"I can't complain about that," Christopher smiled.

At 8 am on Sunday morning the family gathered for the customary breakfast ritual. Elizabeth, however, was absent. "Rebecca, could you please wake your sister up?" Christopher assumed she had been reading rather too late.

"Dad, come quick!" Rebecca shouted from the doorway. "She's really sick!" Christopher left the table with George hot on his heels and joined Rebecca at Elizabeth's bedside.

In the bed Elizabeth lay motionless with a pool of vomit on her chest. "What are those red marks on her face," cried her brother.

"Elizabeth," her father called as he placed his hand on her forehead. The girl stirred and spoke.

"I'm sorry Dad."

"Don't be silly." Christopher cleaned her up and tended to her care while George and Rebecca reluctantly returned to their breakfast. Two hours later Elizabeth was still pale but was up and talking. "There's flu going around at school, Dad. I must have caught a bad dose."

"Well, we'd better get you to the doctor."

"The surgery's closed as it's Sunday," Rebecca reminded them.

"Well, we can take you to the Chicago hospital."

"It's not necessary Dad," Elizabeth volunteered. "I'm feeling quite a lot better now and we don't need to drive forty-five miles and wait for hours." Hospitals were expensive and the little girl knew her father could ill afford the charges for emergency treatment.

"All right for the moment but if you feel any worse let us know immediately," Christopher intoned.

Later that evening the invalid's temperature had increased and it was certain she wouldn't be well enough to go to the School awards. She was however resting comfortably and Christopher made the decision to bring her to their local doctor's surgery as soon as it opened at 8 am the following morning.

Christopher awoke at two o'clock and instinctively went to check on his child. As he turned on the light he gasped. The red rash that had appeared earlier as a temporary blemish had now engulfed almost the entirety of her body. Her breathing sounded desperate and labored. Christopher woke the other children and carried Elizabeth to the car for a dash to the hospital.

Thirty-five minutes after the family's arrival and twenty minutes after filling in admission forms and guarantees of payment a young doctor emerged. "Mr. Daly, bring your daughter in here please." The examination room was a violent expression of white and no signs of life presented themselves. Rebecca and George reluctantly resigned themselves to the reception area.

After ten minutes or so, the doctor called for an emergency team who whisked the ailing child to an intensive care bed. "I'm sorry, Mr. Daly, your daughter is critically ill. She has contracted Meningococcal disease."

"Meningo..what?" an increasingly alarmed Christopher blurted out.

"Meningococcal disease. It is a moderately rare but highly dangerous bacterial infection. If it is detected quickly it can be effectively treated with antibiotics. Unfortunately, from what you have said, Elizabeth has been exhibiting symptoms for more than twenty-four hours and the disease has progressed. It will be touch and go for her survival and if she pulls through she may suffer long term effects."

"We all thought it was the flu," her terrified father stammered.

"The symptoms are fairly similar and that is what makes Meningococcal so dangerous," came the reply from the intern. "The disease spreads very rapidly. We have administered massive doses of antibiotics already and all we can do now is wait and pray."

When he returned to his other children and broke the dreaded news Christopher was greeted by a sobbing Rebecca and stone-faced son. After quickly having some coffee in the canteen the entire family were ushered to Elizabeth's bedside to begin the vigil. It was 6:30 in the morning when Elizabeth's young body finally gave up the fight. Tears streamed down the cheeks of all three watchers and Christopher silently cursed the Almighty.

Tuesday slid into Wednesday and on till Saturday announced its arrival. All three surviving Dalys existed through the intervening days in a melancholy fog. Christopher had accomplished the necessary arrangements without even being aware of the fact. It was two hours before the funeral and Rebecca had begun to howl again. For an undemonstrative lass she produced a surprisingly physical show of emotion. "Have a cup of tea, Becky. You'll feel a little better." The girl just shook her head at her father's offer. By one' clock she had run out of tears and joined Christopher and her brother for the heart-breaking journey to the crematorium.

Apart from Susan, the late Mrs. Daly's friend and two of Elizabeth's classmates along with their mothers, there were no guests other than the immediate family. The minister coughed and began to speak.

"Dearly Beloved, …. I'm sorry." Quickly correcting his nervous gaff the man of God continued. "It is our melancholy duty to lay to rest this young girl cut down long before her prime. The passing of children is always especially sad and so it is on this occasion. It is difficult to understand the Lord's divine plan for each of us at such a time. Elizabeth was a bright and happy girl, loved by all who knew her. God's plan for Elizabeth is perhaps beyond our understanding but we can all draw comfort in the knowledge that she is now at peace with her Maker."

At the conclusion of the service Elizabeth's two classmates approached Christopher with their mothers and offered their condolences. One of the little girls, Cindy, reached for his hand. "I know Elizabeth is with God now, Mr. Daly because she truly believed."

"Thank you dear," was the muted response from the bereaved and shattered man.

"Really Mr. Daly, I'm sure. You see, what happens to people after they die is exactly what they believe will happen to them."

"That's an interesting thought Cindy but how do you know that?"

"I just know it and I've always known it since way back when I was old enough to know anything."

The tiny assembly of mourners then bade their farewells and returned to their respective lives.

Once back in his desolate enclave Christopher made tea for his two children and poured himself a strong bourbon. The three continued the artificial business of pretending to be busy while inwardly embracing nothingness. Rebecca cleaned the entire house twice that afternoon and George insisted on mowing the weed-lawn. Christopher, with tears lining his eyes, forced himself to pack up Elizabeth's belongings and lovingly store them as securely and neatly as he could manage. A small silver urn stood on the center of the lounge room mantle. It was all that remained of a much-loved child.

The death of their mother had been a cruel blow from which the family had barely been able to recover but recover it had. Elizabeth's sudden and tragic departure seemed almost malevolent in its meaninglessness. As night fell over the decaying white-planked dwelling a pregnant moon shone in through the windows. "That's weird." George pointed to it while summoning the attention of his father and Rebecca. "I've seen plenty of full moons before and I've even seen one that was blood red but this moon is the grey of granite." The other two showed little interest in the grey moon and it simply kept on shining with only the boy's exclamation to mark its unusual nature.

As the post-Elizabeth days passed into weeks and months a semblance of normalcy returned. Rebecca returned to her former silence and George turned rebellious. "Where do you think you've been?" Christopher assertively inquired as his son entered the house at midnight one Friday.

"Around with the guys," came an equally assertive reply.

"You're only fourteen and you should keep civilized hours. If you're bored you could always study. Your school grades are pathetic!"

"I can look after myself, Dad. Why don't you just get a whiskey and watch the telly." Sensing no victory in sight, Christopher actually followed George's sarcastic advice.

Christopher had never actually met any of his son's friends although it wasn't for want of trying. He couldn't say that about his daughter. Her two closest buddies would often call at the house to take Rebecca to a movie or God knew where. Jenny was a tall girl with a slim figure and cropped raven locks. A tattoo featuring a butterfly devouring a snake adorned her left shoulder while a silver stud that looked as if it had once belonged to a knuckle-duster almost covered her right nostril. Of shorter stature but larger build was Skylene. Dark curly hair draped her shoulders and her aquiline nose was presided over by permanently glazed hazel eyes. Skylene was the same age as Rebecca and Jenny a year older. They attended the same school and demonstrated the same lack of propensity for any studious application as his daughter. The beat-up Volkswagen beetle with its prominent Marijuana and Bad Girl stickers that Jenny drove didn't further endear her to Christopher either.

It was late April of the year after Elizabeth's death and the first signs of spring were bursting into existence. Late one Thursday evening a cold northerly wind, but not bitterly so, was rippling the surface of the duck pond in Trout Park. Gathered in a corner of the rotunda was a motley group of youths. A black guy with a blood red bandana was issuing instructions while his white and Latino brothers gazed on in admiration. Two colored girls did their best to add sex appeal to the occasion, giggling and flashing their tits. Every member of the group sported patches of purple with a white diagonal streak on their otherwise mundane hip-hop inspired baggy fashions.

"You all know why we're here tonight Bro's. The 'hood's getting a new member. Also, we got new business. Along with the usual crack we're startin' to offer this new cheap stuff called Wet. It's got Angel Dust in it and Man, it sure is a blast."

At this point the leader pulled a shiny 9mm Italian pistol from his back pocket and placed it on a scarred wooden bench that had survived countless family picnics. "Now we'll introduce our new brother. Our rules say that to join he has to do a hold up that nets at least a grand." A round of whistling and cheers intermixed with expletives formed the applause. The two girls dropped their jeans and flashed their asses to add further effect.

Into the center of the group strode a young man in his middle teens. His untidy blond hair waved in the wind as he reached the leader and picked up the pistol. George Daly had never touched a gun before and was surprised at how hard and cold the blued steel felt in his fingers. It was also much heavier than he had expected.

Chapter Three

Whether born of a promiscuous romantic desire or the real need to understand the common folk of the new country Rick decided to take the long road to Cebu, ship. He might not have made this decision had he seen the headlines of the local papers only a month before. "MV Suragat sinks, 1200 drowned." Not having seen them this innocent made a pure decision unfettered by the grubby statistical dangers of the real world. Twenty-four hours journey time seemed a fair trade off for the considerable price saving over an air ticket.

On the appointed day he caught a taxi to the embarkation point, North Harbor, which was only a dozen or so kilometers from Manila's center. The driver was a surly man in a hurry. "It'll cost three hundred for the trip," he'd said. Having been in the city for just long enough to notice that taxis were equipped with meters Rick had demanded that the driver use it. "Want to run the meter then, do you? Ok!" Over the noise of the motor could be heard a faint but menacing ticking of a rapidity that could have rivalled a Thompson machine gun. At the gate of the port where the taxi dropped him the third-class ship passenger parted with four hundred and twenty pisos and a portion of his dignity.

It was only 1 pm but already dozens of young men appeared from every shadow with faces that desired money and were none too fussy about how they came by it. Women with children and belongings trussed up in hessian bundles vied for passage with numerous urchins, porters and the purveyors of soft drinks and barbecued chicken pieces. Our Mr. Daly, resplendent in a brown safari suit, braved the odds and fought his way through the throng. After only a hundred meters an urchin scampered in front of him. A boy, not more than six years old and wearing little more than decaying rags thrust forward a particularly grubby palm.

"Piso Joe." Foolishly, Rick obliged. He had learned on his second day in Manila that it was totally pointless to take umbrage about being called Joe but he hadn't yet learned some of the finer points. As the coin hit the grubby palm fifty more of the urchin's brothers-in-alms surrounded Rick. Just as he gathered his wits a violent tug announced the sudden loss of the camera around his neck. The youthful crowd vanished as quickly as it had appeared. There was nothing for him to do but keep walking. Fifty meters on and he'd bought a beer from one of the peddlers. Although none too cold it was a just compensation for the loss of the camera. What was more the gangplank was now in sight. A hundred meters to go!

A handsome man in his thirties wearing a pristinely starched white uniform was collecting tickets and checking the passenger manifest. A few paces before reaching this goal, a girl of about fifteen or sixteen, slim and pretty, tapped Rick on the shoulder. Placing his hand on his wallet pocket, he turned. A smile born of sunshine greeted him. "Hey Joe, what about my Christmas?" The girl smiled again in a way that could put a man in jail. From where Rick hailed, Christmas festivities began around about the 15th of December. Unbeknownst to him, in the Philippines, they run from October to February. Being not in the best of moods his brain fired quickly. "How about a mixed-blood baby," he replied. The girl vanished and Rick reached the gangplank and the man in the white uniform.

Once on board Rick felt a little safer. He located his assigned bunk, a stretcher bed on one of the middle decks and deposited his belongings next to it. Both his gaze and arm remained attached to the small suitcase until some minutes after the ship had sailed. As the inter-island ferry negotiated its passage out of Manila Bay Rick felt his belongings were secure enough to do some exploring.

The MV Krisco was a not uncommon example of the passenger ships that regularly ply the green waters separating the thousands of islands that make up the archipelago. Approximately 20 years old it was a vessel that stood three stories high and boasted a length of half a football field. The face that she showed the world consisted of a very dark hull topped by layers of green and white painted steel. The outer area of all the decks was open to a height of two meters; a potential vacuum that was instantly filled by the torsos and faces of a sea of humanity gazing at loved ones left behind in the far distance or merely sampling the sea spray. Almost all activity was exclusively performed by those in uniform. Unless in the midst of some overwhelming moment of danger or excitement Filipinos are blessed with the uncanny ability to instantly find relaxation in almost any setting and the passengers bound for Cebu were no exception. Elderly women and teenage boys sat or lay seeking the solace of dreams. Children ate sweets and read comic books while groups of men gathered around the several canteens drinking San Miguel and chatting.

"Marcos might have been a villain," asserted a grandfather who wore a bandana and the clothes of a farmer, "but at least he was able to maintain order and provide some semblance of security. This Aquino is simply a rich idiot. We never know what tomorrow will bring." Removing the bottle from his lips, a bespectacled student in his early twenties retorted. "If Marcos had stayed in power another few years the entire Philippine economy would have been locked in the vault of some Swiss bank."

"And is Cory any better?" The elderly farmer would not be shaken in his conviction. "One of her cousins is now the head of the Philippine Long Distance Phone Company, the rest of her family are stealing everything they can and the country is descending into chaos. A crooked leader who can lead is better than a crooked one who can't!"

Rick couldn't resist the temptation and invited himself into the group. His offer of beers for the group that was half a dozen strong proved to win instant acceptance. "Is there anybody who could govern this country honestly and effectively," he inquired. A couple of burps and a chorus of laughter answered his question. The student ventured further elaboration. "Where are you going to find a person with no family or relatives, who possesses ability and who just happens to be honest? If such a person existed he or she would never be elected to any office of any importance."

"Why not?" mumbled Rick. Luckily for him the group were of a patient mentality. "You Americans don't understand the nature of our society," replied the farmer. "In every family, rich or poor, the breadwinners are expected to provide for all of the others. Everything must be shared. For example if you have a million pisos and 200 relatives how much money do you really have? Even the richest of families never seem to have enough money."

After his fifth beer and the fifth round he bought for his companions Rick excused himself and sought out the toilet. A rusty iron door with bent hinges opened onto a small windowless space with a hole in the center of the floor and a rudimentary flushing mechanism above. Naturally enough there was no toilet paper or soap. "Hope I don't have to do a number two before we dock," thought Rick to himself.

Back at the canteen he ordered another round of beers. Gripping the bottles in his fingers he set forth to rejoin the conversation. After only three steps he tripped over the end of a rusty pipe. Bottles and their precious amber contents leaped from his hands and made their return to earth in the most anarchic of manners. A scream announced the advent of disaster. A young woman in her late twenties with shoulder-length hair was staring in disbelief at the small torrent of liquid that was now running down her previously-pristine white dress. As she looked up Rick noticed that she was more than attractive with generous velvety eyes of brown, flawless skin and the fullest of curved lips.

"I'm so sorry. How clumsy of me," he blurted out at the visage of beauty overlaid with a flash of anger. "I'll have to change and I have very few clothes with me. Thank you for your carelessness." More apologies escaped Rick's lips and he looked such a helpless and pathetic sight in his embarrassment that the girl couldn't stifle a small giggle that had welled up in her throat. Her lips parted in a radiant smile that revealed her pearly whites. "It's all right," she said softly. "It was an accident and the decks on these tubs aren't exactly uncluttered. I'm Marilyn," she announced. "Marilyn Delgado; and you are?"

"Rick Daly." The girl cut short further attempted apologies and the offered money to pay for the cleaning. "We don't see many foreigners travelling third class. In fact almost all of them fly. The few that do brave these ferries travel first class with a cabin. Strange, you don't look particularly poor and I'm sure you've got money anyway!"

Quickly disclaiming poverty, the now less-embarrassed spiller of drinks told the lass of his planned business and desire to understand the normal folk that made up this chain of islands. "It'll take you years to understand this nation if ever," Marilyn proudly asserted. "We Filipinos are a complex although poor people."

The sounding of the ship's gong interrupted their conversation. Marilyn answered the unspoken question suggested by the look of puzzlement on her new companion's face. "It's the dinner bell. You get dinner and breakfast on this trip."

"May I buy you dinner? It's the least I can do," Rick offered.

"It's included in the ticket but you may join me if you like, after I've changed." The girl then disappeared for ten minutes. On her return the pair made their way into a vast dining room with the barest of decorations. Steel tables bolted onto the floor were accompanied by iron seating trestles. The endless queue filed past a small line of cooks who quickly equipped each diner with plate, fork and spoon, rice, thrice cooked eggs and some indeterminate vegetables.

Sitting on a trestle opposite his newfound friend, Rick made an observation on their repast. "I hope we don't get food poisoning from this lot!"

"If you wanted American food you'd have travelled first class," answered Marilyn tersely. "I'm not that hungry anyway." After consuming two spoonfuls of the mix Rick laid down his cutlery. He couldn't help thinking of that foul smelling lavatory and didn't want to tempt Providence.

"Do you live in Cebu?" Rick asked to keep the conversation going.

"No, I live on the island of Samar, which is another twelve hours by ship from Cebu."

"What were you doing in Manila?"

"I needed to buy some small pieces of equipment for my parents' store and they're much cheaper in Manila than in the provinces."

Rick informed the young lady of his business plans in detail although she hadn't asked. "Why don't you make a business in your country?" was her rather natural question. "There are more opportunities here and less regulation than in Australia," was the reply. A slightly sardonic smile escaped Marilyn's lips. "I wish you luck."

Although mystified by that sudden expression Rick was more interested in the story of this charming creature. "You're obviously educated and I shouldn't imagine you work as a housemaid," he risked. "What do you do?"

"Nothing really at the moment," came the retort. "I help my parents around the home and in their small store." Rick was bemused. "You obviously went to college. What did you study?" Marilyn blushed slightly although blushing isn't much of a problem for damsels with shaded skins. "At first I took Social Work because I wanted to help the poor but when I realized I didn't really empathize with them I changed my course to bookkeeping and accounting." The prospective businessman pricked his ears a little. "With those qualifications you must easily be able to find good employment, surely!"

"If you call a job with a department-store in Cebu for 2,000 pisos a month good employment. My room rent cost me a thousand alone. It simply wasn't worth it so I returned to my parents' house in Samar."

Rick found himself listening very intently at these last remarks. The conversation shifted to more light-hearted topics. After buying Marilyn a Coke and himself a beer Rick made a startling announcement. "As you know, I'm setting up a furniture export business in Cebu and I'll need a bookkeeper."

"Are you offering me a job?" came the surprised reply.

"Yes I am. I'll have to check your papers and references first of course but I'm a good judge of character and I'm sure you are exactly what I need."

"What would be my monthly salary? It would need to easily cover the rent of my accommodation."

"I believe three thousand a month would be fair and as a bonus you can live in my house, if you wish, rent free in return for a little light housekeeping."

"I'll take it," smiled Marilyn but her face showed a certain skepticism since most foreigners lied and tricked Filipinos at every possible opportunity.

"Good. It'll take me a couple of weeks to find a suitable house to rent and premises for my furniture factory. If you give me your phone number and address I'll contact you when I'm ready. What about your family? Will they object at the sudden loss of your services?"

Marilyn was a little taken aback by the definiteness and certainty of this man. In a country where uncertainty is the norm this was rather a shock. "My parents won't mind at all. They'll be happy if I've found real employment and since I'm the eldest my brother and sister won't object. As for the phone number, we don't have one. It takes years to get a phone even in the city and you can simply forget it was ever invented if you live in a provincial area. However you can send me a letter. It should arrive within a week."

Rick pictured Marilyn's family living in a comfortable house with all the usual accoutrements but sans telephone and felt sorry for them. "I hope you're serious," queried the simultaneously excited and doubtful girl.

"Don't worry. I am."

The dining room was now almost empty. The couple adjourned to a nearby deck railing and watched the endless waves competing with the darkness. "A man should never ask a lady's age but I'm afraid curiosity has got the better of me," angled Rick. "I'm twenty-six and turn twenty-seven in February," spoke Marilyn softly. "And what about you?"

"Thirty-five but I feel like I'm a hundred." Marilyn laughed. "You certainly don't look like a hundred but if you are you must be very rich by now." The determined man replied with a laugh of his own. All around the ship a creeping silence was gathering – the silence of a large number of souls who simply will themselves to sleep. "I suppose we'd better do the right thing and hit our bunks," suggested Rick. At that the two of them retired to their humble cots, which were not more than fifty meters apart although that space was occupied by at least thirty persons.

As the sun rose across the green sea sending shafts of light along the decks and across the faces of the reposed passengers Rick awoke. With only a little hesitation he walked over to Marilyn's cot and sat down. Twenty minutes later her striking eyes opened. "How long have you been here?" At the worried strain in her voice he attempted to reassure her. "Only a couple of minutes. I thought we could share the fabled breakfast together."

"Breakfast isn't until 7:30 but the canteen opens in fifteen minutes and we could have some coffee I suppose."

After the coffee the breakfast bell sounded and they dutifully sidled into the dining room. The meal consisted of rice and a crispy dried fish, which, although it wasn't kind to the nostrils, didn't taste too bad. By ten o'clock the MV Krisco was making its way down the channel separating the main island from its nearest neighbor, Mactan. Green fields presided over by acres of palms gradually gave way to a vista of industry and none-too-attractive edifices of concrete and corrugated iron. With the passing of another hour the docks came into sight.

Mothers with children commenced gathering their belongings and an air of expectation hung above the crowds of passengers. Lives would resume, lovers meet again and for many the call of home sounded strongly. Rick and Marilyn patiently waited for their turn to walk down the gangplank.

"I have another boat to catch to Samar," asserted Marilyn. "It leaves at eight o'clock tonight and I'll visit a friend in the city during the day. Since you don't know anyone here I suppose you'll have to stay in a hotel for a while. I can suggest the China Hotel in Colon; it's basic but it has aircon and is not expensive." Rick thanked her for the advice and swore he'd write to her as soon as he was evenly slightly established.

Once ashore Marilyn climbed onto a jeepney while her companion walked to one of the waiting taxis. Marilyn wondered if he'd really contact her as the jeepney sped away towards downtown. Rick's taxi traversed the heavy traffic comprising of tricycles, cars and the odd smoking bus and within twenty minutes dropped him at the China Hotel. The fare of thirty-five pisos seemed ridiculously cheap but he wasn't going to argue. In fact the majority of taxi drivers around the world are honest. It's only the rogues who gather the fame though.

The hotel was an aged affair comprising four storeys of yellow painted concrete. A muted cacophony from dozens of individual air conditioners vied with the noises from the street for attention. To his surprise the hotel didn't have a higher tariff for foreigners. He was checked in to Room 302 on the fourth floor for the regular sixty pisos a night. It was clean and cool and showed no signs of nightlife of the insect variety. The lack of a television Rick considered a bonus. Advertisements, pathetic game shows demanding great humiliation of contestants for paltry amounts of cash, violent soap operas and endless national back-patting – all in Tagalog – were the sole occupants of the screen as he'd discovered in less than an hour of total viewing.

After freshening up with a shower, cold but who needs hot water in that climate? Rick decided to do a little exploring. Diagonally across from the hotel entrance was a modest kitchenette that apart from serving cold beer and snacks provided a measure of sanctuary from the armies of beggars and seedy individuals that populated the grimy street. Seating himself where he could survey the passing traffic outside he ordered a bottle of Red Horse, an extra strong beer that comes in half-liter bottles and a plate of pork crackling in vinegar.

The beer was cold but the comely girl in a smart uniform who served it was anything but. Her gold sash was emblazoned with the moniker, "San Miguel the oldest and the best."

"Why do the breweries send employees to beer outlets?" Rick queried innocently. "Competition for the throats of beer drinkers is extremely fierce in the Philippines," answered the girl. "By the way I'm Sally. What's your name?" Rick introduced himself and added a quick summary of his background and present business. Once the Red Horse bottle stood empty he thought he'd switch to the regular San Miguel. It tasted better and wasn't quite so vicious. Sally was quick to oblige and his order appeared along with her voluptuous smile.

He had just raised his bottle to his lips while gazing at the Promo girl's curvaceous figure when several very loud gunshots rang out. At the end of the narrow road on which the kitchenette stood and in the middle of the intersection where Colon Street met up with a major crossroad lay the prone figure of a uniformed policeman. More shots echoed throughout the late afternoon scene. The regular pandemonium of rush hour traffic was instantly transformed into complete chaos. Crowds of pedestrians were running in all directions and almost magically the vehicles that had been plying the thoroughfare vanished. After what seemed a very long minute or so the wail of sirens echoed between the buildings and dozens of police cars backed up by lorries carrying soldiers converged on the scene.

Uniformed men sporting Armalites appeared in their hundreds. A soldier appeared at the entrance of the kitchenette and ordered the clientele to stay exactly where they were. Teams of police were hurriedly talking to witnesses and hastily searching nearby premises. "How many were there?" asked a police captain of an elderly woman who had been waiting for a jeepney when the violence erupted. "Siguro (Maybe) five or six Sir," the lady replied. "They headed into the cinema over there," she continued while pointing with a bony finger. A dozen or more soldiers were quickly detailed to search the cinema complex and yet others checked the two nearby barbershops. A couple of barbers and the white-uniformed hostess girls who provide services much beyond that of a haircut peered out from their premises as much as they dared.

Thirty minutes later and the customers in the kitchenette were told by the soldier that they could leave. Rick stayed put however and requested another San Miguel from Sally. By this time confused details of what had occurred began to filter in. "What on earth do you think happened?" Rick asked of the promo girl. "Three policeman and one bystander have been shot dead apparently. It looks like the work of an NPA hit squad."

"What's the NPA?" fired his next question. "The New People's Army, a communist guerrilla group that has been fighting the government for over twenty years. They have hit squads called Sparrows and those belong to the Alex Bayancara Brigade." When he inquired as to why they killed the police Sally answered in a lowered voice. "They say they only kill corrupt officials and cops but who really knows?"

After a couple more beers and another hour Rick left the kitchenette and ventured down the street to what looked like a slightly more up market bar and restaurant. 'Our Place' bar and restaurant offered the usual disco music and dancing girls but boasted the added attraction of Western meals. Seating himself at the bar Mr. Daly duly ordered bangers and mash with gravy and peas. Despite only having thus far experienced a relatively short sojourn in the Philippines Rick had already had more than enough of the ubiquitous sardines and cold rice. The sausages and mashed potato went down very nicely indeed. The owner of the establishment was a retired Australian policeman who was married to a Filipina.

With a full dinner on board Rick couldn't face any more beer so he switched to drinking rum and Cokes and settled down to watch the dancers perform. Only one girl would appear on the diminutive stage at any one time and their bikinis stayed firmly in place. The second dancer to strut the boards after Rick's arrival kept smiling at him. When she had left the stage she sidled up to him and while experiencing that well-oiled generosity Rick invested in a ladies' drink. Her lemonade cost Rick fifty pisos but she continued to smile into his eyes. Her name was Lina and she looked to be not much older than eighteen. After the usual small talk she returned to dance again. Slim and with very long straight hair she certainly filled the part of being exotic.

"Been in Flipland long," inquired a husky voice with an obvious Australian accent from the next stool. The voice belonged to a nearly bald man in his fifties and who boasted a stomach that had been trained on countless Fosters and San Miguels over the years. "Nearly a week by now," Rick replied.

"If it wasn't for the cheap beer and lovely girls none of us would spend an hour in this dump." The voice assumed the authoritative tone of one who knows. "I'll admit that there are certain challenges such as the dirt and the beggars but it doesn't seem that bad," Rick answered his neighbor. "And it looks pretty good to me, what with the lovely girls and cheap beer."

"I'm Archie and you'll learn. Pleased to meet you." The obligatory handshake accompanied Rick's introduction of himself. "What do you make of the shooting a couple of hours ago?"

"Shootings are pretty commonplace around here but three cops shot dead in the middle of downtown in broad daylight is extreme even for Flipland." Archie then presented a ten-minute rundown on the insurgency situation. "You'll quickly discover that anything can happen here," he added. "Surprises are so common that nothing is surprising. And by the way, don't fall for the virgin dancer routine. When I first came to this country, I was sold a 'virgin' in this bar in Ermita for about five times the usual bar fine. As soon as she was back in my room I put it to her straight. 'Are you really a virgin?' I said. She replied, 'I was once.' 'How original,' I said. 'For that matter so was I.' Live and learn!"

It turned out that Archie had been living in Cebu for four years and was married to a Filipino woman. "I did the right thing and brought her to Australia," he confided, "but strangely enough she didn't like it. Said that Sydney was too quiet and boring. Like all the other Filipino expats she surrounded herself with other Filipinas. Most of them were ex-bargirls and so dishonest and troublemaking that she couldn't stand them after a while. Said she wanted to get back home where she could quickly sort people out. Some of her girlfriends would go to the doctor when they became sick and be prescribed medicine. However, whenever some Filipina or other told them that the medicine would just make them sicker and they should rub olive oil on their stomachs or some such other crap they would then throw the medicine away and follow the advice of the Filipina. I call this stupid behavior the Filipino theory of truth. This idiocy was too much even for Mercy."

"How could you just move here? What about your job?" Rick's latest question was met with a laugh of derision. "She wanted to go back and that was it. At least she didn't marry me to get to a Western country, clean me out and then latch on to another feller. I was a mid-level bank employee. At that time they were on a round of staff cuts and I was lucky enough to get a voluntary redundancy. When we arrived back in Cebu, after all the handouts to the family and gift giving etc. there was enough for Mercy to buy a small beauty parlor. She makes a living and it keeps her out of trouble."

"Well what about you? Where does your beer money come from?" ventured Rick as he ordered two rum Cokes. Archie continued. "I still have enough left to live on quite comfortably here. Provided, that is, that not too many more financial emergencies happen to Mercy's family."

"What do you mean? Is it ….." Archie cut Rick's question short. "Last year her sister caught tuberculosis and the treatment was pretty expensive. The year before her cousin was involved in some trouble and it cost quite a bit of cash to square it all with the cops."

Suddenly a slender arm thrust itself around Rick's neck and a warm body moist with perspiration plonked itself on his lap. Lina was back from her latest spell of dancing and expressed her desire for more of Rick's company as well as another ladies' drink. "I'm fairly busy right now talking to my friend, I'm sorry." Lina's curvaceous figure flew from his lap with almost the same velocity that it had arrived, a shake of the shiny hair announcing her displeasure.

Turning back to his new companion, Rick was almost stuck for words. "How can so much bad luck happen to one family?" he inquired. "Easy," responded Archie. "Unless a family is pretty wealthy, here things just keep rolling over them. And that's the regular decent folk. There are many foreigners married to Filipinas whose families steal them blind and then when the cash cow finally runs out of milk the wife suddenly abandons the husband to look for greener pastures."

"You're joking," Rick mumbled although he knew Archie was being deadly serious.

The outbreak of a sudden round of applause cut into the pair's conversation. A new dancer, a petite girl who didn't look a day over sixteen had taken the stage to the strains of Kate Bush's 'Babushka.' After only thirty seconds gyration she'd abandoned her bra and panties exposing her small but firm breasts and badge of womanhood to the adoring audience. Archie smiled approvingly and Rick couldn't stop himself focusing on the new performer. From the sidelines Lina was glancing daggers at her latest heartthrob.

"Enjoy it while it lasts," suggested Archie. "Bold dancing as the Flips call it doesn't happen very often in Western owned bars. It's illegal. Mind you it's the order of the day in the Filipino bars across town."

"They sound interesting," commented Rick.

"Only if you like warm beer, girls that can't speak English, no edible food and an even sleazier clientele," came the matter of fact reply.

"What does your wife say when you spend time in these establishments?" Archie pulled himself off his stool a little, whistled at the young naked dancer and smiled. "I'm the boss of my family. I pay the bills and I do as I like. If occasionally I slip up with one of these dancers so to speak, Mercy turns a blind eye. It's the Filipino way. The men are definitely in charge here. Mind you it wasn't like that back in Sydney. I danced for a few minutes too long with one of her girlfriends in a Leagues club and she nearly murdered me. Yet if I took her to a restaurant and she was overly friendly with other guys – she's a good looker – and I complained I was told to grow up. As they say, when in Rome…" Archie stared hard at the naked girl on the platform just before she exited. "I feel the possibility of slipping up tonight," he grinned.

When Rick mentioned his business plans to his newfound friend Archie shook his head. "You're a brave one. That's for sure. At least you don't have any Filipino relatives, which is a plus. But how are you going to open a business without a Filipino majority shareholder? Foreigners aren't allowed to own businesses outright here unless they're multinationals."

"I hadn't really thought about it but I guess I'll have to find a suitable local business partner."

"Be very careful," Archie advised.

It was already 1:30 am and Rick was feeling a tad inebriated and sleepy. After accepting Archie's business card he made his way out of the bar and headed for his hotel. As he walked up the street a girl called after him in one of the Philippine dialects. He turned. It was Lina. "Goodnight," he responded not understanding the insults that had been hurled his way and kept walking. The fifty-meter journey to his lodgings didn't tax him despite an eventful day. There were still the flashing lights and other trappings of a high profile murder investigation but otherwise the darkened streets were quiet with little activity outside of the scattered bars.

A sound night's sleep saw Rick awaken somewhat refreshed at 8:30 am the following day. It was a Sunday and the sound of church bells could be faintly heard in the distance. A simple but edible breakfast of boiled eggs and coffee was more than sufficient to obliterate the cobwebs of the night before. Being Sunday he was certain that it would be useless to pursue any of his assigned business tasks and that therefore he was free to check out his new home. A stroll around downtown with its endless obstacles of street vendors and aimless gathered crowds was terminated when the "Hey Joe's" and "Piso Joe," became too much. By this time Rick was back in the familiar street of the China Hotel. To escape the ongoing harassment he dived into the barbershop next to the kitchenette where he'd been drinking during the assassination of the three cops. He didn't need a haircut but the idea of a relaxing shave appealed to him.

As he parked his backside in a rather comfortable if worn leather chair and felt the warm soapy water on his cheeks several of the white clad girls strolled by suggesting that he might like a massage after his shave. There were two types of massage offered. The first cost ten pisos and was performed by the barber as the client sat in the chair while the second had a tariff of fifty pisos and the added mystery of being conducted by the white clad hostesses in private rooms upstairs. There is only so much mystery one can cope with in a short space of time so Rick decided to let that unknown remain so for a few days. He did however accept the services of the ear cleaning lady, a homely middle-aged matron with an interesting set of tools. A light was strapped to her head and she worked with scrapers and cotton buds to mention a few. The sensation was somewhat pleasant in a masochistic sort of way and at its conclusion Rick felt certain that the sounds of life emanating from the street were louder than before. Between the attentions and attempted attentions of the various employees of Amigos he contentedly sipped on an ice-cold beer. By the time he emerged from his sanctuary an hour had passed and his wallet was only thirty-five pisos lighter and that included the tips.

More out of curiosity than any intention to purchase anything he walked to the nearest large department store, Gaisano Metro, which was only about 200 meters away. "Why would a simple department store need armed guards?" he thought as he greeted the four smiling men in blue uniforms and carrying shotguns that were standing next to the entrance. The Sunday crowds were out in force and movement from one area to another wasn't entirely without incident. Apart from the extreme care to avoid bumping into someone or being bumped in to, or worse still, being pick-pocketed, Rick's attention was focused on assimilating the scene. The goods on sale, in the main, were not overwhelming. However the sporting goods section proudly displayed a variety of spring bladed knives and extremely lethal-appearing crossbows. A variety of handcuffs were also on sale, suggesting that a sizeable portion of the populace were civic minded enough to part with some of their own hard earned cash to equip themselves with the wherewith all for performing citizen's arrests.

The most notable feature of the scene was the sheer number of shop assistants. Three or four dutifully manned each of the half dozen tills on each floor. Almost all were female, young and resplendently good looking in their green uniforms. An ancient looking clock with a viciously white face reported the time as being almost noon. A sign next to the escalators suggested that its readers were probably hungry and therefore should head to the café on the fourth floor. Eager to obey such an innocuously pleasant directive Rick strode the moving stairway to the appointed level and looked for the eatery.

A surprisingly elegant gathering of tables and chairs nestled around a simple fountain and artificial greenery, beckoned. Behind the two young ladies in pink a large board listed the offerings. Rick noticed the phrase, 'Bola Bola,' in between the more common items of hamburgers, toasted sandwiches and various drinks. "What's bola bola?" he inquired of the shorter of the two pink-clad waitresses. "Meat balls, Sir but I bet you know all about it!"

"I beg your pardon," mumbled Rick.

"I'm sorry Sir. You must be new here. 'Bola Bola' is our dialect word for the lies guys tell girls when they are trying to lead them into some wickedness."

"You learn something every day," the smiling Westerner announced. "I never knew that guys would lie to girls in order to seduce them. However the meat balls sound interesting."

"Would you like to order them Sir?"

"Yes please and also a cappuccino, a plate of chips and a mango smoothie."

According to the price list the total would be sixty-five pisos. To his amazement the girl produced a calculator to add the four items and arrived at a total of eighty-two pisos. After a ten-minute lesson in elementary mathematics the lass conceded that Rick was right and he took his seat. The mango smoothie was delicious, the chips passable and the coffee not bad. The bola bola tasted spicy yet bland. After all, Rick considered, the sign didn't say what kind of meat was used in the meatballs!

On his way out of the store he paused at the perfume counter to buy some locally-made aftershave. "I'm afraid we only have the imported ones here," a tall salesgirl in her early thirties consoled, "Local aftershaves are sold in the grocery department." The girl was particularly friendly and inquired as to where Rick came from. After answering her he had a question of his own. "How many hours do you work here?"

"Nine hours a day and we get three days off a month."

"With all that work I suppose you must be earning a very good living?"

"If you call fifty pisos a day a good living," came a rather terse reply. "Out of that we have to pay our room rent and buy our clothes and food. A small payment is even deducted for our uniforms."

"Jesus!" blurted out Rick, forgetting that he was in a deeply Catholic country. "How can you survive?"

"Barely. I share a room with another girl and can just get by. Maybe one day I'll have a husband to support me." Rick quickly bought an American aftershave although it seemed pricey and exited the store. The thought occurred to him that the saleslady's extreme affability might have had an ulterior motive.

Rick spent the remainder of the afternoon on a serendipity experiment. Outside Gaisano Metro he had climbed aboard the first jeepney that stopped. He neither knew the destination nor cared. It was with the thirst of a young child that he absorbed all this new world had to offer. After no more than a minute a passenger rapped the roof of the cabin with his knuckles and the contraption abruptly halted. "Bayad usa," the man called out and handed a piso to the driver. Once again the vehicle resumed motion. Its next stop following the rapping sound was followed with the call, "Bayad tatlo," at which three passengers paid and alighted.

Rick's initial lesson in Filipino language, Cebuano at least, was nearly complete. 'Bayad' meant pay and 'usa' meant one.

Twenty-five minutes later and the jeepney pulled up in a cloud of dust next to rows of wooden houses on one side of the road and open fields leading to hills sparsely populated with coconut trees on the other. "Here we are at Tisa, the killing fields," the driver, who was somewhat of a joker, shouted. This area of the metropolis was notorious for being a favored dumping ground for the bodies of criminals and other undesirables who had been 'salvaged.' An English teacher might explain the meaning of this word as recovering as much as possible from a wreck. Yet the linguistically-mischievous Filipino people use the term to describe the removal by death of an otherwise obstinate piece of human garbage. This was as good a spot as any to jump ship. Besides it was the turn-around point of the jeepney's route before it headed back to the untidy beehive of Colon, the city center. "Bayad usa," Rick attempted as he handed over a piso. "No way, Joe. It's two pisos once you get past Labangon," the driver laughed. On impulse Rick gave him two more pisos. "The ride was worth three anyway."

A brisk two-kilometer walk saw Rick pass Sari Saris, tiny general stores that sold simple food, soft drinks, beer and the like, diminutive factories that appeared more as junkyards than premises of production and rows of barbecue stands. "Manok, baboy," one old woman with a frail stature challenged Rick as he passed. He wasn't hungry so he passed up the offer of chicken or pork. As he continued his meandering a burst of noise and an emanating dust cloud caught his attention. In a vacant lot there was a crowd of sixty or seventy persons, almost entirely male, excitedly cheering, exhorting and bewailing simultaneously. Quietly the Sunday explorer strolled up to the pulsating throng. His arrival went either totally unnoticed or was ignored. Through a gap that appeared between the torsos of denim clad men he could see what was generating the dust. Feathered wings were flying furiously in all directions, razor-equipped claws were digging for blood and violence and the immanence of death filled the air.

It was a sabong or cock fight, the Sunday pastime of many an inveterate Filipino gambler. After a few more seconds the loser, a white rooster, lay dead in the dust and wads of money changed hands. Not being a great devotee of blood sports Rick left the gathering with the same stealth and speed with which he had arrived. It was already dusk and the numbers of young men who gathered on street corners waiting for something to happen were on the increase. Rick suddenly felt very, very alone. The quickened pace of his walk back to the jeepney turnaround point was only interrupted by a solitary small girl spouting the familiar "Piso Joe." The smile on her face betrayed the fact that this was more of a childhood amusement than a serious activity for her.

By the time a jeepney headed for Colon reached the stop it was night. It was as if a switch had been flicked. Climbing aboard Rick noticed that two passengers had paid the driver but stayed on board. More joy riders, he thought of the two rather well decked out youths in their smart white T-shirts and ironed pants. There were very few passengers getting on along the way back to the city. The low-wattage bulb in the cabin cast the faintest of lights, just enough for passengers to be able to see their money.

Although there was plenty of room the acquisition of a nurse on her way to work caused the youths to move right along so they were seated next to Rick. The nearer of the two started to read a newspaper. Didn't their mothers warn them about the perils of reading in poor light, Rick mused to himself? After what seemed twice the amount of time taken for the outbound journey the jeepney reached Gaisano Metro and Rick alighted. A passing teenage girl in her church clothes pointed to his pocket and laughed. Looking down Rick noticed that there was a long slashing cut diagonally running across the hip pocket of his jeans. Luckily his wallet was still inside, trying to get out like a newborn escaping after a caesarean. Shifting the wallet to another pocket Rick cursed. A brand new pair of jeans ruined.

Back at his hotel he took a shower and on dressing, looked at his watch. Eight o'clock. He thought he'd head back to the restaurant and bar he'd visited the previous evening. Simple Western food always beats tasteless cold rice and fish that were probably starved to death. To his surprise the owner's wife remembered his name. "What's your choice for this evening Rick?"

He consumed a chicken schnitzel with baked potatoes and peas washed down with a cold ale. Dinner done, Rick returned to the ground floor bar area and once more propped on a stool, prepared to absorb the disco music and general proceedings. Looking around he couldn't see any sign of yesterday's companion. In fact there were very few customers at all tonight. Thus undivided, his attention was only forced to alternate between the stage and ordering beers. A procession of slender 'maidens' shook their booty to the tunes of their favorite songs. After an hour or so Rick was in the process of deciding to have an early night. Just as he stood up Lina appeared on the dais. Her smiles in his direction were even more intense than the previous night. She must have gotten over her aggravation. He resumed his seat and gazed back. Five minutes later and the girl was seated in his lap and kissing his neck in between mouthfuls of very expensive cola.

It was a warm evening. Mind you it's always warm in that part of the world. There are only two seasons, as someone once said, hot and hotter. Rick still felt that his bed was calling but since he hadn't had a woman for a while he thought he might bring Lina with him. The payment of the bar fine and the passage of fifteen minutes saw Lina glancing around Rick's hotel room for a television. "There isn't one, Rick smiled wickedly. I'll guess we'll just have to start on our own entertainment immediately."

Lina peeled off her clothes, disappeared into the compact bathroom for a few minutes and returned with beads of moisture glistening on her body. Staring at her nude figure Rick asked if she had any children. "One," she replied, "a four-year old boy. It's the usual story. My boyfriend promised to marry me and seduced me. When I became pregnant he ran away and I was left in disgracia. My family were horrified and the neighbors talked so much that I had to leave my village and dance; so here I am."

"Sad," murmured Rick. "To look at your figure I'd have thought that you hadn't ever had any kids." With a flurry of activity Lina dived on Rick, forcing him onto the bed and removing his clothes with such force that his shirt sustained a tear. The girl's enthusiasm didn't belie her performance. Near on two hours of intense activity passed before the pair fell asleep.

In the morning the man gave the girl two hundred pisos. "For your son," he mumbled. Lina took the money and kissed him hard on the mouth. "I have to go home and do some chores before it's time for me to return to work," she stated. "Remember, you're mine. If I see you with another girl I'll kill you!" At that she departed down the corridor. Rick made a mental note to avoid Our Place for a week or two.

The next few days saw him actually performing an activity approximating work. Dutifully he scanned the Sun Star and the other city newspapers looking for a suitable house to rent. Although a house was the first priority he was also searching for suitable premises to establish his factory. By Wednesday morning he had inspected five houses and two business premises without success. That afternoon he came across a house in Labangon that appeared perfect; four bedrooms, a tiny garden and its own water supply courtesy of a spear pump and tank. The asking rent of 12,000 pisos a month was reasonable enough so he took it. Three days later and one of the bedrooms was converted into an office and he moved in. It was good to see the back of hotel living for a while and his new abode was only four kilometers from the city center.

Another ten days had passed before he'd located a suitable factory site. Located in the famous Tisa area it was close enough to his house and relatively cheap. Setting up the equipment and hiring tradesmen was going to be a much more demanding endeavor. Yet he'd made a good start.

Chapter Four

Crammed into a miniscule space on one of the two parallel benches of the crowded jeepney Marilyn had thought what a fine figure of a man Rick cut as she caught a parting glimpse of the foreigner approaching a waiting taxi. Most likely his job offer was merely bola bola and the only logical thing to do was forget about it. Yet, the young woman desperately hoped and forced herself to believe that he might have been sincere.

She made her way to her friend's boarding house situated on P. Burgess Street. As luck would have it Rosie was at home. Marilyn and she had studied together at the University of Eastern Samar and as they hadn't seen each over for over a year they had much to catch up on. "Still no boyfriend?" inquired Marilyn. As both girls were in their late twenties the question of marriage prospects hovered in the background of their consciousnesses, all the more so due to the increasingly less subtle hints and pressures from their families. Rosie's mother had warned her about the dangers of turning thirty. "As you are well aware there are many more eligible females in this country than men and half of those men are worse than useless."

"Not a glimmer of romance I'm afraid," confessed Rosie. "The closest I seem to come to finding true love is the vulgar wolf whistles of the standbys on street corners."

"How about you?" Marilyn shook her head and the conversation turned to other matters. In addition to the countless fiestas held by the various communities in city and province alike, Cebu City held a yearly festival, called Sinugba, in January. Processions, music and dramas lasting several days prevented the population from feeling too deflated after the cessation of the formal Christmas festivities. The thought of all the gaiety and social intercourse held fast in the imaginations of both girls. "I suppose you'll go home to the province for Christmas?" remarked Rosie. Her companion replied in the affirmative. "I have to stay here unfortunately," bemoaned

Rosie, "as my company has so many unfilled orders to catch up on that we are only getting three days off over the entire Christmas period."

"When does your ship leave?" Rosie asked. "Eight o'clock," replied her guest. "Let's go to Fort San Pedro. You have time," Rosie continued. "They have a fun fair and rides at the moment and it'll be better than sitting in this dump."

Within half an hour the girls were strolling beneath the stone walls of the sixteenth century Spanish fort with its towering battlements. After buying some fairy floss from a vendor a rusty Ferris wheel caught Marilyn's eye. Up, down and around they revolved against the spectacular city view. "This is great," sighed Rosie. "Mind you I'm always scared that the thing will collapse while I'm on it."

"Don't be such a chicken," scolded Marilyn. "There've only been six fatal accidents involving amusement rides in the entire country this year; so what are the odds?"

A sudden cracking sound caused both girls to scream. The wheel stopped turning and their brown complexions turned decidedly pale. Before either could speak it began to move again. Another two rotations and they were back on terra firma once more.

Marilyn looked at her watch. "Six thirty. I'd better go to the ship." She had been determined to say nothing of her encounter with Rick on the journey from Manila to anybody. Tsismis or rumors grow in this land like tropical weeds. Yet the secret inside was burning a hole in Marilyn's entire being and cried to get out. "I've been offered a job here in Cebu by a tall handsome foreigner," she confided. "Is he rich?" joked Rosie. "Since most foreigners are rich forget about the job and work on getting him to marry you."

"Stop it. I'm not like that. It was probably just bola bola about the job anyway but then maybe it wasn't. A decent job is almost an impossible ask these days so I thought you'd be happy for me if it comes off."

"I am," apologized Rosie. "I was only teasing you."

After leaving Fort San Pedro and reaching the downtown area it was time for them to part. A quick hug and both girls caught different jeepneys.

Marilyn arrived at Pier 9 by 7 pm and boarded the Calbayog ferry. Unlike the behemoths that ply the Manila route this vessel was little larger than a motor yacht and had a legal limit of 100 passengers. The last of the 120 journeyers had boarded at 7:45 pm and the San Juan sailed with unusual punctuality for these waters at eight sharp. Black water met black sky and only the white foam crests challenged the darkness of the scene.

Marilyn woke from her slumber just on sunrise. For breakfast she consumed a boiled egg and some sticky rice purchased from a dockside vendor before the ship had sailed. The sun was strong and bright when the ferry berthed at the long jetty linking Calbayog city with its oceanic horizons. Only stopping for a coffee at a nearby stall Marilyn made hasty steps to the market square from where all provincial transportation emanated.

Slowly her jeepney filled up; a man with one leg, a boy struggling with an oversized rooster, two schoolgirls, an elderly nun and a soldier whose M16 was nearly as big as him. With a pregnant lurch the vehicle slowly left the square, snaked its way past a glistening white church, the dusty city hall and a mid-sized park of pale green bordered by rows of pink bougainvilleas and increased speed as it hit the concrete highway. Rocky hills frowned over this manmade intrusion framed by the backdrop of an azure sea.

Through an endless succession of villages and settlements, interspersed with sections where the road's only companions were green fields dotted with groves of coconut and nipa palms, the motley collection of humanity rolled. Periodically the collection changed its composition. A sun-wizened farmer replaced the nun while an American missionary occupied the seat previously warmed by the schoolgirls. When the village of Cagmanipis loomed into view and Marilyn called for the driver to stop only the soldier remained from those at the market square. Who knew the destinations and lives of those people and who cared? Not Marilyn as she ran with her baggage towards an adequate cement building on the corner of a small lane. "Mama, Papa, I'm back," she called out.

Her mother left her position in the store that formed half the front of the house and hugged her. "How was the trip? Did you get all the items we requested and what was the final cost?" Business, family, emotions and life all seemed to merge together in one single care. "It's all here; the cheapest price was in Santa Cruz. The total was P3, 500 and I've brought back five hundred pisos left over." Flora was impressed and gave her daughter another cuddle as she ushered her through the doorway that led into the house. Awoken from his customary siesta Ronaldo, her father, joined them. "We're very pleased to see you back Honey," he crooned as he kissed her.

The three then sat down to a customary lunch of dried fish, rice and some bitter greens. Juliet, Marilyn's younger sister, was over at her fiancé's house while Jun her only brother worked for the government in Calbayog and rented a room there. After talking for a while Marilyn took over her mother's role in the store so she could have a rest. The nightly repast was generally held around 8 pm and spared from the vagaries of television the family would retire early. Most days passed in a similar vein. Sundays provided the bane of the wives in the form of the sabong. Mysteriously, even the most impecunious of the unemployed males who owed money around much of the village would turn up at the gathering with wads of cash to wager. No criticism of such a mystery would ever be mouthed during the sabong. Sunday is an extremely religious day in most of the Philippines and the afternoon sabong is as least as sacred to its devotees as the morning church service with its sermons of hellfire and brimstone and exhorting the parishioners to suffer all in this life in exchange for a fair go in the next.

Out of all the disruptions to tedious daily routine vicious gossip was the most common. Every so often one of the villagers, on the pretext of buying a small bag of ice, would spend at least twenty minutes reporting the sad tale of the latest village girl who had fallen pregnant after being seduced by one of the worst of the local boys. The only objective judgment on the veracity of these tales lay in the faces of their principal characters. If the boy was seen drinking and loudly carrying on with his buddies and the girl was seldom seen at all and if so, seen crying or otherwise carrying a dejected countenance the tsismis or gossip could generally be believed.

Cagmanipis, like many of the other villages that dot the coastline of Western Samar, is officially a fishing village. As a result of years of atrocious practices such as the use of dynamite the few tiny fish that remained to be caught wouldn't support a litter of kittens let alone a settlement of a couple of thousand people. The young men, apart from a fortunate few who had gained the chance to become seamen, remained as layabouts and drunks who called themselves fishermen. Remarkably, considerable numbers of the teenage girls travelled to Manila or Cebu to work as maids and were able to send home enough money to support their families. No-one in the entire village would ever dare to start a tsismis about the activities of any village girl who was working in Cebu or Manila. It was an unwritten law that these daughters or saints of the village could never be criticized for bringing the cash that the community needed to survive.

The Wednesday morning following Marilyn's return saw her seated at the side of her mother in their store. A middle-aged woman with a sour face rushed excitedly up to the counter. "Susan's back," she said. "You know the girl who went to Manila and married an Australian airline pilot."

"I'd heard about Susan marrying an old foreigner but I didn't know he was a pilot." Flora wasn't quite as big on gossip as most of the women. "He's a pilot all right and you should just see the money and gifts that Susan has brought her family. She's only been in Australia for two years and already she's back visiting. They're having a bathroom added to their house and they're opening a store." Flora's heart skipped a beat at the sound of the last word and Marilyn appeared uncharacteristically stern. She'd never cared much for Susan or her family who were a bunch of no-goods. Such tales seldom bring joy to anyone.

Back in Wollongong, Stan, a retired steelworker, at that very moment was readying the latest model airplane he'd built for the weekend's test flight. He could ill afford the money he'd given his wife for her trip home but there was no way he could've refused it. Fresh from her journey from Manila Susan was sleeping in her parents' house and constantly dreaming that she'd become pregnant from her recent tryst with one of her old boyfriends.

After the sour-faced woman had left Marilyn spoke up. "Don't worry about that new store being any competition to us, Mama. The father and his friends will drink and gamble away all its capital in a month or two."

"I suppose you're right," agreed Flora and lightened up a little. "However, talking of marriage, you'll be thirty next year and I don't see any marriage prospects on the horizon. Your father and I sacrificed to send you to college. As an educated woman you should be attractive to a man with prospects."

"Don't start that again Mama," Marilyn intoned. "I simply haven't met anyone suitable yet." The daughter was in two minds about mentioning Rick's offer. On the one hand it might never come to fruition but on the other it demonstrated the fact that she was keeping an eye out for possibilities. The next two weeks passed with an almost absolute boredom. Marilyn had given up all hope concerning Rick and the promised opportunity. She'd have to keep helping her parents and sitting in a store in a godforsaken village waiting for some eventuality to turn up. Opportunity is one of those unjust creatures that slaves feverishly for the wealthy and powerful but makes a determined effort to pass locations like Cagmanipis by.

"I don't see any letter from your new beau," Juliet had cruelly teased. Marilyn rued the moment that she'd told her sister the story. "Your fiancé, Dodong, promised to marry you last year and I don't see any wedding date yet," she retorted. "We're still trying to save money but at least he's real." Juliet exited the room to feed the pigs leaving her sister feeling more miserable than she had for a very long time.

Christmas with all its outpourings had faded away and Marilyn had hardly noticed its passing. The celebrations, the firecrackers and increased drunkenness in the village had all left her feeling jaded. "Show me a Filipino who's lost interest in Christmas and I'll show you a Filipino who's lost interest in life," a Manila newspaper columnist had once quipped. New Year came and went in the same fashion. Going through the motions with a somewhat catatonic soul Marilyn set off for Calbayog one Saturday morning to make some routine purchases for the store. On her return shortly before dusk, Juliet excitedly greeted her. "There's a letter for you." Her sister thrust it into her hand and crowded her so that there was no possibility of a private reading. Marilyn held it fast for a while and then excused herself to answer a call of Nature. Having fought for and won a modicum of privacy she ripped open the envelope.

Dear Marilyn,

It was such a pleasure to meet you on the ship from Manila. I must apologize for the delay in writing but it took longer than I had expected to find a suitable house and longer still to locate premises that would serve for a factory. The house is at 34 Narra Street, La Paloma Subd., Labangon and the workshop will be established only a few kilometers away in Tisa.

Luckily the home I have rented has a telephone (7-92-51) so please give me a call when you arrive. I do hope that you haven't changed your mind. In either case please contact me as soon as possible.

Warmest Regards,

Rick Daly

The letter was dated eight days prior so there was little time to lose. Marilyn's heartbeat had noticeably increased pace as she returned to her sister in the lounge room. "It's from him," she triumphantly exclaimed "and he's serious about the job." Juliet was pleased for Marilyn although still apprehensive. "You must be very careful with foreigners you know," she proffered by way of advice.

Marilyn broke the news to her parents over dinner. Her brother was also there that day and Flora had cooked up a local delicacy, Chicken Adobo. Marilyn was chewing on some of the smaller bones as she made her announcement. "I've been offered a real job," she blurted out as a bone somersaulted out of her mouth onto the plate. This news was such a shock that her mother failed to chip Marilyn about the impoliteness of speaking while chewing. "A job. What kind of job. Where?"

"Don't worry Mama, it's a respectable job as a bookkeeper in Cebu. I met a foreign man who is in the process of setting up a furniture factory for the export market."

"Did you now?" her father chimed in.

"How do you know what his intentions are?" Flora added.

"I consider myself to be a good judge of character," Marilyn added defensively. "Besides you are always telling me I should advance myself and if I stay here I shall eventually rot."

"She's right Flora," Ronaldo conceded. Jun, visiting from Calbayog, added his support to Marilyn's accepting a new opportunity and without too much further reflection the parents gave their consent and blessing to the venture.

The following Tuesday afternoon saw Marilyn struggling aboard a Calbayog bound jeepney with an oversized suitcase after hugging her parents and sister. By 6'oclock she was already seated next to her bunk on the Juanita, sister ship to the San Juan, and as she gazed at the setting sun the girl wondered what the coming months would bring. What real choice do I have? she pondered. Sitting in a remote village where nothing ever changes would simply amount to a living death in which the body ages faster than the passing seasons can justify and the soul atrophies by degrees. She wasn't surprised at the ironic fondness demonstrated by the inhabitants at the sound of trouble or some localized disaster; as long as the trouble or disaster wasn't descending on them or theirs. Anything that can relieve unremitting boredom is generally welcome until its true colors prove worse than the boredom it displaced.

Right on 8 pm the Juanita sailed. Exact punctuality twice in a row, Marilyn observed to herself. I hope it isn't some sort of negative omen. The night crossing was no more eventful than the trip over. Sleep nonetheless eluded her. Too many thoughts, hopes, fears and dreams buzzed endlessly through her head. As the first rays of the coming day struck the vessel's deck the demure adventurer had just released her mind's hold and drifted into a dream of her youth. The vision of endless coconut groves surrounding the effervescent play of innocent childhood vanished at the crash of the lowering gangplank. She was back in Cebu.

With the berthed vessel framed by a very blue sea Marilyn sat down to a meal of fish and rice. This particular quayside store boasted a telephone. It was a full ten minutes after she'd finished her repast before she'd been able to find the courage to ring Rick. She held the line for almost thirty seconds. No answer. Her heart sank. She ordered a coffee and simply stared at the Juanita. The ship appeared virtually demonic in her imagination. In the Philippines time generally passes more slowly than it does in other lands and on this occasion it was true to form. As Marilyn drained her coffee she glanced at the modest watch on her wrist. "Ten-forty." It was only fifteen minutes since the unsuccessful call. After a second coffee it was only ten-fifty. Still she tried again, her hand shaking as it held the receiver.

"Hello." It was Rick's voice, strong and masculine, at last. "It's me, Marilyn," the girl whispered. "Where are you?" the voice inquired. "Here at the docks in Cebu," she murmured. "When can you come?" the voice continued in a confident tone. "I can be there in an hour."

"Fine. I'll be waiting."

As she replaced the receiver and handed over two pisos for its use to the storeowner Marilyn could hear her heart beating so loudly that she was afraid everyone within fifty meters could hear it also. It was done. She was committed for better or for worse.

Chapter Five

The dockside jeepneys were jam packed with passengers and the admittance of Marilyn with her overly generous valise was simply out of the question. Resigning herself to the expenditure of thirty pisos Marilyn solicited a cab. The sun, hot as ever, was directly overhead as the still trembling girl arrived at Rick's new abode. A concrete bungalow with a tiny front lawn, a few flowers and high fence adorned with spikes and broken glass greeted her.

Even in this middle-class subdivision doorbells were somewhat of a rarity. "Ayo. Ayo. Hello!" she called. A tall man with a blue shirt and cream-colored trousers emerged from the front door and strode to the gate. Rick was even more handsome than she remembered. "I wasn't sure your offer was genuine," the girl stammered as the gate opened and Rick hauled her belongings inside. "It's genuine all right. I can't make this business happen on my own."

Being a reasonable host Rick brewed two cups of green tea and then sat down to talk to the new arrival. "The factory's leased but not established yet." He almost lost his train of thought as he looked at this girl. Wearing no makeup and clad in a simple yet stylish business dress of beige Marilyn looked every inch the lady. "First things first, I suppose," he ventured. "We'll get everything set up here and then progress to Tisa." The girl nodded automatic approval.

"How remiss of me," he apologized. "I haven't even shown you around the house yet." At that, he uplifted Marilyn's oversized case and took it to her room with the girl close on his heels. The room was modest with a bed, table, reading light and electric fan. Marilyn's mind raced. I hope he won't try to take advantage of me. This thought kept recurring. After all, foreigners, especially Western men, can't be trusted. Yet I'm a shrewd judge of character and he seems all right. These fears were partly laid to rest when the pair came to the office. It was air-conditioned and the latest 286 computer beamed up at them from its desk. This hall of accounting, word processing and paper-based labor separated her bedroom from the sleeping quarters of her new boss.

"What do you think?" Rick looked hard at Marilyn. "It's fine," she replied. "Does the TV in the lounge room work?"

"Of course. You can get cable, including CNN and the BBC, as well as the local channels. You like television then?"

"We don't have it in the province so I enjoy watching it if I have the chance," Marilyn asserted.

As the sun dropped from sight in the west Marilyn was feeling a little more settled and confident in her future. She offered to cook dinner but when she explained it would be fish and rice Rick insisted that he would perform the deed. Into the oven he placed a chicken along with some potatoes. "What's that?" Marilyn asked as the oven door was opened. "What do you mean?" Rick queried in turn. "That – the place you have put the chicken."

"Haven't you seen an oven before?" Rick suddenly became very worried about his new employee's skill set. "Not really; only in movies. Only very rich people have ovens. No one in our place does." Marilyn felt her olive skin turning slightly ruddy.

Ninety minutes later and the chicken was served. Marilyn politely refused the potatoes and insisted on cooking up some rice. "Filipinos can't live without rice," she explained. Dinner accomplished the pair spent an hour or so watching the dreaded box. Being tired from her journey Marilyn requested permission to retire. "You can sleep whenever you like, except during working hours," Rick joked. Safely tucked up in her new bed and with the door bolted Marilyn was quickly asleep, once more dreaming of her childhood. When she awoke the morning sunshine cast a warming glow on her new abode. After dressing she ventured beyond her immediate sanctuary into the lounge-room and kitchen. Everything was silent.

Two more hours passed by before Rick showed himself. Four steps led from the sleeping area to the dining room and thence the kitchen. Rick was on them. Marilyn gasped. "Good Heavens, It's ten-thirty and you're still in your pajamas."

"One hour of the day is as good as any other for anything," came the retort. As it was somewhat too late for breakfast Marilyn brought her new boss a coffee and told him to wait another hour and a half for lunch. Rick amused himself watching CNN on the TV until the appointed time. An endless succession of very expensive hotels occupying all four points of the compass filled the screen interspersed with the news that mattered according to the right wing and capitalistic American establishment. In short, the only news not pertaining to the U.S. mainland to which Rick was privy was a short item about Palestinians attacking Israeli settlements.

After a simple lunch of French fries and scrambled eggs Rick announced, "Since I'm going to be in the Philippines for some considerable time I'd better get a driving license." Marilyn merely smiled. "Please do some grocery shopping as we're low on food. Catch a taxi home." Rick handed over five hundred pisos for the shopping and another twenty-five for the cab fare. Dressed in very new blue jeans and a faded khaki shirt he bade Marilyn a temporary goodbye, exited the gate and strode to Tres d'Abril. Within five minutes a jeepney pulled up and he clambered on. Save for three exceedingly pretty nurses the vehicle was empty. Expanding himself into a largish area of seat he settled down to enjoy the eye candy. By the time the transportation arrived at the LTO (Land Transportation Office) on the highway a kilometer and a half shy of the city center all three nurses had directed vicious visual darts in the direction of the Westerner passenger and proceeded to look at anything and everything not tied to the quadrant where he was seated. Can't win them all, Rick smiled to himself as he alighted.

A dusty area interspersed by the odd weed led from the road to the vividly white building with a green tile roof, which was the Cebu office of the LTO. After waiting fifteen minutes in a queue of two Rick approached the counter. A middle-aged man with a kindly face was waiting. Rick spoke first. "Good afternoon. I've come to live and do business in Cebu for a number of years and I will need a local driving license."

"Ma-ayong hapon Joe, I mean good afternoon Sir," replied the beaming face of the office clerk. "Can I have your residence certificate Sir?"

"Residence certificate. What's that?" Rick mumbled. "To be eligible for a license you must have a certificate showing residency."

"Is that a residence visa in my passport?" queried Rick. "Hell, no. You'd never get one of those under Miriam Defensor Santiago anyway. A certificate of residency can be obtained from City Hall for about ten pisos as long as you have a proper residential address, not just a hotel."

"That's a relief," said Rick, "but who is Miriam Defensor Santiago?" The clerk smiled again. "She is a close friend of Cory, our president, and is the Commissioner for Immigration and Deportation. Let's just say that she doesn't care for you white folks too much."

Thanking the man for his help and vowing that he would return before closing time Rick sped off in the direction of City Hall. A fifteen-minute jeepney ride followed by a brisk five minutes on foot saw the city hall looming large behind a tidy park whose natural greenery was spoiled by the pillaging of numerous concrete paths.

Inside a three-storey colonial building numerous ceiling fans whirred comfortingly while rubber stamps were raised and lowered, slowly. As he reached the counter a woman of about forty smiled at the only foreigner on the floor. "I would like a certificate of residency," he explained.

"Do you have any proof that you are really a resident?" the lady replied. "I can tell you my address but I don't have anything on paper."

"You have an honest face so just fill in this form and come back here when it's done." Five minutes later Rick returned with the document. "That'll be twenty pisos thank you," beamed the lady as she filed his form. Ten minutes later Rick left that humid sanctuary with his new certificate.

Closing time for the LTO was four-thirty. It was already three-forty five before Rick returned. The same gentleman was manning the desk. "Got it," smiled Rick. A Polaroid photo, twenty minutes and 200 pisos later and Mr. Daly was the proud possessor of a Philippine driving license. On the far side of the room a group of young men were being instructed on traffic principles.

"What are they doing?" the foreigner inquired.

"Oh them. They're jeepney drivers being trained for their accreditation." The desk clerk was becoming increasingly amused at Rick's demeanor. Just as he was about to depart Rick had a sudden thought. "I'd better get a copy of the road rules," he imparted earnestly. An uproar of laughter from both the trainees and the entire office staff met his request. Rick bid them good day and set off for home.

Not far from his jeepney stop stood a cool looking kitchenette. Since it was a hot day, like all days in the Philippines, Rick thought that a refreshing ale might be in order. At the next table sat a group of military men who invited him to join them. "It's always pleasant to find a foreigner who's not too proud to drink with we Filipinos," announced the Colonel, the senior officer of the gathering as Rick took his seat. "Not at all," responded Rick. "I enjoy the hospitality of the Filipinos."

A thin man in his fifties with a kindly face and thin grey hair, the Colonel pushed over a bottle of San Miguel to Rick's corner. "Are you a tourist here or on business?" ventured a gentleman with thick wavy hair and a heavy gold necklace that graced his uniform. "Business," replied Rick, who then proceeded to give a three-minute summary of his mission. The Major, for that was the rank of the gentleman, smiled. "I wish you luck, for you'll surely need it." At that point one of the junior officers from the table embarked on a joke that somehow linked Cory Aquino's soiled underwear with a popular nude actress, Didith Romero. The uproarious laughter that followed left Rick fairly non-plussed since the joke was relayed in a Philippine dialect interspersed with occasional English phrases. The joke teller then courteously retold it entirely in English so that their new companion could also laugh.

"What do you think of all this coup business then?" inquired the furniture novice. "We all work at the military office across the road and such subjects are a little sensitive right now. Let's just say that Cory doesn't have many friends in Cebu city or in the Visayas as a whole. It isn't surprising as most government money is spent closer to her home province of Tarlac. We Cebuanos sometimes feel like a forgotten people." The conversation reverted to lighter matters and then a waitress with a winning smile and the kind of sexual mouth that can spell doom brought the next round. It was Rick's turn and he gladly obliged. Rick had been in the kitchenette about seventy minutes and had already consumed seven beers. Somewhat emboldened with the amber fluid he pointed to the major's necklace and spoke. "That's one hell of a necklace. Aren't you afraid of its being stolen by snatchers?"

"Not particularly," laughed the major as he raised his shirt a little, exposing the menacing black steel of a .45.

Night had fallen by this time and promising to return another day Rick took his leave. "We're here most days after work," the colonel said as he waved goodbye. Susan, the waitress with the dangerous mouth, directed a flashy smile in Rick's direction as he made his exit.

When he arrived back home Marilyn looked somewhat frosty. "You like your beer don't you?" she announced. "It's rather late for dinner but I'll make you some sardines." She didn't feel it her place to make any further comments about the cloud of brewery odors that emanated from Rick's mouth every time it opened. "I've had something to eat already so I'm fine thank you."

Marilyn retired early that evening so Rick sat in front of the TV alone. Settling down with a rum and Coke he lit a cigarette and watched the spirals of smoke swirling at the bidding of the ceiling fan. By 11:30 Rick was fast asleep.

The next morning Marilyn's familiar smile was back. "Here's your breakfast sir," she beamed as she served Rick bacon and eggs. "Cut out the 'sir' business but thanks for the breakfast. I suppose I should check out your papers for the sake of form." Marilyn excused herself for ten minutes and returned with a plastic folder containing her hard won educational accomplishments.

"Very impressive," commented her boss as he quickly perused them, "yet these certificates show that you will turn twenty-nine next month not twenty-seven as you told me on the boat." Marilyn laughed. "It isn't good to tell the truth all at once, especially to strangers. Please forgive me." Rick chuckled to himself. Stifling sounds of further merriment he spoke seriously. "You can return those papers now. I didn't really need to see them anyway." Rick felt safe enough now to proudly display both his residence certificate and driving license. "You were certainly fast enough in acquiring them," murmured Marilyn.

The next task was to establish the business and hire workers, so that very afternoon saw Rick in the offices of Pablo, Ameraldo and Sanchez, attorneys at law. Before leaving Sydney he'd had the foresight to seek recommendations for a suitable legal firm. Jun Pablo greeted Rick as a secretary offered him tea or coffee. Between sips of the rapidly produced beverage Rick digested the bad news. "As I see it Mr. Daly, you are not an international corporation but are simply an individual wishing to establish a business in the Philippines."

"That's correct," confirmed the client. "Under Philippine law," continued Mr. Pablo, "foreign citizens are prohibited from any outright ownership of any business or land holding. You may however own up to forty-nine percent of an enterprise provided that the other fifty-one is owned by a Filipino citizen."

"That's somewhat of a problem then," intoned Rick as he then remembered what the Australian guy in Our Place had said. "It's a simple matter to find a silent partner who qualifies under the law," stated the attorney. "However, finding one you can trust is another matter entirely."

The image of the lovely Marilyn sprang to Rick's mind. "Assuming I can find a suitable partner is there any way that I can mitigate the risk of being double-crossed?" Jun Pablo was a silent for some seconds, deep in thought. "You could always require the silent partner to execute a mortgage document over the business in your favour; a mortgage whose payments and nominal interest you would never enforce unless the worst happened."

Angel, Mr. Pablo's secretary, brought two more cups of coffee. "That might be just the solution then," purred Rick optimistically. "Normally, such a mortgage document is used as a protection over real estate," Jun continued, "but I can't see why one couldn't apply to a business that is registered to a Filipino citizen. There are no legal constraints against foreigners being beneficiaries of mortgages." Rick's faith in his new country's processes was somewhat restored.

"I'll double check the relevant statutes and call you at home this evening." Jun then shook Rick's hand and bade him a good day. In somewhat of a hurry to return home Rick hailed a passing cab. "La Paloma, off Tres d'Abril," he instructed the driver, "but first I'd like to buy some flowers." The compact green Daihatsu taxi sped off in the direction of Carbon market. Just shy of the market complex it halted. An elderly woman sat behind a tiny bench in front of which was a riot of color; roses, jonquils, azaleas, daffodils and all manner of tropical hues as well. "She needs the business," the driver explained. "Her prices are only slightly higher than in the market and her flowers are generally better presented."

Clutching a dozen roses ranging from subtle pink to blood red Rick returned to the cab. Buying flowers for Marilyn at this time may have been somewhat of a shrewd gesture but Rick simply wanted to. The impulse had been as irresistible as it was sudden. On reaching his home he gave the driver a generous tip and called from the gate.

"Have you found a girlfriend already?" Marilyn teased as she let him in. "No, the flowers are for you." Marilyn looked slightly embarrassed. "For me? I can't think why but thank you anyway." Once inside Rick sat down to watch the news with an ice-cold beer. The local channels presented an endless array of crime stories interspersed with a glowing account of Cory's latest achievement. That item didn't take long to tell. Switching to the BBC Rick discovered that the huge empire of the Soviet Union was collapsing. Boris Yeltskin was in charge of Russia following a failed coup attempt by army officers opposed to Glasnost.

Over dinner Rick asked Marilyn what she thought about the collapse of the Soviet Union and its possible effects on the world. "I only have a vague idea of where Russia is," replied the girl "and I don't know what it means for the world. I'm not all that smart anyway."

"Oh yes you are," asserted Rick, "but I suppose we don't need to concern ourselves about events that we have no control over." Marilyn nodded in agreement. "Closer to home I do have a matter that I wish to discuss with you." A pair of dark brown eyes suddenly lit up a lovely face. "What do you mean?" she stammered. "Have I done something wrong?"

"Not at all," Rick reassured her. "I have come across a fairly solid stumbling block to my plans. Apparently, foreigners are not allowed to own a majority share in any business so I require a legal partner, a person of integrity."

"How can I help you with that?" a puzzled Marilyn queried.

"You are a Filipino citizen, I presume, and a particularly talented and attractive one at that." Rick Daly couldn't help himself sometimes. "Yes of course I am but I don't see…" Rick cut her short. "Would you be willing to take a fifty-one percent ownership of the business subject to a mortgage that I won't enforce?"

"I don't know. I'm not sure." The elegant woman on the ferry now looked like a stunned teenager. "Well," continued Rick, "my attorneys, Pablo, Ameraldo and Sanchez, will prepare a set of documents that you can then take to any attorney of your choice to double check. I'll pay for the cost of that of course."

Somewhat hesitantly Marilyn agreed to Rick's proposal. At that point he opened a bottle of wine and suggested a toast and mini-celebration. "I don't drink," responded the girl, "but you go ahead and I'll toast you with Coke." The phone rang. It was Jun Pablo. "Hello Rick. I've checked the statutes and I was right. You can go ahead and nominate a silent partner."

"I'll bring her in tomorrow," promised Rick. "Her!" The attorney was at a loss. "Yes it's a lady."

"That's fine. I was just surprised that's all. See you tomorrow then."

Eleven o'clock the next day saw Marilyn, resplendent in a blue floral dress, and Rick in his jeans at the law offices. "You can take the papers to an independent attorney," suggested Rick, "and be back here in an hour." Marilyn read the documents very carefully and finally spoke. "That's not necessary. This firm has a good reputation and I don't see any problem. Besides I don't have any property or money that would be at risk anyway." The documents were then duly signed and the participants were photographed. "Why are our pictures being taken?" Rick asked Jun. "In the Philippines this is a standard practice," came the reply. "We take all precautions against any possible problems."

The clock on the wall showed 1 pm. Rick suggested that they adjourn to a suitable restaurant for a celebratory lunch. Jun Pablo, his secretary, Marilyn and Rick took a taxi to the Lighthouse Restaurant. Under rattan fans a surprisingly tasty array of dishes at very moderate prices appeared. "This is very good. What sort of cuisine is it?" Rick was no travelling gourmet. "It's Filipino food," stated Mr. Pablo proudly. "It's certainly much grander than the usual fish and rice," Rick demurred. Angel the secretary, dared to speak at this juncture. "The Philippines has many wonderful dishes but mostly people can only afford to eat the simplest of meals at home."

"Quite right," said her boss and Angel once again fell silent.

Fourteen days passed before the business was officially registered. During that time Rick had spent over 60,000 pisos acquiring an old jeepney to use as the business's general transport vehicle. When the notification was finally received Marilyn felt obliged to inform her parents of her situation and her latest achievements. She was very discrete about posting the letter so that Rick wouldn't see it. The next few days saw Marilyn and her senior interviewing prospective workers for the factory. Following only one placement of an advertisement in the Sun Star newspaper, what seemed like unruly crowds turned up at the gate, the phone rang hot and life was anything but serene. At the end of the mayhem two cabinet-makers, one foreman and seventeen skilled woodworkers were engaged. "You'd better put in place a bonus system for performance," Marilyn had suggested. "Why?" her superior had responded. "Up to you but if you don't you'll see." Reluctantly Rick agreed to establish the principle of a performance bonus of 100 pisos a month, much smaller than the sum proposed by Marilyn.

Rick routinely assigned Marilyn the task of doing the shopping. Without fail she would depart and return via jeepney unless the sheer amount necessitated a taxi. Late one afternoon with only two bags of groceries a cab had pulled up. As Rick left the house and opened the gate he noticed that Marilyn was crying. "What happened?" Before the girl could answer he observed a small blood stain on the sleeve of her blouse. "On the jeepney near Colon," sobbed the girl, "a snatcher grabbed my necklace."

"Was it valuable?" the pale face inquired. "No it was just a costume necklace costing about ten pisos."

More tears ensued. "When the man pulled off my necklace he looked at it for a second and then threw it on the floor of the jeepney. He yelled 'Fancy' and then slashed my arm with a knife."

"You poor darling," intoned Rick. He seated the girl down on the best couch in the lounge room and brought her a cup of green tea. "Have you been to the police?" A shake of that black, shiny hair affirmed the negative. "Well we must report this attack tomorrow." Marilyn between sobs tried to explain that small crimes such as this were entirely beyond the capacity of the police force and that reporting was merely a waste of time. Rick would not be put off. Accordingly, at 9:30 am on the morrow the pair took a taxi to the nearest office of the local constabulary. San Nicholas Police Station was certainly not remarkable as far as overt appearances were concerned. A fence of barbed wire protected a single storey concrete structure.

Marilyn was reluctant to tell the story so Rick spat it out for her. "What I don't understand, Sergeant is the fact that after taking her necklace the thief, rather than simply running away, threw it on the floor and slashed her arm with a knife."

"You are new to the Philippines I assume Mr. Daly?" the sergeant postulated. "I've been in the country about six weeks," Rick answered.

"Things are a little different here than where you're from, wherever that is. In the Philippines a whole layer of criminals exists who consider that it is their right to be able to rob you unhindered. If you thwart their wicked desires, to their way of thinking, you have somehow stolen from them and are evil." Rick looked confused and Marilyn showed a pretty but blank face. "You'll probably never understand it," the sergeant continued, "but that's the way it is here. To most criminals it is never their fault that they are pursuing this way of life. They have been forced to it by a never-ending list of possible circumstances. Any person whom they perceive to be more fortunate than they is guilty of a heinous crime in their eyes. And that goes doubly, no triply, for foreigners." He looked straight and hard into Rick's eyes.

"I really don't understand." Rick sounded apologetic. "We foreigners who come here are either tourists spending money or else folk who wish to operate businesses and employ Filipinos. Can't even the poorest people here see that?"

"I'm afraid they can't, Mr. Daly." The sergeant was a sufficiently educated man to understand the almost universal ignorance of Filipino customs and ways exhibited by foreigners. "It's not like your place. I'm afraid you will have to adjust."

Rick and Marilyn both thanked the sergeant and left the station. "I told you so," remarked the girl. "This is some country," Rick replied. "It's different but not bad," answered Marilyn. "Seems moderately lousy to me on certain points," Rick responded. "As you like Sir." Marilyn fell silent and the duo made their way home.

As Marilyn was preparing the dinner Rick spoke. "I just realized that my tourist visa is about to expire. I suppose I'll have to go to City Hall to renew it."

"I'm not very knowledgeable about such matters I'm afraid, Rick." Marilyn appeared ever-so-slightly embarrassed.

At the city hall Rick was informed by a pleasant young man that there was a separate immigration office for the processing of foreigner visas but that extensions of tourist visas could only be performed in Manila. "You mean I have to go all that way just to extend my visa," blurted Rick. "Yes Sir, the local office used to have the authority but after Cory was swept to power it was decided that all matters concerning foreigners should be only dealt with in the capital."

Somewhat flustered, Rick thanked the clerk and made his way out of that dusty, fan-swept colonial edifice. He wasn't terribly happy. So far he'd spent at least P300, 000 and didn't really have too much to show for it. A trip to Manila would cost how much? After the last experience Rick didn't want to travel by ship. Besides he didn't have a couple of days to waste. Accordingly, Marilyn was dispatched the next day to the Philippine Airlines' office.

"My boss would like a return ticket to Manila," she stated ever so politely when it was her turn to approach the counter. "Morning or afternoon?" was the automatic reply. "I think morning would be better as he has a lot to do before he can come back." The ticket was issued and exchanged for the sum of P1760. Marilyn had never in her entire life flown on a plane or bought such a ticket so the amount didn't shock her. Rick set off for Cebu's airport on Mactan island the following day, a Tuesday.

"Turtle-shell guitar Mister?" shouted the first of many peddlers. The scene inside the terminal was a little less chaotic. Two male tourists in Hawaiian shirts were arguing about their tickets with a counter clerk, a party of nuns was patiently seated in the main lounge and business types rushed to and fro. The clientele was certainly more up-market than that which swarmed up the gangplanks of the inter-island ferries.

In less than an hour Rick strode onto the tarmac and walked to the Manila bound Airbus 300. He couldn't help but notice groups of military aircraft at various stations in the sea of concrete. Helicopters and Tora Toras outnumbered the civilian aircraft present. The ninety-minute flight was uneventful and by 10 am he emerged from the ancient terminal building in the nation's capital. Beset by would-be porters although he wasn't carrying any bags Rick fought his way to the taxi queue. A shiny yellow cab with very cold air-conditioning took him to the Commission on Deportation and Immigration, close by the sixteenth century stone walls of Fort Intramuros. "Four hundred pisos!" he exclaimed at the driver's statement of the fare. "This distance is normally less than two hundred."

"You are correct Sir but this is an airport taxi and we have different rates." Reluctantly Rick handed over the amount and strode to the dilapidated structure that awaited his business.

Lines of people that snaked from one room into another matched dozens of rows of windows, most shut but some plying their trade. A general hubbub and clamor rose from the spot, second in intensity only to that of the Sunday sabong. It took Rick a full thirty minutes to learn the location of the necessary forms to fill in and thence to discover the queue he should join. By 11:30 he'd finally reached the window. "I'm sorry, aliens must produce three passport size photographs with their applications. There is a machine across the street." Rick thanked the man and hurried away. It was 11:55 by the time he'd rejoined the queue and again reached the window. Just as he stepped up the window shut with considerable force. Behind the glass a wooden sign proudly showed itself. "Closed for lunch. Reopening at 2 pm."

There was nothing for it. Rick exited this bastion of confusion and adjourned to a kitchenette for a few cleansing beers and some pork crackling. He was unable to even abide the thought of dried fish and rice or chicken adobo with its abundant bones. Settling down in a chair he opened a newspaper he'd bought across the street. "Philippine democracy stable says Cory," blared the headline. It was page two that caught his attention. An article reported on the corrupting influence that male foreigners were having on the nation's schoolgirls. In conclusion the story suggested that foreign nationals should be prohibited from placing advertisements in newspapers seeking pen pals.

The reading of that article necessitated another San Miguel and more pork crackling. By the time Rick had reached page four he felt like screaming. "Miriam Defensor Santiago, the CID commissioner says that aliens who have become separated from their wives should automatically have their residence visas revoked." This piece also announced that the price of tourist visas was to double the following week. "Good aliens don't mind paying for the privilege of visiting the Philippines," Ms. Defensor Santiago was quoted as saying. "The sort of aliens who don't want to help the Filipino people and who come here to prey on our women we simply don't want. The pride of our people demands that these corrupting influences are minimized as much as possible." The story ended with Ms. Defensor Santiago's advice to the wicked type of alien to visit other countries; not the Philippines! "We will make life very hot for them if they insist on coming here," she was quoted.

After the fourth San Miguel Rick glanced at his watch. "1:50 pm," the hands told him. Hoping to be at the beginning of the inevitable line he charged across the street and entered the fray once more. His hopes were soon dashed. The queues were as lengthy as before despite the fact that not a single window was yet open. Most of those forming the lines were young Filipino men and girls clutching several passports each. A tall man of about forty-five with wavy brown hair was immediately in front of Rick. "This business is a real hassle isn't it?" Rick said when he'd caught the man's eye. "You're not wrong," said a voice with a heavy German accent. "I'm on my fourth visit to the Philippines and although it's a great country in which to relax any business or legal formalities are an utter nightmare."

"Who are all the Filipinos with handfuls of passports?" Rick inquired.

"Some are travel agents but most are simply fixers," came the reply.

"What's a fixer?" Rick was serious.

"If you don't mind paying about five hundred pisos extra you can get one of these people to do all the standing in line and bureaucratic bullshit fulfilment for you."

"Really? I'll remember that for the next time." Rick was perspiring heavily in the stifling humidity. "Is it easy to qualify for a residence visa instead of dealing with this tourist visa crap?" he asked. Gerhard, for that was the name of his kindred spirit, laughed in a hearty Germanic manner. "In the Marcos time it wasn't too difficult but you can just forget it now. Firstly, you need to be married to a Filipina and secondly have to submit a book of reasons as to why you should be granted this huge privilege along with wads of money. Besides you probably don't want a residence visa anyway."

"Why not?"

"Well, if you do have residency, every time you leave the country you must pay P1600 travel tax with a maximum of P3200 tax payable per year."

"Anyone'd think that foreigners came here to steal money from the Filipinos," commented Rick. "Who's this Miriam Defensor Santiago anyway?"

"You mean Saint Miriam," Gerhard said sarcastically. "We call her the patron saint of foreigners. She's the boss of the Immigration Department." Gerhard then lowered his voice to just above a whisper. "She's a real bitch who hates white people and doesn't care too much for men either. Unfortunately, she's a close buddy of that other troll, Cory, so here she is. Miriam's a meteor job. Somewhere out there in space there must be a meteor with her name on it!" Rick's level of confidence in his newfound home and optimism for the success of his business venture suffered a heavy blow at the receipt of these remarks. This German guy seems on the level and then there were those newspaper stories, he thought to himself. Rick showed Gerhard the story about the corrupting foreigner influence on the country's schoolgirls. "Hah!" laughed the German. "It's like Filipino men would never frequent bars or take advantage of women. In fact the youngest girls are to be found in the Filipino bars in Caloocan and Santa Cruz a long way from the tourist belt. The girls seldom speak English but their bodies are young and warm and they're cheap."

Rick made a mental note of this advice. "There's honest and dishonest corruption in this country," his new friend continued. "This immigration nonsense is dishonest corruption of the worst kind."

"How can you have honest corruption?" interjected Rick. Gerhard appeared like an elder statesman. "Well, consider the fact that the police in this country aren't paid enough to support themselves and their families. They're forced to make more money somehow. If you give them a tip for performing their job well in some matter that concerns you and for upholding the law, that's honest corruption. When officials earn money by obstructing the law or the normal processes, that's dishonest corruption. This place under St. Miriam is a temple of dishonest corruption." Just then it was Gerhard's turn at the window. Five minutes later he'd paid his money, bade Rick goodbye and disappeared.

At last Rick was on the verge of having his visa renewed. A woman whose short cropped hair stood out from the flowing locks of all the other females in the building eyed Rick suspiciously. "Your visa forms are in order but you will need to have your onward plane tickets checked at window 17."

"I don't have a confirmed ticket to leave the Philippines," stammered Rick, "as I'm planning to do some business here."

"In that case," the short-haired demon replied, "You'll have to go to window 18 and show documentation to support your claims. By the time you have done that this window will be closed. I'm afraid you'll have to come back again tomorrow."

Fighting the impulse to swear and scream Rick bit his lip and embarked on the nightmare that was window 18. After nearly two hours he'd shown his business documents to a young lady who'd then stamped a piece of paper. "Reasons for extension approved," the blue ink declared. He thought he might just make it back to the other window in time but the moment she caught sight of him running into the hall the short-haired woman thumped the window shut.

As he phoned Marilyn to explain that he would not be returning that night Rick remembered the experience he'd had in the Bank of the Philippine Islands when he'd arranged a telegraphic transfer of funds. In hindsight the three hours in the bank appeared the very pinnacle of efficiency. The incidental costs of his venture were mounting too rapidly for comfort. With that thought in mind Rick asked the taxi driver if he could recommend a modestly priced hotel. "Sure," said the driver, a dark-skinned fellow in his twenties. "The White House hotel in the tourist strip only costs three hundred a night." His passenger quickly assented. The Intercontinental had cost P1200 a night, free bullet holes and all.

To his surprise Rick found that the reception desk of the White House was staffed by an elderly Englishman who looked like he'd had one gin too many over the years. "Welcome to our humble abode Sir," the white-haired octogenarian had announced. "You'll find it comfortable enough, ceiling fan, bathroom with cold shower. I'm afraid the beer garden next door generates a lot of noise but it shuts at 3 am and anyway it drowns out the moaning noises from the adjacent rooms." After checking in, Rick mentioned the need to purchase some clothes. "Robinson's Department store is only a kilometer away," suggested the elderly gent. Entering the concrete monolith the erstwhile shopper checked the store directory. Men's clothing was listed as being on the first floor.

Alighting from the escalator Rick spotted rack upon rack of shirts and trousers. The sizes were invariably too small but he located one garish shirt and a pair of faded jeans that looked as if they might fit. Clasping them firmly he strode to the cash desk. The girl had barely read their prices when the lights went out. The soft hum of air-conditioning fell silent and all was in darkness.

"What happened?" asked the customer.

"A brownout Sir." The girl's look of resignation bore the hallmark of familiarity. "A what?" Rick hadn't heard the term before. "A brownout. The electricity supply often becomes overloaded here and they turn off various sectors in turn. Don't worry the power'll be back on in about thirty minutes probably."

"Ok," replied Rick. "I've selected my purchases already so it won't matter anyway."

"I'm sorry," intoned the salesgirl. "Our registers will not work until the electricity is restored and we can't make any sales. You'll just have to wait."

"Wait; be buggered." Rick surrendered the shirt and jeans and departed the store empty-handed. He returned to the White House.

After eating two toasted ham and egg sandwiches Rick walked out of the hotel and strolled down the street. He'd never been to the Ermita area before and was stunned to notice bar after bar, disco after disco and armies of Western men strolling. Del Pilar at that time still boasted as many houses of sin as any street in the nation although Cory was doing to her level best to reduce their numbers.

The first stop was Lovebirds, an establishment whose dancers always performed in red and white striped bikinis and whose air-conditioning was the coldest in town. Next Rick visited the Thriller bar, which was owned by one Mr. Michael Jackson (not the singer but a Michael Jackson who was born white and who was destined to leave this earth some years later at the wrong end of a .45 during a Christmas party). Thriller was the name and thrilling was the game. Never before had Rick seen such bold and sexually aggressive dancers. Before he'd finished his first drink he was almost raped by a girl called Christy. She said she was sixteen but looked even younger than that. The years spent in Australia had caused Rick to become a total sucker for affordable sex. This girl's English was limited and her knowledge of the world even more so but her firm young body made up for the sins of the mind. Rick apologized that he had an appointment with a friend in another bar but promised he would return and buy her a ladies' drink.

The temporary tourist had merely wished to do more exploring. He proceeded to eat a hot dog at the immortal Raymond's Fast Foods, one of the preferred hangouts of the hunting girls – freelancers who didn't work in any bar. Next on the unfolding list of experiences was Bubbles; a bar with more than thirty dancers strutting their stuff on three stages at any one time. The Australian manager of Bubbles expired less than a year later of Deep Vein Thrombosis after returning from a trip to Sydney. After Bubbles came Papa Joes, a Filipino-owned bar and disco that catered almost exclusively for Westerners and was a mid-sized house of sizzle. The cards destined that the eldest brother of the three owners was to die of a sudden and extreme case of lead poisoning.

Blissfully unaware of the precarious balance that Ermita held between life and death Rick continued his carousing. As the bewitching hour had already passed he thought he'd return to the Thriller bar and take out the young hot body that called itself Christy. He ordered a vodka and looked around for the object of his desire. She was nowhere to be seen and when he asked the manager where she was he was answered very directly. "Oh Christy; she's a star performer. She was bar fined by an American guy about an hour ago." Temporarily devastated, Rick resumed his bar hopping finally reaching the northern end of Del Pilar around two. A decidedly tacky and grimy operation known as the Yellow Butterfly beckoned. The drinks were half the price of those in the other bars, the girls were mostly on the ugly side and the place was smoggy and hot. Yes, the Yellow Butterfly displayed the Philippine hospitality industry with some accidental commitment to truth.

After two warmish beers Rick made his way to the toilet. Unseen a plain girl with shortish hair and a thin wiry body followed him in and locked the door behind her. The very second that he'd finished pissing the girl declared that his appendage was an ice cream and she just had to lick it. Being too drunk by this time to resist Rick was forced merely to oblige. The creature then forced him to the ground and thrust herself on top. Five minutes later she extracted one hundred pisos from his wallet and disappeared.

As he staggered the eight hundred meters or so up Del Pilar back to his hotel Rick hoped that he hadn't picked up a dose of something. He also thought of Marilyn and what a classy girl she was. Thank goodness she wasn't here to witness any of this, was a recurring thought that played across his mind. A loose piece of concrete found Rick's unsteady foot and he fell in an untidy heap on the pavement. As his left hand propelled itself forward to break the fall a sharp pain pulsed through it. A jagged piece of glass had found its accidental mark. Pulling himself up he glanced at the wound. Quite a steady trickle of blood oozed from it. It would need stitches. On the five hundred meter journey to the nearest hospital he passed a roadside stall and thought a coffee would do him good. He drank the warm and sickly fluid and with his good hand passed over a five-piso note. The stall owner, an elderly man, looked at Rick's injury and refused to accept the money. Half an hour and three stitches later and Rick was in his cot.

It was almost eleven the next day when he again presented himself at the Commission on Immigration and Deportation. His head was mildly painful and it had been a struggle to rise from his bed. He'd brought no change of clothes with him and having failed in purchasing new ones he somewhat resembled the unswept cage that he'd only just escaped from the preceding evening.

"That'll be P1, 500 Sir. Your visa is now good for another six months."

"I beg your pardon. Isn't there something else I have to do?" Rick was dumbfounded. "No. You just have to pay." A middle-aged woman who resembled a schoolteacher took his cash and stamped his passport. Two hours later and Rick was on a flight back to Cebu City.

Less than a week after his return the factory was able to open. Machines had been installed, workers were in place and a large supply of cut rattan lay stacked in a corner. The factory office was exactly as Marilyn liked. After all, she'd been the one to set it up. On the first Monday after commencement Rick noticed that nearly half of the employees were missing. "I wonder why they didn't turn up?" Marilyn stifled his wonder. "There was a neighborhood fiesta last night down the road. The missing workers are probably still recovering."

"Make sure that their time sheets are adjusted," Rick announced. "Of course Rick." Marilyn knew what she was doing.

The following Monday saw one of the cabinetmakers absent. He arrived for work on the Tuesday. "I'm sorry about yesterday Mr. Daly. My sister's baby had her christening and I was obliged to attend." When Rick questioned him about the possibility of giving advance notice or of phoning he'd merely looked blank. "That's the way it is," Marilyn had informed him. "Family matters and celebrations always take precedence." Rick's eyes rolled upwards. His silence and disconsolate expression spoke volumes.

Tuesday rolled into Wednesday and by the end of the week no more absences had been recorded. Moments of fancy saw Rick day-dreaming; "Daly's Exotic Furniture, a business that had its origins in the most humble of circumstances in Asia makes take-over bid for U.S Cabinet Makers, the world's largest manufacturer of wooden furnishings." Rick could almost smell the first whiffs of future success. Three-quarters of the boss's time was spent in the office, studying statistics and answering the phone. His bookkeeper come secretary performed more than admirably. Virtually every time she looked at or spoke to him her face would light up with a spontaneous smile that revealed the whitest of teeth framed against a flawless skin, a sure sign of a healthy lifestyle.

To say that Rick was impressed with his silent partner and principal employee would be more than an understatement. For a hundred and fifty dollars a month back home I couldn't even employ a cleaning woman who wouldn't poison my pot plants out of spite, he fondly mused. Marilyn's smiles brought extra sunshine into his day and he much preferred the time in the office with her than that spent in a supervisory capacity on the factory floor.

At home this dark-skinned angel seemed to have overcome her initial fear and reticence about sharing a house with a foreigner. In fact she appeared to be even more comfortable with their domestic arrangements than he. The constant smiles worried him though. It wasn't that they might be false. He was sure in his guts that Marilyn was sincere. He just didn't know how to take them. The smiles almost suggested more-than-friendly cooperation but he didn't want to risk damaging his business set-up or appearing a fool. The worst time was when they happened to sit down together to watch television. Rick found that his eyes simply couldn't concentrate on whatever program was running. The girl didn't appear much more focused on the electronic medium either. Their conversation had ranged from religion to politics. "Do you believe in God?" Rick had asked. "Of course, I'm a good Catholic," came the reply. "Don't you think the greedy rich people are stealing the lives of the poor in this country?"

"I cannot imagine how else things could be run as most people here are simply too lazy to ever get ahead." Marilyn appeared somewhat sheepish at her own remark.

Marilyn had retired to bed early as was her custom and Rick felt a sudden attack of complete and overwhelming boredom. The bright lights of the city's discos and bars were calling. Sneaking out of his own house Rick moved like a ghost among the shadows until he reached the very public ground of Tres d'Abril. Climbing aboard the first passenger vehicle that passed, a jeepney, Rick headed for the noise that seemed the real soul of the nation. "Bayad usa," he proudly announced when handing over his piso.

Still careful to avoid Our Place Rick made his way a few kilometers to the north until he found The Club. As he passed through the door the excitement of the high point of a party overwhelmed him. A dozen foreigners were singing along with the beat as six very shapely females were giving it their all on the floor. For some uncharacteristic reason Rick didn't feel talkative and all but ignored the other customers. Transfixed, he stared at the array of flesh while consuming a considerable number of beers.

"Enjoying this Mate?" a direct voice interrupted. "Of course." The voice belonged to Ronny the Rat, the owner of this establishment and renowned throughout a particular stratum of the world for his love of grog and underage girls. "Just don't enjoy it too much for it's what we love that usually kills us. In my case it'll probably be beer." Time later proved him right. At least he was spared the indignity of being hauled before some court or other for sexually interfering with minors. "I don't plan to expire from sheer enjoyment just yet," replied Rick somewhat tersely. His enjoyment or otherwise was then left in peace. Rum and Coke followed beers and Rick's gaze toward the stage took a greater intensity. He was merely there to amuse himself and he did appreciate the moves and fine bodies of the girls. No intention of succumbing to carnal desires entered his head this night.

Four hours later and a girl in her late teens took the dais. "What a body," Rick thought through his drunken gaze. The briefs of her blue bikini appeared to mock his manhood. It wasn't too much later than the owner of the blue bikini was seated next to him explaining the toughness of her life and that of her family. Three ladies' drinks later saw Rick succumb. Despite vowing to limit his spending the foreign hopeful insisted on paying the girl's bar-fine, almost against her will. "What's your name anyway?" his mouth slurred. "Merly," was the answer. "You have any kids?" a liquid voice inquired.

"No, not yet." As the mix of liquor took increasing hold of his mind Rick fondly thought that a girl who'd hadn't had any children would be a lot tighter and better. There was just no way that he would have ever brought a girl if he'd been in his right mind. Firstly, he probably wouldn't have done so at all in his present situation and then, if the only muscle worth mentioning in his entire body simply would not be stilled he would have taken the girl to a hotel and made his excuses later. Not being in his right mind Rick thought he'd save a hundred pisos by bringing Merly home to his own bed. Besides, it must be impressive to bring a bargirl to a house rather than a hotel, his bemused mind asserted.

It must have been at least 3 am when Rick installed the girl in his bed and, as best as he was able, performed the deed. By four our drunken Daly was sound asleep. By five the sun had arisen and Marilyn was outside Rick's bedroom window watering some plants. Being in a strange bed and hearing the sound of the water Merly awoke and turned around. "Ma-ayong Buntag (Good Morning)" said Marilyn. "Who are you?" Merly's barely functioning mouth managed. "I work for Rick," was the abrupt response. "I suppose Rick found you somewhere last night?" Merly answered in the affirmative and after having explained the reasons she needed to dance Marilyn felt a little sorry for her.

Having received her performance bonus in advance the night before Merly dressed and exited the house somewhat rapidly. By the time Rick awoke the sun was bright and hot and he was alone. Confused for a second he then remembered. Anyway his aching mind was happy that Marilyn wouldn't learn of his folly. Another hour saw a bedraggled rendition of himself emerge from his sanctuary for lunch.

"The girl you brought home last night was quite charming. I talked to her this morning while I was watering the garden."

"Oh.. I see," mumbled Rick. "Boys will be boys I suppose," hinted Marilyn "but I thought you were a little more self-controlled." The shamefaced foreigner said nothing for a while. "I don't wish to appear judgmental," intoned Marilyn, "but perhaps you should manage some of your physical needs a little better." At that moment Rick summoned the courage to inquire into her personal life. "What do you do? You're nearly twenty-nine. I assume that you've had boyfriends."

"I had a boyfriend when I was seventeen but we only held hands and cuddled a bit."

"You're kidding me," challenged Rick. "You're not trying to say that you're a virgin at twenty-eight?"

"I am and I'm proud of it. The first man that gilling-gillings me (Filipino slang for the sex act) will be my husband." Her boss was simply nonplussed. "As you know I respect you very much and would never do anything to damage or hurt you." Marilyn smiled again.

The rest of that day passed like any other non-working day. The house was quiet and the noises from the street sent their assurance that life was continuing. Saturday came and went and then it was the Sabbath.

Sunday saw the echoes of music and merriment in close proximity. "What's going on?" asked Rick. "It's the La Paloma fiesta," replied Marilyn. "Don't you want to join the fun?" suggested Rick. "Not particularly, I'm happy to stay home," was the response. Firecrackers shattered the tranquility and skyrockets lit up the night sky. Marilyn had tuned the TV to the karaoke channel and Rick hadn't objected. Staring at the image Rick had felt some intrinsic boredom when an electric impulse shook his entire being. There it was.

Marilyn's hand ever so lightly placed on his thigh but nonetheless on his thigh. The stirring in his loins overwhelmed the shock and embarrassment. Nervously he turned to Marilyn and pulling her toward him kissed her hard and passionately on the mouth. Seconds went by as a natural chemistry began to assert itself on the situation. Marilyn then pulled violently away and began crying. "I shouldn't have done that," she sobbed. "It's all right," consoled Rick. "Besides what is the problem?"

"I'm not that sort of girl and I work for you."

Discretion being the better part of valor Rick apologized and promised that it wouldn't happen again. The ensuing hours were so quiet that the house could have been a morgue. Few words were spoken over dinner or after. For once Rick thought he'd hit the hay early and excused himself. The next day was a Monday and the pair oversaw activity at the factory as usual. As he emerged from his shower that evening Rick passed Marilyn in the kitchen. She slid her body between him and his intended passage and placed her hand below his belt. Rick lowered his automatic responsive kiss from her lips to her breasts, after dislodging her T-shirt. Without being large they were full and boasted large nipples. His hand reached inside her shorts before she stopped him. Both of them looked embarrassed and Rick continued on his way without saying anything.

Nothing was said at the factory and Marilyn demonstrated a greater coolness than previously. Rick was burning inside but put down the situation to one of those teases that Life torments us with. Almost a week passed until Saturday saw increasing numbers of youths hanging around street corners and the not rare foreboding of impending activity and trouble. After a few beers following dinner Rick had bade Marilyn "Goodnight" and retired to his bed to read. The humidity seemed to suffocate him as his eyes grew weary of the pages. Less than five minutes after he'd surrendered the book and doused the light his bedroom door silently opened.

The nude figure silhouetted against the faint glow of the ambient visibility was obviously female and in addition was lithe, firm and lovely, even in the near dark. As the figure approached closer Rick could make out her wavy locks. Slim and taut for a woman approaching thirty her almost bony hips framed a thick bush of black pubic hair. Without a word this lovely silhouette lay down on his bed and kissed him. Rick had known since the first moment he'd laid eyes on her that this was some woman. Yet, the site of her naked body was more than his imagination could possibly have conjured up.

Chapter Six

Slowly and hesitantly Rick's hands reached for the girl. From her shoulders down across the twin igloos with its prominent nipples and on across the flat stomach his fingertips continued their movements. As his left hand traversed her navel the girl shook. Rick stopped. Her mouth on his convinced him that it was safe to continue.

Ever so hesitantly his fingers crossed a thick, black foliage with a moist cave in the center. A short distance in and Rick realized the girl had indeed told the truth. Incredible as it was this girl was still a virgin a few weeks shy of her twenty-ninth birthday. Everything came to a halt. His finger in her inner sanctum had been too much for Marilyn. Strongly she pulled his hand aside and without even blinking performed an almost instantaneous one hundred and eighty-degree turn. Her hot mouth riding his manhood sent her boss into a frenzy. His tongue dived through the bush with its dusky hills above shaped against the feint light until it struck the pinkest of oysters. Marilyn moaned but kept up the sensual pressure on Rick's straining tower.

Before this sudden development could reach any conclusion Marilyn bolted upright and disappeared with the surprise and shock of her arrival. Rick was flummoxed. Confused he left his room and ventured as far as the kitchen. Marilyn's bedroom door was shut fast. Extracting a beer from the fridge Rick pondered one of the most surprising and frustrating experiences of his entire life.

Over breakfast Marilyn smiled intensively at Rick until he couldn't help himself. "Why did you leave so suddenly last night?" Marilyn's face darkened. "This is wrong," she whispered. "You're my boss, we're not married or anything. This is just wrong." If he hadn't been immune to blushing Rick would have done so. The business rolled along with only a few absences. Sometimes when Marilyn spoke to Rick she would ever so lightly place her hand on his arm. Above the waist Rick was ever so grateful for the savior of his business plans. As regards the nether regions he wasn't so sure. To keep himself sane he visited several barbershops although he hadn't required a shave or a haircut. To be fair, there are some services that can be rendered quickly and efficiently in an otherwise slow country.

Three days later when Rick was fast asleep his door clicked open once again and Marilyn in all her natural glory sprang upon his bed. The moment she touched him every hair on his body asserted itself. If this was the devil's temptation, bring it on, his sacrilegious mind countenanced. His touch on the girl seemed to produce a similar wicked desire. The heat of their bodies somehow bound them together under the blanket of the universal tropical steam bath. Just as his hand stroked the fur on her sacred mound Marilyn quickly turned until her shapely buttocks framed Rick's face, her lips closed on his pulsatingly engorged penis and his tongue found itself hard at work exploring her delicate and pink Holy Grail. Rick was barely about to cement their physical relationship when Marilyn stood up and began crying.

"I'm so ashamed and sorry, Sir. I just couldn't help it. Please forgive me." Struggling to find levels of sensitivity that had long lain dormant Rick soothed the distraught girl. "You've no idea how smitten I am with you," he said, "but I'm so sorry if I've somehow offended your morals."

"It's my fault, not yours," continued the tearful refrain. A few more kisses and therapeutic rubbings saw the stricken secretary fall fast asleep still in Rick's bed. As the pair awoke almost simultaneously the next morning Rick felt an evil sense of accomplishment.

Unspoken, an extra bond between the pair evinced itself. The mutual smiles even attracted notice from the factory floor. "The boss is human after all," remarked one of the cabinet-makers. Fortunately both Marilyn and her superior were out of earshot at the time. Sensing a vulnerability the pair expertly established a more formal relationship at the work site. The very workers who had first sensed a scandal soon thought they had been mistaken.

Back at La Paloma the situation was very different. Every evening Marilyn would come to Rick's bed and share her bodily warmth and some of her fluids with him. Naturally enough the boss's body and mind wanted more. Yet every time he attempted to penetrate her with either his swollen member or even a finger she would close her legs fast. "Not by this time," she would say. Ultimately it is always women who control men and Rick had just to grin and bear it. Luckily the lies about masturbation sending you blind were false. Otherwise he wouldn't have been even able to tie his shoe laces. She was an admirable employee, a so-far honest business partner and a thoroughly stunning woman. Yet Rick's emotions were now more than mixed. He hated the fact that she frustrated him so often. Yet he loved what she was. To him she was the archangel of perfect womanhood. If only he could truly possess her. The churning of the lathes and resultant production of furniture entirely faded away from his priorities.

March transformed itself into April although no change in the season was apparent. Nothing had changed either at the factory or at home. Mr. Daly was constantly sexually teased while doing his level-best to reach his goals. One Saturday morning in the swelter of late May Rick had ventured to the south of the island to where the waves broke over black rocks, revealing brief patches of yellow sand and where holiday makers, some families but mostly young men with their girls, temporarily made merry in the simple thatched huts that dotted the shore. Rick had not come to appreciate the natural beauty or the sounds of eco-love.

His mission was merely to arrange shipments of cane from the scattered holdings that lay ever so slightly to the interior of that one star pleasure arena. He'd driven his recently acquired jeepney for the four-and-a-half hour journey. A day later, after spending a night in one of those primitive thatched huts alone, Rick's vehicle was loaded to the brim. Fractionally unsure as to how simple country folk who have been denuded for centuries by rich city slickers could have driven such a hard bargain with him Rick shoved the machine into gear and headed north. Fifty kilometers short of Cebu City the rains hit, somewhat early. It was still bucketing down when he reached his home gate and shouted for Marilyn. A human cry somewhat disappears against the torrents of nature and a full ten minutes passed before an umbrella-clutching secretary appeared. Dinner finished the all-too-familiar-sexual repartée passed between the business's principals.

As the following dawn broke Rick was still fast asleep. Marilyn in her role of garden nurturer however was abroad. "Shit," she yelled at the top of her lungs. Nothing stirred from Rick's quarters however so she rushed back into the house and pushed open his door. Her nipples still pressed hard against her white T-shirt and her shorts clung tightly to her thighs showing her legs of color to their best advantage. Yet even a bleary-eyed Rick could see that her sudden visit was business not pleasure related. "Marilyn Mahal, darling," he stammered as he roused to consciousness. "What's the matter?"

"The water pump's been stolen."

"The what?" Rick was simply unable to grasp what had occurred. "While you were away and it was raining I had to go down town to buy some food. It was only two hours later when you returned. I didn't notice that anything was amiss until I turned on the tap this morning and nothing came out. Thinking our water tank needed refilling I hit the pump button. Nothing! I tried again. Nothing! So I checked the pump in the yard. Gone! Thieves must have made off with it while you were away and I was shopping."

"How much will it cost to replace?" Rick's tone conveyed disappointment. "Ten thousand, more or less. It wasn't my fault." Marilyn stared at Rick with a look he'd never seen before. "It's never safe to leave a house unattended here," she added. "Why didn't you say this to me before?" Rick challenged. The girl blushed underneath her swarthy skin. "It's not my place to tell you what to do Sir."

"You work hard enough with the business, let alone the house, Marilyn. Perhaps we should hire a maid." A platonic smile escape Marilyn's lips. "That's a good idea Rick but you can't employ just anybody."

"Do you know of anyone whom you can recommend?"

"My family and friends are in Samar and I can't think of any girl who would come to Cebu at short notice."

"I suppose we'll have to advertise then," said Rick with a tone of resignation. Following an advertisement in the Sun Star there were six applicants; four short girls who looked in need of a wash, one tall Amazon who Rick ruled out on the grounds that she'd be able to beat him up and one nurse.

One by one the interviewees were admitted and sent off until the nurse arrived with her starched uniform. Her English was excellent and she was a smooth talker. "I don't quite understand," said Rick. "Why would a nurse want to take a maid's job?" Cecilia, a pretty thing of twenty with smooth shoulder-length hair fluttered her eyelashes. "I have completed my exams but it will be six months or more before I'll be qualified and able to start work. In the meantime I must seek some other employment." Rick was sold. The lass's demeanor and superb English had convinced him. "I'm not so sure," whispered Marilyn but Rick would have none of it.

Cecilia was duly hired with the understanding that most likely she would have to leave in six months' time to take up nursing duties. "She's a bit too smooth for my liking," Marilyn intoned, "but if she can guard and clean the house I'll be happy enough." Marilyn was eager to have help with the home duties considering the hours she put in at the factory. Mind you she wasn't so keen on having a younger girl sharing the house with Rick and herself.

Within a week Cecilia announced that on Thursdays she regularly attended karate class and if it was permissible she would like three hours leave of absence. "Certainly," the Westerner replied. "It's good that you keep fit."

"Would you like to check my bag Sir?" Cecilia asked on her way to the gate. "That won't be necessary. Enjoy your class." Rick sounded like a pontiff. "You should check her bag," Marilyn whispered. "Let's not be crass." Rick cut her short.

On a Saturday morning the postman arrived at the gate with a letter, for Marilyn. As she tore it open and digested its contents she was unable to contain her glee. "My sister's wedding has finally been announced," she blurted. "I must go home for a week." On seeing Rick's less than joyous expression she added. "You can come too if you want." Secretly in her heart the girl strongly desired that this man accompany her home to the province to meet her family. Requiring little prompting Rick agreed and the pair left Cecilia in charge of the house and the foreman to oversee the factory for the time.

Marilyn's journey on the Juanita this time was considerably more to her liking. She had Rick to cuddle on the green canvas cot. The sunshine as the boat pulled into the quay manifested more than a usual warmth. Marilyn's world had never appeared brighter. Children stared at Rick and giggled on the jeepney ride. Foreigners were not often seen in these parts. From the moment he alighted in Cagmanipis to the time he disappeared into the

Delgado house this blond-haired man had been an object of wonder to a throng of at least a hundred children.

"Sort of like being a movie star without the money," he said as he was introduced to Marilyn's father. He was treated more like a treasured possession than a visitor but Rick enjoyed every second of it. Naturally enough the star value of his arrival was soon subjugated to the performance of the wedding. Juliet was, for the next couple of days, the queen of the house. "I told you that it would happen," she confided to her sibling. "Not a moment too soon from appearances," Marilyn returned. Juliet did appear to be either pregnant or else a victim of sudden weight gain.

The wedding itself was flash enough by village standards. The groom, William but known as Dodong, dutifully presented himself on time, a hundred guests ate, drank and made merry and the church bell received some exercise. During the reception Rick's arm enveloped Marilyn's waist until a violent pinch suggested that it might be politic for him to remove it. As the sun set over the bay and the happy couple disappeared from view an elderly woman approached Marilyn. "It looks like you'll be next and to a wealthy foreigner too." Marilyn scowled at her and walked on with Rick at a discrete distance behind her heels.

On the following morning the entire village appeared late on its daily start. By eleven there was still no notable movement anywhere. The sun burned fiercely. Marilyn was counting stock from her parents' store when Rick finally presented himself. "Where are your parents?" inquired the bleary-eyed body. "They've gone to church to pray for blessings on the marriage." Marilyn appeared to have a devilish wink in her eye. "We could go swimming. Do you know how to swim?" Rick laughed and apologized that he'd brought no swimming togs. "Your underwear will do," stated the girl. "There are no crowds of onlookers at our beach, such that it is, anyway."

"Where is it?" cried Rick as the duo reached the shore. "There!" shouted his girl, pointing at small patches of sand that obtruded between endless rocks and mounds of seaweed. Clad only in a white T-shirt and denim shorts she thrust herself into the brine. A few seconds later the foreigner stripped down to his jockettes and joined her. The tepid water barely felt cool to the touch but had quite an effect on Marilyn's shirt. The points of her nipples pinnacled now as they splashed about. Golden sparkles of light danced on the surface of a still sea. After a considerable time of frolicking the couple emerged from the waters. Hauling his torso on to an expansive stone sill Rick noticed that only a short distance away a girl in faded jeans and a floral shirt was staring intently at him. She came closer still with a fixed gaze. By this time Marilyn was at Rick's side. The girl was Lina, the dancer from Our Place. Before Rick's lips could move Lina's scornful countenance sprang into action. "Kalumbri ka na pisti." Shouting the curse she turned on her heels and disappeared towards the village.

"Why did Maria curse you like that?" Marilyn was shocked and confused. "How does she know you?" Nervously, Rick spoke. "She is a girl who hassled me for money not long after I arrived in Cebu." Marilyn was suspicious but said nothing further. Back at the house the family was gathered for lunch with the exception of the bride and groom who had departed for a week's matrimonial bliss in a modest resort on the isle of Leyte. The midday meal was accomplished with a little more levity and good cheer than usual. Marilyn's brother and father left to attend the sabong while Flora minded the store. Rick and Marilyn took up positions in hammocks in the yard for an hour's siesta.

As darkness fell that Sunday and Flora was preparing dinner she called Marilyn into the kitchen. "I just heard the most alarming tale." The daughter turned pale. "It seems that the girl Maria, the one who left Cagmanipis not long after giving birth to a son in shameful circumstances, knows Rick. Apparently, he is her boyfriend and promised to support her and her child."

"That can't possibly be true," Marilyn, murmured in a quivering voice and her face betraying a fear. "It must be just more of the foolish tsismis doing the rounds."

"I daresay we'll find out soon enough," remarked Flora. A few minutes before dinner was to be served a grim-faced Marilyn sought out her employer and guest. Keeping her voice low she whispered, "They say that Maria is your girlfriend in Cebu and that you'd promised to help support her family. Is that true?"

"Who says that?" snapped Rick.

"They…, people here," replied the girl. "What a load of crap!" retorted the foreigner with a dawning realization that he'd better tell the truth and quickly. "She told me her name was Lina. She was a bar girl in Cebu with whom I had a one-night fling. That's all!"

"You obviously keep your brains in your pants!" An angry Marilyn just managed to smother what would have been a shout. "I'm sorry. I thought there was something strange about that dancer." Rick kept apologizing until Marilyn had more than had enough and walked off. Hardly a word was spoken during the meal and to even eat a few spoonfuls of the food in front of him was an agonizing ordeal for the very embarrassed guest. After it was over Rick followed Marilyn out of the house and again attempted to explain. "No-one here will believe you," she told Rick. "Maria was always a good provider to her parents. I, however, think you are telling the truth but that will make little difference here. The damage has been done."

If the Sunday had been problematic Monday was worse. Marilyn and Rick were due to return to Cebu that Wednesday. The departure date couldn't arrive soon enough for the survivor of a day of almost total silence and frosty looks. By lunch time the story had turned another notch on the screw. "Marilyn your new boss has some kind of dark past. He was in Cebu before; more than six months ago." Staring at her mother in disbelief Marilyn was dumbstruck. "He met Maria in a restaurant there and they had quite a violent romance. After they had been together for a considerable time Maria fell pregnant. It was then that he dumped her. The shock and scandal was such that Maria lost both the baby and her job. She arrived home a couple of weeks ago and was recovering despite the further disgrace and emotional turmoil. Recovering, that is, until she saw Rick – with you!" Not wishing to confront their guest Flora's growing displeasure was again conveyed through the intermediary. "Rick we must talk." Marilyn's voice had sounded urgent.

Although strongly suspecting the veracity of this tale Marilyn still harbored fears. "Have you been in Cebu before?" she challenged. Seeing the look on her face despite his denials her boss produced his passport. The document was at least two years old and bore only one entrance stamp for the Philippines. Keeping it company was the ink that represented the hard-won visa extension. "You see. That girl is a liar and a loony one at that," trumpeted Rick with an air of finality.

Although Marilyn was convinced, her mother wasn't quite so certain. Her father stayed out of the whole business as far as humanly possible. Flora pointed out to her daughter one ugly and inescapable truth. Regardless of the tale's authenticity the villagers would always take the word of a local girl who supported her family against that of some foreigner. No matter of prior disgrace could ever mitigate Maria's intrinsic advantage in this matter. The tsismis would go on and almost certainly become worse.

"You must resign your job and come back here," Flora ordered. "If you don't, the scandal will make life more than uncomfortable for us."

"That story is a load of rubbish," the daughter answered back. "I'm not going to abandon the first employment with any prospects that I've ever had on account of stupid village gossip and the aspirations of a deranged girl."

Flora appeared singularly unimpressed and pushed her husband into reissuing the directive. Marilyn's response was the same. By the Wednesday morning Rick felt that he'd been in an invisible solitary confinement. Marilyn's parents had virtually worn out their tongues in fruitless attempts to convince her to do the right thing. Her brother had returned to Calbayog the day after the wedding and Marilyn too, felt spiritually alone.

Even a short stroll for Rick from the confines of the modest home produced considerable numbers of interested onlookers. Unlike on the day of his arrival, the village girls weren't idolizing him, there were no galleries of smiling folk and no star status. Whispers followed his every step and the giggles of children, louder than before, suggested an overpowering and amorphous malice. Rick spent his last hours in Cagmanipis staring at the most isolated wall he could find in the Delgado home. When the hour arrived for his and Marilyn's departure there were no hugs or well wishes from the girl's parents; just a growing silence from which it would be a miracle if they could escape.

As a Calbayog-bound jeepney pulled up and the disconsolate pair climbed in, a sea of faces appeared from every window and each possible vantage point. Perhaps even the dead were watching from amongst their overgrown graves and piles of bones (the cemetery had run out of space some years before) and throwing silent curses at the departing duo. As the vehicle disappeared down the ribbon of concrete the whispers seemed to grow louder and louder. Even the trees were gossiping in the wind.

As they waited for the San Juan's departure, Rick spoke. "Thank you for coming back with me. I wouldn't have blamed you if you'd followed your parents' advice."

"It's not for you that I'm here. I'm not going to sacrifice a proper job and rot in that hell hole because of some stupid tsismis."

"I see." Rick's demeanor bore all the hallmarks of a chastened penitent. The San Juan sailed at 9 pm, a full sixty minutes late. For that tiny piece of normality Marilyn felt truly grateful. Little conversation passed between the two and Rick didn't even drink one beer on the entire voyage.

It was with a sense of overwhelming relief for both of them when the rented domicile in La Paloma came into view. Rick reflected on his life thus far. Outside of Asia he'd never been particularly successful with the fair sex. He'd met most of his girls in discos and wine-bars. The fact, that underneath those smiling faces and luscious bodies lay human beings had never occurred to him in any deep sense. It was always the chase and the conquest that had occupied his thoughts and actions.

There was Cathy, an Australian virgin of twenty-two he'd deflowered and dropped after a furious three weeks. A vision of a country lass who'd succumbed to his advances next came to mind. He'd faithfully promised to call her the next week but Rhonda had spent more than an hour relaying a conversation with her mother about finding the One. Rick performed a vanishing act and never contacted the girl again. Even the thought of her had disappeared until now.A couple more victims of his lust paraded themselves across the screen of his consciousness. Perhaps, he considered, if sex hadn't been so difficult to obtain in the sunburnt country I'd have been a little kinder and more sensitive to women folk. It wasn't as if he was any kind of Casanova or Don Juan. Most weeks he'd slept alone and the amount of time, money and effort he'd been forced to expend in attempts at rectifying the situation had been horrific.

"We're here." Marilyn's matter-of-fact voice awoke Rick from his mental perambulations. The taxi was paid and the pair entered the house. All seemed to be in order. The factory had survived their absence. There were no signs of heinous burglary. Everything was the same save that Marilyn smiled less at her boss. Work resumed, Cecilia ventured out to her weekly karate class as well as to the occasional party and Life trudged on.

Chapter Seven

The now infamous foreign celebrity and his local accomplice had been gone from the community for less than two hours. Smoke rose from a small hole in the ceiling of a modest bungalow boasting only three rooms and a thatched nipa roof. Maria's mother Violetta was frying some singularly small fish over a portable wood stove. The sickly sweet odor of burning coconut husks and leaves mingled with competing scents. At the back of the house two lean mongrels snarled.

Maria's father, Rodolpho, a lean and wizened man with the manner of one who has pretended to have worked hard all his life with little to show for it, was savoring a glass of cheap rum. As the dinner was placed on a wooden bench numerous children appeared and the Cruz family began to eat. In each corner of the room with its extremely natural floor lay neat little piles of discarded fish bones.

Extracting a bone from her teeth and tossing it with precision into the corner Violetta raised her considerable frame with its generous covering of flesh a few centimeters in her chair and spoke to the gathering. "Some people here are beginning to look us down. A rich foreigner dumps our Maria and takes up with Marilyn Delgado of all people."

"It ain't right," concurred Rodolpho as he washed down his bland meal with the last of the rum.

"It ain't right that you lose four hundred last Sunday either!" Violetta's stern gaze forced her husband into silence. "If you continue to lose large amounts I'll ban you from going to the sabong all together and then everyone'll laugh at you." Having regained control of the assembly Violetta continued. "Those stuck up Delgados are richer than us and therefore have better luck."

"Don't worry, Mama, I'll get another foreigner soon enough even if he is a bit time-ripened." Maria's jaw movement suggested resoluteness. She had barely completed her sentence when the single light bulb that lit the dwelling turned itself off. Plunged into darkness the matron of the nipa castle felt her away to another bench and returned with two candles. "Power's off again." Having stated the obvious and therefore making it official Violetta lit the objects.

"What's more," Maria continued by candlelight, "I'll make that asshole Rick pay." In the flickering glow an otherwise vibrant face cast a sinister apparition. "The wicked shall be cast into the fires of hell," slurred Rodolpho as he gazed into his empty glass. "Perhaps you could clean up after the meal since you don't do enough work to be tired," suggested his senior partner. Rodolpho disappeared. "In a few days I'll return to Cebu," Maria declared.

The children began to hold their noses. The tropical-night air's acclaimed scents of hibiscus and frangipani had been swamped by an unmistakable aroma of human excrement. The evening breeze had veered. Not unlike many of the dwellings of rural folk, that of the Cruz clan possessed no toilet. Time-honored tradition held that when an individual felt compelled to answer Nature's call he or she would make their way some distance into the coconut trees to complete the task. A distance of a hundred meters or more is probably the norm but laziness can, alas, shorten it.

Half a kilometer away down a dusty track that convoluted its way among dwellings, mounds of garbage and a number of natural obstacles the hollow block domicile of the Delgados was host to an animated discussion. "People are saying that Marilyn is some kind of prostitute," Flora lamented in the eerie light of a kerosene lamp. "Well there isn't much we can do to correct the views of the malicious and credulous," her husband retorted. "It's your fault. You should have been much firmer with Marilyn. She might have listened to you." Flora's normally genial countenance prickled with anger. "What's more it's starting to affect the store. More people come by but fewer buy anything."

"How could I have stopped her? Her mind was made up. Anyway, I don't entirely blame her. Why should she abandon a proper job because of some spiteful neighbors here?"

The raised voices of the couple competed with a transistor radio that was distributing the dulcet tones of Vilma Santos's version of Kylie Minogue's song 'Locomotion.' 'Buy Filipino' was a slogan of the Cory government. 'Buy Filipina' was an interpretation dearly held by foreign men who appreciated the beauty of the nation's women. 'Play Filipino' was merely an unannounced practice of the country's radio stations.

Growing tsismis and the potential social ruination of their family dominated most of the conversation that passed between them to the point that Ronaldo did his best to avoid communication. "Ayo. We're back," declared a voice one afternoon. The happy couple were back from their honeymoon. Between the jeepney stop and the house the newlyweds became apprised of the blossoming scandal. By the time they were inside and asking questions Ronaldo had excused himself. "Is this true?" Brushing her flowing locks away from her face Juliet sounded a little concerned. "Who knows?" answered her mother. "We had a lovely time in Nayad-by-the-Sea, Mama. There was just so much to do. I never knew that Imelda Marcos was from Leyte."

"That's wonderful dear," Flora interrupted, "but we must persuade Marilyn to come home."

"She's old enough to make up her own mind. As I was saying that Nayad resort was out of this world. Waiters appeared like flies with drinks before you even knew you were thirsty. The swimming pool had a spa Jacuzzi set-up and you could sit there with the bubbles effervescing between your legs."

Flora gazed at her second daughter disapprovingly. "They even had a swim-up bar where you could get all these fancy cocktails." At Juliet's last remark her mother had given up. "I hope it wasn't too expensive," was all she could manage. Juliet babbled on. "As you know Dodong landed a construction job in Calbayog and he'll earn good money. In fact we've decided to move there rather than Dodong's having to commute. We've rented a small apartment."

By the following Monday Dodong and Juliet had vanished to Calbayog, henceforth only to be an occasional but welcome interruption to the fabric of their lives. The Delgado house was now an empty home populated with two empty people. The store had become a beacon for popular discontent. When one of her friends stopped by with the latest on the scandal Flora had listened intently before telling some secrets of her own. "You know Maria's experienced disgracia before. However it is our Christian duty to forgive past transgressions."

"Yes, yes. What?" the woman excitedly queried. "Well apparently as well as sleeping with numerous men Maria is a lesbian. She got the job in the restaurant by sleeping with the female boss."

"What? Maria a T-bird! I'd never have guessed."

"What's worse is that apparently she was fired out from the restaurant for selling drugs. That family'll do anything for money."

"Well I never..." The friend disappeared down the dusty road.

It was a full two days before the latest hit Ronaldo's ears. "What the devil are you playing at?" he challenged his wife. "Just fighting fire with fire," came the reply. "You've no evidence whatsoever for the stories you're now telling." Ronaldo's face revealed a fragment of contempt. "Neither do they," Flora shouted back. "Ah yes, but Maria did know Rick, didn't she?" Ronaldo then left the house.

As the days rolled by Ronaldo's presence appeared directly tied to the necessities of eating and sleeping. "You wouldn't mind the store in an iron lung!" Flora had once hurled at him. Worlds may collide but they can also drift apart. The ghostliness of the home seemed at kin with the silence from the cemetery with its mounds of skulls and bones.

"I'm going fishing," Ronaldo announced early one morning. "Fishing for what?" retorted his paramour. "If I catch something you'll be the first to put it on the table and count the pisos you've saved." Ronaldo disappeared into the morning sunshine. Ten minutes later and he was positioned on a suitable rock with his line dangled into the evergreen water.

A gurgling sound attracted his attention. A short distance away a small girl lay face down in the incoming tide. Diving from his temporary abode into the unknown Ronaldo swam to the child and hauled her onto dry land. Less than three years old it was no wonder that she couldn't swim. Several minutes of coughing and wheezing saw the child come round to her normal wayward self. "Sancha where are you?" A tall woman wrapped in a red shawl was searching the shoreline.

"She's here. She nearly drowned." Ronaldo carried the child to the mother. "Jusko (God)" was all the figure could manage. Restored to her mother's arms, the little girl was howling. "I don't think I could've ever forgiven myself if anything had happened to Sancha."

"Well it very nearly did." Ronaldo, a fifty-three-year old with a beer gut, stood as tall as Superman. "I didn't see her leave the house. I'm sorry. I'm Vicky, Victoria Guyen." The woman was in her early forties and despite being the bearer of four children held a proud figure. In Cagmanipis almost everybody knows almost everybody but there are always the few who slip between the cracks. Ronaldo felt almost certain that he'd never seen this woman before but was glad that he did now. "I've lived here for more than twenty years but I've never met you. Who's your husband?"

"Ricardo Guyen, but he died in a fishing boat accident two years ago."

"I'm sorry. I remember that event." Ronaldo looked at the sea for a second to remind his audience that he understood its wickedness. Vicky with her daughter thanked him once again and left. Ronaldo resumed his fishing.

"What did you catch?" shouted Flora on his return home. "Nothing." He purposely didn't mention the rescue of the child. "I thought as much. You should do what many other Filipinos do to support their families; go to Saudia Arabia to earn dollars." Ronaldo didn't bite. During the days that followed he went fishing more often, occasionally returning home with some semblance of a catch. Always, however, he managed to pass Victoria's hut and was generally invited in for a quick morning coffee. Sometimes there were chores and odd jobs that obviously needed doing and required the service of a man. He was happy to oblige. To feel needed and appreciated is one of the rewards of life.

The Cruz household had been keeping itself busy as the authors and bearers of news. "I see Maria has left again," remarked the next-door neighbor one morning. "It's a wonder she doesn't miss her son." Violetta raised her a bulk a little preparing for battle. "Of course she misses her son but money comes first. She'll find a position in another restaurant. She's a very skilled and highly paid waitress you know." The neighbor quelled for the time being, Violetta resumed hanging her washing.

"Gang plank secured," shouted the deckhand. The San Juan had berthed at pier 9. Along with the other nefarious passengers Maria strode the plank, her head held high. Without blinking she climbed into a waiting taxi and headed for downtown Cebu. After paying the driver without any added tip Maria walked down the narrow roadway that led to Our Place and became Lina once more.

Patrick had barely risen from his bed when the knocking began. "We're not open yet!" he yelled as he reached for the door. "It's me, Lina. I'm back," a feminine voice replied. The door opened and Lina was admitted. "Are you ok now?" the owner asked. "I'm fine Sir. Can I have my room upstairs back?"

"Sure. Your job and room are still vacant." Lina and her smallish bag then ascended the stairs. An hour went by and the official owner of the establishment appeared. Corinna, her translucent nightgown hugging her slender body, was still rubbing her eyes. "What's the commotion?"

"Lina's back."

"I see."

Patrick looked into his wife's morning face. "Three weeks off for a simple abortion after being knocked up by a Russian sailor. I really don't understand why these girls don't use contraception."

"We're Catholics darling and it's a sin." Corinna thought her answer was self-explanatory. "Isn't an abortion a sin or selling your body?"

"The girls sell themselves because they financially have to and of course they hope they don't fall pregnant." Patrick laughed. "So they are accepting one sin, gambling on another and making a deal with the devil when they lose?" Corinna's blank look emphasized a cultural and religious divide.

Our Place like many discos had its own generator and when the frequent brownouts occurred it was able to function normally save for the air-conditioning. A week after Lina's return saw her make four bar-fines. Three were profitable. The fourth saw a bruised and bloodied girl arrive back at the bar the following morning. "What happened?" queried Patrick with as much sympathy as he could muster. "That Canadian was a moron. Drunk as a skunk he wasn't able to perform and then said it was my fault. Then he hit me, several times. He didn't even pay me. Can we get the police?"

"Hold on girl. It's difficult to prove assault and any arrangement you had with him once you left here is nothing to do with us."

Following her flirtation with disaster Lina took four days off work. On her return she marked a redheaded man with an Irish accent. She performed the rotations between stage duty and his lap admirably. By the time the customer had bought her four ladies' drinks he'd consumed seven beers and three rum and Cokes. When she sat on his lap his right hand would disappear down the back of her bikini briefs in the roughest of manners. "If you don't cut that out Shamus, I'll give you a Filipino haircut."

"And what would that be me darlin'?"

"I'll cut your hair by removing your entire head." Lina's expression revealed an element of seriousness. Shamus's offer of a bar-fine was met with a stern refusal and his resulting anger forced Patrick to intervene. At the departure of sudden drama routine always fills the vacuum. All of the girls regularly received their pink card health checks and Lina's brown behind had experienced the odd jab of antibiotics.

◇◇◇◇◇◇◇◇◇

A week had passed since their arrival back in La Paloma. The factory operated normally and the house seemed as it should with one difference. When Rick lay in his bed in the minutes before slumber overtakes the mind nothing happened. The door didn't open and Marilyn's gorgeous body failed to appear. "What's wrong?" whispered Rick one morning over breakfast. "Haven't you caused enough trouble? Besides Cecilia might see me approaching your room." Rick said nothing more.

Every evening when Rick and Marilyn returned from the factory Cecilia would bring Rick a beer and some nibbles. The favour was not extended to Marilyn. Cecilia was always polite and respectful to Marilyn who was her senior but she constantly smiled at Rick. "You should be much richer than you are Sir," she casually remarked one evening. "And why is that?"

"Well Sir, you are very handsome and even clever enough to run a large business."

"That's not quite the way the world works my dear," Rick laughed. Cecilia's friendliness to Rick did not go entirely unnoticed by Marilyn.

Occasionally Rick would leave the factory early on some pretext or other and travel home via Alfred's Kitchenette where he'd previously met the soldiers. This was one place where he could truly relax. One time the Major challenged Rick's impressions. "And what do you really think of our illustrious country?" Rick's reply was studied. "The Philippines is like a woman. You love her and hate her at the same time." A chorus of approving laughter informed Rick that his answer was indeed a good one.

Early one evening while the maid was out shopping Marilyn passed by her boss in the kitchen. In the confined space between a wooden bench and tiled sink-top her body clad in her customary house clothes of shirt and shorts brushed hard against his. Instinctively she pulled him to her and unzipped his fly. While she playfully teased him Marilyn's lips touched his. Rick responded with a passionate tongue-on-tongue exploration and then lifted her shirt so that his lips could fasten on the nipples of her ripe breasts. His right hand squeezed itself betwixt the top of her shorts and the flesh beneath. Pressing his fingers hard against her cotton-clad mound of Venus Rick felt his blood beginning to boil. As his fingers worked their way beneath her cotton briefs Marilyn disengaged herself, lightly kissed him on the cheek and continued her journey.

The frequency of such moments of feely, touchy tantalization increased over time. The house office, Rick's shower and even the living room were all silent witnesses. Nowhere at home was off limits. The passage of the seasons saw the rainy months disappear and almost endless sunshine return. "Let's catch a movie," Marilyn whispered one Saturday afternoon. "There's a Michael Douglas film showing in Colon."

With a casual "Why not?" Rick prepared to go. "Cecilia, Marilyn and I have a business matter to attend to downtown. We'll be gone for about three hours." On the secretary's return from her bedroom the pair departed. Smartly decked out in an olive skirt and cream blouse Marilyn looked a picture of elegance. Once they'd reached a discrete distance from the subdivision the girl reached for Rick's hand. They looked every inch a couple of lovers on a weekend stroll.

As the pair approached the Vision cinema a group of standbys yelled something in a Visayan dialect at Marilyn. Rick was unable to understand a word but Marilyn pulled her hand away from its embrace with his and began to cry. "What's the matter? What did those yobos say?" questioned Rick. The tears fell faster than ever. "They called me a foreigner's whore," she sobbed. "Just ignore those idiots," advised Rick. "That's easy for you to say but for a Filipina a good reputation is everything." Rick added to his advice. "You know that what they say isn't true so why should it bother you?" The girl's weeping slowly began to diminish. "You don't get it do you? What people think of you matters more than the reality."

Rick indeed didn't get it but twenty minutes later they were ensconced in the movie theatre and Marilyn had forgotten about the unpleasant experience. Against the background of constant chattering and giggling Marilyn felt just able to follow the plot. Rick didn't care too much for celluloid pleasure. His arm was firmly around his girl and to feel her warmth was entertainment enough for him.

❖ ❖ ❖ ❖ ❖ ❖ ❖ ❖

Barely had the two figures disappeared around the corner and Cecilia laid down her broom. Picking up a small green brush and metal dustpan she headed for the home office. Carefully placing them on the table within easy reach she searched for the petty cash tin. After a full ten minutes she located the item. Filthy bastard, she thought as she extracted the tin from beneath a pile of Playboys in the third drawer. Hastily removing the lid she extracted a bundle of notes leaving lonely a miserable pile of coins. Her mind was racing. "A large pile of hundreds, a smaller collection of fifties and a mid-sized heap of fives, tens and twenties. If I take any of the hundreds they might notice." With a religious precision her slender fingers with their cream-painted nails extracted two fifty-piso notes along with six twenties and eight fives from the respective stacks.

Cecilia placed these pluckings into her purse and replaced the piles in the tin and thence the tin under the Playboys in the drawer. A medium-sized safe of grey steal beckoned her from its corner. Not knowing the combination and lacking the skills to bypass such niceties she regretfully ignored the challenge. Carefully scrutinizing the remainder of the office for possible targets the nurse-in-waiting collected the brush and dustpan and exited; not in the direction of Marilyn's room as stealing from a Filipina was too damned risky, nor back to the kitchen. With a deft movement of her left hand Cecilia opened the door to the master's bedroom. It was never locked. "I suppose I'll find a large supply of condoms in here and probably some jelly as well," she chuckled to herself.

At that point her mind wandered. This particular foreigner was a little more together than Sven had been, even if his house was a dump. Sven's house was a three–story affair of white stone set high on the cool hills of Lahug and he owned it. What a view was there for the asking from almost all windows. From the rear of the structure you could see the entire city. While still pursuing her studies she had worked as the principal household help in the home of this Swedish man. Poor Sven, she laughed internally. He just had no idea. Between beers he spent all his time running that stupid bar while his wife's relatives stole sixty percent of the money. He could never understand why a well-populated bar failed to show any profit. He'd just sit and stare at the fish tank for hours.

Apart from an unrealized disillusionment with his family, the Philippines and life in general Sven used to drink too much, far too much. One of Cecilia's duties had been to assist him home after the bar shut. Although he was a six-footer Sven was thin and she was able to manage. This individual had inherited a considerable sum of money as a result of his parents' untimely deaths and his situation as an only child. Only fractionally over thirty Sven had taken a long vacation encompassing several countries. On the Philippine leg he'd only been in the capital for a matter of hours when he'd fallen in love with Leilin and decided to save her from her life of poverty and sin. Sven had paid a considerable sum to the Brown Fox bar as a severance before bringing Leilin back home to Cebu. They had married within a month.

Two days before the wedding Sven had noticed a new stereo in the wooden shack where Leilin's extensive family resided. "How were they able to buy that?" Sven had inquired. "Credit," Leilin had replied. The wedding went ahead and Sven enrolled himself on a treadmill. From less than a week after her employment Cecilia learned a secret, an open secret to Filipinos but nonetheless a secret. From his wife herself to her mother and father, siblings and cousins Sven only possessed a financial value. The question of inheritance was never openly discussed but it was apparent that in the event of Sven's demise they would inherit everything. Without uttering any words the entire family made it plain that they would be truly beholden to any individual who hastened the acquisition of what was rightfully theirs.

As Cecilia glanced around Rick's bedroom her thoughts continued their reverie. It was a terrible accident after all; that night when Sven was so drunk that he fell over the outside stairs and dropped twenty meters. I didn't mean to push him when he fell against the rail. It just happened. I meant to pull him back to safety of course but my hands somehow moved the wrong way. Sven would have certainly died but a compact mound of garbage had lessened the impact. Even then he'd struck his head on a jutting-out piece of pipe. After ten days in a coma Sven regained just enough consciousness to be officially classified as a vegetable. Leilin's family quickly consigned him to a sort of home. The occasional bringing of groups of patients to church broke an otherwise minimal standard of care. Prayers were muttered over the collection of shattered human beings and then they were hastily returned to their routine.

Questions had been asked about the accident. "It's a terrible thing," muttered Leilin. "It'd have been much better if he'd died." Some tongues had wagged at the time but the downfall of a rich foreigner was probably an act of God and, besides, there was no evidence of foul play.

Cecilia was still deep in thought. That whole business was a damned shame. Sure, the family gave me a handsome bonus when they let me go. Without Sven they simply didn't need me. What hurt most though was the vaguest of suggestions that the ongoing expense, however little, of Sven's care in the home was somehow to be blamed on me. I could just feel that they would have given me really big money if the accident had killed him. A sharp crash brought Cecilia's consciousness back to the present with a jolt. She had somehow bumped a crystal glass from the table. It's shattered remains lay on the parquet floor. She swept them up with her trade tools and continued her purpose. Her daydream had seemed long and detailed but in reality had lasted no more than ninety seconds. Her keen eyes cased every visible surface and a calculating mind produced a mental list of priorities.

The wardrobe revealed a modest collection of handmade belts between an endless array of shirts, trousers and other male paraphernalia. Two of them sported zippers on the inside for safeguarding cash. Would these be missed? Her hands still stroking the leather the hired-helper was somewhat unsure. Yet she'd never seen such finely made leather items. As her left hand was about to return them to their place her right clasped them and directed the items to a pouch of her apron. One bottle of cheap aftershave and two packets of cigarettes completed her haul. Less than a minute later the cleaning tools were back in their homes, her booty was carefully stored inside her karate bag and Cecilia was back at work in the lounge room. A popular soapie was showing on one of the television's local channels.

Kris Aquino, the daughter of the president, was playing the part of a slum dweller who'd just been raped by a neighbor; performing the part very badly. "Kris is just wonderful." The rich and famous always managed to blindside Cecilia despite her greater-than-average intelligence. By the time Marilyn and the boss returned from their business the show had finished. Still with her broom in hand the maid hastened to the gate to admit them. "Was your business successful, Sir?" she inquired. Marilyn's cheek muscles managed to stifle a spontaneous snarl. "Yes thank you Cecilia. Our meeting went well."

From the moment she opened her eyes in the smallest of rooms at the back of Our Place's restaurant area to the time she closed them again Lina worked feverishly on her project to ensnare a foreigner. The pitfalls and potential dangers sometimes caused her to worry though. That unfortunate business with the Canadian stayed long in her mind after the bruises had gone down.

What can I do to protect myself? was a recurring thought in her mind. Carrying any sort of weapon was impractical as well as illegal. The answer came to her after viewing an old Bruce Lee movie on a friend's Betamax. I'll learn karate. Between performing both vertically and horizontally and considerable periods of sleep or rest there were few free hours in Lina's day. Nonetheless considering the fact that she didn't begin work till 9 pm she could make the time for lessons.

It was a Monday evening just after six when the determined dancer fronted up to the premises of Cebu's Shaolin School of Martial Arts. "Karate classes are held Monday and Thursday," said the head instructor, "and cost P800 a term."

"That's chickenfeed," scoffed Lina as she handed over her payment. "There's a beginner's class starting tonight," replied the instructor killing any further conversation.

During a halftime break the students from various classes stood in the corridor around two ancient soft drink vending machines and engaged in a hotchpotch of social interaction ranging from political conversations to serious flirtations. As she approached one of the drink dispensers a heavily perspiring Lina bumped into a girl whose smooth shoulder-length hair dangled over her crisp white suit with its green belt. "I'm so sorry. I didn't see you there; too much sweat in my eyes I suppose. This is my first class."

"No problem," responded the girl. "It's hard work but it's worth it. I've been studying this discipline for over three years. By the way, I'm Cecilia." Lina in turn introduced herself before the motley group dissipated into the various rooms that responded to classes of each level.

Every Monday and Thursday Cecilia would flirt that little bit harder with Rick before asking in an unnaturally accommodating voice for permission to go to her class. "Of course," the boss would say. "You don't even need to ask. In the unlikely event that something has come up and we can't do without you for the few hours I'll let you know." With a toss of her shiny and sleek hair Cecilia would pick up her bag and disappear through the gate with a "Thank you Sir. You are too kind."

The maid often left the house at 4:30 in the afternoon although classes began at six. Less than half a jeepney ride away she would alight and walk a hundred meters or so to an extremely modest cement dwelling. "Mama," she'd call, "I'm here."

"What did you manage to extract today?" was Dolores' answer on one occasion. "Two hundred and fifty pisos, an ornament and an alarm clock," Cecilia replied to the corpulent frame from whose loins she had begun life. "Not bad." Dolores considered herself a small-scale social revolutionary whose weapon of choice was theft. "We'll be able to buy a color television soon," she added. "Your father just never understood that life offers its rewards to those who'll take them. His habit of allowing others to take advantage of him was what ultimately led to our separation. Honesty he called it. Stupidity was what I said."

"Never mind, Mama, that was long ago." Dolores would not be put off her piece of bitching however. "Just look at your father today. Almost eighty years old and lives in a ramshackle shack. A lifetime of serious toil and he can barely afford two meals a day."

"I have to go to class now, Mama." Cecilia kissed her mother on the cheek and walked back to the stop to resume her journey.

By the time that Christmas began its final approach Cecilia had nothing but contempt for the stupid foreigner and his stuck-up secretary. He wouldn't notice if I stole his dick from out of his underpants, she thought to herself. Taking down assholes like him is just so ridiculously easy. Not much of a challenge really. Almost every time she left the gate for her class her bag was heavy with booty. Her neat karate uniform lay carefully folded on top of the treasure. One time she even lifted three beers from the fridge. "The boys around my mother's house will be grateful for the gesture," she giggled aloud.

Attendance statistics for those who toiled under the iron roof of the Tisa factory were running at about seventy-five percent by the end of October. While not approaching those of similar operations in Germany, Japan or the U.S. Marilyn reassured Rick that they were somewhat impressive for the Philippines. By the time All Souls' Day and its paramour All Saints' Day came knocking the warehouse was reaching its storage capacity. Light but sturdy settees, tables with matching cane chairs and tropically inspired coffee stands of fair-to-good workmanship lay in ever increasing towers.

"Why on earth are we heading for a cemetery at nine o'clock at night?" Rick quizzed his significant other. "It's the duty of all Filipinos to pay their respects to the Dead," answered Marilyn. Even in the sooty darkness of evening her beauty still shone. "Besides, you'll find the experience somewhat interesting." Gripping the girl's hand Rick resigned himself to his fate as the gates of the Tisa cemetery beckoned in the distance.

From the sixteenth century onwards the Catholic Church had attempted to stamp out the pagan tradition of All Souls' Day and failed dismally. In a lethargic spiritual truce the Church had finally allowed this ancient custom and by way of recompense had introduced its own All Saints' Day to immediately follow the ancient holiday. Come the first of November all thoughts of labor, enrichment and business fade unequivocally from the minds of Filipinos. All Souls' Day is an occasion on which the living pay homage to their dead relatives and ancestors.

As the pair reached the gate a collection of popular disco tunes sallied forth into the night air at considerable decibels. Flashing lights competed with thousands of candles and vast hordes of living humanity appeared to be celebrating the party of their lives. "The living certainly outnumber the departed tonight," remarked Rick. "Shsh, this is a serious occasion," chided Marilyn. Rick's tall frame was happily hidden by the dark but his loud English speaking voice was not. "To see all this merriment you'd think that everybody hated their dead relatives and were glad to see the back of them. Look, there's even a stall over there selling refreshments." A sharp pinch into the mound-of-Venus of his left hand managed to silence the sacrilegious foreigner. "Of course we are sorry when our loved ones are taken from us and go to the Lord," explained Marilyn, "Yet we believe that by having this giant party we are sharing our enjoyment with them. This celebration is a triumph of Life over Death. It is the acceptance of the inevitable that gives rise to immortality."

"Do you have any relatives here?" asked Rick, "or are we merely sightseeing?" A filthy glance that knifed its way through the blackness reached his eyes. "Most of my family are laid to rest in the Cagmanipis burial ground but there are two of my kinfolk here. The first is a great uncle of mine called Alfonso Revera who was killed in a freak accident a long time ago and the other is a distant cousin who passed away only last year after a mysterious illness that she'd caught while serving foreigners in a disco-restaurant. The family were so afraid that it might be infectious that they insisted she be buried in Cebu." Marilyn's disapproving glance intimated to Rick that the girl wasn't merely a waitress.

"We'll go and visit Alfonso's grave first." Marilyn grabbed Rick's arm and led him along a maze of earthen corridors each with a crowd of revelers making their vigils. For once Marilyn's dress matched Rick's. They were both sporting faded denim jeans. Marilyn's however hugged her contours tightly and demonstrated the aesthetic qualities of her rear end.

Her great uncle's resting place was an unremarkable slab completely overwhelmed by a thriving colony of weeds. Before Marilyn had finished uttering a simple prayer the voice of boorish curiosity boomed from her side. "What kind of freak accident saw him off?" Seeing that Rick would not let this matter go Marilyn honored him with the truth. "Many years ago this part of Cebu City was covered with lush forest and some small farms. Alfonso would arrive from Samar to sell fertilizers and pesticides to the farmers. He'd trudge for hours with his wares atop his buffalo. Most nights he'd sleep in this little nipa hut atop a cliff as it was central to his daily meanderings. During a particularly heavy storm one night the hut's foundations had become a sodden mixture of clay and mud and the structure was precariously poised on the edge of the precipice. Finally it slid off the cliff and crashed into the valley below."

"Wasn't he aware of the instability of the hut during the storm?" posed Rick, expecting his girl to be able to answer for her long-deceased kin. "Who can be sure?" came the natural reply. "People at the time seemed to think that a violent rocking of the hut's solitary bamboo bed caused the structure to fall. Anyway along with Alfonso's corpse in the wreckage was found the naked body of a young woman. Alfonso's wife in Cagmanipis was so incensed that she refused to have anything to do with his burial. At public expense he was interred here."

Another brisk journey through the throngs of merrymakers found the couple paused beside a fresher disturbance of the earth's crust. "Here we are at poor Remy's grave," Marilyn announced. "She was the heroine of her family and a village role model until she took sick and died that way."

"Sounds like it could have been AIDS," muttered Rick disrespectfully. "I don't think it could've been that," responded Remy's living relative and visitor. "Remy didn't use drugs." Catching his comment deep in his throat Rick decided that it was not a suitable moment to educate Marilyn on health matters.

The process of paying homage, soaking up the atmosphere and generally basking in a totally surreal experience took more than a couple of hours. At one point Rick risked a sudden attack of lumbing, a violent series of pinches and other tortures inflicted by females on their lovers, by fixing his gaze on a luscious body in her late teens. Her vibrant curves only slightly masked by a short skirt formed a curious contrast with the gravestone behind her. The way of all flesh, mused Rick and then shuddered.

"I just can't believe it," he mumbled on the way home. "Fiestas here, fiestas there and even a fiesta for the dead."

"If you want to put it that way I can't stop you," scolded Marilyn. "You know why we Filipinos consider these observances important." The jeepney ride back to their home reminded Rick somehow of the Ghost Train the first time he'd ridden it at Sydney's Luna Park. Nothing seemed real; not life; not even death itself.

As the sun rose on All Saints' Day Marilyn dutifully headed off to church. Rick drank beer and watched the cable TV. Cecilia made a point of serving her boss his drinks and snacks. "I should go to church too," the maid remarked in the afternoon. "By all means go then," said Rick between sips of beer and engrossed in a Major League baseball game. The girl snapped back, "You really shouldn't drink so much. I had an uncle who solved his midlife crisis that way. By excessive drinking he turned it into an end-of-life crisis and died." Cecilia and her familiar bag accordingly made their exit. After visiting her mother she did indeed go to church.

Rick Daly was feeling increasingly optimistic about his fortunes. Whether falling asleep to the monotonous buzz of mosquitoes or waking up in a pool of sweat he felt a surge of hope and expectation. Some months before he'd applied for an export license and also done the spade work for his intended markets. Import quotas were granted from a number of western countries. Furthermore Brigg's Furniture Wholesalers of Memphis, Younger Bros. Rattanware Importers of Leeds in the UK and YZ Imports of Sydney had all agreed to purchase moderate quantities of his product once the sample shipments had passed quality assurance.

He'd had to make the Manila trip once during this time to again jump Miriam Defensor Santiago's obstacle course for aliens. This time he'd approached a travel agency in the capital and handed over his passport along with thirty-five hundred pisos. Freed from the insults, innuendo and endless waiting and secure in the knowledge that his passport would be delivered, with visa extension, to his hotel, Rick relaxed. The gin veteran behind the bar of the White House Hotel could certainly be trusted to safeguard his passport. A day as well as another night on the town was certainly preferable to the alien-angst dance at Intramuros. "This was certainly an example of honest corruption if it was corruption at all," Rick decided of the additional five hundred pisos it would cost him.

The Del Pilar walk went pretty much according to schedule; a quick beer in Chicks' Bar where Charito, the one dancer who manifested a dislike for Rick, dropped her panties revealing a miserable little collection of pubic hairs and refused his offer of a drink, a brief sojourn at Raymond's to watch the hunting girls and down some of the cheapest alcohol on the planet and the odd high-priced beer in the street's swankiest establishments. They say life moves in a cycle and where you are on the wheel, when it stops for however briefly, decides whether a spoke skewers you or not. Between bars and with eyes fixed firmly on the pavement, more to avoid tripping on unfortuitous apertures than in the amorphous hope of finding money, Rick found himself accosted by a somewhat grubbier than usual child-beggar. "Five pisos, Joe," the creature challenged. "What is this? Inflation," retorted the Westerner as he pushed the obstacle out of his way.

Early the following morning our Mr. Daly was wending his way southward along the famed street when a violent bump with a shadow saw his wallet fly from his pocket. Despite being a little the worse for drink, reflexes sprang into action that the owner of the wallet never knew he had. His left arm sprang from his side and retracted baring a small boy of less than five years in its grasp. With the wallet back in place Rick decided to teach the child a lesson. He would not let him go but hauled him along the dusty and sin-soaked pavement. What he was actually going to do with the trussed quarry had not so far actually entered Rick's head. Most likely he'd have released him at the end of a block or so.

Swish! A flash in the dark saw a considerable tear in his shirt. Swish! This time he saw it. A double-bladed butterfly knife was attempting intercourse with his heart or other vital parts. In a weak moonlight the blade glinted in the scrawny hand of a pathetic skeletal creature. Rick's grip released the child but the attack didn't stop. A hundred meters or more a spectral female figure pursued him, lunged at his torso and slashed. As he reached

Raymond's the blond six-footer grabbed a stool and thrust it toward the relentless blade. From behind, three deaf-and-dumb girls who sometimes frequented this most famous spot in Manila disarmed the wretched mother of the thief-in-training. Soon all had vanished into the night, Rick included.

Before making his bed fall at the White House a shaken foreigner had snuck back into Chicks' bar for a constitutional drink and a quick squiz at his tantalizing enemy, Charito. A rum and Coke had barely stopped his shaking hands when a Filipino man in a stained T-shirt and ancient denims had accosted him. "Hey Joe. You're CIA. I know that people like you are here to destroy our country." Not bothering with the niceties of logic, which would include such salient facts as that the CIA would be much more interested to hire suitable Filipinos than highly noticeable Westerners Rick just turned his back. The unpleasant and intoxicated brown figure had tapped Rick on the shoulder at least three times before Roger, the doorman, was called upon to show him the night air.

◇ ◇ ◇ ◇ ◇ ◇ ◇ ◇ ◇

From the window of the plane the scattered and aggregated signs of settlement that make up Cebu City never looked so good. A couple of unfortunate happenings besides, Rick felt confident that things were on the up and up. Marilyn greeted him as his taxi pulled up at the gate and Cecilia was all smiles. Surprisingly neither production nor attendance were down during his absence. In fact the warehouse was somewhat replete with items awaiting their final homes.

The first indication of brewing inertia was a letter that arrived from Rattanware Importers. The brief document pointed out that the promised sample shipment had not yet arrived. Brian Small and John Bedford, joint managers of the Leeds-based wholesaling operation, drew attention to the fact that the passing of deadlines meant that Rick's product, missing both Christmas and January sales, would be compelled to wait almost a year before facing the arbiter of consumer choice. A few days later and a similar communication arrived from the U.S. and another from Germany.

"There's some weird sort of disaster," Rick mouthed to Marilyn after reading the first letter. "The stock we sent hasn't arrived."

"I don't know about such things Sir," responded Marilyn with her formal voice. "Perhaps we should begin our inquiries with our shipping agents here in Cebu. That's all I can think of at the moment." The secretary bookkeeper was duly assigned the task of chasing down the missing furniture. "The goods were dispatched to the docks in accordance with their bill of shipping," a junior clerk explained. "We've received no notification of any problem. You could always check with the Bureau of Export licensing." After thanking him for his help, Marilyn phoned the bureau. The Cebu office, disclaiming responsibility, referred her to the head office in Manila. Seven phone calls and two hours had gone down by the time Marilyn had located the cargo in question. "It seems that there was some irregularity with your consignment," an anonymous voice had claimed. "According to our records it lacked an official clearance stamp and has been impounded in the government bond stores at the Cebu docks."

"What's an official clearance stamp?" a nervous potential entrepreneur asked of his shining star. "I had no idea either so I rang our attorneys," replied Marilyn, her cream-colored shorts betraying the shapely thighs within. "There is no such clearance stamp."

"I don't understand. Why didn't our goods ship as scheduled then?" A greyness in his face revealed a deeper than usual concern. Rick looked puzzled. "Sometimes, quite often," Marilyn murmured as she stroked the inside of Rick's left thigh, "people here in official positions feel the need to earn extra money. Their salaries are very low."

"Nice one! No wonder this place is regarded as a banana republic that sells rotten bananas," was all Rick could manage. "What should we do now?" Marilyn appeared scared. "I have no idea. It's not fair of you to expect me to know all these things."

"I'm sorry." Rick apologized. "Could you bring me a bourbon and Coke then, please," he muttered as though this would provide a solution. Since Cecilia was at karate class Marilyn obliged. More than that, she kissed him and touched his body.

"My best guess," she purred, "is that we ask Attorney Pablo." As the cooler temperature of late evening descended Marilyn was once again in Rick's bed protecting him from his demons while exposing herself to an attack from hers. As the sun rose on the denuded hills opposite Narra Street Marilyn returned to her own bed for another hour's sleep, a fearful shuffle across a distance smaller than ten meters, while demonstrating an extreme concern that the watchful eyes of Cecilia might notice.

It was Rick, not his number two, who phoned the lawyer. "What do you suggest?" The disquieted voice of an-almost-successful businessman was begging. "I'm not exactly sure how to put this," the senior partner replied. "Business and legal matters do not exactly move in straight lines. You have perhaps made an enemy in the relevant government instrumentality." Jun Pablo hesitated to give any further advice.

That same evening, a Wednesday with an unseasonable downpour, witnessed Rick drowning his sorrows in the Scandinavian Bar. The brown, skimpily clad skins of the dancers and waitresses alike suggested an attachment to northern Europe born of a desire related to nothing more than money and the weather-inspired hopes of European holidaymakers. Through a San Miguel and La Tondena Rum inspired fog a hazy gaze could barely focus on the flashing bodies. A tap on the shoulder brought Rick back to the present. "You look like you need a drink. Let me buy you one." An exceedingly handsome man only a few centimeters shorter than Rick was smiling. This was a face that Rick would have fallen for if he were a woman. However he wasn't and didn't. "I beg your pardon," Rick turned to face his accuser. "I'm in great form except for my hearing. Did you offer me a drink?" The striking personage of Marco Gordon introduced himself and reiterated his offer. "Thank you," slurred the businessman on a mental precipice.

"These girls are cute enough," remarked Marco, a gentleman with Eurasian features and exceedingly good English, "but there's more to life than just women."

"Right you are but I'm not sure I've found it yet." The boy from almost everywhere could always manage an attempt at humor no matter how pissed. "I couldn't help but notice that you don't look very happy," Marco continued. "You've hardly looked at the girls." Through tired eyes Rick acknowledged his benefactor's efforts. "I've got all this shit going down with my business. Many thousands of dollars and a year after my arrival here my business is stalling because of some greedy vultures in a government office."

Marco bought Rick another drink even though it should have been the latter's turn. "Conditions in the Philippines are very different from those in western countries," Marco exclaimed. "I should know. My father was a Scotsman and my mother a Filipina. My father could never cope with conditions here but couldn't bring himself to leave either. From my mother herself to the general society in the Philippines, for him it was a kind of fatal attraction."

"You said was," observed Rick.

"Unfortunately, it all got too much for him and he died of drink," observed Marco somewhat dryly.

"I'm sorry," Rick slurred politely. Three rounds later and Rick insisted on paying.

"I didn't quite understand the gist of your trouble," Rick's Eurasian friend continued. "It's disgustingly simple but there's no solution," the would-be furniture king spat out.

"There's always a solution to any problem. That's a basic mathematical law." Marco smiled and prepared to listen intently. "I've got all this furniture ready for export, licenses, shipping arrangements and everything done but the bloody stuff can't seem to leave Cebu's docks. They must have glue on them or something!"

"Have you thought of paying a consideration to the relevant officials?" Marco's voice took on the tone of a schoolmaster. "What do you mean?" Marco's expression denoted an impatient amusement at the incompetence of a novice student. "Bribes."

"If this country wants to get ahead such immoral practices aren't go to help it any," was all Rick could manage. "If you want to be a philosopher then go ahead but if you desire to operate a successful business here then you'll have to become more pragmatic." The Scandinavian Bar's headmaster-emeritus had spoken. "How the fuck do these finer points help me?" An inebriated Daly was beyond esoteric cultural observances. "Well I used to work in the local office of the tax department before I left to start my own 'buy and sell' business." Marco appeared confident in his own capacity. "I have many, many contacts in most levels of government in these islands," he went on. "I can probably solve your problem in less than a fortnight."

Rick's head had begun to hang but on hearing these words he raised it, winked at the current three dancers and turned towards Marco. "Could you really do that?" his voice quavered. "Sure, but it'll cost you."

"How much?" The price seemed much less important to Rick than the imminent failure of his operation. Thoughts of Marilyn returning jobless to her parental home also flashed across his consciousness. "If you can trust me with ten thousand I think your goods will find their ships," the Eurasian returned. More out of desperation than belief Rick agreed to the deal and asked Marco to come to his house on the morrow.

It was 3:30 in the morning when Rick crashed through the gate of his domicile. Before he could reach the front door Marilyn, awoken by the noise, pulled it open. Drunk though he was, Marilyn was pleasantly surprised that Rick was alone. No ripe slip of a girl stood in the shadows. She promptly put the boss to bed alone and returned to her own little cot.

Rick didn't mention his meeting with the government fixer to the feminine head of operations. Perhaps it was pride. When Marco presented himself Rick introduced him as a friend who was a labor consultant by trade. Marilyn kept smiling at Marco during the half-hour morning tea. Her boss was even less amused when he noticed that his visitor was directing most of his attention to the girl. "Marilyn could you go to the store and buy some beers please?" Rick thought he'd wrap things up. "That's Cecilia's job," returned the secretary. "Where's she? Don't tell me karate class is now in the mornings."

"Cecilia's had a death in the family and I've given her five days off." Marilyn failed to look either sympathetic or convinced. "Please Marilyn." With a glance of cynical resignation Rick's guiding angel excused herself and left the house. "I'm sorry to be a little rushed," Rick apologized, "but I've got some work to do." He handed over the ten thousand and showed his guest to the gate.

"Where's Marco?" asked Marilyn upon her return with a basket of beers. "He had to leave as his niece was having a christening this afternoon," lied the boss. Jealousy aside, he couldn't wait to see his bookkeeper's expression when he informed her that the red tape problem had been solved. Her approving looks meant more to him than he was aware.

Slightly after eight in the evening, two days later, the phone rang. Cecilia picked up the receiver. "It's Marco for you Marilyn," she announced. Rick's eyebrows furrowed as if an earthquake had hit them. "Hello." Marilyn's voice into the hand piece sounded a fraction sweeter than normal. Rick's mind was racing. "You wanted to speak to Rick?" he heard Marilyn say. Grabbing the piece of black plastic he challenged, "What's the idea of asking for Marilyn rather than me?"

"What do you mean?" Marco was genuinely puzzled. "I asked your maid to get you and then Marilyn picked up the phone."

"Oh, I see." Rick was now on the defensive. "Do you have any good news about our consignment?" A brief silence followed. "Well?" reiterated Rick.

"There's a problem," a muted voice echoed in the receiver. "They say that considering you have many thousands of dollars tied up in the bond store ten thousand pisos isn't enough. They need twenty more."

"That will definitely fix the whole thing then?" returned Rick. "Sure. Your goods will be gone within the week."

"All right then. How can I get the cash to you?"

"I could come by your house tomorrow. Your secretary's brownies were truly delicious." A savage cough heralded Rick's opinion of this arrangement. "That won't be necessary. I'll bring it to you. Where will you be?" Ten seconds of silence followed and Rick repeated his question.

"You can bring it to me at three o'clock at Mila's Fast Filipino Foods restaurant on the main drag near the Capitol building."

"See you then." Rick replaced the receiver and called for Cecilia. "Yes Sir," the beaming maid replied. "Why did you say that the call was for Marilyn when it was for me?" The future nurse wrinkled her face and then spoke. "Mr. Marco asked to speak to the person in charge and I assumed he was referring to the domestic aspects of our household. I'm very sorry Sir." Cecilia adjusted her blouse to propel a bit more skin into visual range.

"That's ok, but in future, if in doubt please refer anything to me." Cecilia wiggled her more-than-reasonable tits. "Certainly Rick but don't you think you should drink less." Marilyn dragged her life's hope aside like a stunned mullet before he could react to this effrontery. "What's going on? I can sense some funny business." Rick mollified her by gainsaying and commenting on how stunning she looked that day.

Seven sunrises and sunsets later and the imprisoned furniture was still bound fast. When Marco rang again he was apologetic. "As you know there is currently a culture against foreigners. Cory and Miriam blame most of the ills of our nation on overseas interests. This is rubbish but it doesn't alter the facts on the ground. Your goods aren't going to move unless another 30,000 is forthcoming." It is difficult to pick up your heart from your underpants but Rick seemed to manage it. "You're sure that this will be sufficient and the goods will move?"

"Absolutely." The voice oozed the confidence of an insider. "Well I'll see you tomorrow, same time same place."

An entire week passed after the transfer of the pregnant envelope and Rick's furniture was still stuck fast to the soil of Cebu. He was now more than impatient. He was annoyed. "Where's the good corruption in this?" he wondered. Picking up the scrap of paper with Marco's address details he made a phone call; attempted to make a phone call. The number was nonexistent. The address was real enough so Cecilia was dispatched to check it out. "The family that live there are called Reyes and they say they've never heard of any Marco Gordon." Her satisfaction on delivering this negative news went unnoticed by her boss but registered with his secretary.

The next three nights saw Rick bar hopping with a nasty urgency. The Scandinavian bar knew Marco by sight; he'd been in there two or three times but nothing further. The other bars nearby had never heard of him. Dejection, drunkenness and depression coupled with the availability of cheap and persuasive female flesh can only have one outcome. By the time Rick's fruitless search arrived at the Silver Dollar bar he'd given up. A sixteen-year-old stunner restored his faith in the nation's value. "Not La Paloma, this time," Rick wisely swore to himself.

The taxi pulled up outside Fiely's Welcome Inn. With its forty pisos a night tariff and no questions asked, the wooden edifice with its tiny rooms and ineffective ceiling fans was more than Rick could have demanded. The sun was casting its bright presence on the following day by the time Rick fumbled his way through the gate. On reaching the door he spent another thirty seconds scrabbling with the key. Entering the hallway he noticed everything was quiet; too quiet. There was no sign of Cecilia anywhere. Not wishing to be quizzed by Marilyn he snuck up the steps and disappeared into his room. When he awoke it was after midday. The house was still deathly quiet.

"Could Marilyn have gone off somewhere with that smooth serpent?" Rick's mind raced. A miserable clammy chill burst from his bones and expanded through his entire body. The thought was intolerable. Beads of terror formed on his face. "Marilyn," he yelled. Amidst acres of noise only the Philippines can produce the kind of silence that can burn into the soul.

◇ ◇ ◇ ◇ ◇ ◇ ◇ ◇

"Good to see you dear," Dolores intoned. "How did you do this week?" The nurse who would soon enough be entrusted with lives disgorged the latest unofficial bonus from her employment as a maid. "That's a very fancy watch and the cufflinks have inset diamonds. Won't your boss miss them?" A sneer of derision greeted her mother's question. "That guy wouldn't miss his ass if it was on fire." The fat woman was placated. "Don't take the TV dear. Even fools would notice that." Cecilia grinned. "Very funny, Mama. By the time this guy and his business implode we'll have moved on to richer pickings. Maybe, within five years we'll be able to live in Lahug."

Back in the tomb-like house not a moment's thought concerning the helper had escaped Rick's mind. Marilyn where are you? You couldn't have hooked up with a slime ball. You must have an explanation for being gone. If the factory had burned down he couldn't have cared less. The deathly silence continued, mocking his fears. A rum fortified coffee stilled his shaking somewhat. A hasty self-prepared bacon and egg sandwich washed down with two beers saw the return of some semblance of composure.

When Marilyn's ever-so-sensual face appeared at the gate Rick's heart leaped. "Where were you?" he stammered, half afraid of the answer. "Help me with the shopping," came the mundane reply. "I couldn't get any cheese. It was this week's special. Out of stock!"

"You haven't seen that Marco fellow have you?" was Rick's next question, desperately hoping that the response was negative. "No, should I have?" Marilyn gazed hard at Rick's ashen features. "What's wrong with you?" Keeping his innermost fears to himself Rick spilled out the rest. "Almost sixty thousand pisos down the drain in an attempt to bypass the export blockage."

"I thought that guy looked too smooth." Marilyn couldn't help feeling a tad superior at that instant. "You smiled at him often enough when he was here." Rick's jealousy would not be stilled so easily. "He's very good looking but that doesn't mean that you should give him large sums of money." Marilyn quickly retreated into her role as bookkeeper come secretary. "Humph!" Rick could say no more and retreated to his bedroom to lie down.

It was a full hour before the door opened and Marilyn entered. Pulling off her shirt and slipping down her shorts, she lay on the bed next to Rick clad only in the briefest sky-blue panties. Her boss hadn't moved at her arrival. Her hands slowly began to caress him and her lips gently, ever so subtlely commenced to kiss his near-naked torso. "I'm not serious about anyone else. You know that." Her breasts rubbed his body as she moved.

Rick's physique responded before his mental processes.

Marilyn's soft touch carried more intrinsic chemistry than ever and her kisses invigorated any portion of Rick's being on which they landed. Neither of them spoke. After a considerable amount of every conceivable kind of caress and electrostatically charged sensation of skin on skin Marilyn swung her shapely torso around into the couple's time-honored sixty-nine position. The twin hills of her tan buttocks formed the softest backdrop to Rick's vision. After some minutes of allowing his tongue to tease the soft opening in her black grass he raised it a little higher until it reached another opening. The girl's star shaped volcano smelled as sweet as the rest of her being. Hesitantly, the darting tongue reached its rim and flickered, ever so slowly in a circular fashion. "Oooh!" Marilyn's soft voice broke into a more intensely aroused murmur. The darting sliver of flesh then proved brave enough to approach the volcano's opening.

He had never done that to any woman before in his entire life. Rick's spontaneous actions surprised him. "I love you." The words spoke themselves. A faint voice gurgled from a full mouth. "You already know my feelings."

"I feel so stupid about Marco," Rick confided during the daylight hours of labor. "There's not much you can do about it now." The bookkeeper's voice was rather matter-of-fact. "But nearly sixty thousand pisos down the gurgler; that's more than two thousand U.S. dollars." A wistful smile escaped Marilyn's lips. "What's worse; our exports are still sitting at the docks. Soon they'll grow mould."

"Try Jun Pablo again." Three hours later, acting on her suggestion, Rick was sipping on a cup of tea in the law offices. "What I'm about to say is absolutely confidential," the senior partner had intoned. "There are people in the bureaucracy who can fix these problems and require no consideration until they are resolved. If you can trust me with thirty thousand, cash, we'll see what we can do." Rick nodded. In his situation he'd have done the same if asked to walk round the Capitol building naked.

In the intervening days between this meeting and the resolution of the export matter events at home took a nasty turn. The clock on the lounge room wall declared the hour to be half past four. Cecilia with her usual bag and accoutrements was in the throes of departing for her karate class. Earlier that afternoon a visibly stressed Rick had been contributing to the coffers of the San Miguel Corporation. Generally this precious fluid came in small robust bottles. However it could be obtained in cans from the supermarkets. In response to Marilyn's question about paying more for cans than bottles he'd replied, "They chill a lot faster in the fridge." A few of the empty aluminum vessels presumed an unintended mission in life. They rolled from the coffee table where Rick had carefully placed them and lay about the floor. The maid would have cleared them away but she was, after all, getting ready to depart for karate. Her bedroom door opened and with a skipping motion and a singsong "See you this evening Rick," she bolted for the door.

Her right foot came down on the edge of a miscreant can and her carefully groomed personage performed the proverbial 'ass over tit' fall. Cecilia's karate bag was never zipped up when she left the house. After doing two somersaults that would have earned a seven in an Olympic diving competition it obeyed the law of gravity, coming to rest on its side. Out of its stomach rolled a tacky plaster pig given to Rick by his late mother and two full cans, bearing the famous moniker of the sixteenth century saint. The pathetic little collection shouted its silent accusation such that the Pope himself would probably have been able to hear it.

The aspiring furniture magnate stood and stared, his mouth agape. "What are you doing with those my dear?" was all he could say. "Er…er…er.. umm…" For once the eloquent Cecilia was stuck for a sensible reply. "I'm just borrowing the beers Sir as one of my cousin's has a kindergarten graduation and the ornament needs professional cleaning so I'm taking it downtown." A reddish glow appeared on the boss's cheeks and his voice ratcheted itself up two notches. "I'm surprised to learn that toddlers in your family drink and Henrietta is as clean as the day my mother gave her to me."

On hearing the raised voice Marilyn awoke from her well-earned nap and descended the four steps. "What's going on?" Before any answer could escape the lips of the protagonists her eyes spotted the dumb accusers. Striding over to the prone bag she upended it and shook the wretched container as violently as her strength could manage. Two lipsticks rolled out. "They're mine," she declared triumphantly. "No they're not. I bought them at Gaisano last Sunday," a quavering voice returned. Retrieving the lipsticks from the spill and placing them on the table Marilyn appeared a full three centimeters taller than her regular stature. "You'd better pick up your uniform and get to class." Her refined lips couldn't hide the semblance of glee. Cecilia bolted for the door as if her life depended on it.

"I never liked her but I just thought she was lazy." The secretary called a mini conference with her boss. "Before we fire her out we'd better do a full inventory of household items." After agreeing Rick checked his room for missing personal effects. Marilyn's belongings save for the lipsticks had been untouched, so she commenced the inventory in the kitchen. An hour and a half later, possible casualties of the internal marauder were duly listed on paper. "The way I see it," stated Marilyn, "At least P20, 000 worth of household items are missing and your vanished personal items add another ten thousand. And that's not even counting various amounts of cash. I always thought that the petty cash tin needed refilling too often but I've never had the time to check it properly."

"Well, we'd better sack her then." Rick was resigned to the fact that the flirtatious smiles were those of a leech. "I'll leave you to perform the task."

"Not so fast, buster." Marilyn looked truly angry. "You hired her. You fire her. You might like some of the missing goods returned while you're about it as well. Forget the cash though." Reluctantly he agreed. Marilyn made a point of retiring well before Cecilia was due back from karate class. Not being experienced nor adept at necessary unpleasantness Rick prepared himself. Four more San Miguels and three rum and Cokes went down the hatch before the scheduled return of Cecilia.

"Ayo. I'm back," broadcast the errant maid as if nothing'd happened. She'd let herself though the gate with her key and stood beaming at the front door as it opened. "Class was really good tonight. Being in the final stages of the most advanced level we were entrusted with the knowledge of how to deliver fatal blows." She was still smiling as she entered the lounge area. Funny how a snake can have such voluptuous curves. The thought escaped Rick's mental processes before he could stop it. "Welcome home my dear. Come and sit down. I'll fix you a drink. What would you like?"

"Bourbon and Coke, please." Expecting a request for tea or soft drink Rick was taken aback. Nevertheless he obliged, returning from the kitchen with two stiff drinks and a switchblade. "Here's your drink. Now, I want all my stuff back."

"What do you mean? I never took anything." Cecilia adjusted her blouse to reveal a section of bosom as she spoke. "Cut the crap. Approximately P40, 000 of goods and cash have walked out of the house in the last year. You know nothing about it I suppose?"

Cecilia looked stern. "Of course not. Maybe Marilyn took the missing items." Rick was not amused. He moved closer to the girl and put his arm around her. Like a lightning strike the fingers closed around her left breast and pinched its nipple. Cecilia screamed. Normally Marilyn would have burst onto the scene at such an event but not this time. Rick had a carte blanche. "Just checking in case you've stashed jewelry in your blouse."

"You wait, I'll report you to the police." Cecilia's eyes fixed hard on Rick's face. "Go ahead my dear. I believe they call your crime 'Estafa' in these parts." After delivering his last remark Rick pinched the backside of the errant female as hard as he could. Another scream and an attempted exit followed. Forcing her back down on the couch Rick groped her crotch area. "I bet I'm not the first to touch this spot," he laughed. The wretched creature was really struggling now but her boss wasn't quite done yet. "You keep telling me not to drink so much," he laughed. "We'll see how sober I am. Let's play a little game." The click of the switchblade was distinctly audible. "Your karate won't help you, bitch." Holding her left hand fast on the table Rick spread its fingers. "If I'm drunk, I'll undoubtedly spear one of your digits," he mouthed. "I don't suppose you remember where any of my missing belongings are?"

"Fuck you Joe!" The nurse in waiting was undaunted. Down came the blade, again and again, each time just missing her outstretched and unnaturally pale fingers. Realizing that the game wasn't going to produce the desired results Rick groped the girl's crotch one more time in a gesture of parting.

A few seconds after the ensuing scream he removed his hand and pulled himself up straight. "I suppose you realize by now that you're fired?"

"Fuck you, asshole!" The defiant manner of this educated thief surprised him. "If you don't return everything you've stolen within seven days I'll lay criminal charges." Cecilia's mouth tightened and her jaw took an unusual rigidity. "If you make any trouble you'd better just watch out!"

Rick appeared confused through his haze. "What do you mean by 'watch out'?" Cecilia's lips curled into the most scornful of smiles. "Life is cheap here, especially that of foreigners!"

Following thirty minutes of banging and crashing an erstwhile maid appeared in her nurse's uniform with her case. "Fuck you Joe and your tart," were the last words she uttered as she was let out of the gate and disappeared down the street. "We'd better be careful," Marilyn commented upon her reappearance. "About what?" responded the man. "It's possible here to arrange a murder for only a few thousand pisos. There are many addis addis (drug addicts) who'd slit your throat for spare change." Rick didn't want to lose Marilyn and especially not by his own death and winced.

The very day after Cecilia's departure the phone rang. Marilyn picked up the receiver. "It's Jun Pablo for you."

"Hello." Rick's voice was less confident than usual. "Good news, Rick. Your consignments are on their way."

"That's great but I've another problem at the moment."

"How so?" Jun's voice sounded incredulous. "Our maid was stealing us blind and after we fired her she issued death threats against us. What are the chances she'd be able to organize our murders?"

"Less than ten percent. I wouldn't worry too much," reassured Mr. Pablo's voice. Not particularly comforted Rick rang off.

As dusk settled that day Rick's hearing was the sharpest it had ever been. The slightest sound of footsteps in the street outside saw him pull back the curtain to peer out. A palm frond fell and he flinched. This display of nervousness was too much for Marilyn. "Good night darling," she murmured and disappeared. The rustling of leaves in the wind seemed to conspire at the foreigner's downfall. A slight but grating creaking sound from the roof produced nothing short of panic. Rushing to his office his nervous hands dialed the combination of the safe. Underneath modest bundles of notes lay a Smith and Wesson .38. Not a real Smith Wesson but a paltik, a local copy freely available for less than a thousand pisos. "Made in Massachusetts USA," its barrel proudly exclaimed. The only obvious sign that it wasn't a genuine piece lay in what it lacked. No serial number was evident anywhere on the blued metal. It was in fact a perfect CIA gun.

Replete with the loaded paltik in a snappy green shoulder holster he'd purchased from Gaisano and a bottle of bourbon, a bottle of Coke and a glass Rick waited for the imminent approach of foul murder. The clock ticked. Minutes passed with all the baggage of hours. The night was unnaturally silent. No laughing or cursing of workers, standbys or the ubiquitous human traffic that is synonymous with life in the Philippines was to be heard.

The next day saw a repeat performance and the day after. Any movement or sound after dark saw Rick approaching his own abode with all the adrenalin of a combatant in a war zone. Two days earlier a maid had been stabbed to death in a home not a thousand meters away. Fortunately Rick didn't know that. As the days rolled by he'd surrendered his nightly vigil but remained as concerned as ever as he and Marilyn took the jeep ride to work.

Concerning the prospects of employing the law to recover the stolen property Jun Pablo's advice had been highly specific. "Without concrete evidence it's just a waste of time and money," he confided. Accordingly Rick cut his losses and placed an ad in the Sun Star. "As of the 5th December 1991," it read, "any contractual arrangements made on behalf of Rick Daly or Daly's Furniture by one Miss Cecilia Crisputa will no longer be honored by Mr. Daly or any of his instrumentalities." A stunning photograph of the criminal maid accompanied the notice. Cecilia had always been proud to be noticed in her party attire. Hence Rick had taken a happy snap a week or two before the discovery.

The phone rang on the afternoon of the notice's publication. "You're dead meat," a husky male voice with poor English had pronounced before ringing off. The gun was pulled back into service and the nightly waiting game resumed. "Phhph.. bang!" Hammer back, the black steel was aimed squarely at the roof. Loud and merry voices followed by more explosions revealed the mundane truth. Firecrackers are a favorite pastime of the poor.

When Marilyn snuck up on him and grabbed his testicles in the factory office one Wednesday all Rick could do was yawn. "If they were going to murder us and were able to they'd have done it by now." Reluctantly the furniture king was forced to agree. Nights at home were passed in the customary manner with all the promise and pitfalls that entailed. No more firearms were produced at nightfall and the cooler Christmas season came and went.

Despite his attorney's advice about the uselessness of laying charges against Cecilia Rick undertook a solitary journey back to San Nicholas Police Station. The desk sergeant, a clean-cut young man in his early thirties listened with patience to Rick's tale. "From what you say it's a clear cut case of Estafa and a fairly gross one at that. Yet, without any tangible evidence, we can do nothing." Looking up from his typewriter Sergeant Colo smiled. "It might be an idea for you to have a word with our captain. He's had quite a deal of experience with foreigners." Rick was shown to a compact office that was completely devoid of any luxuries.

"Please take a seat Mr. Daly." The captain still appeared smart in his tan uniform despite a portly midriff that portended the onset of middle age. "Captain Frederick Fernandez at your service. I'm afraid that what my sergeant has told you concerning the lack of evidence is true. You will have to take this episode as an expensive lesson. Before you take any person into your home you must be absolutely sure of their honesty. In the Philippines it takes a considerable amount of time to be sure of such things." Rick leaned forward in his chair, obviously impressed by the level of education and experience demonstrated by this man. "Are you suggesting that personal referral of one honest person to another is the only successful way of approaching human relations here?" Captain Fernandez tapped a ball pen several times on the table. "More or less. Where you come from the norm is to assume a person is honest until proven otherwise. Here, unfortunately, it is necessary to assume the worst until it is disproved. Personal networks are the only means of making any progress. This applies to politics, employment, friendship and even your love life itself. Always, you must invest time to be sure. Any shortcut you take is fraught with peril." Rick thanked the captain for his advice and departed.

The preceding months had seen the odd letter from Marilyn's parents. The tsismis had finally died down and therefore she was more or less forgiven. Her sister and her husband had visited once but they didn't stay. With the thaw in family relations Marilyn set sail once more on the Juanita. For Filipinos a Christmas not spent at home is one that didn't happen.

A shout from the roadside caused Rick to duck in the jeepney. Embarrassed, he straightened himself and sat like a Buddha for the rest of the trip to work. It was only two days after Marilyn's departure that the factory shut down for the season and he was left alone in the house with his thoughts. Risking burglary he'd ventured downtown a few times and on occasion brought home a bed warmer.

The cable television evinced boredom. Even the karaoke channel with its parade of scantily clad love-lorn girls left Rick emotionless. Small but rapid explosions outside convinced him that something was up. Without any more stupid reactions he opened his door and looked out. La Paloma's Christmas fiesta was in full swing. A parade was passing by. Fine lasses in even finer costumes, lively lads and a host of musicians were filing past his residence.

"If you can't beat them...." Rick scolded himself for being churlish and headed for the throng. The parade had ground to a halt at the basketball court area diagonally opposite his abode. All manner of sweetmeats were on sale along with cold beer to wash them down. Smiling and laughing faces were everywhere. The fiesta queen was radiant despite an application of whitish powder detracting from her natural brown beauty. Strolling through the crowd Rick felt suddenly alone. He could observe the highs and lows of this country but he could never belong to them. "Another white face I see." Rick spun round. The Midwest-American accent belonged to a portly gentleman in his late forties with a cherubic face.

"I'm Ralph, Ralph Winton. There aren't many foreigners in this area and we like to keep tabs on them." The hearty laugh that followed this utterance revealed that the sentiments were joking ones.

"Rick, Rick Daly. I'm in furniture." His response produced an even heartier laugh from Ralph. "I'm retired CIA myself. CIA beats furniture anytime." Rick removed a piece of barbecued squid from his mouth and stared, askance. "If you're really ex-CIA is it wise to be telling people?"

"As I said I'm retired and I can look after myself." The cherubic face oozed self-assurance. A few beers and some snacks later and Rick poured out a portion of his soul. "I lost almost P60, 000 to a Eurasian conman who spoke perfect English." Ralph's laugh was disquieting. "This is the Philippines my friend. I learned this truth the hard way. I've been robbed by foreigners as well as locals on more than one occasion. I learned one thing. Once your own mother sets foot in this country you can no longer trust her."

"If that's the case how can I trust your advice?" the rattan philosopher stated. "Maybe you can't." An even heartier laugh convinced Rick that the guy was probably ok. "I notice that you've hardly eaten anything. Is there some reason for that?" As he answered, Ralph smiled. "I suffer from vicarious anorexia nervosa." Rick's visage conveyed his confusion. "My wife thinks I'm too fat. Hence I'm on a beer only diet. Besides, most of the food here sucks." Rick was impressed by this guy's insidious understanding of his surroundings and said so. "It's not a racial thing," Ralph went on. "My wife is a Filipina and is probably a lot smarter and more honest than me. However there is something in the air in this place that promotes both stupidity and dishonesty. A couple of weeks ago I was walking through Colon and I saw a group of youths staring at a man welding scrap iron. 'Aren't you afraid of damaging your eyes?' I asked them. One of them replied, 'No problem Joe, the man doing the welding is wearing a mask.' You see what I mean about this place?" Rick couldn't help but laugh at the tale of the welding incident but he retrieved an element of seriousness.

"This place according to you is a real dump then?" he challenged. "Not entirely. You've ridden jeepneys in peak hour. Where else can you feel up a fourteen-year-old schoolgirl without even trying?" Ralph's lips parted showing neat plastic teeth. "While I'm giving you advice let me relay a story that says it all. An acquaintance of mine was particularly proud of his performance with a bargirl. He'd happily just shot his bolt when a moaning voice loudly begged, 'Don't stop! I haven't finished yet!' He pulled out of her and remarked, 'Who's paying for this fuck anyway?'" By eleven thirty the show was winding up and both Ralph and Rick departed. Back home once more, the fiesta ended, Rick twiddled his thumbs and waited for the return of the woman.

Chapter Eight

Marilyn was due back in a few days. A bored Rick was sipping beer and watching CNN early one afternoon. A gigantic crashing sound shook him. It came from just outside his gate. His first thoughts were that it must have been a car accident. Another crashing sound exploded and then another. They were gunshots. Several seconds passed. Rick cautiously opened his door and peered out. A fat woman was howling in the street like there was tomorrow. Her husband must have been killed, crossed Rick's mind. Before he could venture any further more gunfire erupted. Volleys of shots echoed through the neighborhood. Rick closed his door somewhat quickly. Thirty seconds went by. More shots were followed by others but they sounded somewhat further away. Ducking through the doorway Rick sprinted to the wall of his yard and ever so gingerly peered over. He couldn't see anything so he just stayed where he was. One minute passed and then two.

From the very moment the shooting had stopped a huge crowd had gathered not more than a hundred meters from Rick's residence. With fake nonchalance he strolled over and pushed through the humming throng. On the ground lay two bodies, a short distance apart. Both were clad in red stained polo-top shirts and inexorably the stain spread into the parched earth. With wide eyes and numb mind Rick just stared. "Rick!" The call snapped him from his shock. Captain Fernandez and Sergeant Colo along with a few other officers had taken charge of the scene. "Rick. What are you doing here?" It was Captain Fernandez's voice. Rick looked up. "My house is only a few meters away and I could hardly avoid the disturbance. What happened?"

As Captain Fernandez spoke the crowd hushed. "We were doing a routine patrol along Tres D'Abril when we heard three pistol shots. As we rapidly swung our mobile car into La Paloma we happened on a crime-in-progress. Three addis addis (drug addicts) had held up a woman and stolen her necklace. As our car approached the hold-uppers shot at us. We returned fire and they lost."

"What about the woman's husband they killed?" inquired Rick. "What husband? Nobody was killed apart from the criminals."

"The crying I heard from outside my gate was like it was the end of the world." Rick was genuinely puzzled.

Sergeant Colo smiled as he spoke. "The victim has lost a diamond necklace worth more than P20, 000. Around here that could be conceived as worse than the loss of several husbands."

The disposal of the bodies occurred without fanfare. Regardless of their motives the criminal drug addicts that almost invariably hail from the lowest stratum of society are, whenever the opportunity avails itself, removed with the exact same feeling of satisfaction that one experiences after a long and tiresome cleanup. Remembering his manners Rick invited Captain Fernandez, Sergeant Colo and the squad for dinner when they had a quiet evening.

Marilyn was due back in three days and Rick was desperately looking forward to her return. It's amazing how barren any life can be devoid of appropriate female coloring. Days of labor were just that. The only solace he could find was in consuming three or four glasses of rum and Coke whilst watching the karaoke channel. The booze enhanced the imagination to the point where the luscious singing girls could be disrobed at the speed of thought.

Rick had just arrived home from the factory as the cloak of evening had gently laid its mantle. Before he'd managed to drink two beers a 'whip-whip' sound reached his ears. Drawing the lounge room curtain he saw a flashing red light in the dark. A police mobile car pulled up at his gate and seven Armalite bearing officers got out.

"Ayo!" Like a school child in times past, on hearing the voice of the teacher, Rick opened the door and greeted his gun-toting visitors. "What's up?" escaped his mouth, his voice betraying a degree of nervousness. "Nothing," replied the captain. "This evening fortunately is somewhat quiet so we thought we'd take you up on your offer. My men are desperate to watch the FA cup final on your cable TV."

"You are most welcome. Please come in." Rick's manner demonstrated the utmost of graciousness. The tidy little troop dutifully filed inside stacking their M16s against the lounge-room wall and taking their places, some seated according to rank, and some standing, in front of the TV. "What would you like for dinner?" asked the host. "Nothing thanks. We've already eaten." Rick then offered them beer but was met with the standard police-on-duty polite refusal.

While his guests were transfixed with the violent scene of leather, boots and football hooligans Rick disappeared into the kitchen. He returned in less than twenty minutes with burritos and enchiladas for the guests. "Watching football always makes people hungry," was all he could manage as he offered the goodies. After responding with thanks on behalf of the group Sergeant Colo added, "Your current maid is a great cook." Rick's downcast expression evoked a measure of embarrassment.

"I haven't found a replacement for the 'karate-killer' yet," he responded.

The captain glanced up from the TV. "A man who can cook and a foreigner at that. We are impressed." The assembly of the Philippines' finest were transfixed as the striker for Manchester United took a shot at goal. The dying of the light was as instantaneous as it was unexpected. A scrambling flurry of men and guns occurred in the darkness. By the time Rick had struck a match and lit a candle his guests were ready to re-fight the Vietnam War.

"I'm sorry," remarked Captain Fernandez. "It's just a brownout. However we never know if it's an ambush. Between the criminal gangs and the various rebel groups our lives depend on our alertness."

"Of course," responded the host as the guests re-stacked their weapons against the wall. "That lousy Visayan Electric Company charge like wounded bulls but deliver a service that would make a politician feel proud." The sergeant and the men looked upset at missing the game. "Excuse me just a minute." Rick fired up the recently purchased generator and the party was on again. The striker had missed the shot and it was now Arsenal who took the advantage.

In less than an hour after their arrival the brown-suited men excused themselves and returned to their duty. When he'd had time to think about it Rick was more than grateful for the making of these new friends. He remembered the loss of the water pump and countless other smaller episodes. On average the mobile car pulled up outside his residence twice a week, sometimes on a Sunday, sometimes a Wednesday and maybe a Tuesday. Strangely enough the incidence of local crime directed against the businessman's castle suddenly vanished.

The budding friendship between the police captain and the stranded foreigner was evidenced by a dinner invitation to the captain's humble home. Marilyn had finally returned and accompanied her boss on the visit. Simple Filipino foods but nicely done were served. Francisca Fernandez, a well-covered woman just staving off middle age, was an unusually frank hostess. "Fred doesn't get home much. Between work and a kabit, that's a girlfriend you know, he doesn't have too much time for us."

"Cut it out," responded the captain. "I don't have any kabit but my work keeps me occupied for most of the day's hours. You should just ignore the stupid tsismis. Being a policeman I have many enemies and they'll do anything to get back at me."

Changing tack with the spontaneity of the weather Mrs. Fernandez questioned Marilyn. "It must be difficult working for a foreigner. How do you cope with all the gossip and jealousy?"

The complexion of Rick's companion lightened by at least three shades before she responded. "I can't say it's been easy but Rick has given me the first real job I've ever had."

"Captain Fernandez, it's very kind of you to entertain people such as us in your home." Rick's tone conveyed a smidgeon of embarrassment. "Call me Freddy and you're more than welcome. I must just apologize for the extreme simplicity of my abode. A policeman's salary doesn't buy much."

"I'll say that again," interjected Francisca. "I'm not exactly sure how much he gets but what he brings home certainly won't propel us into the rich and famous." A couple more San Miguels were followed by instant coffee and the clock was striking one as Rick, with Marilyn in tow, departed.

The following weeks saw several visits from the police mobile car at Rick Daly's place. The routine was usually the same; Armalites against the wall while the men watched sport on the cable TV. The NBA basketball from the States was a big favorite. Soft drinks and nibbles were served but beer or whisky was always politely refused. Despite being a gracious hostess Marilyn was partially lacking in enthusiasm for the acquisition of the new friends. "The police here always want something," she dryly commented one day. "You'll see as time goes by."

She couldn't argue with the new found security arrangements however. After the advent and departure of Cecilia with its attendant trauma the question of hiring a new maid had remained rather silent. However Marilyn broached the subject one evening over dinner. "Rick, I know of a girl who'll work here. Although she isn't a relative, she's a relative of friends of my family and she's honest."

"Good," murmured her partner. "I hope she isn't pretty and when can she start?"

"She isn't exactly ugly," responded his secretary come bookkeeper come consort, "but she isn't going to become Miss Philippines either."

"When could she come here?" Rick again inquired.

"Within a fortnight. She'd be happy with the same salary or even less than you gave to that criminal." Marilyn felt a twinge of spontaneous national pride at solving a problem that had stumped her foreign boss. Ten days later, Leticia, a short girl barely out of her teens, fronted at the gate and was summarily employed.

The next bond between Rick and an indigenous person was formed out of somewhat more pedestrian circumstances than the last. Much as he loved Marilyn the frustration of their relationship began to tell on Rick. More frequently than in the past he would exit the house of an evening to roam the watering holes and houses of sin for which the Philippines is justly famous. Having an exploring nature he'd often venture further afield than the comfort zone of the expat bars. Our Place never saw his patronage again.

On one such evening sojourn Rick found himself imbibing warm beers in a bar on Mactan Island, less than four kilometers from the airport. The scents of earth and fresh bamboo had greeted his nostrils as he arrived in what must surely have been just a tropical version of a shed. Stepping inside, Rick found that the outer appearances belied the reality. A sound system second-to-none produced a furious beat, a sequence of flashing lights almost induced epilepsy and half a dozen bronzed teenage girls were strutting their stuff completely naked.

Accompanying the flashing flesh, vibrating disco lights and frenetic beat was a musty odor that emanated from the dirt floor. The patrons were seated on garish red plastic chairs that bordered the stage on all four sides. It was a classic example of theatre-in-the-round. The nude starlets whirled around to provide each section of the audience with views of breasts, shapely buttocks and pubic mounds, bushy or otherwise. As the show increased its intensity lights, sounds and objects of desire blended into a single sensory buzz.

With her long hair swinging, a dancer sprang from the platform, cart-wheeled and somersaulted her way along an earthen corridor that divided groups of cheering and leering customers and landed her naked brown butt straight in Rick's lap. Shock caused him to drop his beer, the fluid running in a stream along the dirt. The brazen hussy rotated her behind on Rick just long enough to produce a highly visible erection on his part. The girl sprang from his lap leaving his embarrassment visible to all. As she returned to the stage, a chorus of laughter echoed throughout the establishment. A businessman in blue trousers, offsetting his regulation starched-white shirt, was seated next to the embarrassed-foreigner and laughed louder than the rest. "Some guys have all the luck!" he exclaimed. "It was probably the blond hair that attracted her to you. Very few foreigners ever patronize this place."

"I'm not so sure about the luck bit," Rick replied. "This is the first time I've suffered this sort of humiliation since I was fourteen and popped my fly buttons at the bus stop when a schoolgirl with a mini skirt turned up."

"Take it in a spirit of good humor my friend," the businessman advised. "As you can see we're a pretty broadminded mob here. By the way I'm Philippe Lopez but call me Noy." Rick introduced himself in turn. "What brings you to the Fly On The Wall?" Philippe, a man in his forties with a generous stomach, rotund face and thinning locks, inquired. "Most foreigners hang round the air-conditioned joints uptown."

"I enjoy experiencing new things." Rick's response was somewhat matter-of-fact. "There are certainly some lovely things here tonight," Philippe laughed. "I'm on my way home from work and I enjoy a few beers first. You could say that my time here is product appreciation."

"What do you mean?" Rick appeared puzzled. Philippe or Noy continued. "I'm a manager at the San Miguel plant in Mandaue and I live here on Mactan."

"I suppose there is a lot involved in producing this precious drop. I'm in furniture manufacture and export myself." A glimmer of pride appeared on Rick's face. "Export? I suppose you've already experienced the red tape barrier?" Noy ventured.

"You could say that," commented the rattan-industrialist. "Any pointers you could give me in that arena would be more than welcome." The conversation between the two continued for more than an hour. As the time was rapidly approaching eleven Rick prepared to leave. "I must be going also," commented Noy. "I'd like to invite you to dinner at my home. My wife Rena is a great cook. Here's my card. Just give me a call."

"That'd be great," smiled Rick. "May I bring my secretary? She lives in my house."

"Of course." Noy shook Rick's hand heavily and disappeared into the darkness. It was a full thirty minutes before Rick alighted from his taxi and discretely entered his abode. The prevailing silence convinced him that Marilyn must already be sleeping.

"By the way," he remarked the next day at the factory when Marilyn approached him with output figures, "I made a new friend yesterday and we've been invited to dinner."

"Where?" the girl asked.

"On Mactan Island. My friend is a manager at San Miguel in Mandaue. His wife apparently is a wonderful cook."

"I'd love to come." Marilyn appeared genuine.

Ten days and a phone call later and the invitation was finalized. At seven o'clock in the evening Rick and Marilyn arrived at the Lopez family residence in the Sea Mist subdivision. Ushered inside, the couple were introduced to Rena and Noy's daughter, Alma, a sprightly youngster of nine years. "Mr. Daly what country do you come from?" asked the child. "It's a long story Alma but more or less you could say Australia."

The Chicken Ariscaldo soup was delicious. A fine broth with tiny pieces of poultry and grains of rice was served at exactly the correct temperature. As the gathering of five enjoyed their repast Rick couldn't help but notice that Alma was continually staring at him from her almost black, almond eyes. She asked him several more questions until her mother scolded her. The main course of local beef, thinly sliced, held its own with the soup. "How do you find conditions here Rick?" Rena asked during a lull in the conversation. "All I can say is – interesting – it certainly is a fascinating land but it does have its share of problems."

Marilyn's figure sat stiffly in her seat and she seemed oblivious to the current topic. The piercing gaze of the nine year old was still directed at the Westerner. Four hours after their arrival the visitors conveyed their thanks for the hospitality and departed. During the taxi ride home Marilyn glanced at Rick with a strange expression on her face and remarked, "You certainly seem to have some kind of magnetic attraction for all females, regardless of their age."

Rick was defensive. "I don't know what you mean."

"You mean you didn't notice the way Alma was totally preoccupied with you? It was unnatural."

"She's only a child and one who obviously hasn't been told that it's rude to stare at people." Rick was confident that this unjustified suggestion of potential pedophilia had been adequately dealt with. "Still, it was very strange," Marilyn added. Once home the pair retired to their rooms without the usual sensual repartée.

Rick's friendship with Noy grew over time. Sometimes the two of them would go bar hopping. The family visited Rick's home a couple of times and

Marilyn and he sampled Rena's culinary skills on a number of occasions. "You're such a clever man Mr. Daly," commented Alma during one visit to Rick and Marilyn's abode. "I've never known a foreigner like you before." A furrow appeared on Marilyn's brow. "Anyone for brewed coffee?" Rick had appeared with a jug. When the time arrived for the guests' departure the group was standing outside the gate. As the thankful visitors climbed into their ancient red Nissan, Alma was the last one to speak to Rick and Marilyn. "I had a lovely time, honest. I wasn't bored at all despite all the grownup talk."

The seasons such as they are in this land had rolled by again and by July 1992, the wet season had commenced. Earlier in that year a presidential election saw the back of Cory Aquino as her term had expired. Fidel Ramos, the former army-chief-of-staff, replaced her. Rick silently hoped that anti-foreigner sentiment might slowly begin to diminish.

Almost every afternoon and night torrents of warm water dropped from the skies. As the rain bucketed down outside one evening Rick and Marilyn were partaking of a simple dinner. "You deserve a break Marilyn. Would a few days in a resort appeal to you?" The smiling eyes across the table were answer enough. "I made some enquiries and, as it is the off season, we can have four days in Dakak resort in Mindanao for less than P7, 000 including the plane trip."

Marilyn had paused with a look of concern. "I know that place. It's in northern Mindanao near Dipolog and somewhat close to the Islamic separatist and kidnapping groups." Rick appeared disdainful. "Don't be such a pussycat. That resort is very secure and while we're there we won't have to venture outside." Sufficiently mollified Marilyn again resumed a manner of anticipation. Before they could actually go, of course, there was the smaller matter of purchasing the package. Besides, the preparations for a pleasurable event can often be more enjoyable than the event itself.

After waiting for some twenty minutes in the offices of All Star Travel in F. Ramos Street it was the couple's turn to be served. "We would like to buy a four day package to Dakak," Rick announced confidently. As the girl was collecting the relevant materials a Rolls Royce and two Mercedes pulled up outside. With barely an "Excuse me" she rushed out along with two other staff members. Disgorged from the Roller an obese Filipino man of around sixty and wearing the barong shirt favored for its simple formality was immediately surrounded by the bodyguards who'd alighted from the cheaper vehicles. With a putrid reverence, the fawning staff members instantly ushered the new arrivals inside and immediately served them. Consigned to a couple of seats in the corner Mr. Daly and Miss Delgado were less than impressed. After thirty minutes the rich man still hadn't actually bought anything and was preparing to leave, along with his entourage. The girl who had previously been serving them spoke in their direction. "I'll be back with you in a few more minutes." The couple stood up and headed for the door. "Don't bother," shouted Rick. "We'll buy our tickets from some place that has a semblance of customer service." The travel agent looked confused.

"What was that all about?" Rick queried of his consort. "Rich people probably trying to get something for free," responded the equally disgusted Marilyn. The pair had more success at Lucky Travel, a short cab ride away. Their mini-vacation package secured they headed home.

It was a viciously hot sunny morning as the propeller plane took off from Cebu with its load. The majority were other holidaymakers. Forty-five minutes later the aircraft disgorged its cargo at Dipolog airport. A three-room building saw the comings and goings of humanity. Pushing through the humming crowd a relaxed Marilyn dragged her boss by the hand. A placard emblazoned with a single word, 'Dakak,' greeted them. Dutifully the driver collected seven or eight persons and ushered them into the interior of an avocado-green L300 Mitsubishi minibus.

The journey took in barren hills, interesting dirt roads and sundry other objects but, surprisingly, lasted less than twenty minutes. As they drove through the opened gates Rick noticed an extremely prominent sign. 'No outside foods or drinks allowed.' The meals must be overpriced here, he thought. At the check-in counter the new arrivals were met by an overly smiling young man and an equally youthful woman who hardly spoke. "I'm sure you'll all have a wonderful time here," the smiler declared. "We have quite a few famous people stay with us. Only last week Vilma Santos was here for three days." A gasp of wonder escaped the lips of a Filipino family standing behind Rick and Marilyn.

Each group was shown to their quarters by the requisite boy. A white stucco cabin with a fake thatched roof awaited Rick and his lady. It was a simple affair but the ceiling fans whirred comfortingly and the bed was generous. From the doorstep the view over modest cliffs and thence a sandy beach reached a spectacular conclusion over an endless speckled sea. "It's lovely." Rick smiled at Marilyn's approval. "Thank you darling." Her hand, wrapped around his waist, felt warmer than usual.

That afternoon they took a dip in the ocean, and strolled around taking in the tennis courts, archery area and a private Jacuzzi with cracks in the walls offering hope to potential voyeurs. A candlelight dinner in the Sea Change open-air restaurant at dusk saw the lovers communing with Nature and each other. "What can I bring Sir and Madam," the waiter inquired. Rick requested the sautéed prawns whilst his paramour ordered Chicken Adobo. "And your drinks?" continued the waiter. Noticing the price list Rick quickly consigned himself to a few days of sobriety and drank only one beer. Marilyn asked for a non-alcoholic tropical cocktail.

It was almost midnight on the first day when the couple retired to sleep. Marilyn was surprised at her partner's lack of molestation attempts. Even as he lay down Rick was groaning. Thirty minutes later and he was disgorging his dinner down the toilet. For the entire next day and half of the day after, he was laid low. Marilyn, between bouts of concern, amused herself as best she could.

Back on deck at last, Rick was determined to make the most of the remaining time. He defeated Marilyn at tennis, nearly shot a passing waiter with a stray arrow on the archery course and insisted that Marilyn and he risk the 'private' Jacuzzi. For dinner that evening he ordered an extremely well-done steak. Marilyn bravely ate fish.

Between mouthfuls, a disturbance from three tables away reached both their ears. "I ordered a rum cocktail not a tequila sunrise," a particularly slender girl with too much makeup shouted at a confused waiter. "Don't worry," soothed a fat foreigner in his thirties. "No way. I want the correct drink and I want it now!" The waiter beat a hasty retreat.

Looking up Rick noticed the outspoken girl. It was Maybellene. She must have struck it lucky in Manila. Mind you her customer didn't inspire the slightest degree of envy. Maybellene acted as if she hadn't known Rick and the latter certainly wasn't going to disturb this status quo. "That girl is revoltingly loud," commented Marilyn. "She's obviously a prostitute." Rick concurred and added, "We've been so lucky with the weather. Rainy season or not we've had such balmy evenings. Are you ready to sleep?" Their empty plates stared upwards and the bill had been signed. "Not yet. I'd like to go dancing." Marilyn winked mischievously. "There's the Coco Disco with a resident combo."

Without any overdose of enthusiasm Rick assented. Marilyn looked a treat in her black evening dress as the pair whirled and swirled and Rick trod on her toes. It must have been nearly 2 am before the couple strode the path leading to their bungalow. Over the bed the fan emitted its reassuring beat. On a moonlit wall the largest gecko Rick had ever seen darted after mosquitoes. The couple showered together and, once dry, proceeded to the beckoning object of horizontal comfort. Clad only in underwear they embraced each other. It took less than five minutes for Rick to remove Marilyn's and his briefs. A not unfamiliar licking and sucking accompanied the mutual exploration. A warm earthy scent rose from Marilyn's left buttock as Rick's tongue ran over it.

When his fingers reached the area guarded by her flower Marilyn snatched them away. "Not by this time! You know how I feel about losing my virginity." More kissing and teasing followed and Rick lost control. Climbing on top of the owner of the shapely curves and inviting bush he attempted to mount her. He thrust hard and felt he'd hit the mark when the girl disengaged herself and leaped to the floor. Huddled in a crouching position she began to cry. "You forced me. You forced me." Rick spent the next half hour consoling, apologizing and declaring his love.

The transgression of the darkness had been forgiven by the time the Sun rose. That day was spent in all manner of frolicking and the ensuing night was passed in moments of tenderness but without exhibited lust. In the morning the minibus carted them away at eleven. An hour and half later and the pair were on their way home from Cebu's airport.

Seated in the lounge room or sala as the Filipinos call it Rick opened a small box in front of Marilyn. Inside, a diamond ring glistened. "I want to marry you," he blurted out, forgetting any rehearsed and more romantic lines. The girl picked up the ring, paused for several moments and then slid it on her finger. "It'll be some time before it can happen after that business in my village," she smiled, "but yes I'll marry you."

That night when Marilyn came to his room for physical reassurance Rick again approached her inner sanctum with a measure of force. "Not until we are married!" Marilyn was both tearful and angry. Without another word she disappeared into her own room. The fact that they were due back at work did not cause her to open her door the next morning when Rick knocked. He was forced to turn up at the factory alone. "Where's Marilyn?" the foreman inquired. "We went to a christening and family celebration last night and she got drunk. She'll be here tomorrow." The foreman and several workers laughed loudly, the more so because the thought of the modest Marilyn overindulging amused them.

"You can have your stupid ring back," declared Marilyn on his return home. "Why? I gave it to you because I love you and really want to marry you." Rick was worried. "If you really loved me you'd respect me." Marilyn appeared sterner than usual. "I do respect you but I can only withstand so much temptation."

"We must avoid sin." Marilyn appeared determined so Rick said nothing further.

It was the fifth of August. The day had been so humid that the factory closed early. The house was so hot that it threatened to fry any creature bold enough to venture within. Rick closed the windows and the curtains, fired up the air-conditioners and after turning on the stereo, extracted a cold San Miguel from the fridge. Beads of sweat showed through Marilyn's T-shirt and she removed it leaving her clad in only bra and shorts. With a little encouragement from her suitor those were soon discarded followed by the cotton briefs. Buck naked she faced Rick. Removing his own clothing he embraced her feeling sure that the moment was near. The nude couple danced a waltz around the room to a love song. Rick clutched her body to him hard. Poof! The lights went out, the stereo was silenced and the air-conditioners died. In the darkness Marilyn giggled and disappeared. The Visayan Electric Company had struck again. By the time Rick was able to operate the generator Marilyn had gone to sleep behind a locked door.

A week of work and sexually-charged evenings passed. Marilyn never wore her ring to work or at all in public. She was the model secretary-come-accountant with all the attributes of propriety. At home she'd make a point of showing it to Rick. "I don't understand why you still resist me," he commented. "I want the man who first has me to be my husband," she replied. "I'll marry you whenever you are ready," the foreigner assured. "It's not as simple as that. My parents and other relatives must approve and that could take some time." Rick's disappearances some evenings failed to give her the hint although she was able to guess what he was up to. A conundrum of sexuality and morals weighed heavily upon her.

Despite standing firm at the final hurdle Marilyn was always ready to run the race. Some business problems saw Rick preoccupied one night. Rum and cola was followed by more of the same. At 2 am Marilyn's door opened and standing above the steps she spoke. "What happened to you? I was waiting."

"I've got some thinking to do. I'll come shortly." Rick poured another drink. "You mean drinking, don't you?" Marilyn then retreated.

By the time of the next occasion when Marilyn requested his personal touch Rick was prepared. Remembering a boyhood trick he'd secreted a small bottle of baby oil under his pillow. Marilyn appeared at the steps as Rick drank below. A look of puzzlement grew on her face. Rick abandoned his glass, walked up to the girl and kissed her. Without speaking he led her to his room. The sound of their bodies rubbing competed with the hum of the air-conditioner. Loving caresses and sensual tongue-lashings occurred as usual. Ever so discretely Rick extracted the tiny plastic bottle from his pillow and liberally applied its contents to his member. The next time he embraced the challenge of Marilyn's body he was armed, and struck. Deep, deep into her vault he slid. "You tricked me," cried her voice. Oblivious to the criticism Rick continued on. The bed vibrated for at least five minutes despite the necessitated haste of an important mission.

As the creaking subsided and Marilyn gazed at Rick in the dark, dumbfounded and confused, the white man smiled with spiritual satisfaction. "You're certainly not a virgin now; so that's one hurdle gone." There was no reply. A few more kisses of tenderness and Marilyn was sneaking back to her own room, terrified that Leticia might become aware of her movements.

To Rick's dismay their nightly encounters didn't produce any more instances of actual penetration. Marilyn seemed determined to keep unavoidable sin to a minimum. Almost but not quite, Rick thought to himself. He wasn't sure if he was thinking about Marilyn or the country that bore her. Before the frustration had sufficient chance to kill him he found it necessary to leave Cebu for an entire week. Hoping to find cheaper supplies of cane he'd organized a trip to Bacolod on Negros Occidental. He'd departed from the gate with the usual formal goodbye that was performed for the benefit of the neighbors.

The business side of the escapade was uneventful. He'd found a few more potential suppliers of cane at an acceptable price. Bumpy bus rides in ancient jalopies along the roughest of dirt roads always kept him informed as to the state of his latest meal. Bacolod is an interesting city. The most prominent thoroughfare is named Tucson Street after a wealthy family whose tentacles run right through the town. One of its most aggressive daughters, Rose Lacson, went to work as a maid for an Australian mining baron, stepping-stoned, married him, oversaw his death and despite countless court battles in that southern land, emerged with millions in inheritance. Not realizing the famous family from which she hailed, some local residents in Western Australia's Perth assumed that she was merely a Filipina tart who'd struck gold.

Whilst the fortunes of its most famous family were of no concern to Rick the town that oozed its way at the base of their stronghold provided more enlightenment. Girls smiled constantly, men grinned, old ladies nodded and the entire compliment of the town seemed to sincerely welcome visitors. His second day's work done, Rick rapidly consumed some solids and headed into the dark. The preceding evening had seen him disgrace himself with a fifteen-year-old girl from a local bar. Not only had she been unenthusiastic, her teenage twat was only blessed with a minimal covering of a dozen hairs. "Strictly a commercial and learning experience," Rick had concluded.

The Lonely Belle Bar and Disco sucked in Rick's patronage after he had only walked a kilometer or two from his modest accommodation. As two dancers strutted their usual stuff, tugging their bikini briefs and generally trying very hard to persuade a somewhat disinterested audience Rick consumed two rather cold provincial beers. Before he could embark on the third a handsome Filipino man had approached him. "We don't see many tourists in these parts so we try to welcome them. I'm Ricardo Caldez. May I buy you a beer?" Instantaneously deciding that the approaching personage wasn't gay, Rick accepted.

"I'm not a tourist by the way. I'm here to look for supplies for my furniture manufacturing business." Rick attempted to appear proud. "That's great," replied Ricardo. "I didn't meant to offend you but I'm sure you realize the Filipino thing; all Westerners are Americans, all Americans are tourists and all tourists are rich." Rick smiled. "No offence taken but as you can imagine I'm heartily tired of being judged as something I'm not. I was actually born in the U.S. but I left when I was three."

Ricardo commented further. "We have the same name and neither of us are the average Joe." Rick laughed and inquired as to the background of his companion. "I'm the governor's eldest son. I do some administrative work, oversee some social welfare programs and occasionally enjoy myself like anybody else." The furniture king smiled again but said nothing. Ricardo was obviously reasonably-well-educated. He'd even heard of Sydney.

The pair hardly had time to glance at the flashing forms on the stage. Ricardo had more in common, apart from their names, with Rick than the latter would've cared to realize. "I admit the USA abuses its power somewhat," remarked the simply dressed Filipino, "but it is the world's only superpower and it must be dealt with by any aspirants of virtually anything unless they wish to always remain in a cloud of pipe dreams."

Rick left the Lonely Belle in the company of his latest acquaintance. At the next bar the pair remained in earnest conversation as strobe lights, bare tits and flashing fur burgers danced before them. Round for round Ricardo kept up his end of the financial obligation. When the last dancer removed her slender body from the stage of the last bar they were still talking. "You'll never change this country without changing the way that the ordinary people think."

"Right on bro'," slurred Rick in response. "I suppose that means education but what groups of rich people will pay for an educated lower class that could catch them at their game?" Ricardo laughed so loudly that a waiter came over. "Like life itself, isn't it?" he joked. "Everything changes all the time but nothing ever really changes. On that note I must excuse myself for a few minutes while I go to the CR. (comfort room or toilet)."

Finding themselves on a blackened street in the latest hour of night the pair still managed to evince a thirst. "I know a quiet kitchenette that is always open and their beer is cold," suggested Ricardo. "I've got a 7 am plane in the morning," moaned Rick. "Don't worry you'll make it even if you lose a few hours' sleep," reassured his companion.

The Ever Sweet kitchenette was still serving beer to the pair as the waitresses shook their heads. Two drunken customers were not unusual; two drunken customers without any sign of being armed were not a rarity either. Still a plain girl in her late twenties with large breasts that her uniform couldn't hide kept staring at Rick's companion. It was probably less than an hour before sunup that a group of different drinkers arrived. Clad in simple farm clothing and all wearing hats a clan of ten or more men took their places after nodding to Ricardo and he to them.

"We have to leave," Ricardo commented quietly but earnestly. "Why?" retorted his companion. "I haven't finished my beer yet." Ricardo looked extremely serious. "Those guys that just came in and said hello to me are NPA. We have a friendly standoff but the governor's son can't be seen at the same place as them. You must understand."

More baffled than ever Rick gulped the remainder of his bottle and followed his friend out. The next all-night dispenser of drinks was much quieter than the last. An elderly waiter with a kindly face served only three customers, including the latest arrivals. Four rounds later and the world's problems still remained to be solved. "My God!" exclaimed Rick as he attempted and failed to stand. "I've only fifteen minutes to get to the airport. I'll never make it!"

"Calm down. You'll catch your plane. There're still two beers on the table. Let's down them first." Bottle to mouth Rick looked two shades paler than he'd ever done. As the pair abandoned the last waterhole the sun had not only risen but was applying its own version of global warming to the scene. It was a full forty minutes before a taxi could be found. Achieving refunds for anything is a tall order in the Philippines and Rick didn't like his chances of recovering anything from a missed plane. "Could you step on the gas mate?" he mumbled after Ricardo had directed the driver. The taxi proceeded at a leisurely place in the correct direction and the pale-faced passenger merely bit his lip.

Discharged from the rusting scrapheap on wheels the duo hastened into the terminal. Not only was the flight closed but the plane, a Bacwan 11, could be spotted on the runway in the final seconds before takeoff. "Shit!" yelled a thoroughly drunken foreigner, not able to stand unaided but still in command of his vocal chords. "Relax," replied his Filipino friend as he requested and was given a priority phone connection. Through an alcoholic haze Rick's eyes failed to believe what they saw. Two hundred meters into its takeoff run the silver bird halted, reversed and taxied back to its departure point. Rick Daly was poured onto the plane like some vital but almost-forgotten cargo and then, ten minutes behind schedule, the titanium structure lifted into the air.

Back in Cebu once more a still rather pissed foreigner was trying to make sense of the experience. 'He really was the governor's son!' was all that he could come up with. By the time he reached his own gate and Marilyn let him in, the stench of alcoholic vapors was overpowering. Marilyn didn't bother to ask about the success of the trip. She merely put him to bed.

"How's your head," she dutifully inquired when he surfaced late that afternoon. "I'm not too sure," came the response. "I suppose that'll teach you!" The sun finished its arc in the sky and went to its rest. Rick returned to his cot and succeeded in reading a few pages of a novel before returning to his temporary death.

Business is business, work sets you free and the Lord helps those that help themselves. Life under the endless tropical sun continued as it does, despite the woes, struggles and deaths of thousands. Leticia was always the perfect maid, noticing the throb of the household but saying nothing. "Sir, can I get you something?" or "Maam, is there anything you need?" The work was done, nothing disappeared and both Marilyn and Rick were free to concentrate on other matters.

Yet a pair of eyes is always a pair of eyes. Rick had begun to suspect that Marilyn had grown somewhat cold towards him she'd been so proper in the last few days. Resigned to his fates Rick was showering his particularly grubby body one evening when the door swung open. There was Marilyn, with a bucket and mop in her hands. As Rick's eyes fell on her she abandoned these tools of manual labor and pulled back the shower curtain. Without speaking but with a knowing glance that demanded silence she pushed her head into the cubicle. Her lips closed around his manhood just long enough to turn it from a three-storey building into a skyscraper. Bucket and mop in hand once again she was gone.

Always fearful of Leticia's innocent eyes Marilyn's movements around the house were somewhat subdued. If Rick hadn't known better only their business relationship stood between them. Like most helpers in the Philippines, Leticia was granted Sunday off. She was free to do what she would. Obviously it was not possible for her to visit her family so she enjoyed her freedom in the city, totally unfettered. It was two in the afternoon as Leticia caught up with the tsismis emanating from those of the locality's maids that were known to her. "An attorney and all, he raped his helper while his wife and children were sleeping," said one of a story that had passed her ears. "A helper was murdered in Lahug, along with the entire family of her employer," mouthed another. Remy, one of the most garrulous of the gathering turned to Leticia. "What news have you got for us?" Her eyes burned.

Leticia was quiet. "My boss had some trouble with the government over export regulations and he has a lot of business meetings at night," was the best Leticia could manage. "That's nothing that would make a priest's hair stand on end," retorted Remy. "My life is boring," bemoaned Leticia. "What can I do about it?" The arrival of an ice-cream seller distracted the group. As darkness fell Leticia took her leave from her friends and prepared to catch a jeepney home.

Approximately two hours after Leticia had left the gate Marilyn was doing odd jobs around the house and Rick was reading in his room, book and beer in hand. The noonday heat was even more stifling than usual. Rick had replaced his bottle, dropped his book and begun dreaming of other times when reality called. "Rick! Rick! Please come here." Not too surprisingly, considering the population of the house, it was Marilyn's shout that woke him. Dressed only in a shirt and underpants he strode the ten meters past his office and to the door of the Queen's bedroom. Ever so politely he knocked on the door. "Quick! Come in!"

Rick turned the handle, which was unlocked and entered. There was Marilyn clad only in underpants standing upright on the bed. "There was a mouse in here!" she exclaimed. "I can't see any mouse and besides I should've thought that, in this neck of the woods, mice would be the least thing to fear." Marilyn smiled and, dropping her undies, lay down on the bed. "I thought you'd never come." Not too reluctantly, and sensing his obligation, Rick stripped off and joined her. A miniscule alarm clock on the dresser proudly declared the hour to be half-past two.

Without too much kissing and cuddling and with naked abandon Marilyn performed her not unusual 180-degree turn and sucked for all she was worth. The gentle afternoon light flickered on the mounds of her buttocks. The flickering sunlight danced on an ever so-gently mottled brown ass. Pausing, after offering the regular tongue-lashing Rick raised his mouth. "You have a beautiful labot," he remarked, deliberately choosing the Visayan term for a girl's backside. Disengaging her lips from their quarry a feminine voice returned, "How does it compare with others you've known?"

"Possibly the best I've ever seen," Rick remarked, balancing the required compliment with the smallest measure of objectivity. Marilyn lips resumed their task as did Rick's tongue. By the time Rick had rotated himself and prepared for an even more intimate sojourn Marilyn had firmly crossed her legs.

This beautiful naked girl often lay in his bed but the natural consequence almost always eluded him. Somewhere in the nexus between Marilyn's body and soul some demon of the Catholic Church demonstrated its power. Rick would often excuse himself of an evening with some paltry reason if Marilyn's figure was there or simply sneak out if it was not. Somewhere at the back of his skull a childhood voice reminding him of the intrinsic dangers of self-abuse kept his mind focused outwards and he'd sally forth in quest of the answer to the question posed by his physiological yearning.

At best it was a tricky dance; keep the one you love dangling while draining your juices elsewhere. He'd been in the Philippines long enough to understand the power of tsismis and Rick's occasional nocturnal missions occupied an ever increasing circle. If he had the faintest idea that Marilyn would suspect that he was carousing in a particular section of the city he'd simply travel another five kilometers before indulging himself. Although the warm beer was hell on earth Rick had begun to enjoy the honesty of the scattered Filipino bars. The women bared their all; they didn't pretend to be enamored of the customers and the prices were a damn sight cheaper.

In October of 1992 Rick effected one such nightly sneak-out that led him to the industrial area of Mandaue. His jaw dropped a centimeter or two as he alighted from the taxi. The Earing Earing bar was a glorified tin shed with a few tables out front masquerading as a beer garden. The stench of long expired diesel fumes hugged the ground whilst the wispy clouds overhead gave up their industrial secrets.

Of course these night-time ramblings in search of a necessary scratch, on occasion, resulted in absolute failure. Generally failures marked Rick's return home with the same degree of discretion as he had left. He'd never departed from the most forlorn establishment however, without at least downing one beer. An unspoken worldwide law of conduct governs even the most prodigal of sons or daughters.

Fearing the worst Rick entered the shed. To the left and right on the flimsiest of stages were passable young women in the barest of G-strings. In the center was one of the ugliest performers ever to grace publicity. A gross creature firmly seated in middle age strutted about as if she was seventeen. The hanging boobs and the midriff that suggested the birth of countless children shook themselves to the point where the gut feeling of wanting to throw up overtook Rick. The cheers of the crowd at the creature's self-humiliation did little to settle his stomach. The disappearance of the offending item and the advent of a girl, no more than fourteen, reinvigorated the entire audience. A skinnier body Rick had never seen in his entire life. If she'd been a foot taller she would surely have made modelling's big-time. The miserable lass moved legs and hips to an invisible rhythm and threw, first her bra and then her panties into the crowd. What her pubic hairs lacked in number was compensated for by their thickness and enthusiasm.

Just looking at the sparsely covered and bulbous crack made Rick feel guilty. He downed the last drops of his tepid beer and departed. Escaping into a larger morality he reached the patio that bridged the house of sin and the street. "Leaving so soon!" a hearty voice challenged. Glancing to the right Rick noticed a lightly built gentleman sitting on his own at the front of the building. "Come sit down here and have another drink." The man was European and elderly, an unusual combination in this particular locality. With the same delicacy as one reluctantly accepts the overtures of a worthwhile charity Rick joined him. "I'm Rick Daly, Sir and you are...?"

"Hans, Hans Werttenburger. I'm very pleased to meet you."

The guy was obviously desperately lonely so his pleasure didn't surprise Rick too much. "I have to work tomorrow, I mean later today, so I can't stop long."

"Das macht nicht, I mean no problem," replied the face of age.

Two more tepid beers were promptly ordered and just as they were delivered a huge roar emanated from the shed.

"They've probably got a thirteen-year-old on now, I suspect," ventured Hans. "Aren't you afraid of missing all this?" proffered Rick in hope of a speedy departure. "Hell no! Been there, done that and worse." The elderly man hoisted himself up a bit in his chair. "Drink your beer sonny," he challenged. "You have a trace of an accent. Yugoslav?" queried Rick. "German, my friend," came the reply. "Your English is pretty good," Rick complimented the man. "So it should be. I spent more than thirty years in the States."

"What are you doing here?" asked Rick. The reply was as short as it was vicious. "I'm minding my own business, ever so quietly. How about you?" Rick responded with his standard explanation. "A furniture factory with export leanings is the rather mundane excuse for my presence in this land."

"Daly. You said your surname was Daly. I don't suppose you have any connection with Christopher Daly of Elgin in the Chicago area?"

"He's my uncle. How do you know him?"

"What a small world," smiled Hans. "I used to be his boss on the railroad until a number years ago when I was fired because of the asshole Jews."

"What do you mean?" Rick's level of sobriety rose a notch. His elderly companion leaned forward as though about to share a secret. "Jewish interests on the board unearthed the fact that my time in the war was spent in the Waffen SS and not the Wehrmacht as I'd claimed when arriving in the U.S. in the fifties."

"Two rum Cokes," Hans beckoned a waiter who occasionally checked the doorway. "My friend'll need it soon enough." Oblivious to the ongoing exchange the waiter obliged.

"I've never met any man who admitted to having been in the SS during the war before," commented Rick. "Lucky you," was the terse reply. "You don't look like a mass murderer to me." Rick felt he was smoothing the waters. "You are stupid enough to believe the Hollywood version of the Second World War then are you?" The older man stared at the younger with an intensity that burned.

"How would I know what to believe about events that occurred before I was born?" Rick placated. Hans stretched a bit. "Well sonny, if you'll listen I'll tell you the truth as I know it." Rick's expression and folded arms indicated assent. "How could you have willingly contributed to an attempt at genocide?" Rick was unable to quell his interruption. "Genocide!" shouted Hans not caring who may have heard his voice. "Genocide is what Hollywood did to the truth. Why do you think I'm spending my remaining years in this place? The fucking Americans and their Jewish masters had made my life so miserable that to leave the Land of the Free was a pleasure."

"Are you telling me that you still believe it was ok to murder the six million?" Rick leaned forward innocently but with a degree of earnestness. "Nobody murdered six million, more's the pity," retorted Hans. "If I had known the way the world was going to turn out, I and the Führer, and all of us would have fought much harder than we did."

"Judging from the war footage I've seen, many of you fought hard enough," said Rick, his impatience to depart dissipating.

Hans' voice was raised loud enough to compete with the sounds of sin emanating from the shed. "It was not like that! The lies they tell could make a person sick." Rick's subdued face waited. Armed with yet another rum Hans continued. "Hitler was more or less right, although I think he placed too much emphasis on the question of blood and race. The Jews have the same blood flowing in their veins as you and me. What's wrong with them is more a matter of culture and religion than a racial thing. The Fuehrer, on some level, realized this. His chauffeur, Emil Maurice, was a member of Hitler's bodyguard, as was one of his brothers. They had a very high proportion of Jewish blood. Accordingly, Himmler wanted both of them booted out of the SS. Hitler refused, saying that they and their entire family had proven their loyalty to the Reich. There has always been a fundamental confusion about the cause of human behavior – nature v nurture. How much of what we are is determined by birth and how much by our education and life experiences? In the Third Reich most of us very largely came up with the wrong answer to that question but so did almost everyone else in the world of that day. If our struggle had occurred today rather than in the '30s and '40s our enemy would probably have been termed, 'Zionism and Global Capitalism' rather than 'Judaism' per se.

"It is because we came so close to destroying the corrupt world order that has dogged mankind for centuries that the 'Holocaust' was enshrined in crystal. The symbol of the Holocaust was designed against possible further attacks on the world order. Communism was never as great a threat, due to its own weaknesses, as the main economic tenets of National Socialism. Just as the American civil war was essentiality about the right of secession rather than the morality of slavery so was our struggle primarily about cleaning up the world order rather than attacking races other than our own. The loss of the war was an absolute disaster. Luckily for me I was only a corporal. If I'd been an officer I would probably have been hung. As it was I was held in a camp in Scotland until 1947."

"Surely no prisoners of the Western Allies were held that long," queried the listener.

"You have to be joking. At our holiday camp in Scotland we were divided into three grades: 'A' stood for conscripts and politically unaware soldiers, 'B' represented the volunteers and those who had fought hard before being captured while 'C' was assigned to diehard and committed Nazis."

"Really?" Rick attempted to verify the drift. "That's fine sonny if you want to live in a world of lies and theft." Hans appeared as an elder statesman. "As I was saying, the A-graders were soon allowed to return home, those who were awarded a C rating were held in camps for years and the B's had to hope for the best. I was rated as a B-."

"You got to return home to your family not too long after the war then?" postulated Rick. "I don't want to talk about that!" Hans glared at his temporary companion. Emboldened by drink Rick couldn't help himself. "What about the Holocaust then? How could you have been a party to that?"

The expression on Hans' face was a hybrid of contempt and compassion. "What Holocaust? Hitler was more or less right. I'll grant you in hindsight that things didn't go exactly according to plan." Rick failed in his attempt to follow the dictates of his manners. Rudely interrupting his companion he blurted out, "Are you saying the Nazis didn't kill six million Jews?"

"Yes!" The only sound that broke the silence generated by that remark was the slithering of rum quietly poured down gullets. Hans continued in the face of his totally dazed audience. "The Holocaust is largely a Hollywood myth and hey, who runs Hollywood?" Rick meekly nodded. "Sure, hundreds of thousands died in camps, most of whom shouldn't have." Hans' countenance had taken on the cast of a teacher. "It's the nature of war and we didn't start it. You have to remember how Germany was treated after WWI." A somewhat incredulous listener evoked more passion from the elderly gent. "The Holocaust was an accident of human weakness and nature on all sides. The Russians killed more people than we did and the Americans and British did their share."

Rick smiled with a rum-soaked cynicism. "I've seen footage of the death camps. I just can't understand how people like you could do that to other human beings." The redness of Hans' face angrily stood testament to Rick's casual accusation. "Do you want to hear the truth or do you simply desire to suck the American lolly?" At Rick's apology Hans continued. "As for the myth of the six million Jews, if we had really killed such a number there wouldn't be so many of the bloodsuckers now taking their pound of flesh every chance they get." Rick's face was almost as ashen as that of the dead. "There wasn't even enough fuel to burn six million corpses," declared the old soldier triumphantly. "I estimate that possibly 500,000 to one million people expired in our work camps. In all probability American fighter planes killed huge numbers of people on their way to the labor camps when they continually attacked our trains. Not wanting to admit such a possibility they grossly inflated the numbers who perished in the camps and added the lie about the work camps being death camps where Jews were sent for the sole purpose of execution. When you think about it, it would be logistically absurd to transport millions of people huge distances in a time of war just to kill to them. Any real attempt at mass murder would logically have been carried out at more numerous and smaller centers. There was no aim for mass murder. The millions of prisoners were needed to work for the Reich. Alive they had a value; dead they had none. 'Arbeit macht frei' (Work sets you free) is a wonderful slogan. That was the essential idea. We wanted to reform parasites and transform them into willing contributors to the social good. Admittedly, the real Holocaust, such that it was, is not a shining example of German achievement. It is likely that in the struggle to attain power the Nazi Party went too far with the whole anti-Semitism thing, creating a monster over which they lost control. This is evidenced by the fact that Hitler was forced to personally protect his beloved mother's doctor who was Jewish. Herman Goering also saved a number of Jewish families whom he personally knew. Goering's brother, who wasn't a Nazi, saved hundreds of Jews."

"What about the Final solution then?" Rick challenged. Hans again stretched himself in his chair. "The Final Solution was to deport these recalcitrant exploiters, minus their ill-gotten wealth, to Palestine. Two shiploads actually went. When the Allied Powers declared war on us this was no longer an option. As I'm sure you are aware the whole thing degenerated from there."

An incredulous gaze escaped from Rick's face. "Are you saying that there were no death camps, ovens and mass graves?" Hans appeared bemused by his companion's naivety. "There were camps and people died in them. Maybe a majority of the people who lost their lives within their confines didn't deserve their fate but neither did the millions who expired at the hands of the Soviets or the Western Allies. Remember Dresden?" Hans continued, ignoring his own rhetorical question. "You like what the USA does to the world? Just as when pest exterminators clean a house most of the vermin move next door rather than die, so it was with those bloodsuckers. Before Hitler Europe had the problem. Now America, and hence the whole world, has it! By the way not all camps were death camps as you call them. There were some settlements for Jews who had proven their loyalty and service to the nation and the Reich. Their lives were as comfortable as any. There was never any intention or attempt to commit genocide. Hitler never desired that the entire Jewish race should disappear from the earth. He simply wanted to reform them."

The wary listener maintained a steady silence. "You might not be the religious type," Hans went on, "but I'm sure you've heard the bit from the bible about the Israelites and the golden calf. Well, according to the Good Book, God was going to destroy those sons-of-bitches because of their corruption and greed. Moses talked him out of it and suggested that it would be good PR to give them a second chance. What a pity! They didn't change. Their love of gold and power is worse than ever."

"You are painting an entire race as a vampire nation," Rick remarked, sternly.

"I like bats, even vampire bats," observed the old SS man. "They only take what they need. They're not parasites. If only Hitler had been around when Moses was having that conversation with God. I don't think God is Jewish. Despite quite a few injustices on all sides there has always been a Jewish problem, which needs solving if we are to have a better world. At the core of most of the worst excesses of capitalism you often find Jewish interests. These people feel it is their God-given right to feed off others. The majority of them are the world's original racists. Chosen people! Bah! What a choice!"

With the air of an academic, Hans delivered his next remark. "Most of the combatants ranged against us had no idea of what they were really fighting for. To be brutally honest many of those who fought on our side didn't genuinely understand either. Personally, I was fortunate enough to have been able to realize what it was all about. The cost of our defeat shows up daily as this world continues to deteriorate."

"Were you at any of the camps?" Rick bravely inquired.

"No, I was in the Leibstandarte division of the Waffen SS under Sepp Dietrich. We fought on both the western and eastern fronts and our reputation for behaving honorably far exceeded that of any of the Western Allies or of the Russian divisions. The Leibstandarte was commanded by Dietrich and he took his orders directly from the Führer. Himmler had almost no input into what we did."

"You can't seriously be telling me that so many history books and movies are wrong?" Rick challenged.

"That's exactly what I'm telling you. The good guys don't always win wars but the winners always make sure that they go down in history as the good guys!" Werttenburger smiled at his lesson on historical logic. "Once long ago, I met a Lithuanian man who claimed to be both Jewish and to have fought for Hitler. It didn't exactly surprise me. Unbeknownst to most of humanity there were many foreign divisions of the Waffen SS. There were French, Russians, Dutch and Lithuanian just to name a few. In the International division there were even two Englishmen; one a lorry driver from the Midlands and the other a London cab driver and that's not even counting the brigade of British known as the British Frei Korps or BFK. The whole enterprise was an attempt to make for a fairer world."

Rick's face made it apparent that he wasn't entirely convinced. With the hostile glare of a schoolteacher Hans took a sip from his fifth rum and Coke. "The extreme Zionist elements of the Jewish people already just about run the USA. It's going to get worse, mark my words, and bodes ill for the future of the world. This group will never make do with what is fair and reasonable. Rather than not take the lion's share of the world's wealth they would sooner see everything destroyed. You can't reason with them. As soon as you ask a Jew a question he or she simply answers it with another question."

"I've had that experience myself," interrupted Rick.

"As I was saying," continued Werttenburger; "in their little minds they are, as a matter of definition, always the good guys. They have a moral blank check and possess the right to do anything they want. To this end they have beat up the whole holocaust thing to the point whereby the world sees them as the only serious victims of atrocity, a largely exaggerated atrocity although it was. If they are caught red-handed in some gross evil they simply say, 'Remember the holocaust,' as if that automatically meant that whatever they did henceforth was bound to be wonderful."

Rick took a hearty slug from another bottle of beer and lit up a smoke. "It sounds like you still believe in Hitler," he commented dryly. Almost appearing angry at his student's stupidity Hans answered, "Dead men don't lie. Anyway the world certainly wouldn't have been any worse than it currently is if Hitler had won. It would probably have been a little better, in my opinion."

An incredulous Rick Daly posed a more mundane question. "I never thought in all my born days that I'd see someone who drank more than I do. How do you do it?" Hans smiled deeply. "Although I always followed the politics of Hitler I emulate the drinking habits of Churchill."

The unlikely pair laughed simultaneously. Serious once again, Hans looked Rick straight in the eyes. "I always felt guilty about disappearing from the States without saying goodbye to my old gang. Although I promised that I would catch up with them I was so damn depressed at being fired that I just wanted to melt away and hide."

"How exactly did you lose your job?" Rick finally managed some sympathy for this strange individual. "As I told you before, when I emigrated to the US after the war and when I joined the railroad company I'd stated that I spent the war in the Wehrmacht. I never mentioned the SS. Anyway to cut a long story short a filthy Jew on the board discovered my true past and engineered all sorts of phony performance accusations against me."

"That doesn't sound very fair," mumbled Rick. Werttenburger's expression of derision preceded his next words. "There isn't too much in life that is fair," he remarked. "What humanity does in the name of God could give the bastard an excuse to destroy the world. By the way, when you next communicate with your uncle, please convey my deepest apologies for disappearing like that. I think he'll understand." Rick agreed and, after swapping addresses, promised to see Hans again.

Back home in La Paloma Rick had cause to reflect on the night's proceedings. His uncle's foreman, who'd disappeared years before, turning up in Cebu of all places and proudly wearing his service in the Waffen SS to boot, was definitely a shock. His uncle Christopher was perhaps the most straight-laced person Rick had ever heard of. It was ironic that Christopher worked for years under an unrepentant Nazi.

The next surprise in store for Rick Daly was just as unexpected and crept up on him even more quietly. He'd discussed with Marilyn the chance encounter of his uncle's ex-boss but none-too-surprisingly, she had little to say about it. The clock showed a quarter to eight on a rainy night when a loud call emanated from the gate. Drawing the curtains ever so slightly Marilyn was able to spy a police mobile car parked outside. Opening the door she found Captain Fernandez on the step, minus his squad. "They're back at the station," he explained to her obvious question.

"Come in," ordered Rick who was standing just behind his more luscious housemate. Freddy obliged and took his place on a leather chair in the sala. "What can I get you to eat or drink?" inquired the host. "A beer would do very nicely, please." Rick instantly obliged although he noticed that Freddy was in uniform and obviously on duty. "I'm not quite sure how to put this," mumbled the captain. "I've got a problem that perhaps you can help me with." Rick instantly thought of the donations he'd made to the police basketball team and hoped that no more were required at this moment. He'd never begrudged the odd few hundred pisos though as it was a very cheap price to pay for the sudden zone of law and order that now surrounded his house.

"What's the matter?" he ventured. "It's a personal problem. You know my daughter Carla. You met her briefly when you visited my house."

"Yes," affirmed Rick. "Please go on."

"Well she had an accident while playing netball. She broke her leg so badly that a bone was showing through the skin."

"My God," sympathized the host. "Well," continued Freddy "She was admitted to the Our John of God hospital, which is privately run. She was only there for three days. To cut a long story short the hospital is trying to bill me for P30, 000, which is three times the proper price." Rick looked amazed. "Why would they dare to do that, considering you're a police captain?" he posed. "That's precisely the reason that they think they can get away with it. The public and press here are so focused on stories of police corruption that the hospital figured that I wouldn't dare complain but would just pay up. They're right in one respect. There is nothing officially or legally that I can do. That's why I've come to you with the problem."

"How could I possibly help?" intoned Rick earnestly. "I couldn't afford to pay that bill at present either." Captain Fernandez leaned forward with the most honest expression that he could muster. "Of course I wouldn't expect you to pay my daughter's bill. However, you are a foreigner and, I hope you don't mind me saying so, you are fond of the odd drink. If you could go down to the hospital and make it plain to them that they shouldn't try to rob people I would be very grateful." Rick grinned. This sort of challenge was right up his alley. "I'll see what I can do," he confirmed. "Can I get you another beer?" Freddy refused the offer and, replete with his mobile car, disappeared into the night.

The next morning, around eleven, Rick called on Captain Fernandez's house to tell him he was ready to visit the hospital. As it was a Sunday the entire family were at home. There was Carla, a pretty nineteen year old, lying on the sala couch with her leg in plaster from hip to toe. "How could you have done that playing netball?" Rick asked as delicately as he was able. "I tripped over an opponent's leg and fell very, very badly. The pain was agonizing and I could see the bone and blood everywhere."

"How long will you be laid up for?" Carla answered Rick with a despondent look. "Six weeks at least." Rick Daly the foreigner was treated like a local who was an old friend in this particular home. The family insisted he stay for lunch and when he finally departed at two Freddy thanked him once again for his promised assistance. Back in La Paloma once more Rick said nothing to Marilyn. Some things are best planned and executed alone.

Some fortitudinal drinks were obviously required. Three San Miguels, two cans and one bottle, were followed by four rum and Cokes. Rum is one of the staple optional diets of the Philippines as it is cheap and good. "Don't you think you should drink less?" His secretary and life's love appeared genuinely concerned. "For crying out loud Marilyn, it's a Sunday. Give it a rest!" Just for good measure Rick thought he'd better drink a couple of shots of his imported bourbon. Well-oiled and primed for the important adventure Rick waddled around the corner and hailed a taxi in Tres d'Abril.

Fifteen minutes later Rick alighted after giving the driver fifty pisos for a thirty-piso fare. Saint John of God Hospital presented a similar façade to the world to that of its other private hospital brethren. A six-storey concrete structure painted in white dwarfed a modest entrance that led through the shortest of corridors to a compact reception area, staffed by wizened clerks that would have made old Werttenburger smile. Other corridors led off to the sides and along these numbers of crisply uniformed nurses were strutting their stuff. For once Rick remained oblivious to the temptation posed by dozens of starched darlings running around and remained faithful to the task at hand. Turning left he encountered a large waiting area peopled by a composite mix of sick and hopeful humanity.

Being an admirer of the philosophy of overkill Rick had allowed himself to bring two bottles of San Miguel into the fray, one in each hand. With one bottle discretely under his left arm and the other open and in his drinking hand Rick faced the gathering. "I would like to warn you good people that this hospital is notorious for overcharging. They even dared to charge a police officer three times the correct price when his daughter was admitted. I hope your wallets are deeper than your ailments." Rick smiled at the by-now-disturbed gathering and disappeared back into the corridor. Quickly finding the anteroom off to the right of that alleyway he faced a new crowd of people in need. "Good afternoon," he addressed the miserable throng. Almost everybody in the Philippines can speak and understand some basic English. "Mayong Hapon, Joe" replied a teenager, who appeared to be suffering from a minor stab wound, in the vernacular.

"My friend, lucky for you your wound is minor. Otherwise your wallet would be empty and your body expired," returned Rick. The bottle in his hand was by now empty and he let it smash on the floor. "How clumsy of me. I'm so sorry," he pronounced as he replaced it with the one from under his arm. "They don't call this hospital Saint John of God for nothing," he added. "The customers here are likely to see their maker soon enough!" Just as he was enjoying his performance Rick heard a siren and the screech of brakes.

Brown uniformed police, four of them, entered the building. The hospital had rung the cops due to a disturbance in progress by a foreigner. Rick was rapidly handcuffed and led out to the smiles of the wizened administrators. The crowd left behind simply didn't know what to make of it all.

Once seated in the back of the mobile car Rick's handcuffs were quickly removed and the vehicle sped off. Sergeant Colo spoke first. "That was quite a performance evidently. The captain will be very pleased." Another officer spoke next. "Rick, after we take you home can we come in for a few minutes to watch your cable TV?" The agitator was only too happy to oblige and all passed a pleasant late afternoon.

"Er …umm…it is with great pleasure that I address this august gathering." Not since his teaching days had Rick performed any public speaking. Yet here he was at the San Miguel chapter of the Toastmasters. Noy had invited him to appear that Thursday evening for some finger food and samples of their famous product. Nothing about speaking to an assembly had registered in Rick's consciousness. Thankfully the listeners only numbered fifteen. "I must confess that I didn't prepare any interesting topic and by way of an impromptu address will consider the subject of a 'Foreign perspective on the Philippines.' Firstly, being an outsider here instantly cloaks one in the mantle of unwanted notoriety. It is difficult to function simply as a person among many." Some hearty laughter accompanied a burst of applause. These Filipinos understood. "Life is always a battle and generally the answers lie within. Yet so many folk here look to a salvation from outside themselves; whether it be in a simplistic approach to religion or in some amorphous cargo cult surrounding foreigners." A middle-aged man whistled at this remark. By the time Rick concluded his address he'd won over the listeners entirely. "For the Philippines to move forward as a nation the bulk of the people must believe in themselves and act accordingly."

At the conclusion of the speaking episodes the company sat down to a goodly number of gratis San Miguels and some nibbles. When the assembly broke Noy demanded that Rick promise to visit his house on the coming Saturday for dinner. The dinner date was fixed and the pair departed for their respective homes.

Rick alighted from his taxi at precisely ten past seven. It is always good form to turn up ten minutes late for dinner at a friend's home. Marilyn had been feeling poorly and Rick conveyed her apologies. Ushered inside he was accorded the usual deference. The meal was superb as always. "Obviously, good Filipino food exists," Rick thought to himself "but most of the people simply don't eat it most of the time."

An especially succulent morsel of Chicken Caldareta had just reached his taste buds when a noisy and urgent rapping on the door intruded. Noy opened the door to find Enrique, a neighbor from five doors down, in an agitated state. "I'm sorry to trouble you but I know you've got a car. My eldest son Alfredo has taken very ill suddenly and we need to take him to the hospital."

"Of course," replied Noy. Turning to the family and his guest he relayed the story. "I'll accompany you," insisted his wife. Rena naturally wanted to be of assistance in such an hour and also desired to make sure that her husband returned promptly. She didn't like his solo outings of an evening. She didn't like them at all. As the pair departed Noy apologized to Rick and instructed Alma to look after their guest for the hour or so that the couple would be gone.

"I'm very pleased to play hostess to you, Mr. Daly, even it is only for a couple of hours," spouted Alma who had turned twelve eight months before. "I assure you Alma, I don't need much taking care of," flew the response. "Well we could watch TV; I don't mean the regular programs as they're too boring; I mean we could watch one of Papa's videos." Rick assented. "Papa didn't offer you any whisky but I know where the best bottle is. Please let me get you one. He wouldn't mind and besides, he won't know." To keep the peace, the by-now-nervous guest agreed.

Still seated at the dining table Alma put an Irish whisky in front of her guest as she started the video. A young woman in a blue dress was speaking to a man in a suit.

"Governor," she said, "I'm so thrilled at this chance to interview you. I've only been a journalist for six months." The man in the suit just leered. "Do you take dictation?" he commented. "You must let me make you more comfortable for this important interview." At that remark the suited man reached over and undid the girl's dress. He lost his suit at about the same time as he put paid to the interviewer's underwear. "Oh Governor," was all she could manage standing there in the buff.

"I don't really think that this is a suitable movie for us to watch," suggested Rick paternalistically. "Why not? If it's good enough for Papa surely it's good enough for me!"

"He's a lot older than you." Alma appeared aggrieved. "What's age got to do with it? However, you are the guest and if you don't like the video, I'll put on some music instead." The TV returned to its image noir and the strains of popular Filipino love songs filled the room.

"Would you care to dance Mr. Daly?" The precocious girl smiled acutely into the guest's tremulous eyes. "I'm very sorry my dear but I hurt my leg at the factory." Rick sank as hard as he could into his chair. "All right then, we can play some games." After Alma beat Rick four times at Hangman and twice at Noughts and Crosses, the lass produced a set of rubber bands and began playing with them on her fingers. "You have to put your index finger here," she said presenting her guest with a taut and tangled mesh of rubber. Somewhat reluctantly Rick obliged. Snap! The largest of the bands broke. "Oh Dear!" Alma smiled. "You've broken my virgin band." The best that an increasingly uncomfortable Rick could manage was a nervous laugh. "I'd like to watch the Filipino news," he requested. "You don't speak enough Tagalog or Visayan to bother," Alma retorted. "However, the guest is always right." The current crop of violent gibberish was still flashing across the screen when Alma's parents returned. Rick was unable to prevent a sigh of relief.

"How's the boy?" he inquired. "Just a severe case of food poisoning," Noy replied. "He'll come home tomorrow." The next thirty minutes saw a hasty dessert and coffee arrive, after which Rick was on his way and gladly at that. He liked Noy a lot and admired the stoicism of his wife but was developing an unnamed terror for the daughter.

Never had the humid, sweaty confines of his rented bungalow in La Paloma felt so good. Once inside the house Rick glanced around for the presence of the maid, and finding none, kissed Marilyn speedily on the lips. "Don't worry darling, she goes to bed at nine. What's wrong? You look strange." Rick confided the evening's events and Marilyn looked severe. "Be careful Rick! That girl's trouble. I sensed it the first time I laid eyes on her. I don't care how young she is. She's dangerous." Rick was quick to agree and the subject was dropped.

Against all the odds the business was making its way if not exactly prospering. While the maid was washing dishes one night and Marilyn was watching television Rick had forced himself to do some paperwork. The open calendar on the desk glared at him. November 5th, 1993 it mocked. What had he achieved? Comforting himself with the adage that Rome wasn't built in a day he finished his tasks. Largely to fulfil his visa requirements he'd dutifully returned to Sydney twice a year. Each time he visited Australia he understood with increasing intensity how the WWI soldiers must have felt on their scarce furloughs. The familiar world was phony and surreal. The war zone was the real world.

There is something about the sunrise over La Paloma. Denuded hills past Tisa seem to add to the conspiracy. However it is accomplished, by 8 am the heat threatens to fry all and sundry. "Ayo!" It was the postman and Marilyn rushed to retrieve the mail. Returning from the gate she exclaimed, "I've got a letter from Juliet and there's one for you from Australia!"

Marilyn was already reading the lilac pages of her communication in a corner of the sala by the time Rick had opened his envelope. A minute's silence followed and then his eyes narrowed and he screwed up his letter and its covering and threw them on the floor. Marilyn looked up. "What's wrong?" Rick's face took on a particular pinkish hue and he coughed. "I don't know how to put this but I have a daughter of seven years old. Her mother is a Filipina. The letter is from a neighbor of mine in Sydney who knows her. Apparently to save the costs of child rearing she took Jasmine to her mother's place in a remote province of Mindanao and left her there."

No words could describe Marilyn's face, her own letter forgotten. Mouth agape, all she could say was, "You've been lying to me. The stories about you being in the Philippines before are all true. No wonder Maria was so upset with you. You are a bastard!" Rick swallowed hard.

"Maria or Lina's accusations are utter crap! For what it's worth I hadn't ever been in the Philippines before the trip on which I met you."

"What about your daughter then?" challenged the keeper of the books. "I met and married a Filipina in Sydney many years ago. She was a disco bird and the marriage failed. Do I need to say more?"

"Yes you do," returned Marilyn. The sorry face of the boss told a thousand tales. "I paid maintenance for years as that bitch screwed me. I found out a year after I'd married her that she'd been a bargirl." Marilyn's anger was apparent. "Why didn't you tell me this before?" Rick mustered the lamest of smiles. "It's not good to tell the truth all at once," he threw back. "It's not the same thing. A couple of years about my age is very different from your having a sordid past you didn't tell me about."

For the following ten days there were no sensual encounters in the shower or office, no signs of affection in the home or factory and Rick thought that life couldn't possibly get any worse. In a feeble attempt at atonement he'd almost entirely abandoned his nightly escapades and cut down on his drinking. Over lunch one day at the factory Marilyn raised the subject again. "What do you propose to do about your Jasmine?" she accused. "You have a responsibility to your child."

Rick swallowed hard and mumbled, "I'm not sure. Her mother Emily just dumped her in Mindanao and then returned to Sydney. That woman would do anything for money!" Marilyn laughed. "She's not alone there. The Philippines is full of such creatures."

"To answer your question," Rick continued, "I'll insist that the grandmother and her relatives allow me to send her back to Australia where she obviously has a better future. I'll go down there next week. As far as Australian law is concerned we have joint custody. I'll need an interpreter but I don't suppose you would consider accompanying me?" Marilyn coughed. "Against my better judgment I'll go."

Once again the business was left in the hands of others and the pair turned up at Mactan airport. Amazingly, the propellers of the flimsy aircraft succeeded in their intent and fifty souls shrouded in a titanium envelope were born aloft. As the plane approached its destination of General Santos City, or Dajungas as it was formerly known, the intense competition between expanses of jungle and the vast tracts of denuded plains owned by an American pineapple and tomato-producing company became apparent. The arrival was no more pleasant. Barely out of the lounge Rick spotted a dog that had obviously been attacked by a machete or bolo as the Filipinos call it. "This is Mindanao; there are a lot of Muslims here," Marilyn whispered.

The jeep ride itself to Polomok, the settlement in question, took less than thirty minutes. Dropped in a dusty market-square both Marilyn and Rick constantly glanced over their shoulders. The prevailing atmosphere that greeted them could almost be described as one of absolute lethargy. A few chickens scratched in the dust, an old woman lit a primitive cigar and a couple of youths were drinking warm beer.

The challenge of finding the address proved difficult. Considering the number and distance of the streets the pair had hired a tricycle for an hour. Forty minutes into the bumpy journey a miserable residence faced them as the tricycle halted. "This is it," commented the driver proud of his detection skills. "Ayo! Ayo!" Marilyn screamed at the gate. Eventually an elderly woman with a bowed back appeared and admitted them.

"Jasmine!" cried Rick as he spotted the child. The girl threw her arms around his torso. "Kumustaka Papa?" Rick flinched. In less than a year she'd forgotten her English. Translating, Marilyn asked if she wanted to go back to Australia and the child's face lit up. "That's settled then. I'll pay for her ticket home. She can go back to her mum's place." Rick looked in the grandmother's eye with a measure of finality.

The simple door opened and countless people, men, women and children poured in. The granny rapped away in the local dialect and a muscular man in his thirties then engaged Rick. "There seems to be some problem here," he asserted. "There's no problem," replied Rick. "Jasmine has to go home. That's all." The muscular man who introduced himself as an uncle of the child smiled. "Emily wants her to stay here to learn more about Filipino culture." As Rick politely refused and he and Marilyn took the seven-year-old's hands the crowd of relatives moved forward and encircled them. "You are one, we are many," the muscular man's voice intoned. "You lose, we win."

"At least we're still alive," remarked Marilyn as the empty-handed pair took a jeepney back to General Santos. "And what about Jasmine?" Marilyn had never before seen such a sincere look of concern on her man's face. "I guess you'll have to try another tactic," she replied. The trip back to Cebu passed like a funeral without a body.

Chapter Nine

Another world away and a couple of years earlier the only other surviving members of the Daly clan battled through each and every day. The calendar on the lounge room wall declared the date to be Wednesday 11th December 1991 while the accompanying clock chimed its two cents worth. "Five minutes before six," it said. The evening sky outside was gloomy and sported a bitingly chill wind. Rebecca and Christopher were about to sit down to an early dinner. "George is late again," the father remarked. "Where's the surprise in that?" added his daughter.

How a doorbell can be rung with menace is one of those smaller mysteries of life. The Dalys' sounded at that instant with all the emotional force of an attack. Before Christopher rose from his seat both Rebecca and he knew something was wrong. The chill wind hit Christopher's cheeks as he pulled back the hinged timber and metal object that separated his sanctuary from the outside world. There on the doorstep stood two uniformed police officers, one heavy set and approaching middle age and the other an altogether slimmer and more youthful figure.

"Mr. Christopher Daly?" the more senior of the pair asked. "Yes. Is there some problem?" The generous frame of the officer introduced himself as Officer Ragan and his companion as Officer Sandford. "I've some bad news for you, I'm afraid. Your son George is in serious trouble."

"Has there been some kind of accident?" Christopher queried. "No accident," Officer Ragan replied. "George was arrested downtown after participating in a failed armed robbery." Christopher's jaw hung agape. "I know George is a troubled teenager but I just can't imagine him being involved in anything like that. Are you sure it's him?" The younger of the policemen then spoke. "We're certain, Mr. Daly and we'd like you to come down to the station while we interview the boy as he's a juvenile."

Christopher called over his daughter and quickly explained the situation. "My God," cried Rebecca. "Shall I come with you?" Her father shook his head. "I think it's best that I go alone. I'll call you as soon as I know anything." Reluctantly the girl agreed and Christopher accompanied the officers to the station. After some preliminaries he was shown to an interview room and, a short time later, George was led in. His hanging head spoke volumes and he could hardly look Christopher in the eye? "What mess have you got yourself in now?" the troubled parent voiced. George remained silent.

Two plainclothes officers entered the room and introduced themselves. An unkempt man in his fifties with short, dark hair spoke, "Detective Sergeant Harrigan and my partner is Detective Bronsky." A thirty something fair-haired gentleman, whose suit appeared to have been neatly pressed, nodded. Bronsky set in motion the video recorder with the utterance, "Juvenile interview commenced at 7:30 pm on the 11th December 1991."

"George William Daly," pronounced Sergeant Harrigan, "We are required by law to read you your Miranda Rights again. You are not obliged to say anything but anything you do say may be used as evidence against you in a court of law." Christopher sat bolt upright. "Shouldn't we have an attorney here for this?" he asked. "That's your right Mr. Daly, if you so desire, but you will have to pay the attorney yourself as in juvenile cases the court will not appoint a public defender," replied Harrigan. "Well I guess that's settled," responded Christopher. "I certainly cannot afford to pay a lawyer."

Commencing the actual interview Harrigan looked at the boy straight in the eyes. "George," he said. "You were arrested in the doorway of the Green Meadows Betting Agency. At the time you were wearing grubby blue jeans, black sneakers and a white T-shirt with purple patches that sported white stripes. Incidentally those happen to be the colors of the Scarlet Warrior gang. Furthermore, inside the premises we recovered a 9mm pistol that was covered in your fingerprints. A bullet, extracted from the ceiling of that establishment, has been matched by Ballistics to that very gun. Of course we also have eyewitness accounts that establish the fact that you certainly weren't there to illegally place an under-aged person's bet. What have you to say Home Boy?"

"Home Boy!" interrupted his father. "George isn't often around the home. I certainly wouldn't call him a home boy." Christopher's left hand, unseen, reached for and touched the floor twice. "Please don't interrupt with pathetic jokes, Mr. Daly," responded the Sergeant. "This is an extremely serious matter and I'm sure you are aware that 'Home Boy' means a member of a criminal gang."

Beads of moisture appeared around Christopher's eyes. He just couldn't understand why the Lord had forsaken him. His son remained silent for a while and then, realizing that the game was basically up, began to speak.

"Another boy and I – we're both from poor families – desperately needed some money so I foolishly listened to his plan for a hold-up." Detective Bronsky smiled at George and offered him a Pepsi. The boy took the drink and continued. "It was the other kid's idea but I was the one who was to point the pistol." Detective Harrigan seemed to take charge at this point. "George could you please describe to us the events of this afternoon from the time you approached the agency to the time you were arrested."

The boy flashed a nervous look at Christopher. "Well, the other boy stole a car and drove it to within fifty yards of the store. He left the engine running and we both entered. He held a bag and I held the gun. There were no customers inside and I thought it would be easy. I pointed the pistol and demanded that the clerks fill the bag. At that point an alarm sounded. The other kid panicked and ran. He collided with me, knocking the pistol from my hand and tripping me. It went off by accident as it fell. I was struggling to my feet and trying to run after my buddy. When I reached the door he was nowhere in sight and I fell again. That's when the police grabbed me."

Detective Bronsky pushed over a packet of potato crisps to George. "I'm sure you must be hungry," he announced in a reassuring voice. "It would be very helpful if you could provide the name of your buddy as our uniformed colleagues did not apprehend him at the scene."

"I can't do that." George appeared definite. "And why is that?" shouted Sergeant Harrigan at that point. "I'm no squealer," returned George with a defiant look. "George, how the juvenile court deals with you will, in very large measure, depend on how remorseful you are over your action and how much you assist us." It was Bronsky who had spoken. "I'll take what's coming to me but I can't betray anyone else and that's final." Christopher had never seen George look so much like a man.

The senior detective was rapidly losing patience. "You're willing to wreck your future to be loyal to a shitty little skunk who talked you into committing a crime and then caused you to be caught? I don't believe you." George squirmed marginally on his seat. "That's the way it happened!" he loudly protested. "Oh I believe that part," responded Sergeant Harrigan. "I just don't believe that shit about not being a squealer that you're trying to put on us. We know you're a member of the Scarlet Warriors. That gang has been causing us a lot of trouble in recent months and if you can testify against them we can probably convince the DA to drop the charges against you altogether."

"I ain't a member of any gang," the lad's surly voice cried out. "And your colors then?" snapped Harrigan. "I just like them as decorations. They're cool," answered the boy. "Come off it George. I wasn't born yesterday." The sergeant then spoke to Christopher. "He's obviously afraid to name his accomplice or any of the gang members. Please convince him how important it is that he cooperates." Christopher accepted the challenge.

"George, tell them what they want to know. Now is the time to turn your life around, if not for yourself then for Rebecca and me."

At that moment the teenager broke down. "I'm so sorry Dad but I just can't. A bad life is better than no life at all." Everyone gathered in that room understood that George was not going to talk any further and why. "Interview with the said juvenile terminated at 10 pm." Detective Bronsky led George back to the cells and his more senior colleague faced the father. "You're a bit old to have a teenage son aren't you? You must be in your late seventies." Christopher was dazed by the proceedings and could only manage a meek reply. "I'm seventy exactly. I retired five years ago."

Before he'd had a chance to phone Rebecca, a squad car returned Christopher home. As he sat down with a heavy heart his daughter was all questions. "What's going on now Dad?" Christopher didn't speak for nearly a minute and Rebecca fired her question again. Ever so slowly the old man gazed at her through tired eyes. "George has joined a criminal gang which incited him to perform a hold-up and he's too afraid to talk against them. As a result the police and the courts will throw the book at him."

"Is there anything we can do?" Rebecca's obvious concern and genuine sincerity impressed her father. "I'm afraid not my dear. Sometimes circumstances are too vicious and strong to break free from." Rebecca threw her arms around her father and began to cry. "I haven't been the best of daughters, Dad. Maybe this is all my fault." Christopher shook his head. "It isn't anybody's fault; maybe not even George's. There are times in which no matter how hard you try you just can't win. The stacking of the cards ensures the survival of an unjust world."

Little more remained to be said for the present time. Father and daughter both retired to their rooms for the evil dreams that the night was likely to bring. The next morning showed its face with pallid sunshine but no accompanying joy. The family's situation remained unchanged until a trial date was set. Bail had been refused because of the allegations of gang involvement and the young Daly was confined in a juvenile remand center.

By the time of the trial some four months later Christopher had learned that free attorneys were available for juveniles charged with serious offences. In fact one had been appointed to defend George. The police had lied. Notwithstanding that particular shattering of confidence in human good faith all George's admissions were duly read into evidence against him. Without the passionate and tricky defenses demonstrated in television courtroom dramas George's conviction was a foregone conclusion. His sentencing also transpired under the hand of the black god. "Thirty-six months to be served in a maximum-security facility for young offenders," the judge had pronounced. "In cases like this," he had continued, "I only wish that the maximum custodial sentence allowed me under the law was rather more generous. The rot in our society has to stop somewhere and, as far as I'm concerned, the buck stops with the offender."

After the expiration of that day the only contact that Christopher and Rebecca were permitted with their sinning family member was a weekly visit of twenty minutes and letters. However George was never one for putting pen to paper. Rebecca had managed to hold a part-time job as a store clerk after school and more or less became a home body. She spent much more of her free time assisting her father than in consorting with the likes of Skylene and the other friends of her past.

"You should get out more, Dad?" she said one day. "Why is that?" snapped the answer. "I'd sooner stay here than go cruising around and wasting money." Rebecca looked a delicate fraction wiser. "It's good to have fun and enjoy yourself. You can't do it when you dead. However, I can understand the money angle." Christopher looked serious. "There's more to it than just saving money. Life isn't just about having fun and enjoying yourself. There are issues such as responsibility and pursuing worthwhile goals."

"You don't have much to show for all your responsibility and goals," the teenage girl answered. The old man's expression flashed a momentary insight into a soul that bore all the terror evinced by Eduardo Munch's painting, 'The Scream.' "I'm sorry Dad," apologized Rebecca. "I didn't mean it like that. It's just that you deserve so much more for your efforts than what you have." Christopher's face reflected an incremental decrease in despondency but remained very sober. "You're right, Rebecca. There's no such thing as justice and little seems to be fair in this life. Nevertheless we must try to do the best we can." His daughter wasn't exactly convinced but she certainly wanted to help her father in these troubled times. "The last few years have really dragged by," she said. "I suppose it is because of all the dramas we've experienced."

It was late one evening when Rebecca returned from her after-school job and found Christopher sitting in a chair almost doubled up. "What's wrong Dad?" cried the girl with fear in her voice. "Nothing much; just some chest pains that come and go. I've been having them for several weeks." The pain passed and he sat up normally once more. "You must go to the doctor." Rebecca was adamant. She didn't want to mention Elizabeth's fate but it weighed heavily in her memory. "All right, I'll go first thing in the morning." There was no way to persuade him to make the trek to the hospital that night so Rebecca didn't try.

The following day while the daughter was in school the father kept his promise and paid a visit to his local medico. Dr. Stevens knew of the raw hand that the cruel Fates had dealt Christopher. "Don't worry, Mr. Daly. You have a case of angina. It doesn't appear to be immediately life threatening but you will need to visit a heart specialist for a full check-up." Somewhat relieved, Christopher took the referral for a downtown specialist and told the doctor that he'd make an appointment the next week.

Most mornings Christopher made a habit of taking a stroll around the nearest of the local parks to keep his mind off his circumstances. On one such occasion he'd made the acquaintance of Jack Royalson, another retiree. Jack was three years older than he and half a head taller. A thin gent this new friend possessed an even more jaundiced view of the world than Christopher, if that was possible. The two hit it off famously. "Every day you can see the world's deterioration at a speed faster than the grass grows," moaned Jack. "I can't argue with you there," Christopher agreed.

After several casual meetings and conversations that centered on the blows that both men had suffered Jack invited Christopher to lunch so that they could further reminisce over a few beers. The appointed day was the immediate one following Christopher's visit to his local doctor. On learning of the diagnosis Jack advised, "Go to the specialist as soon as possible. Time is often critical in these matters." He then excused himself and returned with two cans of Millers. "It's time for the news," he chuckled as he turned on the radio.

"President Johnson has signed into a law a new social-security bill that will provide greater safety for the less-privileged in our society. In Vietnam today a major battle erupted between Vietcong forces backed by elements of an NVA division and U.S. rangers who were accompanied by several ARVAN battalions. The fighting took place several miles south of the air base at Dao Nang. On the home front the world's largest rock festival opened at Woodstock." Christopher couldn't believe his ears. "Your news is somewhat older than the regular," he commented. Jack laughed. "Yes and, overall, it's a lot better news. I hooked a tape deck to my radio and managed to acquire news reports from the '60's and '70's. The world was a damn sight better place then."

Christopher wasn't really in a position to disagree so he just sipped his can of Millers. His mind bounced back to the principal of the elementary school his children had attended. That man's material comforts all emanated from the fifties but old news; that was really something.

"At our age, in a crumby world such as this, we don't really have all that much to look forward to," added Jack. "The regular news is simply too depressing to bear and if it makes us happy to look back rather than forward what's the harm?" His friend agreed with the sentiment but did not ask to duplicate any of the old tapes. "They say that time flies when you're having fun," added Jack, "but it's not true. Don't you notice that every year seems to pass more quickly than the last no matter what misery it has brought? Each year you get older causes the time to pass faster. Remember when you were a small child and how long a year seemed between Christmases?" Again Christopher found himself assenting. "You see," said Jack, "when you haven't lived very many years each one seems to last a long time but when a year becomes a smaller and smaller fraction of your life thus far, your psychological time sense speeds up."

When it was time to return home Christopher pondered some of the questions raised over the meal. Of course we are forced to live in the present. That's all there is. The fondest memories and most hopeful aspirations are only experienced in the moment of the here and now. He remembered what Rebecca had said about the importance of fun and wondered what the young could see in this miserable world that Jack and he couldn't. It was fall and the leaves on the ground of the park formed a natural kaleidoscope. Jack's house lay at the opposite end of that recreation area from his own. As the wind scattered the fallen leaves into ever changing patterns he was reminded of the transience of not only life but of all things. In February of that year terrorists had planted a bomb in the underground car park of the north tower of the World Trade Center, opening a thirty-yard hole in the concrete and leading to the deaths of six persons.

Still deep in thought Christopher entered his home. It was time for a news broadcast so he switched on his television set as if to remind himself of how bad things had really become on this earth. There was one thing he knew in his heart. "Life has no bottom. No matter bad things are or how far one has sunk things can always get worse." The news presenter announced the collapse of the BGH Corporation, which was a property and stock investment company whose clients numbered many superannuation funds. "An audit has found many millions of dollars missing from company funds and it is expected that criminal charges will be laid against some of the senior executives." The grey-suited man then turned to an account of a hurricane headed for Florida and concluded the broadcast with a brief encapsulation of world news that directly affected Americans. Christopher had stared blankly at the set since the announcement of BGH's fall. He remembered that Trackfast had invested very heavily in that entity, as its profit forecasts were excellent in the eighties.

At the time of his retirement seven years before, Christopher's superannuation, although not exactly stunning in its beneficence, was adequate. His pension kept the home running despite the personal pain that his 'golden years' had brought. The 'Greed is good' mentality that had replaced the hippie ethos of the '70's had nothing to do with him or so he thought. A few more days saw more news of the downfall of BGH, and much worse, the insolvency of Trackfast's superannuation scheme. A spokesman for Trackfast announced that despite the heavy financial loss they would re-distribute their investments and launch a new superannuation scheme. "Trackfast employees have nothing to worry about," he reassured. "Within a year the new scheme will be financially viable." No mention had been made of existing superannuation beneficiaries. The last news of the financial debacle was that a director of BGH, one Simon Rubens, who also held a seat on the failed Trackfast Superannuation Board, was under investigation by federal regulators.

The next Thursday Christopher opened his mailbox expecting to find amongst the usual bills and the odd personal letter, his pension check. It wasn't there. "Oh well," he thought, "it'll arrive tomorrow." It didn't and Christopher phoned the superannuation company. The phone just rang and rang as it did every time he tried over the next week. In desperation he rang the headquarters of the rail company itself. "I'm very sorry Mr. Daly," a telephonist had said, "the old superannuation entity no longer exists and there simply isn't the money to transfer existing superannuants into the new fund. All I can suggest is that you speak to the local office of the Social Security." Christopher put down the receiver without even managing the courtesy of a goodbye.

He mentioned nothing of this subject to his daughter. At the Social Security office a matron who looked like an escaped librarian spoke with all the warmth of an ice bucket. "Mr. Daly, I'm very sorry to learn of the financial collapse of your superannuation provider but these things happen. You do, it seems, qualify for the minimum old age pension. It's your lucky day!" The amount in question was two hundred and fifty dollars a month and was no more than 35 percent of what he'd previously been receiving.

The first signal of an impending domestic financial collapse Rebecca received was the cutting off of the phone. She'd attempted to make a rare call to one of her friends and silence had replaced the normal dial tone. "Dad," she called. "The phone's out of order. We'd better ring the telephone company. It's only a few months till George is due out of detention and he might ring." At this point Christopher came clean. "Don't bother," he said. "It's been cut off because we didn't pay our last two bills."

The look on his daughter's face convinced him that now was the time to break the news. "They can't do that!" she replied. "They could and they did. Somebody stole a lot of money and it wasn't recovered. Trackfast couldn't possibly cover the hole without causing severe losses to its shareholders." Rebecca glared. "What about you; what about us? Don't they care?" Her father managed an ironic smile. "We aren't important or rich. Why should they care? They don't need us."

Although still dazed by the family's personal typhoon Rebecca did manage to ask about when the visit to the heart specialist was to take place. "I was going to go four weeks ago," Christopher solemnly declared, "but after my superannuation checks stopped I simply couldn't afford the cost so I cancelled the appointment."

"How are we going to manage?" inquired the girl, her dark flowing locks brushing across her face. "I don't know," responded the man. "I'll try to get work of some sort but I don't like my chances considering my age."

"There's no choice, Dad. I'll have to drop out of school and work full time." Much as this idea sickened him Christopher had no answer to the proposal and so the idea transformed into reality.

Rebecca was able to land a position in a local supermarket as a checkout operator. The pay wasn't great but it certainly beat what she could bring home from her part-time employment. Her father kept up his end of the bargain. He applied for a janitor's position, a delivery job and so forth. "I'm sorry Mr. Daly," soothed one interviewer. "Your age is against you. We try to replace employees as seldom as possible and it is most unlikely that you would be able to work for more than two or three years."

Rebecca's wages kept the pair out of the gutter and two months before George was due home the old man actually scored some work. It wasn't much; just delivering leaflets on foot and it only amounted to $2.50 an hour. Still, it was additional bread on the table. The wall clock appeared less miserable than usual and the winds of the approaching winter less bitter. The cogs of simple existence clicked over less jarringly. They were able to pay the bills again and, six weeks before his release date, George had phoned. "I don't know what to say, Dad, but I've changed. I'm born again and I think I can become a worthwhile person."

Both father and daughter were thrilled at the call. "We can be a family again," Rebecca had joyously exclaimed. "Now we are at least treading water rather than drowning you should go and see the specialist Dad." A shadow passed over his face. "We're not quite that flush yet and we'll need some savings to accommodate George. He won't have a penny and it's difficult for ex-cons to find work." The conversation ended.

Precisely at 8 am Christopher would set off on his pamphlet delivery round, returning home around three. Dacey Beaver couldn't fail to notice Christopher's latest activity. His dead wife's friend, Susan didn't call any more as she'd found a new relationship and moved to L.A. "One less prostitute in the neighborhood," declared Dacey to herself after noticing the woman's sustained absence.

Less than three weeks after Christopher's new and meagre employment commenced he received a letter from the Social Security office. "Mr. Daly," it read, "It has been brought to our attention that you have been seen working. Any paid employment whatsoever automatically disqualifies you from receipt of the federal pension. Henceforth your pension will be cancelled." Neatly transforming the missive into a paper airplane the long-since-retired signalman launched it at the wastepaper bucket where it silently landed. As the years crept by, Christopher's protestations at what the establishment served up had grown even quieter.

Kinder eyes noticed the pair's plight. It was a sunny morning in the spring of '94 that a knock on the door revealed two uniformed members of the Salvation Army. "I'm so sorry," intoned Christopher. "I would love to give but things are rather tight for us right now." A smiling young man returned, "We are not visiting you for donations Mr. Daly but to see if we can help you." Christopher was shocked. "We're struggling but can manage. Your resources should be reserved for those really in need." Rebecca appearing behind her father spoke up. "Dad we do need help, especially with George coming home in three weeks." Christopher glared at his daughter and returned to his conversation with the Salvos. "It would be simply sinful for us to accept charity that is needed more by others. Thank you for your offer and I bid you Good Day."

The weeds in the front yard of the Daly home stood testament to some malaise. Dacey Beaver could've certainly sworn to that. As the pages of the desk calendar turned, only seven remained before the advent of George.

The next time Christopher raided his mailbox there was only one solitary envelope; no bills, no communications from government departments; the solitary envelope was an airmail one from the Philippines. His only nephew had written to him. The contents caused Christopher to smile.

Dear Uncle Chris,

Life in the Philippines has continued to prove interesting as always. I must apologize for not having written for a year or so but I've been constantly busy. The dramas of setting up a business and factory here would have to be seen to be believed. Nevertheless it is paying its way finally and I think I'm on the verge of success. I have found an excellent secretary and bookkeeper who is the most wonderful woman I've ever met and I hope to marry one day.

A few weeks ago I met an old acquaintance of yours, one Hans Werttenburger. He's been living in the Philippines for years. He wanted me to apologize to you on his behalf for his disappearance all those years ago but he felt that you and the other signalmen on his team would understand the reasons behind it.

There is one sour note however. My ex-wife saw fit to dump Jasmine with her grandmother in a situation of squalor and danger in Mindanao while she rakes in money in Sydney. I went down there to demand that Jasmine be sent home and all the relatives physically threatened me. I suspect that I'll have to plan some sort of rescue.

Love,

Rick

Christopher Daly was pleased to learn that Rick was faring better in the eternal struggle than himself but was concerned about the situation of Rick's daughter. The thought of asking his nephew for financial help never even crossed his mind. Besides money almost never flows *from* the Philippines. Six days later George returned. The homecoming was quite an event with hugs and tears all round.

Christopher's prediction of the impossibility of his son's finding employment came to pass. Armed robbers, no matter how young at the time of their offence, are seldom received with open arms by the business community. No government-assisted training program would accept the young man either. His newfound faith sustained George. He'd spend hours a day reading the bible and would often go downtown preaching to strangers. When his father asked him one day for some help with the front yard he replied, "I'm sorry Dad, I have to do leaflet distribution with my church." The very word 'leaflet' evoked bitter memories with Christopher yet he said nothing.

Rebecca and George found their father grimacing in pain on more than a couple of occasions. "It's nothing," he'd say but they grew increasingly worried. George refused to ever visit Trout Park again but the rest of Elgin saw his youthful figure preaching the message of the Lord. On a grey winter's day the reformed lost boy was calling on the sinners to repent while standing in front of a graffiti-covered wall. Between the 'white guys have small dicks' and 'killing is cool but being killed isn't exactly hot' was another message, totally unnoticed by the amateur preacher. In faded white paint it simply said, 'Hitler was right.'

Chapter Ten

Back behind their door Rick and Marilyn both independently reflected on the failed journey to Mindanao. On reaching home Marilyn immediately took a shower. As the tepid water ran over her shapely form her thoughts waxed towards the philosophic. Foreigners just don't understand how things are here. If Rick had understood the heartbeat of the Philippines he wouldn't have even bothered to make that wild-goose-chase trip. If Jasmine's mother who was a Filipina as well as their kin wanted the child to remain in those circumstances no words from a foreigner would convince them. Law or no law, in the Philippines blood truly is thicker than water. It's thicker than justice, morality or anything else one might care to name. Rick is just arrogant in his assumptions about the way things should and do work. Oh well! They say experience is a great teacher.

While the shower drops were reaching the parts of Marilyn's body that Rick wanted to touch he, too, mused on the useless undertaking. I should have known that the blood relatives of the asshole Emily would behave just as shittily as she always did. Why did I even think that they might be reasonable? Failure is always difficult to bear but when it involves the well-being of one's own child the hurt is an acidic envelope that burns through one's being.

Smelling like roses Marilyn had reappeared, clad in her familiar house shorts and polo top. "I'm making coffee Rick, would you like one?" He had just answered in the affirmative when the phone rang. Marilyn picked up the receiver. A few seconds later she called, "Rick it's a guy called Hans for you." Rick took the instrument. "Hello Hans. How are you getting on?" The voice on the other end chuckled. "Pareho gihapon." Rick was confused. "I beg your pardon." Hans laughed again and spoke in English. "I said in Visayan that I am getting on exactly the same as I did yesterday and the day before that."

"I wish I could say the same thing," returned Rick, "but I've had a few additional dramas lately."

"That's unfortunate," replied Werttenburger, "but around here it's hardly unusual. Anyway I enjoyed our chat the other week and would like to invite you for a few drinks."

"When?"

"How about tomorrow evening?" Rick agreed to Hans' proposal and they arranged to meet at the Cowgirl bar at 9 pm.

The next day, a Saturday, passed very slowly. A machine had broken down at the factory and production halted for four hours while they waited for a mechanic to come and fix it. By the time Rick arrived home he was tired and had a splitting headache. After a shower and the passage of a half hour Rick was sufficiently revived to face the cowgirls. As he left Marilyn had wiggled her backside and grinned. "Have fun. Don't do anything I wouldn't do."

When Rick offered a fifty-piso note to pay for the fare, which was only thirty, the driver smiled broadly and said, "No change, Joe." Rick cursed himself for not having remembered to bring the standard supply of small notes and thus was forced to pay a compulsory tip. After being caught a few times in that manner Rick always kept a supply of change on his person. On this occasion he'd simply forgotten about it.

Entering from the blackened and sweltering street the blast of cold air smacked of the arctic. The Cowgirl was fairly typical of Cebu's foreigner bars; cold air-conditioning, cold beer, warm girls and even warmer prices. Taking a stool close enough to the action to risk the proverbial tit in the eye Rick looked round for Werttenburger. He had not yet arrived. "I suppose I could enjoy the show for a bit," he postulated. One dancer in particular seemed to take delight in thrusting her mound right in his face. The last time she did it she pulled down her panty a few inches and Rick was just about to get a furburger when his friend walked in.

Offending the owner of the potential furburger Rick turned his head to greet his companion. Dressed in a fawn safari suit Hans looked much more the old soldier than a retired drunk. Rebuffed, however accidentally, the sporting nubile body re-hoisted her bikini briefs, performed two somersaults and tried her favorite routine on another customer.

"Good to see you my friend," announced the German as he sat down. "Likewise," responded Rick, noticing how desperately lonely Hans really was. It was ironic, he considered, that in a nation where humanity multiplies with the rapidity of clover that there were so many lonely people. Of course individuals that you can't trust don't ease loneliness and therefore at least eighty per cent of the country's population were disqualified as potential friends.

Rick ordered two beers. "I've been thinking," said Hans. "When we met I told you that we would have fought harder had we known the way the world was going to turn out. We really believed that we could make a better world."

"So?" interrupted Rick.

"Well," Hans went on, "after living in this place for a quite a few years I'm not so sure that anything can ever be changed regardless of the sacrifices of however many people." His companion appeared nonplussed. "Around here there are constant changes; people are killed, politicians replaced and the value of the money alters daily, usually in accordance with gravity. Yet for all that everything is the same. Whether it's a coup or a semblance of an election the result is merely the changing of the guard. We just get a different bunch of crooks stealing the money."

"That might be the Philippines but it's not the whole world," retorted Rick. "It is the whole world." Hans took on a Socratic mantle. "What you see here happens everywhere. Here it is obvious while in most western countries the same practices are conducted more discreetly."

"I can understand what you're saying about the piso." Rick relayed the story of an English tourist he'd met some months before. "According to this chap he was at Manila's international airport in a duty-free store. He'd selected whisky, cigarettes and a hand-crafted model boat and taken them to the checkout. He produced a wad of pisos to pay and the cashier said, 'I'm sorry. We only accept US dollars.' The Englishman then lost his cool and shouted in a voice that rebounded throughout the terminal, 'What sort of country is this that doesn't accept its own money?' The cashier couldn't grasp the notion that they should accept their own currency. Only US dollars are real currency; the rest is just monopoly paper that you play with around the traps."

Hans laughed. "Your story doesn't surprise me at all but it is amusing. However I was talking about something altogether more important." At that moment 'Downhearted' was succeeded by 'Like a Virgin.' It doesn't matter what bar throughout the archipelago a person is frequenting. When that song plays the dancing girls seem to reinvigorate, scream and perform like there is no tomorrow. Why that is the case is open to conjecture. Perhaps they are mentally chasing their past, distant in the case of most of them.

What they call an old lady; a girl in her mid-twenties, strutted in front of the pair, about faced and dropped her drawers directly in front of Hans' chin. There is generally a greater respect for and appreciation of the more mature members of society in this country than in the West. Even a very old soldier could get a look-in, so-to-speak, in this land. "What a great ass!" Rick exclaimed. "It would have been," replied Hans, his face screwed up, "if she hadn't farted."

"I guess you could call that a brownout," chortled Rick. The deadpan expression on the old soldier's face reminded him of the famous German sense of humor. "As I was attempting to say," Werttenburger insisted, "Nothing ever really changes on this planet so perhaps the Führer, I and all the others shouldn't have bothered. I grant you the outcome of war will affect people for a generation or two but in the long run it changes nothing unless the military result is accompanied by education and cultural expansion."

"Very deep, very deep," commented the businessman in his prime. "Look at those tits!" Hans glared at him like he was depraved. "You've got to appreciate the physical beauty of the Filipina," Rick added. "I do, in between drinks, but there is more to life than fun and sex." Hans spoke with the authority of one who knows. "You're quite right," replied his younger friend. "There's work or arbeit as you call it. Without work there is no money and without money there is no fun or sex."

"Crap!" Hans appeared contemptuous. "These girls get plenty of fun and sex. Do you think they come from wealthy families?" Rick missed the point and raised his voice. "They're women! It is we, the owners of the cucumber who have to pay to use it. With no money your chances of even finding love itself are very limited and if you do find it you won't be able to do much with it!"

"It's not wealth that sets you free, it's arbeit! Work!" shouted Hans. Brenda, a dancer who hailed from Mambaling, spoke to the elderly gent with surprisingly-skilled English but smiled at Rick. "Can I come home with you so we can work together?" It was Rick who laughed, spilling a mouthful of beer on the counter. "Work for what? A better world? You have to be joking!"

His companion wasn't joking. "You youngsters just think about yourselves. We were brought up to believe that we owed a duty to the world in which we live. Politics is the art of the possible, not a plan for perfection. I was more than ten years younger than you when I was fighting for our cause, as well as my life, every day. I didn't have time to think about ways to aggrandize my own existence. While I think about it there is one lie Hollywood never levelled against Hitler. They never said he was corrupt. He wasn't, of course. He was sincere. Of how many leaders in today's world can you say that?"

"You've got me there," returned young Daly. "However, I never understood the point of destruction and killing in the name of a better world." Silence isn't necessarily an admission of defeat. Hans would live to fight another day. As a retreating shot however he added, "if you are just going to look after Number One and those immediately connected you might as well become Jewish!"

With an emotion approaching hostility Rick fired a shot across Hans' bows. "You should write a book if you want to rewrite history." Hans laughed so hard that two dancers stopped their movements for a couple of seconds and stared at him. "Do you think that anyone will publish and promote the truth?" he said. "Who owns the mass media?" It was Rick's turn to say nothing. Hans took on a didactic expression. "Communism, or Bolshevism as we called it in my day, failed because of people's inherent laziness. Capitalism will fail because of humanity's intrinsic greed. National Socialism was never given a fair chance! Whereas Capitalism and Communism pit business people and workers against each other Hitler's vision was a world where they both had common goals and could work together." Rick's gaze was fixed fairly on the stage.

More beers, more tits and more naked asses brought back a level of equanimity to the pair and the conversation turned more mundane. Rick was unable to help himself. "On a personal level, I've had a big drama recently," he confided. "You caught the clap?" Hans laughed. Revenge figures as large in verbal repartée as it does in other areas. At his friend's pained expression he apologized. "I'm sorry. Go on."

"I was married to a Filipina once."

"Weren't we all? The operative word is once," interrupted the safari-suited drinker. "Please!" Rick looked worried. Another quick apology from his audience and he continued. "We have a daughter, Jasmine, now seven years old. Her lousy mother to save money, brought her to visit her grandmother here in the Philippines only to leave her there and disappear back to Australia. Apparently, she intends to leave the child for at least ten years."

"Doesn't sound nice," Werttenburger added in a comforting tone.

"It isn't nice. What's more my secretary and I went to visit the relatives and asked them to allow me to send her home. They gathered like flies around a turd and physically threatened me and my girl."

"You mean like Filipinos around money," chuckled Hans.

"Whatever. Anyway we had to come back here to Cebu without the child. It looks like I will have to physically snatch her from the relatives."

"What part of the country is this?" inquired Hans.

"Mindanao." Hans appeared pensive. "Do you know that Mindanao means 'land of promise'? They don't tell you what the promise is, of course. What part of Mindanao is your daughter in?"

"South Cotabato." Hans took on an expression of genuine concern. "That's Muslim rebel territory. Good luck."

"What do you mean?" responded Rick. Werttenburger appeared wise again. "The Jews and the Muslims are just other sides of the same coin. Despite their mutual antipathy they both should be exterminated. What worries me about the Muslims apart from their acquiescence in all manner of violence is the fact that they don't drink. At least the Jews drink. I'll give them that."

Rick looked askance. "What's wrong with not drinking if that's your thing?" he asked.

"Didn't your mother tell you to never trust a man who doesn't drink?" Werttenburger sounded like a sage.

"I'm not sure I understand." Rick was sincerely confused.

"Put it this way" continued the older man, "in this modern world being male is a source of great disadvantage and therefore we men tend to take the odd dram. Those that don't are probably involved in the conspiracy. I'll probably die soon and this country is great for such events." A derisive laugh escaped his companion's lips. "With the amount you drink and smoke I shouldn't wonder." Hans' face suddenly took on a note of sadness that was seldom seen in these parts. "I just wish I had something to die for! When old age and our bad habits catch up on us death is a certainty. There is no running away. Those cowards in Wenck's army and others had a choice but took the wrong one! I miss the Führer." A liquid laugh interrupted his soliloquy.

The old soldier angered. "We fought to prevent the shitty world that we all now have! If only we had prevailed!" Beads of moisture appeared around an otherwise stoic, if drunken, visage. Continuing, the elderly SS man was determined to have his moment. "The freedom that Hollywood and the American government extol so loudly is an illusory concept. Give me a glass of beer rather than an ocean of freedom any day! Seriously though, what is the use of being free if you are hungry?" Rick wasn't going to argue with that and didn't. In reply all he could manage was a rather lame comment on the nature of existence itself. "Why is it that humans generally cry when they come into this world but seldom do so when they leave it?" Hans did not dignify this question with an answer but instead took a hearty slug from his rum and Coke and commented, "In the past great civilizations rose and fell. Today, with globalization, all of humanity's eggs are in one basket. Because of the creed of greed and power holding almost universal sway I suspect that our fall will be every bit as catastrophic as that of the dinosaurs!" It was a quarter past eleven. "Would you like to go bar hopping?" According to Rick the night was yet young. "I don't think so, sonny. I'm feeling tired enough so that the chicks can wait another day or two." The pair then said their goodbyes and exited. After watching Hans disappear in a jeepney Rick still felt disgustingly sober.

His sobriety level caused him to briefly visit two more bars before returning home. It was a Saturday night after all. At two in the morning he passed through the gate and inserted his key in the door lock. Silently he entered. Marilyn woke from her sleep at the sound of the single click and, rising from her bed, opened her door ever so slightly. She observed a solitary figure crossing the sala and heading up the four steps. Good, he hasn't brought back a woman, she thought before re-latching her bedroom door and returning to her dreams.

By the time Rick emerged from his leisurely Sunday lie-in Marilyn and Leticia were in the kitchen busily preparing the noon luncheon. "How's the party boy?" the elder of the two inquired. "Did you have a good time?" Although he secretly suspected that Marilyn was hoping he hadn't, he nonetheless replied in the affirmative. The three sat down to a tastier repast than usual. Boneless bangus or milkfish was served in a coconut sauce and was blessed with accompanying beans and tomatoes. In most Filipino households maids or helpers dine after the family has finished but Rick insisted on a more egalitarian approach.

"Marilyn," spoke up the man of the house between mouthfuls, "I'll have to go back to Mindanao to rescue Jasmine." Marilyn's face showed some consternation. "How do you propose to do that? That's a dangerous area at the best of times and you might get yourself killed." Rick knew that he must exercise his obligation as a responsible parent regardless.

"I don't yet know how I'm going to do it but I will save Jasmine. I'll probably have to employ some combination of force and trickery."

"It won't work. There are many of them and only one of you and Filipinos are very clever people. You'll only cause more trouble." Rick's mind was made up and when he asked Marilyn to come with him he noticed a flash of fear overtake her pretty face. "No. I will not be involved in a foolish and dangerous venture that is probably illegal anyway. I'm sorry but I can't help you this time."

The look on her man's face spoke volumes. His disappointment was obvious and perhaps he saw her refusal as an act of betrayal. "Well, I'll go alone then." There was no more discussion of the subject save for Rick's announcement that he would fly to Davao in three days' time. "Why Davao? General Santos is much closer." Marilyn was perplexed. "That's precisely why," came the answer. "When I take Jasmine the first place the relatives might look is the airport in General Santos."

Without a detailed plan Rick left Cebu at three in the afternoon that Wednesday. Even Leticia appeared concerned for his safety. "Good luck, Sir," she'd said as he left the gate. Marilyn's face was paler than usual. When the silver bird landed in Davao he thought he'd arrived into the middle of a Western. Under a burning sun a seemingly endless vista of space presented itself. The concrete buildings stood in clusters like oases. At the airfield's perimeter, countless stalls purveyed drinks and snacks. At any second Rick expected to see Clint Eastwood dismount from his horse and order a whisky.

Rick knew two things of the coming venture. Firstly it required a lot more thought and second the best possible time to execute the snatch would be very early on a Sunday morning as any muscular would-be heroes amongst the relatives would probably be fast asleep or nursing hangovers. It was with these two preliminary givens that he'd chosen a Wednesday to enter Davao. Four days should be sufficient to organize the enterprise.

The Landview Hotel was certainly no resort. A two-star job at best, its crumbling façade of grey block and yellow plaster played host to numerous domestic travelers, most on business of some sort, but saw only the very occasional white face. It was ideal and was situated only three kilometers from the airport. After noticing a sign in the Men's toilet that read, "Wash your hands before returning to work," and making a mental note not to order any meals there Rick turned in for an early night that day and in the morning did some necessary shopping. When Marilyn and he'd visited Jasmine he'd noticed that a large wire fence and a padlocked gate protected the grandmother's house.

A sturdy pair of bolt cutters was the first item on the list. A torch, batteries and some regional maps completed the purchases. With his new tools in a resplendent plastic bag Rick took a seat in a carinderia. A carinderia is similar to a kitchenette; both serve food and both sell beer. Perhaps a kitchenette serves more beer while a carinderia sells more food. At the next table a young man in faded denims was looking at him. "I'm sorry but we don't see many Americans around Davao." Rick introduced himself at the same time as explaining that he wasn't really an American. "I'm Ishmail, Ishmail Mendoza," the denim-clad youth announced. "Please join me. It's not good to eat alone." Rick obliged.

When the conversation reached the subject of the reason for his visit Rick figured that Davao being three and a half hour's drive from Polomok it would be safe enough to tell the truth in a very general fashion. "I've come to collect my daughter but her maternal relatives don't want to know as her mother pays them to keep the child a virtual prisoner."

"Where is the mother? I assume she is a Filipina."

Rick smiled. "In Australia."

"I'm no lawyer but in that case I would think you have a legal right to collect the child." Rick then asked Ishmail what he did for a living. "I'm a businessman of sorts," he replied. "In fact I'm a smuggler; cigarettes, liquor, electronic goods and that sort of thing." Rick looked shocked, not at the youth's profession but at the fact that he'd so brazenly admit it. "You're certainly brave telling strangers that you have an illegal profession!" As he finished the sentence his mind journeyed back to chance encounters with an odd assortment of characters in Manila's Ermita district. There was the ex-governor of Mindoro who roamed the bars with his three bodyguards bumming drinks and the odd hamburger from anyone who was impressed enough to listen to his story. Then there was Dapper Dan the 'CIA' man who claimed to be able connect anybody with almost every important person on the planet. The gulf separating people from what they claim to be and what they really are can be wider than the Grand Canyon.

His musings were cut off when Ishmail answered his question. "You approach these matters with a Western mind," he remarked. "In the Philippines what is legal, what is illegal and so forth is a giant grey area. It all depends on who you are and whom you know. What is illegal for you may in fact be fine for me." The Filipino man could sense a certain incredulity on the part of his listener. "I'm not exactly a smuggler. That's just one of the things I do. I'm a Muslim and I'm an activist. We are fighting for greater autonomy or even outright independence for large parts of Mindanao. Manila steals too much of the wealth from our land."

"How do you pursue your goals then, apart from smuggling?" Rick quipped. "I was in the MNLF, the Moro National Liberation Front, for a couple of years but the organization was just too corrupt and useless so I joined a smaller, more dynamic group, the Abu Sayef. This group is much more successful in its agitation."

"I don't understand why you are telling me this?" posed the Westerner. "If you're a militant rebel aren't you afraid of being turned in to the military?"

"You just don't get it, do you? Sure there have been battles and people do get killed but generally the conflict is much more subtle. The military know who I am but there is no problem. I leave them alone and they leave me alone. In fact I get on well with most of them."

By this time Rick was looking really confused. "Enemies living next door to each other, so-to-speak. How weird."

"Everything is personal in the Philippines, my friend," stated Ishmail. "Politics here is never about ideologies, despite appearances. It is always personal. Each individual, each family and each community wants to make sure that it is receiving its fair share of the national wealth or better. Whether a person prospers or dies a sudden and violent death largely depends on his personal skills and how much he's liked."

At this point a compelling urge to mention his mission in more detail overtook Rick. "If I were you," Ishmail replied to his companion's soul-bearing, "I'd check things out with the local military first to avoid any dangerous misunderstandings later. I also think I can invite to you visit one of our gatherings if you're interested." Rick smiled. "Aren't you afraid that I might be a CIA spy?"

"I don't think so," laughed Ishmail. "Besides the Americans aren't that stupid. They'd employ Filipinos to help them, not Westerners who stick out like sore thumbs. However, if you want to visit our camp we will have to blindfold you."

"You mean the military don't know where your camps are?" The mystery seemed to deepen. "They don't know and they don't want to know," rejoined the young man. "If they know then Manila will make them attack us. How many soldiers, I ask you, want to reach an early grave for the princely sum of P2, 000 a month?"

Having a day-or-so more than he needed for his preparations Rick accepted the invitation to visit the camp. Early the next morning a diesel-powered vehicle collected him from the front of his hotel. Twenty or thirty kilometers along bumpy and dusty roads they travelled. For the last hour of the journey Rick felt stupid in his obligatory blindfold. For all that however, the more assistance he could obtain for his quest, the better.

As the vehicle halted, his companions removed Rick's blindfold. "Shades of Woodstock," he thought when faced with a tent city surrounded by thick jungle on all sides. Woodstock it wasn't. Instead of the hum of electric guitars and the sounds of multitudes of joy seekers he could see squads of young men and women, dressed in fatigues, training with an assortment of weapons. In the trees the chirping of birds could be heard. The thought struck Rick that the whole time he'd been in the Philippines he'd hardly seen or heard any birds.

Ishmail introduced the guest to a number of their fighters who were gathered around a command tent. One of them was a girl in her early twenties, her long hair trussed up under a dark green cap. The slim profile of the Kalashnikov she was holding highlighted the curves of her full-breasted body. Ishmail had told the group of Rick's plight. "You seem to be a victim of Philippine injustice almost as much as us," remarked Sonia, for that was the girl's name.

Despite the guns and other accoutrements of struggle the Abu Sayef had not yet launched into the series of kidnappings and murders that later established its notoriety. In fact the members were concerned to maintain as a good a relation as possible with the outside world. "Remember what I said about making contact with the local military before taking your child," Ishmail repeated.

Throughout the day, as various members of the group escorted their guest around the encampment and numerous activities Sonia always seemed to be there. "Why did you come to the Philippines?" she'd asked at one point. "A personal quest to operate a successful business I suppose," he'd replied. "Rattan furniture isn't glamorous but it works."

"I think you can see the cancer that is eating this country." The girl's soft eyes cast a warmer glance than her uniform and gun would have suggested. "I wish you luck in retrieving your daughter but I think you might need an interpreter. If you like and my commander gives me permission I could accompany you."

Surprisingly, the relevant officer assented and less surprisingly Rick gladly accepted the offer. As he left the camp the gentle rays of fading afternoon imparted a benevolence to the scene. The blindfold routine was repeated for the first hour of the journey. With Sonia at his side Rick entered the hotel. Dressed in tight fitting jeans and with her long hair flowing free, her beauty was now more apparent.

Over a simple evening meal the rescue planner spoke of one more critical preparation. "I'll need to hire a self-drive car for a couple of days. We'll have to take one tomorrow morning and drive to General Santos where we'll have to spend tomorrow night."

"Hertz have an office here," added Sonia. "They should do."

When the hour came for turning in, Rick pointed to the second bed in the room and said to the girl, "That one's yours." Sonia smiled and hesitantly spoke. "I'm not quite sure how to put this but if it's all the same to you I'd rather share yours." At that moment she gently applied the chastest of kisses to his lips.

Sonia's request was one development that he hadn't at all anticipated. A look appeared on his face similar to the bewilderment of a lottery winner. On seeing his astonishment Sonia explained, "I don't want you to think I'm some cheap sort of girl but I'm a widow. My live-in husband was one of our group."

"Live-in husband?" interrupted Rick. "Yes. We weren't formally married."

"I see, a defacto," he commented. Continuing with her tale Sonia's almond eyes reflected sadness. "Romy was killed in a fire-fight almost two years ago with a squad of Special Forces soldiers sent from Manila." Rick obviously still couldn't see the connection between this misfortune and her request to share his bed.

"I haven't been with a man in all that time and a woman has needs," the girl exclaimed. "But... you live and work with hundreds of men."

"True, but I don't want to form a new relationship and casual encounters would be not only unwise in our situation; they are strictly forbidden." The penny finally dropped about the same time as a pendulum was stirring in his trousers.

The only light in the room was that emitted from a tiny bedside lamp. Sonia deftly pulled off her T-shirt. She hadn't been wearing a bra. Her full, rounded breasts with their erect, hard nipples reminded Rick of Marilyn's tender orbs and he felt a twinge of guilt. Still, it's what you don't do in life rather than what you've done that is the major cause of regret, he philosophized. Besides who could blame me with all the frustration engendered by this woman's to-ing and fro-ing. I have needs too. Sonia's jeans hit the floor with a pronounced 'clunk.' It was only a pity that the buckle on her belt wasn't made of gold.

Basic bikini briefs of the simplest white cotton framed a succulent looking mound and muscular but slender thighs. The female fighter then, ever so gently, removed Rick's clothing until he was as naked as a jaybird. Silently she removed her panties and pulled him onto the bed. A sparse covering of pubic vegetation clearly showed her lower lips in all their sensuality. Fractionally breaking the moment, she placed a condom in Rick's hand. "We don't want any accidents, do we?" The plastic in place, the moment returned. As the man mounted her she moaned, "It's been so long; too long." The moaning increased in volume and intensity until the bed itself was shaking. When the lovemaking had ended Sonia curled up stroking Rick's white torso. A few minutes later and the girl demanded another round. The pair fell asleep briefly. Rick's eyes opened as Sonia's lips were straining on his member so it could perform again.

"Aren't you feeling sleepy?" he softly inquired before realizing the inanity of his own question. "I need more and I have another request." His eyes wide Rick waited. "I would like you to perform a Baby Oil execution." Faced with the male's bewildered expression she explained. "I want you to penetrate my back door." At Rick's hesitation she pointed out that she had showered very thoroughly when they arrived at the hotel. As he obliged the out-of-his league Westerner couldn't help but silently hum the words from that great Neil Young song, 'been a miner for a heart of gold.' It was the first experience that Rick had ever had of anal sex. He couldn't say that he didn't enjoy it but sometimes, enough is enough.

Enough wasn't quite enough. At precisely 6:30 am Sonia dragged Rick into the shower, washed both their bodies, dragged him back to the bed and jumped on him. "Woman on top," she laughed. "It's the Islamic version of Women's Lib." By the time that the day's business needed attending to Rick wasn't altogether sorry. A dull ache in his testicles reminded him that *his* needs had been well and truly met for quite a while.

At the Hertz counter in Davao's office district Rick proudly flashed his Philippine driving license in company with an international credit card. "I'd like to rent a small car for two days but I'll need to return it to the airport."

"Certainly Sir," answered a smartly dressed young man. "That won't be a problem. Just return it in good condition with a full tank of gasoline." Rick agreed and a dark green, manual Mitsubishi Lancer was presented. The paperwork signed, the duo drove away. They'd already checked out of the hotel and headed for the highway. Ten kilometers out of town the bitumen ended and a road of gravel and all manner of dirt awaited their wheels.

"I wasn't expecting this," remarked the driver. "The Philippines boasts many surprises," returned his passenger. The winding track meandered past the odd nipa hut, countless varieties of palm trees and the occasional roadblock where bored-looking soldiers briefly waved them down. After the first Rick realized he was sweating. "Aren't you worried about being grabbed at a military checkpoint," he asked of his companion. "Not exactly," the girl returned. "That's not the way things generally work here. Besides if Allah wills that my time has come what I can do about it?"

Fifty kilometers from the city there were no checkpoints, hardly any signs of habitation and lots more palm trees. "You certainly took me by surprise last night," Rick said with a smile as he glanced away from the road for a second. "I thought I'd explained my reasons," Sonia snapped. "I didn't mean it that way," Rick went on, "but I just wasn't expecting anything like that."

"I'd have thought that being a Westerner and all, you'd have your fill of girls anytime you felt an itch. There are so many prostitutes in this country that, unless your wallet is empty, you'd never experience the sexual frustration that I feel."

"I haven't always lived in the Philippines you know," came the defensive reply. "For most of my life the chase of womanhood was a fruitless and expensive exercise. I'll admit that here things aren't too difficult."

"I'll say," retorted Sonia. "It's a good thing that most of the American military have left, for more reasons than one. They and lots of other foreigners have corrupted our women to the point that many of them will do almost anything for money. You don't have to go to Angeles or Manila to see it. Even in General Santos City and Marbel, which is an hour's jeep ride north, you can find many prostitutes." Rick laughed. "Well Filipinas are certainly attractive." Sonia was not amused. "This isn't a joke my friend. There is a huge problem here."

"I'll agree with that but maybe not for the reasons you think," said the driver with only one hand on the wheel.

Forty kilometers or so before the advent of General Santos the road was blocked. A line of vehicles patiently waited for two graders to clear it. "Mudslide," remarked the girl. "I hope we don't encounter anything like that on the way back tomorrow." There were several variables that Rick had failed to consider. While they waited their discussion continued. "What do you mean that you agree with me but for different reasons about our prostitution problem?" Rick thought it politic to give her a kiss on the cheek before continuing.

"Well, er… umm… when a girl decides she wants a bit she…er…"

"A bit of what?" came an interruption.

"You know, what you'd been missing for quite a while. When a girl needs some of that it isn't particularly difficult for her to find it; and quickly. For us blokes, I mean guys, the problem is much more involved unless we wish to directly use money. That's where prostitution comes in. I once knew a nurse in Australia who pointed to my dick and said, 'See that.' Then she pointed to her vagina and commented, 'With one of these I can get as many of those as I like.' Therein lies the inherent inequality of the sexes."

Before Sonia could speak again the road was clear and the tidy little convoy of waiting vehicles moved off. "Are you saying that it's all right for hundreds of thousands of women, many very young, to be exploited so you can scratch your itch? Mind you I hate those of them who willingly allow themselves to be sucked into a disgusting life for the shallowest of riches. They denigrate the female sex as a whole as well as themselves in the process." As the Lancer picked up speed the sound of gravel spewing out from under the wheels almost drowned her question. "No-one said anything about the exploitation and abuse of young girls being acceptable, but who do you think are the exploiters?"

"The men who buy them of course." For a while at least, Rick was going to have to resume his former vocation on this journey. "Do you think that the stupid former president of this country and her erstwhile sidekick, Miriam Defensor Santiago, with their ill-gotten millions are not to blame for this exploitation?" Sonia looked pensive. The teacher continued his lesson. "In many countries, especially those in the Third World, the ever-widening gap between the rich and the poor ensures a vast increase in the numbers of recruits to the prostitution and bar industries. Those responsible for this widening gap, the wealthy and corrupt people, of which there are many in the Philippines, are ultimately to blame for the fate of those young girls."

Sonia remained silent so Rick went on. "With the huge increase in the numbers of prostitutes supply-and-demand economics takes over and prices become much cheaper and more affordable. As a result more and more males with unsatisfied sexual needs take advantage of this solution. On the other side of the coin this wouldn't happen either if so many women didn't play so damned hard to get."

"I'd never really thought of it in that way. I suppose there aren't many prostitutes who come from even middle-class homes." Her companion smiled as the Mitsubishi hit a bump and she almost landed on the gear stick. "Mind you, I once knew of a Filipino woman from a rich family in Olongapo who, after living for years in Australia, ditched her husband and became a madam in a Melbourne brothel."

"What's a brothel?" Although relatively accomplished in English some words were too arcane for Sonia. "A short-time establishment, like a casa or a barbershop," Rick responded. "Anyway, as I was saying, the exception proves the rule. The link between sexual exploitation and economics is totally undeniable."

It was dusk when the dirt road metamorphosed into another stretch of bitumen and the sky was completely dark when the insipid lights of General Santos came into view. "I haven't been here since I was a little girl," commented Sonia. "Unlike you I had the misfortune to visit only a few weeks ago," laughed the man with the mission. The immediate matter was to contact the local constabulary. Sonia discretely stayed in the car as Rick entered the station. After explaining his situation and showing his passport along with some legal papers Rick glanced nervously at the young officer behind the desk. "As a father myself, I can imagine how you feel. Unfortunately this is a civil matter and we can't assist you. You will have to take your child with your own resources but, provided that you don't hurt anyone in the process, we won't interfere. All I can say is Good Luck." Rick's details were noted on a register and he returned to his waiting accomplice. The next stop was at their intended lodgings for the night.

"We're missionaries with the Church of the Latter Day Saints," declared Sonia at the counter of the Golden Pineapple. "My husband and I have been working in Mindanao for several years." The desk clerk of the hotel couldn't have cared less if they'd been Martians. "Sixty pisos for the night," he declared. "That's expensive," returned the girl before a gentle kick from her male counterpart convinced her to shut up. "Your room is 305 down the corridor to the left. Have a good night's rest." The clerk deposited the cash in a lockable drawer and returned to his magazine.

Not wishing to venture onto the streets at all the twosome contented themselves with cold fish and rice served up by the hotel restaurant, if you could call it that, for dinner. Immediately on its completion they disappeared behind the door of room 305. Amazingly there was a television.

However the single channel broadcast Filipino soaps interspersed with agrarian news. "We must get to sleep," declared Rick. "It's an early start and a big day tomorrow." With that he pulled the plug on the squawking box.

"You're ready for bed then?" intoned Sonia with a wicked gleam in her eye. With the lights out she only required a single performance from Rick for which he was partially grateful. By nine o'clock they were both in the land of Nod. The mantle of night was just beginning to recede when Rick sprang out of bed, waking the girl in the process. "It's five-thirty already. We had best get moving."

The sun's rays were just beginning to offer their warmth when the dark green Lancer with its conspiratorial occupants stopped outside the abode of Jasmine's grandmother. Rick had hoped the child might be playing in the yard. There was no sign of her or of any other stirrings. The stillness was almost eerie in its intensity. The gate was closed fast and padlocked. Getting out of the vehicle Rick put the bolt cutters to good use. Before he could attack the offending lock he was required to remove a goodly portion of wire. Once through the gate he strode directly to the door. Finding it shut fast, he didn't know what to do next. All he could think of was to knock loudly. After a couple of minutes, it swung back and there stood an elderly woman, rubbing her eyes. "Good morning Lola (Grandma)." At that instant the child-in-question ran out of the bedroom and called, "Daddy."

"Jasmine, I've got a new car. Would you like to go for a ride?" When she looked blank, he rephrased the question in his very limited Filipino language. "Mayron Ko ang kotse." The girl excitedly exclaimed, "Yes!" Without losing a second Rick scooped up his daughter and told the granny that they'd be back in thirty minutes. He quickly exited the damaged gate and deposited Jasmine in the back seat of the Mitsubishi. "Success!" exclaimed Sonia. Rick turned the key in the ignition. Nothing! Again, he turned it and the moaning of a bankrupt starter motor was audible. The battery for some reason was nearly flat. Beads of sweat formed on his forehead as he tried a third time. With the kind of hesitation that often makes itself felt in the critical moment between life and death the motor reluctantly chose life.

As the vehicle disappeared down the street there were still no signs of activity anywhere. "Whew!" breathed Rick in a sigh of intense relief as they hit the highway. "That was close but we made it. One hurdle down and only a few to go. It's a good thing that Granny wasn't alert enough to wonder how I'd passed the locked gate." Sonia spoke to the child in Filipino dialect at this point. Her English had become very limited over the last twelve months indeed. "Your daddy wants to take you back to Australia. Would you like that?" The child's instantly happy expression was sufficient answer.

An hour later and the trio's vehicle was again in that infamous no-man's-land between General Santos and Davao. Sonia switched on the radio. Two Filipino songs, one good and the other lousy, were played in succession. Then a husky voice in local dialect, spoke. "You are listening to RVBK General Santos. In breaking news there has been a kidnap of a child from Polomok, South Cotabato. Although information is still sketchy it is believed that the child is the nine-year old daughter of Patrick and Patricia Daly, a wealthy couple who own a sprawling cattle ranch in the north of Canada." Rick's laughter drowned the voice until his accomplice pinched him. "Further, it is believed that the abduction was performed by a Muslim kidnap gang for ransom." The voice finished and Randy Santiago's popular song, 'Babaero Daw,' blared forth from the speakers.

"At least they got one bit right?" smirked Rick. "The bit about Muslim involvement." Sonia didn't quite see the irony. "Ha! Ha!" was all she could manage. Around a winding bend a military checkpoint appeared with five soldiers pointing their Armalites. As the Lancer slowed down the signs of sudden perspiration appeared on the faces of both adult occupants. "Ma-ayong Buntag, Mr. Daly." The soldier smiled. "Have a good journey."

Ten kilometers further on and Rick's hands were no longer trembling on the wheel. Two more roadblocks were just as pleasant to pass. At a point where they passed thickish jungle that the loggers hadn't yet reached but with a few clearings Sonia's hand moved across. The stick that it landed on wasn't the gear lever. "Now that everything is more relaxed could we stop for a bit?" An infinitesimal shudder gripped the driver's being. Surely this whole trip wasn't a setup for a real kidnapping? The question flashed through his mind. "Why should we stop just when things are going well?" Gently rubbing the chosen object, Sonia spoke with the voice of a schoolgirl. "We could stop for a bit of...you know."

"At a time like this and with my daughter on board?" challenged Rick. "We could always go into the bushes," said Sonia earnestly. "I don't think so," was the reply and the Mitsubishi Lancer continued on its inexorable journey.

The wheels rolled as fast as their caretaker could safely push them until the familiar landscape of Davao Airport came into sight. Rick was all smiles as he surrendered the Lancer to a Hertz employee. Straight to the ticket counter the trio then proceeded. "One adult and one child ticket to Manila please."

"I'm sorry Sir; the next two flights are full. We can fit you on the 4:30 pm one though." The Philippine Airlines' girl was courteous and blessed of a winning smile. "That'll have to do then, I suppose. Thank you." Rick paid for the tickets with cash. Outside in the cowboy zone again the unlikely couple, with child in tow, sat down to eat and drink. "You've got four hours to wait. Perhaps we could be creative in how we use them." The shapely rebel looked impish. "This is not the time. We'll just wait here and keep our eyes open for any impending trouble."

One hundred and thirty kilometers away dozens of prying eyes were searching the vicinity of the airport at General Santos. Every imaginable petty figure of authority joined the civilians in their task of saving a child from the criminal infidels. Barangay or local council chiefs, officers of the Ronda, a night-time group of officially sanctioned vigilantes whose job was to prevent cattle rustling and even some schoolboy prefects joined the quest. Oddly enough, those with much more immediate and effective power, the military, had been left out of the loop.

Not long after leaving Polomok Rick had insisted that Jasmine be dressed as a boy in an attempt to prevent possible problems. "Ayoko, Papa, I don't want to be a boy," his daughter had fussed to no avail. Bribed with some chocolates she'd finally allowed Sonia to dress her in the disguise that Rick had brought. Sitting in the darkness of the interior of a tiny carinderia with their faces peering outwards the compact group ate, drank soft drinks and beer respectively and waited.

At a quarter past four Rick and Jasmine stood up to begin the walk to the terminal. "I want to thank you for your help and wish your company all the best," Rick said sincerely as Sonia kissed him. "I hope I see you again but I know it is unlikely," he added. "Please allow me to make a donation to your cause."

Discretely he slipped a bundle of notes, totaling at least P 2,000 into the girl's hand. Reluctantly she accepted the gift and the smallest of tears appeared in her left eye as Rick and his daughter strode out of her field of vision, which was never to behold them again.

While clasping Jasmine's hand and walking quickly Rick couldn't help himself thinking, "It's a pity Sonia doesn't live a few blocks from me. A girl like that could be very useful." Boarding passes in hand father and daughter walked the final few meters to the plane. As the air lifted the wings Rick breathed another sigh.

❖ ❖ ❖ ❖ ❖ ❖ ❖ ❖

Freshly arrived from a day at the factory Marilyn sat over a simple evening meal with Leticia. "I do hope Sir is doing all right with his trip," the short girl exclaimed. "So do I Leticia but I very much doubt it. I'm sure he's out of his depth on this one." Marilyn's fear also showed her own sense of betrayal. "I should have gone with him to minimize the disaster."

"Foreigners think differently from us," was all the maid could add to the subject. "Not too many things have been going well round here, have they?" Marilyn felt that some sort of apology was necessary to the helper. Leticia frowned. "I don't ever remember a time in my life when things were going all that well!"

For an inexplicable reason Marilyn at that precise second wondered how her family was getting along across the waters. All the trouble with Rick and that Maria girl, which was followed by tsismis and more trouble had left some dents in the family's community standing. An incredibly sleepy place is not always conducive to a peaceful soul. Marilyn's thoughts soon drifted away and she and Leticia settled to watch a Joseph Estrada movie. The hour was eight on a Friday evening.

At that instant, across the sea in Cagmanipis, Flora was also looking at her watch. Dinner's been ready for over an hour and my useless husband hasn't yet turned up. What on earth could have delayed his return from his stupid fishing? Flora ate her own dinner before it spoiled any further and resigned the latecomer to cold leftovers.

"You can't go now. We've just finished making love." Victoria was upset. A child cried from the other room. "Go back to sleep, Sancha," the mother yelled. "I've got to go. I'm over an hour late already." Ronaldo was definite. "I'll see you tomorrow." Victoria was visibly upset. "I've got some news for you!"

"It'll have to wait." Ronaldo was gone.

He didn't like cheating on his wife. That's not to say that he didn't enjoy it but he didn't like it. It isn't really my fault, he thought as he walked towards his home. Flora's been rather uninterested for a matter of years and since that business with Rick and Marilyn she turned distinctly cold. Like any other man I have my needs and they should be met. Victoria also had needs and her husband had a very valid excuse for not fulfilling them. He was dead. Besides, Ronaldo's soliloquy continued, the affair was an accident. After rescuing her daughter, we became friends and one thing led to another. Victoria has a really good body for her age and Flora will never find out anyway.

Flora glanced at the clock after finishing her meal. It was 8:45 and still no fisherman. How on earth could he spend so long fishing and hardly catch anything? If he was younger and better looking, I might suspect that he was playing up she considered but as it is he is just lucky to have me. Where would a lazy, pot-bellied man find a woman to put up with him? Even worse he just doesn't consider how important a good reputation is. Any father worth his salt would have insisted that Marilyn quit working for that licentious foreigner. Ronaldo just doesn't seem to know what is really important in life.

As the door opened and a guilty apparition walked in Flora raised her voice. "What do you mean by arriving home an hour-and-a-half late for dinner?" Her husband looked sheepish. "I got my line caught in a deep hole and it took me quite some time to disengage it without damaging my rod and tackle." Flora was not amused. "If there were any barbershops or houses of sin round here, I could just imagine what sort of hole you might have got your line stuck in. Your cold dinner is on the table. Another ten minutes and

I was going to give it to some deserving creatures – the pigs." After forcing down the unappetizing mash Ronaldo went to another part of the house to listen to the radio.

When he'd departed from her abode Victoria was naked and upset. Her thoughts were emotional and all over the place. Typical lousy man; dumps his load in me and then bolts for the door. He takes advantage of my lonely situation and seduces me. Anything to get his rocks off. Then when I've developed feelings for him he treats me like a meal stop on the highway. He just comes around here to go 'fishing' and plumb the depths. He always has an excuse for not giving me proper time and tenderness. Today it seemed like he was here only long enough to perform the deed. The time just went so quickly. I feel sorry for his wife; not because he is unfaithful but in view of the way he treats me she must have a real time of it. I've dishonored my dead husband's memory for this joker. What a mistake! And today of all days he can't spare a few extra moments with me. I wanted to tell him that I'm pregnant. The doctor in Calbayog was certain. Luckily he didn't know I was a widow. Ronaldo just couldn't even wait a minute for something so important. Anyway, he'll find out soon enough and I imagine his wife will too.

The day that followed the night of the cold dinner Flora took more tsismis than sales in the store. While Ronaldo was having a quiet beer on the porch she questioned him. "You were seen leaving that widow lady, Victoria's house one morning a week ago."

"Yes, I know her," replied Ronaldo as he knocked over his beer. "I rescued one of her children some time ago and I occasionally visit to give her a hand. She has really struggled since her husband died."

On the next occasion that the hunter of the sea called on Victoria she broke the news of her condition on his arrival. "I don't know what to say," was all he could manage. "I thought you might not. Strange about that!" There was no illicit sex that day and very little ever after. Two months later and Victoria's expanding belly was noticeable. The tsismis quickly caught up with it. "Buntis, I tell you," exclaimed a woman who was an expert on such matters when she passed by Flora's store. "She's obviously very pregnant. Her husband's been dead for two years so it must be a bloody miracle," laughed the expert. Although most Filipinos do not question the existence of miracles a woman in Victoria's situation was not likely to be considered the partner of the Holy Ghost. Flora did her best to hide her feelings of shock and terror.

Confronting Ronaldo with the news, Flora just knew who the culprit was. "You've obviously been giving the widow Victoria more than a hand. How could you? How could you?" Ronaldo broke down and confessed all. "It was an accident that just happened. I'm very sorry." Flora burst into a cascade of sobs. Ten minutes later when the torrent had passed, she resumed her anger. "You are grounded. No more fishing or any other solo expeditions. You can help me in the store for most of the day."

"Yes dear," Ronaldo meekly answered.

Flora knew the speed and power of the tsismis. She had to tell all of the children the disgusting news before they learned it from others. Jun and Juliet, along with her husband, Dodong, were easy to reach. Flora just hoped that the letter she posted to Marilyn would reach her before the gossip did.

◇◇◇◇◇◇◇◇◇

Flying low over Manila Bay Rick could see the lights of the composite of hopes, dreams, and fears and vice that made that city. Exiting the barren arrival hall with its sheets of iron Rick and Jasmine strode past the waiting taxis and porters and made for the street three hundred meters away. "Ako ay kapoy (I'm tired) Papa. Do we have to walk?" At that he lifted his daughter onto his shoulders, and she giggled. Hailing a passing cab, the pair headed for one of the most expensive Makati hotels. Better safe than sorry, Rick considered. I should act out of character at a time like this.

Remembering his small change Rick had no problems with the taxi. After he'd handed over a modest tip the cab and its moderately-contented driver departed. Before sleeping Rick spoiled the little girl with the most expensive dinner she'd ever had in her young life. At the very least it must have been a considerable improvement on her recent diet.

Sipping his coffee on the following morning the 'kidnapper' kept glancing at the clock on the restaurant wall. Eight-thirty was followed by eight forty-five and then by nine. The Australian embassy would open at ten. Arriving in the

Paseo de Roxas Rick couldn't help but notice how different it looked without the explosions and gunfire.

The embassy was located on the eleventh floor of an unremarkable office tower. After passing through some rudimentary security Rick and the child were faced with a room full of young Filipinas and elderly Australian men. A sign on the wall announced that it was the area for the processing of spouse visas. Obviously he'd walked into the wrong room. A little further along the corridor was a smaller space with nobody waiting. Its nomenclature announced it to be the designated area for passport and citizenship matters.

After Rick rang the counter bell a slender but plain woman in her middle thirties came from an office behind. "Yes, what I can I do for you?"

"My daughter here is an Australian but her mother left her with her grandmother in Mindanao without my permission - we have joint custody you see - and the maternal relatives wouldn't let me take her home. Accordingly I was forced to grab her and obviously I wasn't able to get her passport." Rick was speaking with the speed of urgency. "Not so fast, mate," the plain lady interrupted. "You mean you took the child by force?"

"It's ok," babbled Rick. "I didn't break any Philippine laws or hurt anyone in the process. We just need a new passport."

"You are the Daly fellow then, somehow mixed up in reports of a kidnapping in South Cotabato? We heard about that incident."

"It was no kidnapping. I have a perfect right to take my child." Rick sounded annoyed.

"Where's the mother then?"

"She's in Sydney. She returned there after dumping Jasmine in Mindanao more than a year ago. Once I found out about it, I had to do the right thing."

The consular officer conveyed that calm sense of innumerable obstacles for which that ilk is famous. "Mr. Daly, since Jasmine's mother would need to give her permission for a new passport in addition to your granting permission, it won't be possible to issue one unless you have her agreement."

"That's not bloody likely is it?" challenged the increasingly irate and desperate father. "Besides the mother managed to get the child two passports, I later learned, one Australian and one Philippine, without my permission."

"I know nothing about that Mr. Daly but the fact remains that you will need her mother's permission before we can issue Jasmine with a new travel document. If you like, we can try to contact her in Sydney on your behalf. If you give me your current address in Manila we will keep you advised of any developments."

None too happy about this twist in the tale Rick had little other choice and so obliged. With Jasmine in tow he returned to the Nikko Garden hotel. "Hey Marian, it sounds like you had a live one there," a voice echoed from the rear office. "You know what these dropkick Aussie men, who see Asia as a sexual hunting ground, are like Jill. They're basically losers hiding a pedophile within that's just dying to get out. There is obviously something terribly wrong with the guy. Otherwise he'd have married an Australian girl in the first place. He is also probably one of those who, when faced with a form asking for his religion, writes 'practicing alcoholic'." Jill laughed. "How long will you give him the run around for?" she added.

"As long as possible, ten days at least," Marian responded. "Of course the situation would have been quite different if it'd been an Aussie woman who'd been previously married to a Filipino bloke. In that case we'd have issued a new passport within an hour." Both Marian and Jill let loose with full belly laughs at that point. There was no one around who could hear anyway.

After eleven days of basically being holed up in the hotel Rick received a call from the embassy. "This is Marian Dobbs. We can issue you a single trip travel document for Jasmine as long as you take her straight back to her mother in Sydney."

"That is the only place I can take her," Rick replied "as I have no relatives in Australia who could look after her and I have a business here." He thought he could faintly hear the word 'monkey' on the other end of the receiver but he wasn't sure.

During the preceding days he'd thought about ringing Marilyn and telling her about the mixed success of the Mindanao venture but then he recalled her act of betrayal and decided to let her stew for a while longer. His perfect woman certainly seemed to lack courage. Rick's mind drifted back to a time when they were both seated in a beer garden on Fuente Osmeña. An argument had started between a small group of Vietnam vets and a number of Arab Muslims. One of the vets and an aggressive drunken Arab were on the point of coming to blows as one of the more moderate Islamic group tried to restrain his comrade. Rick thought that he should try to calm down the excitable Vietnam veteran and rose from his chair. "Let's go," whispered Marilyn but Rick would have none of it. He intervened and helped to avoid a brawl. By the time he returned to his seat Marilyn was white-faced and crying. "I don't like trouble," she sobbed. In the back of his mind Rick had unconsciously made a mental note.

The embassy finally agreeing to issue a document, father and daughter once more strode the uneven pavements of the Paseo de Roxas. Two days later the pair flew to Sydney. Rick had finally phoned Marilyn to tell his story and promised he would return to Cebu within three weeks.

It was a hot summer day as Rick and his daughter reached Emily's apartment in Bondi and knocked on the door. A Filipino sailor, clad only in a bathrobe, opened it. "We've come to see Emily," Rick announced. "Just a moment please." The sailor disappeared and five minutes later Emily emerged in a black evening dress.

"Jasmine darling, Mommy missed you so much," she cried as she threw her arms around the child. Rick wasn't sure how much longer she would be able to snow-job Jasmine but she hadn't been able to fool him in years. Turning a hostile gaze to her ex she said, "The embassy told me what you'd done. How dare you upset my family and spoil Jasmine's cultural time there!"

"Cut the crap. You can't leave our daughter in that dump for years on the pretense of learning a dubious culture. I shouldn't think it would take too long to master the valuable portions of it anyway."

Emily looked as if she wished to knife Rick on the spot. She had attempted the procedure some years before during their marriage but was unsuccessful.

"Don't even contemplate taking Jasmine back there and dumping her again," Rick spoke assertively. "If you are foolish enough to do so your family there are very likely to suffer." Emily turned red. "What! You are threatening to have them killed?" Rick produced a laconic smile. "I hadn't actually thought of that but I believe contract murders are relatively cheap in that place. What I was meaning is that I could take legal action against your mother and the gang for publicly calling me a kidnapper on national radio and in the press, endangering mine and Jasmine's lives." Emily merely stared. "I have been in touch with my attorney and he informed me that I would be very likely to win such a legal suit."

"Jasmine will be staying here with me, you bastard. I just missed her so much. Of course it will be difficult with work and babysitting costs." Rick kissed Jasmine and, uttering the shallowest of goodbyes to her mother, turned on his heels. Less than a fortnight later he was in the sky on the way back to Cebu. Much as he loathed leaving his daughter with Emily he simply did not want her growing up in the Philippines and therefore there was no other choice.

Chapter Eleven

Since Rick's departure for Mindanao the seconds had ticked by ever so slowly for Marilyn. The factory had developed problems; production was down and absenteeism had increased. The temporary boss did her best to correct the problems but all she could think about was Rick. She should never have let him go there alone. Why was she such a coward?

Ten days after Leticia and she had found themselves without their customary dominant male a letter arrived at the gate. Seeing that it was from her mother Marilyn smiled and rushed inside to open it. After the first few lines her face changed entirely and her eyes couldn't hide her distress. "What's the matter Maam?" asked the maid. "There is some financial trouble for our family," Marilyn mumbled with a suitable falsehood.

Her own father; how could he do that to her mother? It seemed to be the nature of men. No doubt Rick was sating his inherent lust somewhere or other. I'd have been better off if I'd been born a lesbian or else had entered a convent, as was my intention as a teenager, she pondered. Marilyn now had three sources of consternation, anxiety over Rick, misery over her father's indiscretion and a professional concern over the downturn in the business.

Sipping a glass of wine at 38,000 feet Rick was engaged in a conversation with a bus driver from Adelaide on his first vacation to the Philippines. "Four weeks ago I was sitting in my house in Cebu then, a few days later, I was traversing jungle in Mindanao, and for the last week or so I have braved the vagaries of Sydney. I just don't know where the time went. It seems like yesterday when I left."

"You know all about the Philippines then?" commented the bus driver thinking that he'd been unlucky enough to land a seat next to a proverbial big-noter. Rick took another sip of red and smiled. "Nobody knows all about the Philippines, not even the Filipinos. It's a land of surprises." Not wanting to receive more advice and commentary the bus driver ended the conversation with a sullen, "I suppose I'll be surprised then."

By the time Rick and his bags arrived at the gate of the house in La Paloma it was nine o'clock on a typical evening. Leticia performed the honors of admitting the master and struggling with his case. Entering the sala Rick observed Marilyn quietly watching TV, too quietly. "Have you been up to some mischief while I've been away?" he asked, half-jokingly.

"I feel guilty," replied Marilyn.

"Why what have you done?"

"I should have gone with you to Mindanao. I'm such a coward. I'm so sorry." Rick smiled. "That's fine. I was able to do without you in any case. Forget it." The girl's face was still downcast. "I also received some very bad news from home. My father made a village woman pregnant." She then described the unfortunate episode as Leticia had gone to her room.

After Rick's commiserations and a discrete touchy-feely Marilyn still appeared concerned. "What else could have possibly gone wrong?" Marilyn burst into tears. "The factory has had problems. There were many absentees while you were away and production is down enough that some orders are going to be late in fulfilment. I did my best but I'm only a woman." More tears flowed. "I'm sure we'll be able to repair the damage," he soothed. "It's all right." Very quietly he whispered, "I still love you." At that Marilyn's face brightened a little.

In answer to her questions Rick minimized his little adventure to the point that it sounded quite boring and laborious. "It must have been so dangerous and lonely for you," sympathized his paramour. "Not at all. Piece of cake really. I simply turned up in a car and grabbed the kid. The most difficult part was taking her to her mother's house in Australia."

"Why was that difficult? Did you and her get involved again... you know?" Marilyn looked worried. "You have to be joking!" Rick laughed. "Her Filipino sailor boyfriend was pleasant enough but the bitch herself is still trying to engineer my downfall."

A relieved Marilyn rubbed her hand on his thigh provoking a subtle reaction. "Leticia's asleep. Let's go." She then led him ever so quietly to his room. In the silent darkness Marilyn, for the first time, offered no resistance. He slid into her as neatly as a finger into a glove. The warmth and moistness was almost too much to bear. Then the phone rang. In panic Marilyn disengaged herself, threw on her shorts and shirt and rushed down the steps just as Leticia had arrived in pursuit of the same quarry. It was a wrong number. Marilyn bade Leticia goodnight and went to her room, desperately hoping that the maid hadn't seen the quarters from whence she came.

Nothing was said over breakfast and the boss accompanied by the bookkeeper left for work. Two more days passed. On the evening of the third the phone rang. Marilyn picked it up but the person on the other end rang off. Twenty minutes later it rang again and Leticia answered. Again the caller hung up. An hour later when the girls were sleeping and Rick was sipping bourbon the wretched implement again sprung into life. "Hello," he shouted into the mouthpiece with extreme impatience.

"It's me Alma," a young girl's voice whispered. "I'm sorry to ring you at this hour but it's an emergency. Dad is in Manila on a business trip and Mum has become really strange. She's acting really funny!" Slightly less impatient Rick offered advice. "Why don't you call a doctor?"

"I tried that," the teenager responded, "but when mum saw me on the phone she became violent. I ran out of the house and I'm calling you from a store several blocks away. Could you please come and help? I don't know what else to do!" A sobbing sound seeped through Rick's earpiece.

"I'll be there as soon as I can, probably forty minutes or so. Just wait outside your house." The call ended. Rick left his house and waited for a taxi in Tres. Fifty minutes later and he was outside Noy's house in Mactan. Alma emerged from behind a shrub. "Do you think my breasts are big enough, Rick?" Rick appeared nonplussed. "They're fine for your age but this is hardly the time for such questions." Alma leaned forward and hugged Rick. The taxi disappeared and Rick prepared for a scene. "Relax," said the girl. "Mum seems to be all right now. In fact she went out to visit a friend." The late night Good Samaritan appeared less than amused. "Come in and let me get you a coffee or a drink," the girl insisted. "It is the least I can do."

Reluctantly Rick entered the house, empty save for himself and Alma. No sooner were they inside the door than the fourteen-year-old hugged him again, this time kissing him passionately on the lips. "I'm sorry I had to trick you this way Rick. Dad *is* in Manila but mum's fine. She's gone to visit her sister on Negros for a few days. I knew you wouldn't come if I didn't tell it like that. Anyway, now we are alone, together."

Frightened, Rick resumed his former vocation of teacher of the young. "Now Alma, I think you are feeling confused. This is just not a suitable way for a young lady to behave." The girl attempted to kiss him again at this point and removed her shirt revealing smallish breasts. "You don't understand. I love you. I really love you. I knew it from the first moment that I saw you, even though I was a child then."

His fear increasing Rick tried to defuse the situation. "Think about it, Alma. You are only fourteen. Your father and mother are my friends. There is just no way I would ever even consider deflowering you!"

Alma laughed. "There'd be no deflowering, as you put it, involved. Some boys at school saw to that over a year ago but I don't love them or want them. I want you and I must have you or I'll die. You don't want me to die do you?"

"Of course I don't want anything bad to happen to you and that is the main reason that I cannot do what you are asking." Rick had never appeared so firm.

At that point Alma dropped her school skirt and her panties in quick succession and launched her naked young body at him. Rick fled. He exited the house and literally ran for his life. Eventually he found a vacant taxi and returned home.

The house was quiet. He was relieved, as his absence hadn't been noticed. The girls were still fast asleep. The idea of explaining the incident to Marilyn didn't appeal at all. He wasn't up to an endless succession of "I told you so's." As Rick's troubled head hit the pillow he just hoped that Alma would forget about what had transpired and grow up a little in the process.

Two days later the phone rang at 8 pm. Rick was the closest and therefore the one to pick up. It was Alma. "Why did you treat me that way? You know

I love you. You think of me as a child but I'm not. I know my own heart." Rick hesitated before answering. "The whole thing is just not right, Alma. Think about it. Take my advice and get over it. You'll thank me for it later when you're older." The sound of sobbing could be heard before the click.

There were several more instances of evening phone calls. Sometimes the caller would simply hang up. This invariably happened if Marilyn or Leticia answered. One more tearful conversation between the youngster and Rick resulted in his making a point not to be the one to pick up the handset.

Every evening he lived in dread of the phone ringing. Alma had never tried the factory. Leticia remarked one time, "We've been getting a lot of wrong numbers lately, Sir. It's amazing that they were all so impolite as to simply hang up without speaking." The bookkeeper secretary harbored secret suspicions that the mystery caller was some girlfriend of the boss. Three evenings went by without a single call. On the fourth the phone rang. Rick started in his seat. It was Marilyn who answered. "It's for you Rick. Some guy from a computer company." The caller was a telemarketer suggesting that Rick upgrade his office systems to an early version of Microsoft Windows. "Not at the moment thanks," murmured Rick before returning to his seat and a cold beer that he definitely needed.

Ten days passed with no mystery hang-ups or unexplained calls. Rick began to relax and feel optimistic again. The next phone call wasn't from Alma; nor was it a routine matter. "Hi Rick, its Noy here. A newborn niece of mine is being christened in just over a week and we'd like to invite you and Marilyn." A thousand excuses for not being able to attend crossed Rick's mind but he knew that none would be believed and if he didn't go considerable offence would be caused. "I'd be honored to come. When and where is it?" Noy provided the details. "Eleven o'clock on Sunday June 20th at St. Mary of the Fields Church on Romala Street. See you there."

All Rick needed was a christening gift and lots of courage. Each day between the invitation and the event swelled into a mini version of eternity. The woman of both business and house, in contrast, was looking forward to the occasion. "There'll be so many people there, Rick, including lots of pretty girls," she teased. "Besides, after a christening, wedding or a funeral for that matter, Filipinos invariably hold some sort of party. It'll be great fun."

On the evening of Saturday the 19th Rick consumed four rum Cokes in quick succession and went to bed early. The desk calendar in his bedroom reminded him that the year was 1995 and he was getting older, in case he'd forgotten. Sleep and strange dreams overtook him. The sun was well advanced when Marilyn knocked on his door. "Better get up Rick. We don't want to be late."

Two coffees later and Rick, in his Sunday best, exited the gate with his excited companion. Twenty minutes later and St. Mary's loomed before them. One of Cebu's taller churches, it was well over a hundred years old and built of such strong stone that it oozed solidity and safety. A huge crowd had gathered. Nothing had prepared Rick for the sight of one hundred and fifty people buzzing on the steps. Still, he mused, I remember my mother once saying, 'Safety in numbers.'

The service passed without incident. Rick insisted that the pair sit down the back. "I never feel comfortable in churches," he commented. "Perhaps that's because you have a black soul," answered his lady. Once the spirit of the infant had been thus protected from the forces of Darkness the crowd dispersed only to reform in a large restaurant that had been booked for the occasion. The generous structure of Christopher's Gourmet Philippine diner fairly hummed with rushing waiters, purring ceiling fans and the throng of guests hell-bent on committing at least one or two of the seven deadly sins.

Marilyn and Rick had hardly been seated for five minutes when Noy, his wife and daughter strode over. "Great celebration isn't it?" Noy remarked. Rick agreed but then a knife-edge of terror coursed through his entire being. Alma didn't say anything but was staring at him with the fixed gaze of the insane. Marilyn noticed that his hands were shaking and most likely, others noticed it also. "What's wrong with you?" she inquired when the trio had returned to their seats. "Nothing," replied the man. "For a second I just felt as if a shadow had passed over my grave. I don't know why." One of the finely manicured and slender hands of Rick's personal temptress gripped his in support. Marilyn had never looked more beautiful. Her hair framed her face in the most sensuous manner and the finest frock she possessed hugged her body in lilac bliss.

The baptismal event had, for Rick, passed with the personal horror of the Day of Judgment. He'd hardly spoken on the way home and it was a full two hours after again being ensconced in his domicile before he returned to his normal self. Some jokes and laughter around the dinner table that evening saw the day consigned to the dustbin of history. A tropical downpour of the rainy season seemed to wash away the sins and troubles of the very pavements outside.

School was out on a typically muggy Thursday afternoon and Alma thought she might do some shopping in Colon before returning home. Alighting from the human crush of the jeepney she made her way to Gaisano Metro where she bought some perfume, new underwear and some costume jewelry. The shopping done she thought it might be cool to hang out in McDonalds for a while. Ten minutes later and she was seated by a window, sipping a chocolate milkshake. Her shortened uniform skirt rode high on her brown thighs exposing a triangular patch of blue panty to the view of the world. Her eyes were casting about the scene in an unconscious search for muscular young men. There weren't any. Several obese schoolboys were tucking into their double-cheeseburgers and a number of young females were chattering at full tilt.

Another bored sip of the choco-shake and her attention was suddenly hijacked. Two young women at the next table were engaged in the most earnest of conversations. The one with the longer hair was relaying a story to her overly made up companion.

"This guy actually boasted to me how he and a buddy cemented a two-piso piece to a table in a restaurant with super glue and then moved to another table to observe. According to him, several people sat down and while there attempted to pocket the coin, only to find it stuck fast. Sounds like a remake of the old sword in the stone, doesn't it?" The listener giggled. "Each time somebody tried and failed to pick up the coin this guy and his buddy would laugh uproariously in order to direct maximum embarrassment at the poor unfortunate."

"That's nasty," remarked the made-up girl before the storyteller continued. "Apparently one young man came in, found the coin stuck fast, produced a screwdriver from his pocket and with a swift motion prized it loose and flung it into his pocket. The two foreigners who had orchestrated all this then clapped loudly to again cause embarrassment. Much to their chagrin the youth smiled and bowed. We Filipinos are not as stupid as many foreigners think and, I might add, that tale is pretty mild compared with some things I could tell you about his doings when I worked in La Paloma."

The powdered listener glanced at her watch. "Relax," cried the athletic-looking girl who'd just finished the story. "We still have thirty minutes before our karate classes begin." At that moment a young voice from the next table made itself heard. "Excuse me," Alma broke into their conversation, "You know Rick Daly?" Both females turned their gaze to the adjacent schoolgirl and jointly replied in the affirmative. "Why don't you join us?" suggested Lina.

Alma moved her legs and her milkshake. "I'm Cecilia and this is Lina," announced the athletic girl with the long hair. Taking her seat Alma introduced herself. Cecilia leaned forward. "Don't tell me a young girl like you also knows that creepy foreigner?" Alma appeared embarrassed. "Yes," she replied, "he's a friend of my parents. I thought he was nice initially but now…."

"Hold on kid," soothed Lina. "We both have had unfortunate experiences with this man. He appears charming at first but underneath he is a slime-ball. He was my boyfriend briefly but he treated me like shit. Cecilia, on the other hand, used to work for him and he attacked her before firing her out."

A tear welled in Alma's right eye. "You two have been lucky it seems. He raped me."

"What!" The combined voices of Cecilia and Lina bounced off the ceiling. "How did an asshole like that get his filthy hands on a sweet young thing like you?" Cecilia sympathetically inquired.

The schoolgirl began sobbing and tried to speak through her tears. "It happened three weeks ago but I'll go back to the beginning," she blurted. As the tears diminished she continued. "Rick is friendly with my parents and visited our home quite often. At first when I was young it was all right. However ever since I turned twelve and my breasts began to grow he started paying me so much attention that it made me feel uncomfortable."

"That somehow doesn't surprise me," remarked Lina. "I'm sorry," she apologized, "Go on."

"Well," Alma ruefully stated, "Things remained uncomfortable for the next year or more. It was just unpleasant and scary but I didn't worry too much about it. Then, in recent months, my Dad was out quite a bit at night; you know what men are like; and Mum started threatening to leave him. Dad became scared and began bringing home flowers and all that stuff. One evening Dad suggested that he take Mum away for a weekend like when they were courting years ago. Mum was pleased with the offer but worried about leaving me on my own for even a night or two. They were discussing the idea when there was a knock on the door. It was our Mr. Daly on his way home from the airport after a brief trip to Manila. As soon as he learned of Dad's plan he jumped at the chance and he insisted he could stay at our place from the Saturday afternoon until the Monday morning while they were away. At that point Dad said, 'What about your factory?' Rick replied that Marilyn, his secretary, could take care of it.

"It was all agreed and my parents left on a Saturday three weeks ago. Rick arrived with an overnight bag. Less than fifteen minutes after they'd left and before we'd even had any dinner, he insisted that he and I play some games. I said, 'I'm not really in the mood' and he answered, 'Go on. It'll be fun.' Fun indeed! The first couple of games were really boring and I just wanted to go and watch TV but then he said, 'You study biology in school, right? Well, as an ex-teacher I can show you a game that will teach you the name of every part of the human body.' He then produced a deck of cards and we began playing the local card game Forty-one with a twist. The loser had to name a part of his or her body. When all the visible parts had been named the loser had to remove a part of clothing and name the body parts underneath. If either player couldn't name any part that hadn't been labelled before then that person then had to take off two parts of clothing and drink a shot of rum."

The tap that governed Alma's tear ducts opened again. Cecilia put an arm round the distraught girl and hugged her. "Please continue Alma. I know it's distressing but it's important if you want to see justice done."

The falling drops of water on that McDonalds' table slowed once more. "Pretty soon we were both sitting there in our underwear. I said I didn't want to play anymore but Rick answered that meant that I had to drink another shot of rum. He's a lot older than me. By this time I'd had already had three or four and felt funny. Next thing I knew he was touching me all over and removed my panties. I tried to say, 'No' but he was much stronger than me. He held me down naked on the floor and forced himself into me. The pain was unbearable. It must have only lasted a few minutes but it seemed like hours. I just wanted to die! At the end of it all there were some drops of blood on the tiles. I was so out of it and dazed that I couldn't even cry." Alma's eyes dropped more water at this point. "He just looked at me with this really scary face and told me that if I said anything to anybody, he'd kill me. The guy's a psycho and I believe him on that point. The last thing he said to me at the time was 'No-one will believe you anyway.' When I'd sobered up and remembered exactly what had happened, I just wanted to kill myself. I don't know why I didn't. That asshole left late on the Saturday night and when my parents returned on the Monday morning I didn't want to tell them what'd happened so I just said that he'd had some sort of business emergency and anyway I was quite capable of looking after myself. I am capable of taking care of myself but not with vicious sexual predators like that invited into my home." Another round of waterworks erupted.

By this time both Cecilia and Lina were desperately comforting the fourteen-year-old. "You want justice don't you?" ventured Lina. "Of course," replied the young girl between more tears. "Well then, please listen to our advice. I'm a trained nurse and I know about these things." Cecilia appeared like a saintly Mother Superior. "Have you said anything about this to your parents?" Alma shook her head. "Well don't; at least not until after you've gone to the police and laid charges." The pool of water on the table could have filled a largish cup by this time and Alma looked more frightened than ever. "Why do you say that?" she nervously asked. Cecilia smiled, doing her best to put the child at ease. "You said already that the vile creature was a friend of your parents, goodness knows why, and there is a risk if you tell them first that they will contact him and believe what he says rather than you."

"But I'm their daughter," the schoolgirl half shouted, half sobbed. This time Lina put her arms around her. "The world is a vicious and dangerous place my dear and things just don't necessarily work like that."

"What should I do?" cried Alma. "Think of the embarrassment and social shame of it all." Cecilia took over the conversation at this point. "It's your duty as a Filipina to do your best to stop these barbarians from committing further destruction on our womanhood. You must go to the police and lay formal charges and then be strong."

Alma attempted to sip her milkshake but it was empty. "Would you like another?" proffered Lina. The lass nodded and a few minutes later the bargirl returned with the drink. "I must be going home now," remarked the much-comforted girl. "So must we," replied Cecilia. "We have our karate classes." The schoolgirl burst into tears again. "If only I'd known karate, I might have avoided my fate!"

After some more sympathy and handing over their contact details the bargirl and the martial-minded nurse departed leaving the apparently distraught teenager to make her way home. Alma felt confused as she rode the jeep. Being rush hour the vehicle was bursting. Her slender young figure was forced up against that of a plump Filipino businessman. He apologized for the excessive physical contact but appeared to enjoy it.

The schoolgirl's mind was too preoccupied to particularly notice such accidental invasions of her privacy in any case. The advice of her newfound friends seemed sound enough and there were reasons she hadn't immediately related the incident to her mother and father in the first place. They'd simply never believe her. She was merely a powerless child caught in a sick adult world. Admittedly the whole thing sounded unlikely. If it hadn't happened, she too, would have thought it unlikely. Despite Rick's over-attentions it never crossed her mind that he would stoop so low as to ruin the life of a teenage girl who was the daughter of his friends.

More days of school and pretense passed. Her father went to work and generally came home on time while her mother seemed, if anything, a tad more cheerful than usual. Their weekend away, cursed though it was, certainly hadn't hurt their relationship. Alma even tried harder than usual to smile as she exited the house on her way to school.

It took over a week for the girl to pluck up the courage to follow the advice that she knew in her heart was right. Alma never ever did things by halves. Having made up her mind to lay charges she didn't report the matter to her local police station for fear of parental upset. Instead, after school on a Friday, she made her way to the central police office in Mandaue.

"May I help you, young lady?" inquired a constable in his early twenties. Alma blushed so much that her brown skin virtually appeared red. Seeing the girl's distress the constable invited her to a room, sat her down and gave her a Pepsi. "I can see," he said, "that you are in some trouble that causes you embarrassment."

"I'm not in any trouble," howled the fourteen-year-old. "I was raped! Raped by a foreigner!" The constable started. He would have called a female officer if one had been available but there weren't any. The best he could do was to call his sergeant, a kindly man in his late fifties who possessed all the personal qualities of Santa Claus down to the belly itself. More soft drinks and nibbles were given to the complainant while the pair did their level best to make her feel at ease. "We are very sorry that there isn't a lady officer available at the present time to talk to you," apologized the sergeant "but we will do our best to help. Despite your embarrassment could you please tell us what happened?"

As if it were an obligatory response Alma began crying. After she had calmed down the story began to escape her lips. "He is a friend of my parents," the girl sobbed, "and he abused their trust. Through a combination of Tanduay Rum, trickery and force he took my virginity." At the utterance of that word Alma howled more vigorously than ever. The policemen were sympathetic and gentle. "I'm sorry to upset you further but, for legal reasons, it is vital that you undergo a medical examination." Alma cried poor. "Don't worry," responded the young constable. "It's free." Within an hour the schoolgirl found her uniform replaced by a hospital smock and her nether regions under close medical scrutiny.

"She's definitely not a virgin," noted the chief examining doctor. "However," he continued, "there is no obvious sign of vaginal trauma. Probably because the victim waited too long before coming forward." The doctors were very nice to Alma. They were so kind that the trauma, momentarily, almost seemed worth it. A police car took Alma home and, at her request, dropped her a hundred meters from her house. She made excuses for her lateness to her parents but said nothing further.

The sergeant had asked the girl to come back to the station in four days' time and she duly obliged. "Sit down my dear," he soothed and a Coca-Cola this time was laid in front of the lass. "The results of the hospital tests are back. Unfortunately, they are not conclusive of a direct attack. We will need a lot more detailed statement from you."

Alma poured forth a goodly portion of her soul along with the account of recent events. "I just don't understand," she said as her tears fell on the blotter, "how anybody, let alone a friend of my mum and dad, could do that to me!" Calming her as best they could the officers reviewed what she'd said. "I think we have enough to lay charges," the sergeant confided, "but you must realize that your parents will have to be told." Alma nodded. "You didn't exactly explain why you haven't informed them of this unfortunate business already." An indoor rainstorm occurred. "They'd never, never believe me," cried the girl through pauses in the torrent. "That man is a close friend of my father and even my mother trusts him."

"I see," responded the sergeant with all the delicacy he could muster. "We'll take appropriate steps but you must be strong and never waver from the truth during the court proceedings." The miserable high school girl managed a weak smile and took her leave. The sky was already very dark by this time. The process had been interrupted several times by the flow of daily events, which had included two stabbings, one shooting murder and fourteen robberies.

"You're very late home," remarked her mother. "School finished hours ago. Don't tell me you were required to assist your mathematics teacher again?" Alma knew the truth would **out** and this was as good a time as any. "I've been down the police station," she announced firmly. Rena dropped the glass pot she'd been holding and its disintegration on the floor was less than quiet. "What happened? Have you been robbed?" inquired an earnest matron. "Nothing like that Mum, much worse." Her mother appeared stunned. Alma continued with the confidence of the righteous. "You remember when you and Dad were away recently for a weekend and you left me in Rick's care. Well, he cared too much. He raped me!" At that Rena fainted. With her daughter standing over her she came around. "I couldn't have heard you right. What did you say?"

"Rape!" If Alma's voice had been any louder the entire neighborhood would have learned of the scandal.

For the third time the schoolgirl told her tale while her horrified parent turned as pale as the dead. "It's just impossible to imagine," Rena howled. "I never liked your father's making friends with a foreigner." By the time the beer company manager finished his labors and arrived home the sky was blacker than his house. Before he'd walked two meters inside his dwelling Rena had told him all while his daughter sat in a corner with her head in her hands. "I'll kill him!" was all Noy could manage. "Let the law take care of it," advised his wife. "They know how to deal with individuals like that and they'll get him." The husband and father simply wanted to have Rick murdered and when the womenfolk in his house refused to have any part of that idea, he felt shorter than he had before. At that point Rena found just enough composure to check some facts. "Alma, love, we did ask Rick if he could look after you but he said that he was simply too busy. Also, your father and I thought that you were old enough now to manage on your own."

"I thought so too, Mama," Alma answered as she glanced up, "but I became scared and phoned Rick to ask him to come over."

In the Philippines there is an entire network of law enforcement agencies that are connected more in the manner of a spider's web than that of a standard hierarchical pyramid. It merely happened that the police to whom Alma had reported the attack had virtually no direct connection to those who numbered themselves amongst Rick Daly's friends. "Although the medical examination wasn't conclusive," the sergeant announced after receiving the hospital's final report a few days later, "the suspect certainly had opportunity and the motive is obvious enough as the girl is an attractive little thing. We probably have enough to obtain a conviction and certainly sufficient information to justify an arrest warrant."

It was eleven on a Wednesday morning in late October when several uniformed officers knocked on the door of the Daly household. Seeing the group Leticia asked if they were part of Captain Fernandez's unit. "No," the senior member of the gathering replied. "We have come to see Mr. Daly." Not thinking anything was amiss the maid replied, "He's not here. He'd be at his factory in Tisa." She then gave them the address and the car disappeared down the road.

"Marilyn, could you check on the status of production for the latest of the French orders?" The business was at last showing a healthy profit and the boss felt that all their efforts had been worth it. The secretary-come-accountant had her pretty head down over a pile of papers when one of the floor workers knocked on the office door. "Sir, there are some policemen here to see you." Rick thanked him and thought it must be time for donations to the police basketball team.

At the workshop entrance he was surprised that he didn't recognize a single officer. "Mr. Rick Daly?" the most superior of the group inquired. "Yes, what can I do for you?" came the response. "Sir, we have a warrant for your arrest issued by the Municipal Trial Court of Cebu City. You are required to come with us." Rick was shocked. "There must be some mistake," he muttered. "Unfortunately, there is no mistake and I'm sorry but we are required to handcuff you."

By this time Marilyn had emerged from the factory's office and every single production worker had ceased activity. Several dozen pairs of eyes were keenly trained on the activity at the entrance. "There has been some terrible mistake Marilyn and I'm being arrested. I expect it'll all be cleared up in a few hours and I should be back in the afternoon. Please look after everything while I'm out." The secretary's face was as white as that of a brown-skinned person can possibly be. Her mouth was agape and a preternatural silence had usurped the usual hum of labor throughout the building.

As Rick, in his shiny handcuffs, was driven away the faintest suspicion that this business could have something to do with that weird, sexually aggressive, teenager crossed his mind. He now desperately wished that he'd confided the events of that evening to Marilyn. By the time he was led into the police station in Mandaue and charged his fearful suspicion blossomed into absolute terror.

"Mr. Daly, you are being charged with the rape and illegal penetration of a female minor," the desk sergeant explained while the captive was being fingerprinted. "This is a nonsense," Rick returned with purple fingertips waving in the air. He was able to guess who the complainant was. "Nonetheless, Mr. Daly, we are required to follow the process of the law and I daresay the truth will come out soon enough." The sergeant was very matter-of-fact. "What about my business?" the worried businessman asked.

"It'll just have to look after itself until this matter is resolved." Rick asked how long that might take. "No idea," was the brusque reply.

The prisoner was held in the cells overnight. Realizing that the evidence they had was not entirely that strong the idea of forcing a confession from the suspect quickly emerged. An hour after his arrival Rick was again handcuffed and led into a small room at the back of the station. An officer, smelling of beer and wearing a polo shirt and dirty blue jeans faced the suspect. A few jabs into Rick's rib cage and stomach were designed to encourage confession. "You filthy foreigners aren't satisfied with sating your lust in the bars. You just have to force yourselves on underage schoolgirls." Another blow to the stomach sent Rick reeling. "I suppose you don't have the faintest idea as to how Alma Lopez came to be raped on an evening when you happened to be alone with her in her house." Rick was beginning to realize what had gone down. "I was there for less than twenty minutes and I'd come because Alma had phoned me in what I thought was a state of distress. This girl propositioned me in no uncertain manner but I did the only reasonable thing and hastily left."

"We weren't born yesterday," replied the cop in the dirty jeans. He extracted his revolver from its holster, pulled the hammer back and forced the barrel into Rick's mouth. Becoming instantly aware of his own mortality Rick stood very, very still and merely listened to the further tirade of accusations. "It'd be a lot easier for you if you just to admit to raping this girl," the officer said. When the gun was removed from between his teeth the suspect, with a new shade of pale, replied, "I didn't do anything wrong whatsoever."

The policeman with his pistol back in its holster wrote in a notebook. In a scrawly hand were written the words, "The suspect Rick Daly doesn't consider that what he did was wrong." The interview over Rick was returned to his cell. He was feeling sore and sorry by the time the first rays of sunshine made their way in.

After the boss had been hauled away the bookkeeper, the foreman the two cabinet-makers and the workers had just stood still in shock. Almost two minutes passed before anybody said or did anything. The silence disappeared as suddenly as it had come. Sounds of nervous chatter filled the building. Marilyn was forced to say something, although she was entirely unsure of what that something should be.

"Men, it appears there has been some horrible error here. Whether there has been a case of mistaken identity or some huge bureaucratic bungle I don't know. However I'm sure we'll be able to sort it out quickly. As soon as I know any more I'll inform you." It took the girl nearly half an hour to successfully persuade the assembly to return to work. Once again the hum of lathes and buzz of power saws filled the air.

At home that evening and still with no news of Rick's fate Marilyn confided some of the day's events to Leticia. "I thought those police that came here this morning were somehow connected to Sir's friends," the helper announced. "Far from it, it seems," replied Marilyn with an expression of considerable trepidation. Both girls were unable to even concentrate on the TV soaps and simply went to bed.

In the morning the phone rang and Leticia answered. "It's Enrique Cabilla here from Soldad and Cabalero, Attorneys and Criminal Advocates. We are representing Mr. Rick Daly in the present matter and would like to speak to Ms. Marilyn Delgado."

"She's left for work already Sir," replied the maid. "You can contact her at the factory on 624325."

"Thank you for your help. I'll do that."

Attorney Cabilla then tried the factory's number. A pleasant and youngish female voice answered. "Hello, Daly's Exotic Furniture, Marilyn speaking. How can I help you?" On hearing the attorney's voice Marilyn's body quivered. "What's happened to Rick and why aren't his usual lawyers involved?" Mr. Cabilla explained in a voice that would have remained calm even if WWIII had broken out, "Pablo, Ameraldo and Sanchez do not handle criminal cases and referred Mr. Daly's matter to us. Apparently a young girl, known to Mr. Daly, has accused him of rape and he has been formally charged. The initial hearing is scheduled for 11:30 this morning. As I haven't yet had a chance to meet with Mr. Daly it will be a mere formality to enter a plea and refer the matter to a later date. I won't have any more information until later today. Jun Pablo informed me that you have Mr.

Daly's complete trust and confidence and that I am to keep you updated at all times. My office number is 52387."

"Thank you Attorney Cabilla," Marilyn's soft and heavy words responded. She was surprised at how much her hand was shaking as she replaced the handset. Every bone in her not-so-brave body struggled to make it through the working day. She confided no more than absolutely necessary to the employees. "It appears that the problem is more complex than we initially thought," she told them, "but I have every confidence that the mistake will soon be rectified."

The output figures for the day were well down on usual but they were the least of Marilyn's concerns. As she closed up the factory her head was spinning so much that she couldn't even face the passengers that would be staring at her on the jeep ride home. Accordingly she hailed a passing taxi. "How much is a bit of privacy worth?" she pondered as her air-conditioned transportation headed towards its destination.

Leticia's face spoke volumes. Marilyn told her all since there was little to be gained by domestic-spin-doctoring on this occasion and she simply had to bare her soul to someone. "He couldn't possibly be guilty of these charges, could he?" The tone of her own voice shocked Marilyn. "Sir is a bit of a lad but I can't imagine him doing anything like that," replied the maid. "I'm sure he'll be cleared in due course."

Cold sardines and rice were all that the miserable pair could manage to prepare for dinner. A loud knock on the door disturbed their pathetic feast. It was Enrique Cabilla in the flesh. He was an imposing sight, well above average height for a Filipino with a thick head of hair and a solid jaw line. His dress reflected the formality of his working life, a stylish barong and dark trousers. Despite the determination of the face a hint of kindness lurked behind the eyes. The face of a youngish man with the eyes of the old smiled at Marilyn.

"I'm sorry for not calling first," he said, "but I was on my way home from the office and I thought you'd be in." Marilyn ushered the guest into the sala. "What would you like to drink Attorney Cabilla?" she asked. Despite her burning questions the girl would no more have forgotten such an important gesture of hospitality than spat on the altar of a Catholic Church. "White coffee with two sugars would be lovely, thank you?" Leticia disappeared into the kitchen and by the time she returned with the drink the conversation was well under way.

"So, Miss Delgado, it seems that your boss has somehow arrived in an altogether unpleasant situation. I spoke with him this morning and he, naturally enough, denies the whole business. He was arraigned at the Municipal Trial Court and, as expected, an adjournment was granted. The trial itself will proceed on 23 February next year. It seems he will miss Christmas." Marilyn was clearly stunned. "What do you mean he'll miss Christmas? Won't he, at the very least, be out on bail?" The attorney's eyes briefly focused on the floor. "Naturally we applied for bail but it was refused on the grounds that the accused was a foreigner with substantial means and therefore posed a flight risk."

Marilyn and Leticia both stared out of their dark and exotic eyes. "You mean he'll stay in jail for at least three months?" The attorney's demure nod was sufficient answer. The virgin helper began crying until the older girl put her arm around her and asked her to be brave. "What'll become of us all?" blubbered Leticia. Marilyn's ashen face added further silent testimony to the statement. Attorney Enrique Cabilla wasn't smiling. "I'm afraid the legal process doesn't take such matters into consideration," he blandly remarked. "Marilyn, are there sufficient funds in the business accounts to keep the operation going?" he next inquired.

"Yes," replied the bookkeeper, "if we cut back on staff numbers and basically run a skeleton show." Mr. Cabilla nodded a gesture of approval. "I'll keep you posted on proceedings," he added. "We are preparing a solid defense and I believe that we will prevail." After the last statement he bid the pair goodnight and disappeared into the evening warmth.

It was already mid-November and the pre-Christmas activities were well underway. Marilyn hated the very thought of laying off any workers at this time. There was, however, little choice. After a couple of days of thought and observing activity on the factory floor she decided that the fairest way was to lay off the ten workers with the worst attendance records as well as one of the cabinet makers whose lack of skill had continuously let the business down. When asked of his knowledge about the intricacies of dovetail joints two months into his employment he'd smiled and blankly nodded. Time gainsaid his affirmative answer and anytime the other cabinetmaker had been instructed to teach him he'd taken such offence at any negative presumption about his knowledge the process had foundered. Marilyn understood well enough why he'd lied.

Her announcement on the next Monday caused a tsunami of concern on the shop floor. When she explained the logic behind the layoffs and read the names a sullen ambience immediately made itself felt. She'd asked the ten redundant employees to come to the office to collect their severance pay and the tiniest of Christmas bonuses. Alfonso Verde was the first to collect his dues and complain. "It's not my fault that I had quite a few absences," he explained. "There's been a lot of sickness in my family and quite a few christenings I might add." The bookkeeper expressed her condolences but stood firm.

Three more redundant employees repeated the same tactic but the fourth was more outspoken. "I should never have accepted a job from an asshole foreigner in the first place," he declared. "It's not exactly a surprise that he turns out to be a pedophile and a rapist. It's just a pity that we Filipinos suffer, as usual, for the lust and greed of fucking aliens!" Marilyn rebuked the angry worker and shuffled him out of the office as quickly as possible. After that the remaining labor victims were processed quickly and without incident. The bookkeeper did promise that should things turn around they would be contacted with job offers.

Over the succeeding weeks Marilyn found strength of purpose that she never knew she had. She'd visited Rick a half dozen times in the jail and apprised him of her business arrangements at the same time as he spewed out his version of the Alma saga. "Of course I believe you," she'd said on the first visit, "You're my boss." Rick had glared and Marilyn relented a little. "I do remember that I thought the girl was strange even when she was very young. However, your record as a babaero (womanizer) won't help convince anybody that you could pass up the temptation posed by a schoolgirl." Rick appeared helpless.

"I'm telling the truth, Marilyn," he protested, "and I love you. You know I do." The last statement was more convincing and successful than those that had passed before. The secretary would do her duty to her employer. As

November inexorably rolled into December and the Christmas season was in full swing Marilyn felt sad about the laid-off workers.

One Sunday afternoon she was riding in a jeepney on her way to do some shopping in Colon. Unbeknownst to her, the two young men sitting across the narrow aisle were hold-uppers and killers. They'd killed someone the day before and would kill another on the morrow. As the vehicle passed a church the entire contingent onboard crossed themselves, except for Marilyn who was deep in thought. The killers crossed themselves with a beautiful precision of which the Pope himself could have been proud. Presumably they were safe in the knowledge that their sins so far had been forgiven by this act and were possibly confident that their future transgressions could also be insured against.

On the afternoon of December 10th, the factory closed for the holidays and the remaining workers could now enjoy the holy season. At home that evening Marilyn remarked to the maid. "It's strange. I haven't received a letter from my family for well over a month. Oh well! I'll see them soon enough." Leticia was resigned to staying on over Christmas while Marilyn was away. At least her sister would come to assist her during that period, with Marilyn's blessing.

As the Don Juan sailed for Calbayog Marilyn knew what she wanted for Christmas. "If only this nightmare would end and Rick could entirely mend his ways," she thought. "Eventually we could be married and have our own family." The dark foam crested waves of blue crashed over the vessel's bow with a monotony born of resignation. The Don Juan docked at the correct hour causing a superstitious apprehension to spread among some of the passengers.

They say tsismis flourishes in the dark. Apparently, it also does quite well in broad daylight. In any case it seemed to grow to monstrous proportions as the Calbayog-Allen jeepney neared Cagmanipis. A couple of tiny children were almost crushed by the placards they were holding. "Foreigner's whore," one read while another said, "Death to alien rapists!" Her fellow passengers seemed oblivious to the unfolding drama and were as pleasant as any group of strangers.

The rusting hulk on wheels finally ground to a halt close by the Delgado store. As she walked the few meters to her family home Marilyn could feel hundreds of eyes burning into her soul. She was fighting back tears as she knocked on the door and yelled, "Ayo!" Her mother opened it and let her in but did not speak. Her father was seated in a corner doing nothing but did not greet her either.

"What the hell-sort-of Christmas is this?" shouted Marilyn in colorful language she seldom used. "Am I not welcome here?" The silence of both of her parents answered the question. At that moment Juliet appeared. "We heard all about what happened to Rick," she said. "It seems that for once the tsismis spinners have been outdone by the truth."

"What do you mean?" croaked Marilyn. Juliet quietly continued. "Maria was home two weeks ago and it took a less than a day for the story of how your boss is now in jail for raping two schoolgirls. Since then Maria has been regarded as some kind of living saint around here and her parents are walking a full meter taller than usual."

Marilyn's eyes burned and her nostrils flared. "Two schoolgirls? It was only one!" Juliet emitted a nervous laugh. "He only raped one schoolgirl! That's all right then?" The elder sister struggled to find words. "I mean he was charged with raping one. He's innocent. The whole thing was a setup. I know the girl in question. She's a weirdo." Juliet merely smiled weakly.

Her homecoming was so dreadful that Marilyn didn't even wait for Christmas. Two days after her arrival she set off again for Cebu. Better to spend the festive season staring at a wall, she decided, rather than spend it in this place.

"Why are you back?" inquired Leticia at the same time as introducing her younger sister, Mary, whom Marilyn had never met. "It's a long story replied the boss but suffice it to say I really wanted to spend Christmas here. This place has become more of a home to me than Samar." Neither Leticia nor Mary appeared in the slightest convinced. "Has your return got something to do with Rick's being in prison?" Leticia respectfully inquired.

At that point Marilyn burst into tears. "You've no idea how horrible the tsismis at home is. My own parents won't even talk to me. I'd sooner spend Christmas in hell than there!" In actual fact Leticia and more so, Mary, had a very good idea about the tsismis. Mary had updated her sister on her arrival.

When Christmas day made its appearance the three females did their best to make it a special one. A whole roast turkey had been purchased along with all the other accoutrements of festive excess. The girls even drank beer to the point that the three of them were extremely tipsy by nightfall. At nine o'clock a schoolboy band marched and played their way past the door. Mary opened it and yelled, "Show us your balls!" before collapsing in a heap on the step. Leticia apologized for her sister and dragged her inside while Marilyn mused, that's another one for the fishing industry!

None in the household were less than happy to see the back of the festive season. This Christmas and its lead-up had brought nothing but misery and emptiness. The New Year announced itself with the usual mayhem of anarchic firecrackers, one of which caused a small fire at the gate.

In the city's penitentiary meanwhile Rick had begun to make the best of his new circumstances. Being a foreigner, and one of means, he was accorded all manner of respect. His Christmas dinner in fact had consisted of turkey, Christmas pudding and rum. Generally the warders treated him well. Sleeping with the rank odor of ten men in a cell wasn't quite the same thing as passing the night with one or two naked women but he made the best of it. The hard concrete floor at least lent a coolness to offset the infernal tropical heat.

Days and nights inched by until Rick received a morning visit from Attorney Cabilla. "Your trial date is less than two weeks away," the attorney announced. "I will need to go over your statement yet again and to search for any other evidence that might assist." Rick was happy to oblige. He couldn't think of any other evidence than the fact that Marilyn had always thought Alma to be a strange girl and he remained sure that the truth would ultimately become apparent. "The prosecution case is circumstantial to say the least," Enrique consoled his client. "They have the word of one fourteen-year-old girl against yours. They have the medical certainty that the girl is no longer a virgin. They have the admitted fact that you were alone with the girl for a period of time. That is all they have. Well, it's almost all they have."

"What do you mean, almost?" his client quizzed the attorney. "I'm not quite sure how to put this but the girl is a Filipino citizen and you are a …a foreigner." Rick genuinely appeared puzzled. "Why should that make a difference?" he asked. Enrique just smiled. "How long have you been living here Rick?" he added. "Don't worry though," he went on, "the evidence is weak at best and an acquittal should be a matter of course."

Marilyn, Leticia and the entire Barangay of Cagmanipis in Northern Samar were all well apprised of the trial date. Friday the 23rd of February 1996 saw the headlines of the Sun Star daily read, "Foreigner rape trial begins today," along with the presence of crowds of assistants preparing to help the grapevine pass on news.

The public gallery was bursting at the seams. As the defendant was led into the dock and as his attorney took his place hostile eyes were everywhere. Marilyn, although required to give testimony later in the trial, was busy at work. The factory needed her and she simply couldn't face the drama at the Capitol.

"All rise! The Municipal Trial Court of Cebu is in session, the Honorable Judge Juanita Villens presiding." The Clerk of the Court had rattled off his spiel. A woman in her late forties entered the court and took her place at the bench. Rick couldn't help noticing that she bore an unfortunate resemblance to the since-disgraced Miriam Defensor Santiago. "I declare the trial of Mr. Rick Daly in the matter of the alleged rape of a minor open." A quick smack of a gavel reinforced the point. "The charges have been read and all physical evidence, including written submissions received," the judge added. "It is now time for the prosecution to begin its case."

An extremely handsome young man of no more than twenty-eight rose and faced the judge. "Your Honor," a masculine voice iterated, "it is our intention to show beyond reasonable doubt that the defendant, Mr. Rick Daly, did purposefully and willfully violate and penetrate a minor female without any measure of consent." The judge thanked the young man and bid him open his case.

"Where's the jury?" Rick whispered from the dock to his attorney. "The defendant will be quiet," the lady on the bench ordered. Mr. Cabilla rose to his feet. "I beg the court's indulgence Your Honor, for a few moments. My client doesn't seem to understand an essential part of the process." Judge Villens waved acquiescence to the request and the proceedings were halted for three minutes. Approaching the dock Attorney Cabilla attempted to put his client at ease.

"Rick, there is no jury system in the Philippines. The judge decides guilt as well as any sentence. Before you speak again I'll tell you why. It would be almost impossible in this land to find twelve people of good character and moderate education who were truly impartial in any given case. Blood is thicker than water and virtually all potential jurors would somehow turn out to be related to the complainant or the accused. You could call it familial relativity if you liked."

The defendant whispered so softly that the attorney had to request a repetition. "Believe me, your fate is a lot safer in the hands of a judge than any twelve members of the mob." Rick's face exhibited a measure of concern but he said nothing more and the trial continued.

"Your Honor," the prosecutor smiled, "the defendant had opportunity and motive to commit this crime and it would take a stretch of liberal imagination to believe him innocent. For my first witness I will call to the stand the victim, Alma Lopez." A buzz echoed through the gallery and the judge banged her gavel twice.

The schoolgirl took her place with all the sanctity of a martyred-and-subsequently-resurrected nun. She bowed her pretty head in deference to both the judge and the prosecutor. Her eyes never ventured near the face of the defendant. Mr. Reyes, the prosecutor, issued a soft smile to the witness. "Alma, I realize this is very painful for you but could you please tell the court what transpired on that dreadful evening."

The fourteen-year-old had attended the proceedings in her school uniform but the dress was not the one she'd worn to the McDonalds outlet on that Thursday, months before. This skirt boasted a hemline of at least twenty centimeters longer. No makeup of any kind was apparent on her face and her total presence was that of a perfect maiden.

"My parents know this man and when they were going away for a weekend he offered to look after me. They trusted him and he turned up on that

Saturday evening. Not an hour had passed after they'd gone and he started to molest me. He insisted we play this strip game and began to touch me all over. At the same time, he made me drink rum and Coke until I felt very funny. Then he pulled my clothes and underwear off and forced himself into me. I remember the pain and the blood on the floor and now I have to live with the shame and the fact that no man will ever marry me." The girl began to sob. At this stage Mr. Reyes spoke to his witness. "Yes, yes, my dear but please continue the details of the attack." Alma, choking back further tears described the conclusion of that evening. "He raped me again about an hour later and then while I was lying on the floor, he turned me over and sodomized me. My labot hurt terribly and was also bleeding. Despite what he'd promised my parents he did these terrible things and then threatened to kill me if I told anyone. After that he left the house and went home. I was so ashamed that I didn't tell my parents what happened on their return the following Monday and I made excuses for Rick's early departure." By this time the schoolgirl's tears were so intense that she had to be assisted from the stand.

"A compelling eyewitness account," the prosecutor declared. "Yet there is more evidence. The medical report showed that this girl is not a virgin. At fourteen years of age it would be hard to imagine that she could have lost her virginity in the normal course of daily life. It is much more probable that she has been the victim of a cowardly attack by the foreigner defendant."

Attorney Cabilla had duly lodged an objection against the prosecutor's claim that the defendant had motive. Judge Villens had allowed the prosecutor a little latitude and asked him to explain why the defendant possessed particular motive. "Your Honor," Mr. Reyes had replied, "a young virgin in a school uniform would be a temptation to any man without strong moral fiber and all the more so when the man in question is a depraved foreigner." Another objection was registered on the part of the defense. The prosecutor failed to suppress a malicious smile. "If it pleases the court we can establish that Mr. Rick Daly, the defendant in this case, is a known despoiler of Filipino women who continually frequents bars and other houses of ill repute."

A roar went up from the crowd and again the judge exercised her gavel. The next prosecution witness was the taxi driver who'd driven Rick home on that fateful night. "Mr. Abelera, do you recognize the defendant?" The taxi driver responded with a "Yes Sir, I drove him home from Mactan Island to La Paloma."

"How did he behave and seem?" The prosecutor reminded the witness to tell the truth as he was under oath. "He was extremely agitated Sir but otherwise he was all right. He was reasonably sober and he gave me a tip."

"Did he say why he was upset?"

"No he didn't." The witness was then excused.

Attorney Cabilla thought they'd received the day's fair share of surprises when a familiar face took the stand. It was Lina. She had been introduced merely as a character witness. "How do you know the defendant?" Mr. Reyes opened. "He was a customer at a restaurant and bar that I worked in Sir."

"What did he do to you?"

"He seduced me Sir and left me pregnant. When I asked his help he completely abandoned me." The prosecutor showed his clean white teeth to good effect. "That's all thank you Lina."

The following witnesses were more routine in their statements. A doctor who'd examined Alma testified as to the substance of the medical report. "You cannot definitely rule out the possibility of rape then, Dr. Martinez?" The reply was succinct. "No Sir, I cannot."

The prosecution's opening case lasted two days. By Tuesday 27th February the defense was allowed its turn. "Your Honor and the Court," Attorney Cabilla opened, "We will show that the defendant has been the victim of malicious allegations by a disturbed teenage girl and that his being a foreigner has resulted in him being denied natural justice." The judge cut him short. "I don't appreciate comments of that nature Mr. Cabilla. The courts serve justice and that is why we are here. Foreigners and Filipinos alike can expect to receive a fair hearing at our hands."

The first witness called by the defense was the defendant himself. His recollection of the events somehow sounded more sordid than that of the prosecution's and again the gavel threatened the gallery. At the end of his testimony the judge spoke directly to Rick. "Are you, Sir, asking this court to believe that an innocent schoolgirl was attempting to seduce you?" On his reiteration of that point the judge's eyebrows raised themselves a few millimeters.

The defense cross-examined the complainant with full force. "Alma, are you saying that Mr. Daly attacked you without any provocation or encouragement and forcefully took your virginity?"

"Yes Sir." More tears flowed. "Could you describe his genitalia?" The girl appeared blank. "I mean his thing." The girl blushed. "It was big like all foreigner thingos," she said but could add no more. "So you are saying that it was bigger than the things of most Filipino men?"

"I wouldn't know about that Sir," Alma replied as innocently as she could manage. "Young Lady," Attorney Cabilla continued, "We were obliged to do a little research into your personal history - I am sure you understand – and we discovered that on numerous occasions you kept company with boys after school. I put it to you that one of these boys deflowered you and not my client. Furthermore, I would suggest that you have had a sick infatuation with the defendant and when he refused to have sexual relations with you, that is when you dreamed up these ridiculous charges."

The noise rising throughout the courtroom was then sufficient for the judge to call an adjournment. Five minutes later and serious threats directed at the gallery saw the session resume. "They are just my friends, boys who I do homework with," cried the girl on the stand. "I was a virgin!" Getting nowhere the defense counsel dismissed the witness.

Mr. Cabilla then cross-examined the doctor who'd signed the medical report. "You already said that the examination neither confirmed nor dispelled the allegation of rape. Why is that, Sir?" The doctor told the court that because of the delay between the alleged attack and the examination it was impossible to confirm or deny the existence of vaginal trauma normally associated with cases of rape.

Next on the stand was Marilyn Delgado. Surprisingly composed in the face of such authority, the secretary managed a weak smile in Rick's direction and then faced the defense lawyer. "Marilyn, I believe you've known the complainant for a number of years, as indeed has the defendant. Is that correct?" On the witness's affirmative answer, the counsel proceeded.

"What were your observations of Alma Lopez from the time that you met her until now?"

Marilyn appeared embarrassed. Again, Attorney Cabilla repeated his question. Silence filled the room like a disease. "Well, Sir, she was nine years old when I met her and the way she looked at my boss, I mean the defendant, was strange. It was unnatural. Every time I saw her in the presence of the defendant her interest in him was overwhelming. I even commented about it to him once."

Being the only defense witness apart from the defendant himself the prosecution took considerable time in questioning Miss Delgado. "Were you at the Lopez house on the night in question?" The inevitable answer was returned. "Then Miss Delgado how can you possibly comment on what may or may not have occurred?" Marilyn was visibly shaken. "I was merely making my observations as to the complainant's unusual character and preternatural fixation with my boss." The prosecutor let her answer pass. His teeth then flashed once more. "Miss Delgado, we have already seen how the defendant behaves with women. As well as being employed by him as a secretary you share a house with him and one maid I believe. Is that correct?"

"Yes Sir."

"Miss Delgado, I must apologize for asking personal questions, but they are highly relevant to the case at hand. Do you have, or have you ever had, a sexual relationship with Rick Daly?" Defense counsel objected to the question as being irrelevant but was overruled by the judge. "Miss Delgado," Judge Villens spoke with all the authority that she could muster, "You will answer the question."

Marilyn stood silent for at least thirty seconds. A flash of hatred for Rick crossed her soul. "I must remind you, Miss Delgado, that you are under oath and the penalties for perjury are very severe," Judge Villens stated from the bench. The silence grew. The prosecutor appeared half-a-head taller. Marilyn raised her head and stared him straight in the eye. "No Sir, I do not and never have." No authority in the land could ever match the power of tsismis and Marilyn knew it. After answering the question, the woman bent down behind the stand, out of sight of all and crossed herself. "Is something the matter?" inquired the judge. "I'm sorry Your Honor but I dropped my brooch," replied the witness.

By the fourth day the case wasn't looking too good for the defense but they had one card left to play. Reluctantly, they asked the Court's latitude in allowing them to call, at this late stage, one additional witness. The judge agreed despite the prosecutor's objections. It was almost noon on an out-of-season rainy day when a young woman with heavy makeup took the stand.

"Are you Joy Aguilera?" Mr. Cabilla asked the girl.

"Yes Sir, I am."

"What can you say to enlighten this court as to the matter at hand?" The witness lifted her chin and held her shoulders straight and forthright. "I'm a dancer, you know hospitality girl, at a club in Mandaue."

"Have you seen the defendant before?"

"No Sir."

"Have you seen the complainant before?"

"Yes Sir but it was many years ago when I was dancing in Lapu Lapu on Mactan." Enrique Cabilla made sure that he had the attention of the entire assembly before proceeding. "How did it come to pass that you saw the complainant?"

"Well Sir, you know our industry. I come from a poor family and I have many brothers and sisters to support, apart from my parents."

"Please answer the question." Mr. Cabilla appeared to be losing patience with his own witness. "Like I said Sir, ... Sorry I guess I haven't said yet," the girl smiled. "Well anyway it was more than six years ago when I was first forced into this profession. One Philippe Lopez, the father of Alma Lopez, bought me drinks and then took me home."

"You mean he took you to a hotel?" posed Cabilla.

"No Sir, he took me to his house. His wife was away visiting her sister or something and he said his seven-year-old daughter would be fast asleep in her room. I didn't like the idea much but I needed the money."

"How old were you then, Joy?"

"Thirteen Sir," answered the girl. The prosecutor objected to the line of questioning saying that the complainant's father was not on trial but when Attorney Cabilla promised to show relevance the judge dismissed the objection.

"So, Joy could you please tell the Court what happened at the Lopez home that night?"

"Well, Mr. Lopez, Philippe, was making love to me in a forceful manner on his bed, and it hurt as I'd only had a couple of experiences before, when the door suddenly opens and there's this young child standing there staring. She was probably no more than seven." Attorney Cabilla could smell victory. "What happened then Joy?"

"His daughter just stood there until I pushed him off me and then he saw her. Then she ran back to her own room."

The defense counsel then dismissed the witness. Addressing the court he spoke strongly. "Your Honor the last witness is testimony as to a less-than-ideal home; a home in fact that is highly likely to have caused Alma Lopez to become disturbed. I would venture that her disturbed state has led her to become infatuated with my client and, in turn, after he honorably rejected her advances has caused her to level these baseless charges against him."

The prosecution's cross-examination of the last defense witness was extremely brief. Her recollection could not be shaken and her story stood. As court was adjourned for the day and Rick taken back to his cell the populace buzzed in orgasmic excitement. Before the sun rose the next day the Sun Star's headlines challenged the incredulous. "Foreigner sex scandal thickens: Filipino businessman possibly involved!" the splash sheet read.

Attorney Cabilla was satisfied with the case that he'd presented and had informed Marilyn that, God willing, her boss would back home within a couple of days. Having nothing further to add the prosecution also closed its presentation and the Court retired to consider its verdict. That particular deliberation took two full days. It was ten in the morning when the court convened to announce its findings. Even Rick was smiling in the dock. The prosecutor looked worried and the public gallery was overflowing. Crowds bedecked the forecourt of the building and newsmen were everywhere.

"The defendant will rise," Judge Villens announced with all the pomp that she could muster. "It is the finding of this court that you are guilty of all the charges levelled against you. Both the prosecution and defense relied heavily on witness testimonies and there was no incontrovertible physical evidence. However, considering your undeniable, depraved sexual history and the fact that the complainant has shown herself to be most credible the Court can do nothing but arrive at a finding of guilty. Sentencing will be in two days' time."

The day of the sentencing hearing was no less poorly attended than the others. "Eighteen years," the judge had announced amidst the uproar. Before he was led away Rick was allowed to speak with his lawyer. "We'll appeal against both the verdict and the severity of the sentence," Attorney Cabilla assured, "but I can't see any errors of law that the judge has committed and, considering the anti-foreigner sentiment prevalent in the country, I don't particularly like our chances."

A silent and glum prisoner disappeared back into the system. Leticia was tending her duties when she learned the news. Marilyn had made a point of going to work, no matter what, and was in the factory's office. After ten minutes of solid crying behind a locked door she stoically emerged and spoke to the men. "The news isn't good," she declared. "A miscarriage of justice has occurred and the boss has received an eighteen-year sentence." A group sigh pervaded the enclosure. "Nevertheless," Marilyn continued, "if you continue to work hard this business can still run and your jobs will be safe."

Back behind his prison walls Rick was still reeling from the shock of the verdict. His very foundations of belief in justice and truth had been cruelly shattered. A compressed future can instantly depress anyone and so it was with the expatriate businessman. Yet, conditions behind the walls improved, if anything, after the sentence. The guards were more obliging and talkative than before. All manner of minor creature comforts found their way to the prisoner.

Prisons in the Philippines, like almost every other entity in that nation, exist in extremes. The very sight of some can send despair into all who pass beneath their gates while others scarcely seem like places of confinement at all. Although Rick's abode for the next eighteen years was officially classed as a maximum-security correctional establishment the sight of women and children freely mixing with the inmates surprised him. Stonewalls were not the sum of this place, he realized. There must be other forces to bear here.

Back in La Paloma Leticia was offering advice to her new boss. "Marilyn, that's your ninth beer. Don't you think you should stop drinking?" The accidentally promoted woman took another slug of the amber fluid before retorting, between tears, "You're the maid. Mm...mind your own business." She downed two more beers before throwing up. Leticia assisted her to bed before doing the honors with the mop.

It was a full ten days before Marilyn could bring herself to visit her imprisoned lover again. Two of the intervening nights saw her substantially less than sober. On the morning when she finally acquired the courage to visit her ex-boss she took a slug of rum. The two jeep rides to the establishment of correction were lengthy and involved. An hour and a half later she presented her ID at the gates and, after signing the register, was admitted. Rick's depression lifted a fraction on seeing her.

"You really didn't do it, did you?" she asked. "What do you think?" was the terse reply. Partially satisfied she kissed Rick on the cheek and commented, "Why are there so many women and children in here? On the way in I noticed a scene more reminiscent of a fair than a jail." Rick just laughed. "A Filipina who doesn't understand the Philippines! Come on! Marilyn. The prisoners with the women and children are those with money. You didn't see the others and you wouldn't want to see them either!" Rick and his girl's meeting was taking place in a small courtyard in front of an empty cell. Marilyn still appeared dumbstruck. "I have money, don't I?" grinned Rick.

As she left the confines of Cebu's Correctional Center Marilyn had never been more astounded. Many of those convicts appear to be living more comfortable lives than those of the honest poor, she thought. Images of the homes of the privileged on the cool peaks of Lahug then occupied her mind. Money, work, love and sex; what did it all mean? The answers of the Church seemed shallow and empty. Maybe none of us are close enough to God, after all, Marilyn wondered.

It was more than a week later before the factory boss again visited her former employer. On this occasion she was ushered straight to his cell. The door clanged shut behind her. "Don't worry," laughed Rick, "It isn't locked." Before the stunned woman could react Rick launched himself on her. "Stop! You're tearing my dress," she cried. "You don't know how much I've missed your smell, the touch of your body," he answered, his hands still busily divesting Marilyn of her cladding. "I love you. I love you with all my heart."

Somewhat mollified by the protestations of undying affection the woman allowed herself to be stripped of the remains of her clothing. Standing naked in a jail cell was a totally new experience for her. His hands savagely caressing her buttocks Rick thrust himself deep into her vagina. The standing pair were locked in a classic knee-trembler position. Marilyn was terrified at the situation. Each time Rick thrust deep inside her she imagined warders and other inmates gathering at the door. Her fear and the uncomfortable situation conspired to produce the most intense orgasm of her entire life. "Aghgah! Ahdhg! Oh God! AAAAAaaa!" she screamed. It was Rick who now became nervous. His hand gripped her mouth as he deposited his load.

At the end he just said, "I hope you become pregnant." Marilyn was aghast as she resumed her ruffled clothing. "I love you so much that I want you to bear my child," Rick purred. Life was continually becoming more complex for the honest girl from the fishing village in Samar. Due to the distance and the weight imposed by the factory her visits to the prisoner reduced to twice a month. The last couple were brief and non-physical.

By the time she next made the journey the rainy season was in full swing. Cascades of water splashed her shoes as she made her way to the gate. Once again, she was treated with deference and shown to Rick's courtyard with its private cell waiting in the background. The lovers didn't, however, move beyond the courtyard on this occasion. "I hear," said Rick, "that you've been seen with a young Filipino man." His visitor appeared embarrassed. "That's Roly, the cousin of Nang Cora, our next-door neighbor. He's just a suitor."

The prisoner glared. "What do you mean, just a suitor?" The nervousness of Marilyn's lips showed before she spoke again. "Nang Cora thought that me being alone and single I should be introduced to some eligible men." ('Nang' is a Filipino title of respect for a woman of some note). "What happened between you? Kissing? Sex?" demanded an agitated Rick Daly. "Nothing like that," reassured his lady. "We held hands a couple of times. That's all."

Rick calmed down a little. "Do you want him rather than me?" he asked. "Not exactly," replied Marilyn, "but you're in jail and he isn't." It was Rick's turn to let water flow from his eyes. "I didn't do it Marilyn and I just want us to be together. I know I've been a bit of a womanizer in the past but if I could marry you that's all I'd ever want. Please give the flick to those suitor types."

Reluctantly, Marilyn promised to stop looking for other prospects and departed. Confusion reigned in her mind as she rode the two jeeps that took her home. She loved Rick but how could she be expected to wait eighteen years? His situation was hopeless. The business might be able to survive, especially since Rick had given her power of attorney to act on his behalf, but what would become of her? She wasn't getting any younger. In fact, being in her early thirties already, conventional wisdom dictated that she was almost certainly doomed to remain a spinster into her old age.

A fortnight later when she again visited the imprisoned foreigner she was surprised to notice how cheerful he seemed. "Anyone'd think that you'd won the sweepstakes," she remarked. Rick lowered his voice. "It's as good as…" he whispered. "What is?" Marilyn was losing patience at this excessively good humor from somebody who should be feeling miserable. In a barely audible voice Rick muttered in the woman's ear. "As you know, I have established a good relationship with most of the guards here and money talks. It will be possible for me to leave this place fairly soon." Marilyn was truly shocked. "That would be not very honest and is desperately illegal."

Rick just laughed.

"You're right there, my love. It ain't particularly honest and it is downright against the law. But you just think about it. It's not honest that an innocent man rots away for years either. My proposal is a very fair thing under the circumstances." Marilyn was, by this time, devoting her complete attention to the whispers. "For twenty thousand US dollars I can simply disappear from this jail and leave the country."

"That's a lot of money," the bookkeeper in Marilyn couldn't refrain from saying. "It's the only way," Rick begged. "Can you get that amount from the business?" The pretty face frowned. "Possibly, if I take out a mortgage over the operation and equipment, but if I do that the entire enterprise may not survive. At best it would be touch and go."

Again Rick begged. "Please, please. There is no other way!" Her shiny black hair waved on the slightest breeze as Marilyn nodded her assent. "What do I have to do?" she added.

"Half of the money is to be paid in advance and the rest after the escape has happened. Please bring ten thousand in one-hundred-dollar bills bundled in plain wrapping and don't worry, you won't be searched." Despite her misgivings Marilyn couldn't help feeling excited. Her head was spinning. Back home it was all she could do to avoid blurting out the plan to Leticia. The fewer confidants involved the greater was its chance of success.

Behind the stone-walls, Vilnius Sanchez, a guard who was amongst the closest to this special prisoner, quietly called Rick over. "We've already got hold of your passport and can also arrange a plane ticket in your own name. Since you are in prison it is entirely certain that your name won't be on any airport watch list. Our country isn't highly computerized due to its poverty and the manual systems that we use make it easy for oversights to occur." Rick confided that Marilyn would soon bring the cash necessary to kick-start this operation.

A day after this conversation Rick was assigned to a duty detail that left the prison each day to clean the city's parks and public areas. This detail was a chain gang without the chains. The next fortnight proceeded very slowly. At least he was able to see portions of the outside world again.

It was a sunny September morning when Marilyn turned up at the gate with her modest parcel. "Good morning, ma'am," the gatekeeper greeted her. "Mr. Daly will be very pleased to see you, I'm sure." His lover handed over the package to the prisoner who quickly delivered it to the requisite pair of hands. "Once I've successfully gone you are to deliver the other package to either Warder Orealio or Warder Angayan. This is very important. I'll discretely point them out while you're here so that you recognize their faces."

Marilyn signaled her understanding with a gentle nod. "I'll have to leave the Philippines immediately but I'll make arrangements for you to join me when I can. I think it will be some great length of time before I could ever safely set foot here again." Rick kissed her on the cheek. Before she left he'd introduced her to the two important guards.

Two days later at 7 am as Rick was leaving on his work detail Warder Angayan spoke softly in his ear. "Today's the day. Good luck." The group of forty men accompanied by four guards climbed aboard the prison bus, an ancient Bedford that sported more rust than a shipwreck and whose motor spewed out diesel fumes to a noise reminiscent more of a particularly atrocious-schoolboy-drum band than an engine. To Rick's surprise there was another Westerner in the group, Bill Richards, who was of a similar age and build as himself. Bill was an Englishman doing time for drug offences. What made his presence odd was the fact that there were only three foreigners amongst the entire prison population.

The day's task was the cleaning of basura (rubbish) and weeds from the lawns surrounding Fort San Pedro. Eight-thirty had seen the prisoners dispatched in groups of five or six to various portions of the grounds that were in sight of the prison officers. Rick had been assigned to clean and clear a small portion on the southern side of the fort, alone. "The area is simply too tiny to warrant more than one man's labor," stated the guard as he handed Rick a sack of tools.

First of all Rick extracted a weeding implement and actually spent ten minutes clearing protruding examples of encroaching jungle. Then, protected by the fortress's undulating southern wall, he examined the rest of his kit. Underneath the tools was a fresh shirt and pair of jeans and beneath those was a compact plastic bag containing his passport, plane ticket from Cebu to Sydney, five US one hundred dollar bills and P1,000 in fifty-piso notes.

Quickly changing his outer garments the intending fugitive placed the passport, ticket and cash into his trouser pocket and folded his prison uniform into the bag along with the weeding tools. He thought it wiser to discard the bag somewhat later and further from the scene. Appearing to all intents like an early morning tourist Rick discretely strolled to the edge of the park area and calmly waited on the nearest large road. In less than ten minutes a vacant taxi approached, probably after dropping passengers at the nearby port. The vehicle slowed right down before he'd even had the chance to raise his finger.

"Taxi Joe," the driver shouted. "Yes please," answered the escaped prisoner, the enthusiasm in his voice surprising even himself. "To Mactan airport," he instructed. "You a tourist here, Joe?" the driver inquired. "Yes, as a matter of fact, I am." Noticing the lack of luggage apart from the dark plastic bag the driver made a comment. "I just came down yesterday in pursuit of a woman," the passenger responded. "It didn't work out so I'm going back to Manila now."

The driver offered a wistful smile that conveyed considerable understanding of such matters. "Babae," he said, "are ultimately the ruin of us all. I wouldn't have to drive this cab eighty hours per week if I didn't have a wife and kabit and too many kids to mention." It was Rick's turn to impart a show of understanding.

At the airport he parted with two of those fifty-piso notes, leaving his new friend happy with the included thirty-five-piso tip. As he approached the terminal Rick offered the weeding and garbage tools to one of the beggars who were providing shade for the lower portions of the walls. The fugitive knew that those tools would never be seen again. The uniform remained in the plastic bag and he resolved to carry it with him on the plane to Manila.

Beads of perspiration were forming on his brow as he checked in. "Hot here isn't it Sir?" smiled the man on the desk. "Sure is," mumbled the passenger. Rick thought of his moderately recent experience in Davao when he was forced to wait for four hours for a flight. However, on this occasion he was luckier. It should also be said that there are a lot more flights between Cebu and Manila than between other destinations. "Boarding is in twenty minutes, Sir. Have a pleasant flight." Rick thanked the man and immediately stepped over to a nearby kiosk where he ordered and drank three San Miguels in quick succession. Then another hundred steps brought him to the departure lounge where a generous video screen was showing a rerun of the antics of Bruce Willis in Diehard 2.

Takeoff was more or less on time and another hour saw Rick in that familiar outsized shed in Manila. Strolling out into the late morning sun with forced bravado he wondered where he could lie low until the evening flight to Sydney. He also hoped that officialdom wouldn't be forced to notice his departure from his previous home too soon.

Although his favorite hangouts in the capital, the bars of Ermita, had been forced to close during the reign of Cory there were plenty of houses of sin not far from the airport vicinity, in Paranaque. A short jeep ride saw Rick and his plastic bag enter one of these establishments. Two hundred meters short of this house of ill-repute stood a rare garbage bin. The rotting refuse inside was greeted by the new arrival of the plastic bag with its prison-issue contents.

The Aero bar was dark and dingy, much as you would have expected a daytime operation in wartime Saigon to have been. No dancers strutted the stage but scantily-clad waitresses pushed drinks onto the few customers. The drinks were cheap and other activities were available in back rooms for modest sums. Between beers Rick had disappeared for half an hour with a passable looking waitress in her twenties. On his return to the table his heart froze. There were two uniformed police standing next to it.

The thousand deaths that can occur in a second raced through every part of Rick's body. "Sir," one of the officers spoke, "We are investigating a shooting that happened here yesterday morning and are seeking statements from witnesses who may have been in this place at that time." The sigh of relief that escaped from the fugitive's lungs was so loud that he was terrified that it might arouse suspicion. It didn't. "I'm sorry gentlemen," he replied, "yesterday I was in one of the southern provinces. I'm on a holiday." The police thanked him and proceeded to interview other customers.

All afternoon Rick sat in the semi-darkness. An hour after nightfall he exited and rode a jeepney to Ninoy Aquino International Airport, which was still called Manila International Airport by most expats as a pathetic gesture of defiance against the Cory government when it was in power. Rick strode to the QANTAS counter. Those prison guards really know how to serve it, he thought. QANTAS! The airline where most of the stewards are gay and those that aren't are too busy chatting up the attractive girls to notice male passengers. Well that was how it was in the '70's and '80's anyway.

Much to his relief there were no incidents or hiccups and two hours later he was seated in 37b as the plane taxied for takeoff. "Business class would have been a nice touch but I suppose I can't complain," he internally smiled. For an entire day the escapee's heart had worked overtime. It needn't have. Back at Fort San Pedro the bus had picked up the prisoners and guards at 6 pm. The head count had tallied and it was not until the next morning that Rick's absence had been officially noticed. The guards from the detail were called to explain. "There were two Westerners on that detail, Sir," one said to his superior. "All Westerners look the same and one of them moved position during the count and was counted twice by mistake. These things happen!" These things indeed did happen in the Philippines. No one could argue with that. The guards on the Fort San Pedro trip were officially reprimanded and docked three days' pay.

Rick's plane had in the meantime landed in Sydney after disgorging some passengers in Brisbane. Before he'd left Manila Rick had purchased a canvas bag and a few clothes. He wasn't stupid. Carrying his duty-free grog and cigarettes he approached the Immigration.

Chapter Twelve

"Mr. Daly, you've been away for quite a long time." A youngish female immigration officer, who sported long, dark hair and would have been attractive if not for the look, attempted a smile. "An extended vacation in the Philippines was it?" The look expanded a little, finally settling into a steely gaze. "Business actually," replied Rick as he confined a spasm of terror to his nether regions. "I hope it was successful and have a pleasant day."

Collecting his pathetic excuse for luggage from the carousel the businessman on-the-run made a beeline for the Customs. The green sign beckoned in a friendly fashion. "Nothing to declare," it invited. "Yes, that's me," Rick mused and quickened his step.

The next twenty meters or so was the longest journey of his life. Rick only hoped that any electronic surveillance systems weren't sufficiently sensitive to hear the pounding of his heart. Thirty seconds later when the automatic doors parted, he reached the arrival hall and freedom. He'd made it.

An hour later and he'd checked in at the Kings Cross Backpackers' hostel. So preoccupied was he with the planning of his next move that he barely noticed the two Swedish girls who were laughing in the entrance lounge. It was probably a lucky escape for the pair. Two days and nights at this focal point of Sydney's less-than-wealthy international set passed with the odd beer and chat but nothing else. From the notice board Rick had managed to locate rooms for rent and after a single afternoon's visitations he'd secured an extremely humble attic room in Fitzroy Street, Darlinghurst. Miniscule cooking facilities and a pathetic lounge suite that had obviously just been saved from a trip to the tip, lent the abode the atmosphere of the cheapest of bed-sits in one of London's less than salubrious outer suburbs. Still, the rent was only one hundred dollars a week plus phone and electricity.

Although he had once been moderately familiar with them the sights of Sydney's inner city only evoked the most casual of passing memories. As a young man in his late teens he'd stared with wonder at the neon lights and seedy sex for sale under the Southern Cross in the company of his buddies. Even the most familiar shadow of a prominent lamppost can appear strange in the light of years of absence.

Where was home and did he have one? Within an hour of being ensconced in his new domicile Rick's thoughts flitted backwards. His birth and first couple of years naturally enough eluded him. He did remember his life in England in a blurry fashion however. The pre-school and elementary school themselves were staffed with the ogres of nightmares. Everything was grey from the sky to the buildings to the porridge served at recess. He had just about become accustomed to the vagaries of life in the Farnborough municipality when the family shifted again. Arcane questions such as how does a U.S. Air force officer get transferred to Britain and then to Australia a few years later were beyond the comprehension of an eight-year-old. Being called a Pommy bastard didn't exactly cause Rick to feel welcome at his new school in Windsor, some fifty miles from the center of Sydney.

Once he'd asked his parents how it was that he had no brothers or sisters to play with like other kids. "Having you was a huge effort for Mum," his dad confided. "You'll just have to make do." Rick's junior high school years were relatively normal if anything ever is normal. Without exactly realizing it in black-and-white, it occurred to the adolescent that the nuclear family he belonged to was preternaturally isolated.

An older mind would have been impressed at the transition from U.S. Air force to RAF and thence to RAAF. To Rick the family might have just as well been unwanted nomads. The tragic death of his father four years after the Vietnam War officially ended was as much of a mystery as a loss. His mother, Janice, never adjusted to life as a widow despite the overly generous pension to which she became entitled. "Ask me no questions and I'll tell you no lies," had been the rule around Ben and Janice Daly's home since Rick was old enough to remember anything.

Four years later and his mother was gone, a victim to a virulent cancer at forty-five years of age. Rick was in his second year of an Arts degree at Sydney University when he was left alone in the world. The military pension saw him finish his degree. A year in Europe transpired before he began teaching. It was a job and a challenging one at that. His parents had barely kept contact with his father's relatives in Chicago. His mum's family were a black hole. They had been so incensed when she'd married his dad that she'd simply been cut off.

Life as a teacher had never really suited Rick. The intellectual challenges and daily temptations of mini-skirted schoolgirls were more than offset by another grubby reality. If weekends provided a respite from the stress the long Christmas holidays afforded a chance for a recharge. All in all, his years in Sydney had basically opened his eyes to the country's decay.

The electronic digits of the taximeter displayed $13.45. The trip from Shadforth Street in Mosman to Oxley in Crows Nest had been uneventful. A mere three red lights had marked the course of the journey. A middle-aged woman parted with the requisite sum and thanked the driver. As she was leaving Rick wished her a pleasant evening. His vehicle had done only a single block when he noticed a hail in front of the Crows Nest Hotel.

With precious little cash left after his move into the rented room in Darlinghurst Rick had been forced into sudden employment. Dangerous though it undoubtedly is and with a very uncertain promise of reward, taxi driving offered Rick an immediate source of income, which was not to be sneezed at. Having survived the preliminaries and obtained the necessary credentials he'd found employment with Taxis Combined, Sydney's largest cab company. He picked his cab up at three in the afternoon from the base in Glenmore Road, Paddington and returned it at three in the morning.

After a month in his newfound vocation Rick understood the origins of the urban myth surrounding the Sydney taxi driver. The word around the world has it that most of the cabbies in Sydney arrived, courtesy of a refugee boat, not much before their international-tourist passengers and couldn't find the Harbor Bridge. The more knowledgeable rumormongers generally add the fact that they can't speak English and live two to a bed (day and night drivers take turns) and four to a room. Although Rick's knowledge of the city was passable and he was proficient in English his earnings per shift seldom exceeded eight dollars an hour. "Small wonder," he thought, "that anybody but illegal immigrants would take on such a job." His own situation flashed into his consciousness and prevented his ever complaining.

The fugitive from foreign injustice drove five nights a week. His occupation, although poorly paid, was not exactly uneventful. On his third shift a young Asian girl hailed him in Darlinghurst Road, Kings Cross, the city's red light area. "Where would you like to go my darling?" Rick ever so politely ventured. "Your place," replied the creature in the huskiest of voices. "You want to spend a sum?" the deep voice continued. His body half out of the window in an effort to escape the sliding nature of this passenger Rick drove a couple of hundred meters before she gave up. On the receipt of three dollars and a world of experience later Rick was again alone.

A few boring fares, no interest and no tips followed. It was late in the evening when he picked up a well-dressed blond gent in his early thirties. The man had hailed him on Military Road in Neutral Bay and asked to be driven to the Cross.

As the cab was traversing the Harbor Bridge the passenger began to wax philosophical. "I live by two things," he exclaimed. Snap! The briefcase on his lap sprang open. Inside was a bible. "That's the first one!" Rick glanced at the assembled goodies on his passenger's lap as the southern pylon came into sight. "The second thing is this!" the passenger proudly declared, lifting the cover of the bible to reveal a hideous looking knife carefully placed in a cut out. After his years in the Philippines there wasn't too much that could faze this boy yet he was mildly concerned. However the passenger was well behaved and even gave Rick a tip. The last sight Rick had of the gent was of him approaching girl after girl on the strip. He'd met a collector.

Night after night Rick drove but he hadn't forgotten what he'd been forced to leave behind. Whenever he traversed the Harbor Bridge his mind harked back to Marilyn's pubic mound with its upright hairs. The harbor tunnel evoked deeper memories. The only contact he'd managed with his life's love was the odd telephone call and occasional letter. Phone calls were expensive and a person could grow old waiting for a letter from the Philippines.

There is something about the outer suburbs of Sydney very late at night. Streets that are usually too busy, too noisy and possess that scream of overcrowding are preternaturally quiet. It is as if the troublesome hotchpotch of humanity had suddenly vanished. He'd had a fare out to Bankstown and was cruising back towards the city when a girl in '70's garb hailed him. Rick was disappointed with her destination. Concord was a short trip and not in the direction of the city. Yet her face made up for the inconvenience. Meryl was blonde, nineteen-years-old and of model-like proportions. Her look of desperation as she hailed him and her demeanor during the ride struck a chord with the driver. At the same time as collecting the fare Rick took the details of her address and phone number. He was on a promise.

A candlelit dinner in a Russian restaurant on Oxford Street was succeeded by another kind of rus'in. The speed with which Meryl had accepted his invitation for coffee had flabbergasted Rick. Back in his dingy abode there was no time for such niceties. Barely had the door closed and the blonde stripped. Firm breasts and a pubic mound of generous foliage challenged the host. Rick had almost forgotten what the smell of white girls was like. It was impossible to say who jumped whom. An hour or more of intertwined bodies ensued. The sex was good but Rick was unable to avoid thinking of a more dusky body. When the couple awoke late in the morning Rick served up a brunch of boiled eggs and toast. The lack of complaint about the food or the night's activities on the part of the girl convinced him that this acquaintance was worth keeping.

Meryl was cheap to run. A movie here, a simple dinner there and endless nights of sex. What more could an Australian male ask for? Somehow the 'Getting to know you' routine sneaked up on the pair. Meryl confided that she was a recovered smack addict who had been trying to work as a professional diver in Darwin. "How could you afford the heroin?" Rick innocently inquired one day. "On my back," came the direct reply.

By the time the relationship petered out Rick figured he'd gotten five thousand bucks worth for free. Meryl had signed on as a crewmember on a yacht heading for Indonesia and he never heard from her again. Quiet though their parting had been Rick couldn't help feeling a little sad. After all how often do you find a girl lacking in all the usual jealousies but who will still kiss you on the lips? Working girls often confine their intimate exchanges to their lower regions, the upper ones being reserved for non-business activities. An ex-call girl who takes a shine to a man can provide all the personal touches without the outrageous demands and the ownership thing.

The following months as a knight of the road served as a continuing education for the fugitive businessman. "No wonder the world is a mess," he thought after a young woman cradling a baby in her arms attempted to sit in the front seat. After shepherding her and the infant into the back the trip proceeded uneventfully.

Early one evening as his taxi crawled along the rank at Sydney's international arrivals' terminal he noticed a considerable number of passengers waiting. Yet, surprisingly, the four taxis in front of him remained stationary. To understand why, Rick had to climb out of his mobile office and take a long, hard look. Out of the fifth taxi from the head of the queue the driver had extracted a prayer mat, placed it carefully on the nearby grass and dutifully prayed in the direction of Mecca. In a city where a person who is a second late in moving off in the face of a green light is honked and abused incessantly Rick couldn't understand the complete tolerance with which the present hold up was treated. Four minutes later and the silent drama was over. The taxis resumed moving along the queue fulfilling their functions. As his cab reached the head of the queue a young couple were looking at him. Sensing that they were foreigners he greeted them with, "Welcome to Australia and to Sydney. Where would you like to go?" "Sydney Hilton please," came the curt reply. Once the nefarious collection of baggage was loaded into the boot and the couple installed in the back seat the vehicle did its round of the airport loop and increased speed in the direction of the city.

As it proceeded along Southern Cross Drive the gentleman spoke. "It's our first time here; we are from Berlin but please don't take us around the long way." Rick smiled, "Don't worry Sir; there's enough dishonesty in the world without me adding to it." Nonetheless the cab missed a couple of turns and performed a mini-circuit of the city center before zeroing in on the target. Rick didn't like the Eastern Distributor with its toll. Too many passengers, unfamiliar with the new user-pays approach, had objected to the extra charges. As the taxi snaked its way over the speed bumps and through the 40 kph roads Rick remarked, "The streets are pretty clean for a third world country eh?" The girl spoke. "Australia isn't a third world country. We avoid taking holidays to those destinations." Rick laughed.

"Highest taxes on the planet just about but little to show for it. No well-funded hospital or education system. Our money just pays for foreign wars apart from the portion that is wasted or stolen by various public officials."

"But you have so many resources," responded Gerhardt, the husband. Rick half turned his head and quipped, "It's the country that does the least with the most." That silence born of communicational exhaustion followed and the happy couple were deposited, along with their luggage, at the Hilton.

Since Meryl's departure Rick's social life on his two days off a week had taken an extreme dip. His sex life had been reduced to solitary wanking apart from the one occasion when he'd parted with two hundred bucks for thirty minutes with a glamorous but boring blonde in an upmarket brothel. Between the high price and the establishment-supplied condom of the thickest proportions he'd emerged vowing never again to waste money on a rhubarb sandwich.

He wrote to Marilyn and she replied to his P.O. Box but due to the pace of the Philippine mail service, which runs like a Sunday afternoon, their letters crossed only about once a month. The odd phone call, at considerable expense, witnessed protestations of undying love on both sides but little exchange of information. Slowly, inexorably, his dream woman was moving into that specific medium.

No matter how philosophical the mind might be or how lyrical the heart may wax there is nothing like driving a cab to cement one's spirit in the muddy earth. It had been a long evening, too many drunks and quarrelsome passengers, too many radio calls to addresses from whence the passengers had previously fled and so on. Friday night or not, the business had died at midnight. Inexplicably the streets were empty and vacant taxis passed Rick's vehicle with the semblance of vultures.

His last fare had taken him north over the bridge and Rick was cruising back from Neutral Bay. An old man with a child had taken him to Northbridge. On his way toward the city down Miller Street in Cammeray Rick's attention was caught. An extremely attractive girl in her late teens with medium-length dark hair was standing around a street light like a moth near a flame. Her short pink miniskirt rode her thighs like a rose on satin sheets and made a mockery of her cream colored blouse. His eyes fixed on her and, as the cab drew nearer he noticed her left arm raise itself ever so little. The wheels halted and Rick smiled. "Get in Love."

The gorgeous creature released her hold on the light pole and staggered the ten meters to the open door. "I...I..." Rick smiled as he made sure she was comfortably seated next to him. The girl's name was Evelyn. For some unknown reason the driver and the passenger had immediately exchanged names. "Where to my dear?" Rick had pleasantly intoned. "I live in a rented room in Wollstonecraft," slurred the girl. "I went on a girls' night out and don't have much money left." The cab sped westwards. "Don't worry," reassured its driver. "You are obviously worth a lot in yourself," he grinned.

Evelyn leaned over Rick's torso as they travelled down Falcon Street and took the liberty of unzipping his fly. Silently and with a dedication born of desperation her lips went to work. Despite the failure of the current activity to meet required public passenger vehicle standards, let alone safety rules, the moaning driver said nothing. By the time the taxi pulled up in Milner Crescent a biological explosion had occurred. The girl bid Rick goodbye and attempted to leave. "That'll be nine dollars and eighty cents," Rick asserted in his most professional voice as he zipped up his fly. "But...but..." slurred Evelyn.

"The law is the law I'm afraid and a cab fare must be paid." Rick could have passed for a politician or a policeman.

Under a weak streetlight the girl, with cream all over her mouth, fumbled in her purse for coins. Satisfied with the seven dollars and fifty cents that she had found Rick drove off. Feeling slightly guilty at his meanness Rick wondered if he had become prejudiced against white girls or if life in the Philippines had turned him into an asshole. Then he smiled. "The Philippines is the best teacher on earth," he chuckled.

Days and nights rolled into an endless parade of traffic lights, sometimes real, sometimes apparitions in dreams, but always there. The letters from Marilyn became scarcer and during the rare phone calls her voice had sounded as distant as the miles between them could possibly produce. "How's the business going?" Rick had asked once. "As well as could be expected," was the simple reply. In one respect Rick was lucky. He was about the only foreigner who had any connection to a business in the Philippines not to be asked for money and he would never have been able to save enough to even suggest that Marilyn sell the business and join him. Although the factory was turning a reasonable profit Marilyn wasn't sufficiently wealthy to qualify for a business visa and, under the circumstances, a sponsored tourist or fiancée visa was out of the question.

If you drive a cab long enough you see it all. After nearly three years in the job Rick was certain that he had better ideas on running the country than those of the Prime Minister. During the preceding thirty-six months Rick had only received two traffic tickets. Although such expense wasn't tax deductible, he put it down to an occupational hazard and moved on.

It had been a long Sunday night. Busy yes but not so smooth. Several troublesome drunks had interspersed their presence with the other more easygoing fares. Rick's vehicle had, at one time or the other, during the night reached three of the four quadrants of Sydney's reach. It was with considerable relief that he parked his taxi back at the Paddington base. A dilapidated clock, whose pink face sported freckles born of rust and mounted on an exterior wall, declared the time to be 3:20 am. With his pay-in in hand Rick strode towards the cash depository. "Mr. Rick Daly, I presume." Rick spun round to face the bearer of that authoritative voice. A young man in a grey suit stared at him. Another be-suited individual stood at the speaker's side. "I'm Constable Jones of the Federal Police and this is Constable Mannington. We have a warrant for your arrest and are instructing you to accompany us."

Shock and disbelief effectively paralyzed the tired cabbie from any word or action. Scores of faces looked on. The slightly fresher countenances of the starting day drivers mingled with the weary ones of the returning night shift. Silently bundled into the back of an unmarked cream-colored car, silvery handcuffs, wrapped around Rick's wrists glinted in the moonlight. The police vehicle departed the Glenmore Road taxi base with the suddenness in which it had arrived.

Through the blackened city streets it sped. Glimpses of late night revelers alternated with an eerie stillness. Turning into a nondescript yard it halted and the solitary guest was led into the back of a minacious structure of forlorn grey brick. The charge desk could have come out of a Kafka movie, the individuals manning it could have been police from another world and a lack of visual identifying clues lent the scene a vicious surrealism. No questions were asked of the prisoner nor answers expected. His valuables removed he was placed in a cell whose drabness matched the rest of the building.

As the sun rose and forced an element of brightness on the next morning's scene Rick was presented with an exciting McDonald's breakfast but no information. An hour went by and then another. The heat of a December day had begun to insinuate itself when he was led out of the chamber of boredom, out of the building and into another police car. The shiny metallic restrainers, which had been removed while he was in the cell, were reapplied and the car moved along streets with which he was all too familiar. The State Parliament building, the old Mint, and Sydney Hospital flashed past. As Macquarie Street touched Queens Square the exit and corridor routine began again. Rick did prefer the shiny rose-colored walls of the anteroom in which he found himself to the décor of his accommodation the previous evening.

Through the maze of stone, glass and steel Rick imagined that he heard the calling of his name. Seconds ticked by and two police guards appeared. The shortest of strolls resulted in the opening of a sturdy oak door and Rick was pushed through. The opulence of the room astonished him. Fine timbers were complimented with plush leather trimmings and a number of extremely comfortable seating arrangements. The space in which Rick found himself however afforded only the posture of standing. A solitary robed figure with a wig plucked straight from some seventeenth-century-European scene glared at him.

"Mr. Rick Daly, you have been charged with committing a forced sexual act on a minor, to wit pedophilia, in a foreign jurisdiction. How do you plead?"

"Not guilty, of course? But if it is a foreign jurisdiction why are charges being read against me here?"

The beak glared with even greater hostility. "Mr. Daly, for your edification a law was passed in this Commonwealth earlier this year allowing for the trial in Australian federal courts of Australian citizens who have committed sexual crimes overseas. This is the reason why you find yourself before me. Naturally you will be allowed time to prepare your defense and be given the opportunity to engage legal counsel."

Totally dumbstruck Rick laughed. "Is this all some kind of joke?" The expression on the face from the bench convinced him that it wasn't. The initial hearing that had so briefly occurred had been, unbeknownst to him, his only opportunity to apply for bail and it was gone. Once again he was led away but this time his carriage was a prison van. He found himself in a remand prison where he was placed into solitary confinement for his own protection and was dressed in a drab green uniform. His number was 1217.

An aged black and white TV set up as centerpiece in a covered section of the compact exercise yard lay testament to the logo, 'innocent until proven guilty.' Remand prisoners were allowed a few such comforts as a result of the grudging admission on the part of the authorities that they may be theoretically innocent. The bunks sported thicker mattresses than those of the cellblocks for the convicted and the tobacco allowance was a tad more generous. It was only a few years down the track that, under the influence of the litigation driven anti-tobacco frenzy, the government was further able to cut costs by abolishing even this token gesture.

As an inmate in solitary Rick enjoyed the spacious confines of two meters-by-two meters-by-four meters. In that volume was included the toilet bowl that occasionally could be flushed. This particular prisoner had been scheduled for solitary confinement but not for the protection yard. When it came time for the obligatory daily shower, he was compelled to take his chances with the rest of society's primrose element. For some unknown reason no warders in the world's correctional establishments ever seem to keep watch inside the shower facilities despite the fact that they provide the favorite location for internecine crimes, particularly rapes, that flourish amongst humanity's jailbirds. Rick put down his luck at not being molested to his possession of a particularly hideous ass; pock marked and with unsightly patches of cellulite, which were probably caused by years of bad living.

After the first evening in his new home Rick had provided each cockroach and ant with a name and made firm friends with each and every one of them. Seventeen hours a day locked in the smallest of spaces might seem tough but the intolerable boredom that accompanies each one of those hours is infinitely worse. The ancient copy of a Women's Weekly that Rick had been able to grab from the grubby pile of available reading material after the evening meal hardly provided the stimulation that he was yearning.

The first rays of the sun were rising over the palm fronds that formed the backdrop to Cagmanipis's perch on the edge of the sea. The door of the guest bedroom opened and as Rick raised his bleary eyes the naked forms of two young women strode towards his bed. In the lead was his fiancée Marilyn and just behind her was a girl of sixteen or seventeen. "What are you doing?" he stammered. "It's two days before our wedding!" Marilyn smiled, increasing the natural beauty of her swarthy body.

"It's customary in these parts for bride and groom to get to know each other a little better before the wedding day. My parents won't come anywhere near this part of the house. They are so proud to be having you as a son in law." Rick rubbed his eyes. "Who is the other girl and why is she here?" The sixteen-year-old blushed to the point that even her olive skin was unable to mask it. "That's Gabriella. She's a cousin of mine. Her parents decided that they need more money for the family to survive and that she as the eldest must work in Manila as a 'maid.' Gabriella is terrified of beginning work in a bar as a virgin and she would like you to solve her problem."

The by now wide-awake male body half rose from his bed and surveyed the younger girl. Marilyn continued on. "I've told her how gentle you are and I'll be here to assist you. She'd heard those stories of how girls, who are virginized, especially by foreigners, can't walk for up to a week and was terrified. That's where you come in. I know you have the capacity to make any girl's first time really special and if you love me I'm sure you'll do it."

Love's labors can be strange indeed, Rick reflected before volunteering his assistance. Gabriella possessed a lovely face, smallish breasts, a curvaceous backside and a soft tuft of pubic hair. The shy lass lay down next to Rick while Marilyn deposited her shapely proportions on the other side of the double bed. Rick's hands had ever so slowly begun to explore the task ahead while Marilyn's lips wrapped their velvety texture around his tower of strength.

A crashing sound as the outside bolt was drawn back and the heavy metal door swung wide open caused the prisoner to wake from his dream. Squinting his eyes against the burst of brightness he was just able to make out a spunky blonde in her late twenties sporting the garb of a prison warder. "Get up! It's time for Line Out and Roll Call!" A thought crossed his mind but fortunately he dismissed it.

In the mornings that followed he was awoken by several overly aggressive male warders save for one occasion when the lovely visage of an island girl swung back the door. The days rolled into weeks and then into months. Meals were generally passable except when Chinese food was offered up. There were two fellow inmates who couldn't boil an egg but since they were ethnically Chinese they were tasked with the weekly Asian repast.

Generally, Rick kept on good terms with his fellow unfortunates. Bruce and Brad were exceptions. Those prisoners who proved model crawlers and dutifully assisted the guards in keeping the place clean and tidy were sometimes allowed the privilege of possessing that aged harlot of a TV set in their cells for a night. After lunch one day Brad poked his head into Rick's cell, past the open door. "What have we here mate? A junkyard? You'd better clean it up quick smart." Rick was not amused by the tone of the teenager. "You've been made a cop have you? F... off!" Another pimply youth, vainly attempting to make manhood, joined the ruckus. It was Bruce, Brad's cellmate and inseparable sidekick. They were on remand for snatch-and-grab attacks on elderly women. The altercation reached the point where punches were on the verge of being thrown when a sour-faced warder broke it up. "Don't worry boys. That one's incorrigible. You'll still get the TV tonight and some chocolate."

It is amazing what you can learn in prison. Merely through casual conversation Rick acquired the fundamentals of embezzlement, fraud and armed hold up. Nine months had dragged themselves by since his most recent incarceration and January of 1998 was the epicenter of a viciously hot summer. When Rick was called to one of the air-conditioned offices, he certainly had no objection.

A thin man with grey hair and obviously approaching retirement faced him across a simple wooden desk. "1217, Rick Daly?" Rick nodded. "Your trial date has been fixed for the fifth of April and you will be given the opportunity to hire a defense lawyer."

"I don't have the means to hire a prostitute let alone a lawyer!" Rick blurted out. "Theoretically you will have a legal representative provided by Legal Aid in that case," the thin man replied. "What do you mean theoretically?" Rick inquired.

"In actual fact," continued the thin man with grey hair, "funds for legal aid are very scarce and are usually provided for women, I mean persons, involved in messy family law disputes. In recent months there have been individuals charged with offences such as armed robbery who were denied any legal aid. Almost certainly you'll have to conduct your own defense if you can't afford a lawyer. Don't worry, all the law books you will need are available in the prison library to which you will be given full access." The edges of Rick's mouth curled downwards. "I don't suppose it will make the slightest difference in any case," he muttered. "What on earth do you mean?" asked the man in the most puzzled of tones.

Rick was indeed given access to the necessary law books, even down to the pamphlet that documented the law under which he'd been charged. The thin man returned several times to provide what assistance he was able. On one occasion Rick's dormant curiosity had reared itself. "Why was I arrested in the first place?" The man had promised to seek answers and on his next visit provided one. "Apparently a month before you were arrested the authorities here received a request from the Philippine government for your extradition to that country concerning a crime for which you were convicted there and jailed. There was the mention of your escape from custody in that nation."

"Escape? I bribed my way out after being locked up on the phoniest of charges." Rick's eagerness in imparting this part of his adventures might almost have suggested that he still believed in the possibility of a just outcome.

"Be that as it may, the Australian authorities have decided to try you here under our new pedophilia laws rather than have you extradited. We don't really have any comprehensive extradition arrangement with the Philippines any way." Rick smiled. "That didn't stop the abduction of the former owner of the Aussie Bar in Manila during the second year of Cory Aquino's presidency. I heard all about it. Apparently, he was wanted here and was grabbed by the Federal Police and whisked out of the Philippines before you could say 'bar-fine!'"

It was the man's turn to smile. "I'm sure you are all too familiar with the irregularities that can so easily occur in that tropical paradise, Mr. Daly."

"Touché!" was the only response from the green clad 1217. On the man's last visit before the commencement of the trial Rick ventured another point of information. "I've been doing my legal preparation, mainly to relieve boredom, but I don't understand why my case is linked to any pedophile laws."

"The charges against you relate to forcible sex with, or rape of, a minor who was under the age of consent at the time." The face of the go-between softened for a second. "I thought pedophilia involved sex with prepubescent children," Rick innocently remarked. "You are behind the times Mr. Daly! Any sexual activity with persons below the legal age of consent, which in the Philippines is eighteen, is defined as pedophilia."

❖❖❖❖❖❖❖❖

It surprised Rick how quickly the next few weeks trotted by. Despite the lack of any optimism he thought he might as well play the game as best he was able and did his utmost to provide a defense. The essential problem was this; how do you attack a prosecution based on a lie and bloated with an entire gallery of prejudices and assumptions? He hadn't been able to answer this question to his satisfaction when the day of the trial arrived.

The journey to the courthouse in Queens Square was a familiar one, not that any view could be obtained from the windowless Black Maria. Clothed in a provided suit and tie and clutching his papers in a crisp manila folder Rick almost felt human. By the time he had reached the dock the jury had been called for selection and both the defendant and the prosecutor were given the opportunity to quickly speak to each prospective juror and reject him or her, up until a total of six objections each had been reached.

Rick was relieved at the sight of a jury. Here was his only hope. If he could convince them that he'd been set up and was now something of a political pawn he might just have the barest semblance of a chance. Well over half of the jury group were women. That didn't bode well. He objected to four of the offered dozen of his peers, three of whom were women with that hard, critical stare and one young man who seemed to be a fanatical born-again Christian. Daniel Caruthers only objected to one of the assembled jury group, a middle-aged man with an earring. Caruthers, a thirty-something male, whose thin frame and pallid complexion suggested a life devoid of sunshine, was the Crown prosecutor for the case. His wig somehow seemed a size too large for his head and gave off the impression of a sudden fall of snow. Nonetheless his carriage and bearing bore all the marks of an individual possessed of supreme confidence.

The defendant wasn't pleased to see the four jurors he had rejected and the one cast aside by Mr. Caruthers replaced by four matrons and one young Malay girl. Of the final panel that would decide his fate only three were men and they didn't appear overly sympathetic. Yet, appearances can always be deceiving.

After the briefest of recesses the case began with His Honor Justice Reginald Simpson presiding. Justice Simpson was a man in his early sixties of rotund proportions and a cherubic face. The public gallery was packed. Towards the back a party of schoolgirls and their teacher were eagerly paying attention. With a tap of the gavel the show commenced.

Daniel Caruthers presented the prosecution's opening with a deft air of attempted finality. "Your Honor and ladies and gentlemen of the jury, although this trial is the first one under the new laws and other criminals may have gotten away with similar offences in the past due to shaky policing systems in other parts of the world the demands of justice necessitate that we take our responsibilities in this matter very seriously. Each defenseless child that we can protect from sexual marauders is a child saved. I must remind you that almost all sexual offenders are serial performers. There is always another potential victim waiting for them. The only task before you is to decide the guilt or innocence of the defendant and it is our case that there is overwhelming evidence that Mr. Rick Daly is guilty as charged. I must remind you that in this kind of case we almost never possess the detailed kind of forensic evidence bandied across courtrooms on television." Laughter from both the jurors and the gallery interrupted the prosecutor for some moments. "A lack of forensic evidence," he continued, "does not mean a lack of evidence. Statements from the victim, witnesses and police reports from the area where the crime was committed must be weighed according to their seeming veracity. It is our contention that in this instance the combined evidence points to the defendant's guilt well beyond the possibility of reasonable doubt."

Mr. Caruthers then proceeded to read aloud the initial complaint made by Alma, the police and hospital reports from the Philippines and a summary of the Cebu court's findings. The luncheon adjournment had come and gone by the time he'd finished. For good measure he reminded the jury of Rick's escape from the penitentiary in that distant land. "The defendant's behavior is certainly not that of an innocent person!" Outside, storm clouds were brewing and a ferocious wind whistled by the windows. Clusters of red and brown autumn leaves swirled along the streets.

"Mr. Daly you may now open your defense," instructed Justice Simpson. Nervously Rick wobbled from the dock to his new position in the venue. "Your Honor, ladies and gentlemen of the jury," he began, mimicking the prosecutor's style, "I was unjustly charged in the first place, convicted unfairly and haven't seen the light of day since." At that point Daniel Caruthers objected on the basis of a point of order and the bench agreed with him. "Mr. Daly, you must confine your opening to a denial of the charge and an attempted rebuttal of the prosecution's interpretation of the evidence. You cannot simply tell a story, no matter how earnestly."

Rick began again. "This girl Alma had a thing for me and the police there obviously liked her. Police and schoolgirl combinations aren't entirely unknown there." The judge loudly interrupted him. "Mr. Daly you cannot just tell a story. You must follow the Court's procedures and rules of evidence." Daniel Caruthers smiled at the judge and spoke. "I'm sorry for this Your Honor, these messy time-wasting monologues often occur when defendants choose to represent themselves."

"I couldn't agree more, Mr. Caruthers, but we'll just have to do the best we can."

By the time Rick had uttered a few words that were acceptable to the court all he'd been able to say was that the initial complaint was false and that all the relevant police and court officials in the Philippines had either lied or succumbed to anti-foreigner prejudice. One of the matrons on the jury was clutching some knitting and seemed to be a reincarnation of Madam

DeFarge. As the defendant returned to the dock, he was only too aware of how lame his claims had sounded. In this world, he thought as he returned to the dock, the appearance of truth is worshipped much more highly than the real thing.

Despite all the attention given to this case from the press and the public due to its sensational nature the proceedings only lasted four days. The written depositions from the Philippines were examined in detail. That took less than a day. It wasn't all that wondrous that there were no witnesses for the defense to call. What astonished Rick was the arrival of one, solitary witness for the prosecution. On the stand stood Bruce, one of the two pathetic creatures he'd experienced an altercation with in the remand prison. Bruce was sworn in and faced Caruther's questions.

"Mr. Bruce Wallis, what did the defendant confide to you during your acquaintance in the remand center?" Bruce squirmed a little. "Well Sir, he constantly talked about how you could get any girls you liked in the Philippines, with or without money. He claimed to have raped a number of young girls without any repercussions at all. He admitted raping that Alma girl but said he was just unlucky that she'd had enough courage to complain. He said most girls there were so afraid of losing their reputations that they wouldn't say 'boo' even after being raped."

The prosecutor stretched a little. "I see. Was this admission of the defendant made only on one occasion?"

"No Sir," Bruce went on. "He said it a number of times. It was sort of like he was proud of it." Daniel Caruthers dismissed the witness and it was Rick's chance to cross-examine. He was so caught by surprise at Bruce's appearance that he was still fumbling for words as he began. "I suppose that duo will get a color TV for this performance," he muttered under his breath.

"Mr. Wallis," Rick commenced, although the title 'Mister' sounded ludicrous when attached to that pimply urchin, "I never said any of the things you claim I said."

"Yes you did," came the retort. "I didn't and you know I didn't. You'd say anything to get more privileges and to cause angst for me." At that point the judge cut Rick short and the witness was dismissed.

It was just after lunch on a Thursday when the jury retired. A youngish redheaded woman amongst the twelve remarked to her fellows, "It's just a pity we don't have the death penalty here." The rest agreed with her sentiments. Notwithstanding the fact that they took less than five minutes to reach their verdict they waited an hour over coffee and biscuits for form's sake before returning to the courtroom.

"Guilty!" was the only word that Rick heard out of the score or so that were uttered. He was led away only to be returned a week later for sentencing. His ears closed up at the reading of the judge's damning indictment of his character but did discern the phrase, "twelve years."

His new abode lacked even the modest accoutrements of the remand prison. More boredom, lousy meals and fellow inmates whose movements suggested a lack of hope overtook the hours. He wondered at the price of honesty in a grey world whose half-tones changed faster than the weather. What god had he offended? Was he being punished for all the girls whose bodies he'd tasted or for the one he hadn't? What did being a man mean and what was the curse attached to being white? He thought of Hans and their conversations in the Philippines. Rick slid into a deep depression. He walked and ate, slept and watched his backside. In the protection yard for sex offenders his companions were truly terrifying. "Some of these creatures would molest a teddy bear," he spoke aloud to himself. "It would be better to risk being murdered in the general prison population."

Chapter Thirteen

"Foreigner jailed in Australia for sex crime committed here!" blared the Sun Star Daily's headline. It caught Marilyn's eye as she passed the newsstand on P. Del Rosario Street. There, large as life, under the bold print, was a photograph of Rick. The Manila papers sported the same story as did The Freeman. Quickly purchasing a Sun Star she continued on her way.

The extraction of Rick from her life had not been without pain for Marilyn. Still, financially she had gained. In less than a year the business, which was now hers, had caught up to its previous position and in only two more it boasted its largest ever turnover and greatest number of employees. Less than a year after her former boss and lover's departure she had started seeing other men. Life has to go on, she assured herself.

The glimpse of that headline had brought memories flooding back with the force of a hurricane. She had always believed Rick to be innocent and felt sorry for him. To learn of his new calamity was another emotional burden. Once having completed her shopping she returned home and read the article at length. Tears dropped on the pages as she recalled how happy they had once been.

Being a devout Catholic Marilyn always attended Mass of a Sunday. In recent months she had attended the service at a church in Mandaue. Although it was two jeep rides from her home she had learned that a handsome young doctor whom she'd met after breaking her ankle in a freak domestic accident, attended this particular congregation. Leaving the service one Sunday in June she was amazed to encounter Alma, alone. Seizing the chance, she drew the teenager aside. "I know you lied and sent an innocent man to jail. You'll go to hell for this you know." Alma stormed off without a word. Yet, internally guilt had slowly made its presence felt in the intervening years. Alma had helped her parents more around the home and even reduced the occasions she had sex with her classmates to less than once a month, although that particular change may have been born of fear of discovery.

Both Marilyn and Alma attended confession a couple of times a year. Neither of them had ever offered up their sexual experiences while engaged in this ritual act of cleansing. When her father reminded Alma that she hadn't been for some time the girl argued. "I've been so good lately, Papa, that I don't have anything to confess." Her father, backed up by her mother, insisted that she attend.

Once faced with the cubicle the teenager completely broke down. "Father, I've sinned really badly and I think I'll go to hell." The priest assured the girl of the power of forgiveness and contrition and slowly dragged the full story out of her. To say he wasn't shocked would be a lie. However, he mustered all his pastoral skills and patience. "What should I do, Father?" wailed Alma. At his suggestion that she engage in a bout of truth telling, the schoolgirl, now in her final year, ventured the fear of being sent to prison. "Due to your age at the time I doubt that is a likelihood. In any case it is the right thing to do and the only action you can take if you really want to serve the Lord."

In less than a week's time Alma returned to the police station where she had made the complaint all those years ago and confessed to her malicious crime. No charges were laid against the girl but her most recent statement was taken and, in due course, forwarded to the relevant Australian authorities. Her father beat her within an inch of her life when he heard of the great lie and her mother wouldn't speak to her for a week.

The arrival of the new information from the Philippines wasn't exactly welcomed by the Australian justice system. The new laws were functioning well and wrongful sexual activity was being presented as an ultimate evil, along with smoking. The very idea of the first successful prosecution in this area being overturned wasn't even to be countenanced.

"There is always the likelihood that somehow this cretin has, from prison, managed to bribe the girl or her family into changing her story." Barbara Fellows, a senior justice of the Federal Appeals Court, was discussing the present situation with two of her colleagues over a bottle of wine in a restaurant close by the courthouse. "I agree with you and the political ramifications would be disastrous were we to overturn the verdict," concurred Brendan Smythe. "On the other hand, we cannot ignore the arrival of this new information. The only suitable course of action is to reduce the sentence to time already served and get rid of the guy. I believe he was born in the U.S." The third judge reminded the group that Rick had been an Australian citizen at the time of his trial and that if he hadn't been, he wouldn't have been able to be charged under the new anti-pedophilia laws. "Yet, my learned friends," offered Barbara, "it is actually possible to deport an Australian citizen from our Commonwealth if he or she was actually born elsewhere."

The Attorney General's Department was only too happy to follow the advice offered by the judges who had commuted Rick's sentence. Accordingly, on the first of September 2001 Rick found himself free and on a flight to JFK airport in the States. Well, perhaps not exactly free but the closest thing he had known for some years.

Since a number of Australian government ministers held shares in Qantas the national airline was the carrier of choice for deportations. It had been just after noon when the jumbo and its red kangaroo lurched into the sky. The service was somewhat less than he'd experienced on previous flights. Twenty hours on the trot doesn't do wonders for any cabin crew and deportees were regarded as a blot on the national psyche. For lunch the reluctant passenger was served a left-over kosher meal that tasted worse than pet food and by dinnertime the galley had inexplicably run out of trays. Admittedly the flight was so full that a body could have been forgiven for suspecting that the airline was going for the Guinness record for plane cramming. A particularly sardonic trolley dolly apologized as she dumped three packets of nuts on Rick's tray. Cunningly Rick had persuaded the man next to him to order some spare beers and the deportee at least felt free on that score.

QF 107 touched down in LA around 7 am local time and Rick was removed from the cabin before even any of the First-Class passengers were allowed off. The amorphous mass of glass, steel and concrete took Rick by surprise due to its sheer colossal proportions. As he was escorted from the aircraft and rapidly shuffled through Immigration and Customs, he observed a passenger from an earlier flight undergoing the immigration process.

A uniformed youngster was firing questions. "You checked 'No' on the form's question about criminal convictions but you didn't answer the question pertaining to Nazi activity between 1933 and 1945!" The passenger seemed startled. "As I was only two years old in 1945, I'd have had to have been the youngest active Nazi in history!" he countered. "Ok Sir, I'll just check the 'No' box for you. There is one final question though before we admit you to the United States. What three nice things can you say about our president?" Bemused, the man answered, "He has a nice dog, he has a nice dog, he has a nice dog." Suddenly worried, he added, "and he was never a lawyer."

Leaving the comic scene Rick kept pace with his escorts. After a miserable wait of ninety minutes under strict supervision he was bundled onto an American Airlines flight to New York. Why that particular city should have been the preferred choice for his forced homecoming was beyond him. At 5:50 pm, exactly six minutes late, the wheels of the domestic flight grounded on the tarmac of JFK.

A white minivan was waiting. A middle-aged woman with grey hair greeted him. "Although you are now free, the Corrections Department was certain you would need some assistance after so long away and, unless you have any objections, we will take you to some assisted lodgings until you can find your feet." The very possibility of making a decision for himself eluded the escorted guest and he readily agreed.

Forty-five minutes later and he was deposited in the foyer of a sixties vintage yellow brick building. On arrival a dour-faced man in his late thirties with a strange tattoo on his left arm handed over a bundle of clean clothes and read him the rules; "No drinking, no female visitors and no disturbances of any sort. Remember, twenty steps from here is the street!" Rick took the bundle and was shown his dormitory but all he could remember was the tattoo; red and white patches with a dagger so skinny it could've been a scalpel.

The Sunny Horizons halfway-house provided a minimal modicum of comfort. Three basic meals a day were served and there was a small lounge room that sported a color TV. Previously it boasted a considerable number of educational and retraining opportunities for its guests but with the advent of the Bush Administration, funding for such social niceties was severely curtailed. All that was on offer now was the most rudimentary reading skills program. Inmates were given a weekly allowance of ten dollars and some assistance in applying for jobs.

The first flush of fall saw piles of brown and orange leaves carried down ashen streets on regular gusts of wind. Rick took an afternoon walk on his second day to check out his new surroundings. For once, he was more or less unfettered. Between the hours of 8 am and 11 pm the residents were able to come and go as they wished. The various thoroughfares were littered with the flotsam of American city life; newspapers following the leaves on the wind, discarded cigarette packets and abandoned hypodermics. Discontented faces, mostly black but some white or Latino, stared from the shadows at the residue of the American Dream. The approach of evening had made itself well felt when Rick turned back towards the halfway house. He might have been on the loose but he certainly wasn't situated in paradise.

No sooner than the serendipitous walker had reached the reception counter the dour-faced man who never had introduced himself and didn't seem to need a name called him over. "Rick, there's a letter for you from some other welfare agency." The returnee thanked the nameless man and took the letter. Its contents afforded as much shock as possible to an individual who had spent years swimming in the waters of hell.

> Dear Mr. Daly,
>
> It is with great regret that we must inform you of the death of your uncle, Christopher Daly, on the 30th of August 1999. Apparently he succumbed to a severe heart attack and was deceased before the paramedics reached him. Due to your own misfortunes it was not possible to relay these sad tidings to you any earlier than this.
>
> Yours faithfully,
>
> S.V. Saddington
>
> Dept. of Resettlements and Social Affairs.

Crumpling the paper into a ball and thrusting it into his trouser pocket Rick disappeared without a word into his dormitory and sat on his bunk. Those recently out of jail appreciate this style of bedding as it affords a link with the most greatly known home. The dormitory was empty save for him. He produced and unfurled the paper ball and read it again. He hadn't even heard that his uncle had been ill. The last letter he'd received from Christopher outlined some problems with his pension but nothing further. He did know of George's prison time however. In fact, he felt that George was a kindred spirit more than a cousin.

Rereading the brief lines that told the story in the manner of Fox News reporting the death of a leftist Rick's dark imagination took hold. How did such a fighter suddenly leave this earth? Rick pictured his uncle, a healthy senior citizen, taking up a ruinous health kick and jogging himself to death. Three hours of jogging would be too much for an elderly man. This picture faded back into the realm of Meinong's Jungle as quickly as it had arrived. Christopher had always been a moderate man, even in the face of extreme adversity. He would not have consciously lived any lifestyle likely to kill him.

The next cloud from the ether formed into a vision of George's homecoming. "Dad," the specter of the returned prisoner uttered, "before I was sent to jail, I owed a huge sum of money to the mob and now I'm out they're going to get me!" A passing schoolboy threw a small stone at one of their windows and Christopher doubled up, expiring on the spot.

"Not really likely," mused Rick. His mind then seized on the pension difficulties. He saw Christopher being denied his rights by avaricious and corrupt banks, in league with criminal government agencies. His mind conjured up an amorphous, insidious acid eating at his uncle's life's blood. "It's not our problem, Mr. Daly. This house has been repossessed by the bank and you have had several weeks' notice to quit. You simply have to leave!"

"My children and I have nowhere else to go!" shouts Christopher.

"I'm just doing my job, buddy," says the bank official, while laying a steadying hand on the distraught Christopher's arm. Doubling up in horror and pain Christopher's brave heart gives out and he dies before any paramedics can reach him.

The uselessness of such black ponderings forced itself into Rick's consciousness and he abandoned these miserable reveries. Lying back on his bunk he fell asleep. No dreams interrupted his slumbers and outside, the world moved on.

In actual fact his uncle's fatal heart attack was far less dramatic. Christopher had indeed received a repossession notice from his bank. His mortgage had been largely paid off at the time of his retirement but with the cancellation of his pension unpaid debts, including local government levies, led to an initially modest, but ever increasing, amount. Governed by the logic of the dollar that rules the world, the bank considered that although the debt was by no means huge Christopher and his children would be unlikely to be able to repay. Their decision was automatic. Two days had passed since the repossession notice arrived in the mail. After breakfast one morning Christopher had complained of chest pains to Rebecca. George hadn't been home for a week and all serious matters fell to his sister in any case. Christopher's daughter sat her father down in a chair and phoned an ambulance. He was still alive when the vehicle, with its lights flashing, departed. The banality of truth somehow always surprises even the news media before they tart it up.

By the time Rick awoke a few birds were welcoming the morning and, in any case, he didn't expect too much from life. His uncle had died and he was still living. There it was. What more was to be said? Rick ate the usual breakfast and sallied forth to look for a job. Marks of depression on a human face generally have the effect of instantly deciding the outcome of any job interview but always some slip through the net and such activity is, at least, socially acceptable. The next few days saw Rick attend three interviews; spend an unsuccessful hour in a local bar attempting to attract female companionship and large measures of time feeding the ducks in a nearby pond with hostel left-overs.

The clock on the wall ticked by and the desk clerk, without a name, dutifully turned over the calendar. When the clock showed 10 pm on September the tenth Rick strolled through the door. He hadn't bothered attending any interviews or even trying his luck with the local ladies. His day had been spent staring at the duck pond and attempting to talk to his few friends. The ducks never answered but they did appreciate the scraps he offered.

"This country is the greediest in the world," remarked Pietro, a fellow lodger in Rick's dormitory. "I can't argue with that," mumbled Rick as he drifted off.

Strange dreams overtook his sleeping mind. There was Adolph Eichmann, in a glass booth for his trial on war crimes after he had been illegally abducted from South America by Mossad agents. "Did you organize those train timetables?" bellowed the prosecutor. "You bet I did," replied Eichmann, "and I defy anyone in the world to do a better job of transportation than I have done." Amid Jewish taunts of revenge, hatred and God knows what else, Eichmann stood firm. He knew that whatever he said, he was going to be executed so he might as well speak the truth from his heart.

"I was proud to serve in that uniform," he declared. "I was thrilled to assist the Reich in that way. It was wonderful. We had the chance for once in history to change the world order and we were determined to ensure that every human being on earth, including the most recalcitrant Jews, would accept the change for the better. When your agents illegally abducted me from Paraguay they carried on about the importance of establishing my identity, as, apparently according to your laws, an abductee must admit their true identity before the business can proceed. I didn't deny my real name or deeds because I'm proud of them!"

"So you are denying that you engineered the deaths of six million Jews then?" shouted the prosecutor with fumes of hatred escaping from his breath. "Six million? Did you count them?" challenged Eichmann, his pride intact. "I have told you a thousand times that the camps were labor camps not death camps. The large numbers of prisoners who perished towards the end of the war were extremely regrettable but not deliberate. You must remember that the death rate amongst Germans, including civilians, was also huge. We were starving."

"You are a liar," shouted the prosecutor. "You and your cohorts simply tried to engineer the destruction of the Jewish race!"

"Rubbish!" shouted back Eichmann. "It would be an absurdity to attempt a genocide and we never did. Those Jews who surrendered their parasitic attempts to feed on others and abandoned the racist creed of the Zionists were treated well. If they served the Reich with the same dedication as other citizens they were treated accordingly. You people, through your own warped view of religion and the world, believe that you have the right to lord it over all others and when they resist they are branded as inherently evil." Even in this atmosphere of intense invective at least he was allowed to speak, unlike future interviewees who challenged the worldview of the Bush administration and the Fox News network. For that he was grateful. No matter what he said or had done, or had not done, they would surely kill him. Eichmann spoke further with more spiritual authority.

"You will kill me but not the truth or what I stand for!" he shouted defiantly. "In the future you will kill many innocent people in a terrorist campaign in Palestine. You did bomb the King David Hotel and kill more than one hundred innocent people in a single act of violence. You will then steal the lands of thousands of others saying that you were promised them by God. It is obvious to all that any god that aids and abets such a disgusting group of human beings is not worthy of being a god. All I can say further before you hang me is that I go to my death with a clear conscience, which is more than I can say of you. I do regret one thing however, and it is this. Many thousands of your people perished in the camps without the chance to see why they were there and without the opportunity to change their ways."

"You are a murderer and a liar!" screamed the prosecutor. "You are not fit to breathe the same air as us!"

"Don't breathe it then and die!" shouted back Eichmann.

A vicious banging of the gavel and police threats to the gallery was necessary to restore order. The defendant was led away from the court and, three days later, was hung. His last words were, "Fuck you!" and "Heil Hitler!" The dream moved on. "The Philippines has some good points," remarked the foreigner on the next bar stool. "Where else can you buy a classroom full of fifteen-year-old virgins for less than the price of a second-hand motorcycle?" Then, Rick was back at his former house in La Paloma and deep inside Marilyn. The lovemaking was intense and passionate. Then a second later the vagina he was in was a younger, even tighter one with fewer surrounding hairs. It was Marilyn's daughter. She had been with a Filipino man and produced a baby girl. This girl, Malou, had miraculously attained the age of seventeen and thrown herself at Rick. The moisture and tightness were virtually unbearable and were finished with an almighty crash.

Picking himself up from the floor Rick could just hear the words "Are you all right? Must have been some dream!" Answering in the affirmative Rick climbed back to his bunk. Breakfast seemed tame after the night's imaginations. It was twenty minutes past eight when he was watching the morning news on the communal television and sipping coffee.

A news flash caught the attention of everybody assembled. "A plane has crashed into the north tower of the World Trade Center." Images of smoke pouring from halfway down the building flooded the screen. The worst aviation accident in living memory was discussed with emotional voices. Although the president later claimed to have seen that crash on TV in a Florida classroom he was visiting, the initial impact was not broadcast live and was not available on recorded video for many hours.

Rick and his fellows were transfixed at the screen when another jetliner flew across it, striking the south tower. He rubbed his eyes to make sure he was awake. He was. The entire group were still sitting, transfixed on the screen, an hour-or-more later, when the towers collapsed. The USA was under attack.

"Whoever would want to attack this wonderful country?" sardonically questioned Richard, a black man in his thirties.

"Probably disaffected citizens who objected to the rigging of the 2000 presidential election result," joked one of his fellows. Rick said nothing.

No-one knew it at the time but the attack on the twin towers meant much more than the destruction of two buildings and the loss of almost three thousand souls. It meant the destruction of democracy itself. Those hallowed words from the U.S. constitution concerning unalienable rights to the pursuit of happiness and liberty were suddenly subsumed under the dark cloud of expediency. The White House evoked the apocalyptic terms of good and evil and deemed the withdrawal of long cherished rights as a necessity in the long and bloody war on terror that had already begun. Holy rollers and their fellow evangelistic travelers cheered as the Good Book's prophecy of Armageddon was at last on the way. Armaments manufacturers smiled and the most avaricious of capitalists nodded. The unspoken alliance between Christian fundamentalists and the most aggressive Zionists had begun in earnest. An innocent party could have been forgiven for thinking that the Jewish text the Torah and the Bible were one and the same. Any atrocity committed in the name of God's cause is more than permissible. It is an obligation. Needless to say, somewhere in the badlands stretching from Pakistan to Afghanistan Osama and his followers were preaching the same message.

The nation, including the residents of the Sunny Horizons halfway house, was in total shock for at least a week. Job interviews were forgotten, walks in the park took much longer, meals were a process and the business of life seemed to be on hold. The television broadcast the president's response to the crisis. Somehow Rick was unable to prevent himself from making an educational comparison. George Bush Jr. reads a children's story in a moment of crisis. Hitler had read Nietzsche and Hegel and was a literate man. Rick was engaged in reading the morning paper when they came. Almost a week had passed. Four grey-suited individuals, identifying themselves as Federal agents, handcuffed him and led him away. It was an extreme case of déjà vu.

The mind of the confused prisoner wandered again. He was sorry for deflowering Marilyn, even more sorry for deflowering her daughter, Malou and extremely regretful for not having fucked that tart, Alma. If only he had the chance again. She wouldn't have been able to walk for a month.

"Al Quaeda? What do you mean?" Rick ventured at his first interrogation. "We know about your little sojourn with these individuals some years ago." The light hurt Rick's eyes. "You are a terrorist masquerading as an ordinary criminal. That's some disguise." The accuser wore a military uniform and appeared totally uninterested in any answers that the suspect might offer.

"Might as well spill it all son. If you don't you won't have much of an existence." Rick's spontaneous life seemed to offend the man. Picking himself from the floor and wiping blood from his split lip, Rick tamely mumbled, "What on earth are you talking about? I never screwed that girl and I don't know any terrorists but sometimes I wish I did." Thwap! He was on the floor again. This time a young woman who had just entered the room assisted him back to his stool. "We're sorry for being a little rough but you must understand the urgency of the situation. You have no other choice but to tell us everything."

Rick smiled through the blood and answered, "Do you want the truth or something else?" Again, he found himself on the floor. How had he come to be here? Obviously, life has no bottom. On the bright side that meant he wasn't there yet. Recent years had taught him to expect little from existence and in that expectation, he hadn't been disappointed. Endless interrogations and weeks in the most miserable of nondescript cells passed without the suspect being any the wiser as to what his captors actually wanted.

"Although you haven't mentioned it to us we know you spent time in an Abu Sayef camp in the southern Philippines and have links with global Muslim terrorists." Rick was afraid to laugh and merely dropped his lips a couple of points. "What on earth are you talking about?" His courage in putting the question surprised himself.

"Do you deny that you were present in an Abu Sayef camp in 1994?" The prisoner smiled. "Come to think of it, I did visit a group in Mindanao while on a mission to rescue my daughter. It was a personal and family-law matter."

"Nice try! You want us to believe that you gained assistance from a terrorist organization in some domestic pursuit?"

"That's the way of it but I had never heard of Islamic terrorism or anything similar at that time." Rick was then left alone in his miserable cell for two days without food or water.

When the monsters returned, he was ready to tell them anything. How on earth had they discovered the tiny fact that he had been in Mindanao in that year? A new man appeared, also in some sort of uniform but lacking in any identification marks. "Daly, have you decided to talk yet?"

"I'll talk plenty when I know what it is you are after," the prisoner replied. The new man laughed. "It isn't your place to ask us questions. Just talk!"

Rick thought for a bit and then offered up his sexual liaison with Sonia. "We were waiting for that," smiled the new man. "Please tell us how your fling with Commander Hubib led to your involvement in terrorist activities." Rick's jaw dropped. "I was never involved in terrorism of any sort but how do you know about Sonia and me?" The laughter was abusive. "Sonny," exclaimed the interrogator as he slapped the prisoner, "You obviously haven't heard of Project Echelon. It's no longer a secret so I can mention it. We even know where you, or anyone else for that matter, has put his dick more than ninety percent of the time. I'm afraid that we can't tell you if your Sonia was faking her orgasms."

Rick's jaw fell further. This was just too, too much. Years of maltreatment and prison were nothing compared with this sucking of his soul. A flicker of spirit stirred within him as he remembered his dream about Eichmann. "If you are so good how come you didn't know about the misappropriation of Bill Clinton's appendage?" Another slap subdued his spirit once again.

"For your information, Daly, we scan the world from the White House outwards. You could call the Oval Office an information rain shadow." Licking his blood Rick couldn't resist the temptation to ask further questions. "So, you assholes know, in advance, about multitudes of bank robberies and murders but do nothing to prevent them?" Another nameless uniform who was present, pushed Rick hard to remind him again that it wasn't his job to interrupt or ask anything, before the superior answered.

"We know about most of these things in advance but ignore the information. We don't have infinite resources so we only utilize information relating to direct, significant attacks on the system." Rick didn't know what to say but some words slipped out. "Why are you telling me this?" The laughter, this time, resonated throughout the building. "Where you're going it won't matter!"

Six months slipped by and Rick still had no idea where he was. His mind slipped back to both the Australian and Philippine prisons and he missed them. America, Land of the Free! Bullshit! Land of the greedy rich assholes who hold sway over much of the world! He couldn't tell from his cell if it was day or night so when he was yanked from his sleep on one occasion, he greeted his tormenters with "Good Morning."

"It's 7:45 pm Daly but we thank you for your attempted courtesy. Hopefully you are ready to talk now." Silence was followed by Rick's earnest affirmation that he'd already imparted all that he knew. "You're bloody lucky that you were born in this great land, Daly. Otherwise you'd be sweating it out in Guantanamo Bay!" The senior uniform smiled.

Five months later and Rick again found himself on the street; no charges, no apologies; no nothing. Amazingly, his old halfway house was permitted to accept him. "You seem to have a penchant for trouble," remarked the man-without-a-name. "Yes Sir," replied Rick before disappearing into the lounge room.

Chapter Fourteen

It was eight weeks since Rick had returned to Sunny Horizons and Christmas was approaching. The television news broadcast the fact that Iraq was prepared to readmit UN weapons inspectors. In the Philippines President Estrada had been forced from office amidst charges of gross corruption. Afghanistan had been invaded and the Taliban shrunken from a regime to an insurgency. Osama Bin Laden was declared an enemy of humanity or at least of the U.S. Flowery words about freedom and evil emanated from the White House and the nation was informed that Saddam Hussein's regime must be removed from Iraq before he could use his vast array of terrible weapons.

On a more local level Rick had acquired a job. A man whose acquaintance he made in the park near the duck pond had told him about a vacancy for a maintenance engineer at Brown Bros. nuts and bolts factory. Apparently, the look of desperation on Rick's face was just what the employers were looking for. They had been pessimistic about the chances of finding a human with two legs and two arms for the low wage they were offering. The very next day he was installed as a janitor on their site and performed all the tasks required of him with aplomb.

By March 2003 Rick had saved enough money to bid farewell to Sunny Horizons. He moved into the smallest of one-bedroom apartments on the south side. One morning while walking to work a tall man in a dark suit approached him. "What are you arresting me for this time?" Rick shouted at the surprised individual. "I beg your pardon? I just wanted to ask you the time." Rick apologized. "I'm sorry. I thought you were someone else. It's 7:20." The young businessman thanked him and scurried off.

It was nine o'clock on a Thursday evening, after the day's labors and a few drinks that the thought of contacting his lost love occurred to Rick. It would be seven in the morning there and Marilyn would be preparing to leave for work, he thought. Marilyn did send me three letters while I was in prison in Australia and she probably had no idea of my whereabouts while I was locked up here. I should at least try! His mind was made up and gathering the receiver in his left hand and his heart in his mouth he dialed the numbers. Against all logic he was hoping that the love of his life would have held out and simply waited for his return.

"Hello. Ma-ayong Buntag (Good Morning)." It was the voice he'd desperately missed for so long. "Marilyn darling, it's me, Rick." Several seconds of silence ensued. "Hello, are you still there?" Rick stammered. "Yes Rick, I'm here but I can't really talk. I've got to go to work." Rick's spirits sank. "Can't you spare a few minutes. God, I've missed you so much!" Again, no sounds made their way through the hand piece. "As I said, I can't talk now. Alfonso is around somewhere and he's very jealous." Marilyn's voice had all the warmth of a funeral ovation. "Who's Alfonso?" Rick challenged. Several seconds of empty crackling were followed by an admission. "My husband," said Marilyn in a muffled voice. "We've been married for two years and have a son. He's a businessman. He's a good provider and doesn't drink or womanize but he's very jealous." Click! Without thinking Rick's hand had replaced the receiver on the hook. He'd written off the business as any concern of his years ago but somehow he'd held onto the most romantic of notions that Marilyn would wait for him.

A living shell, Rick Daly stared at the alabaster wall in front of him. The more cogent side of his mind knew that Marilyn was a lost love and had been so for some time. Yet a spark of hope lay dormant in the other half of his brain. Until he was directly told he'd refused to believe that Marilyn would, even could, settle for another man. The futility of existence welled up in his thoughts. Was that the futility of all existence, all human existence or just his own pathetic being?

On the one hand he was merely a speck in the vast expanse of the cosmos and on the other his personal universe had been inexorably shrinking. In fact, the shrinkage was gaining speed with all the power of a big bang in reverse. What would Rick Daly ultimately become? Just another human black hole in the shattered dreams of a collective humanity perhaps?

Looking at himself full stretch in the mirror he felt he'd grown shorter over the last few years. The dial on his watch appeared more compact than he'd previously remembered it as being. Even his menial current employment seemed to provide a significant challenge. There was little left to do but attempt to save enough money to enable a trip to Chicago and a search for his only surviving relatives. That might not necessarily reinject the personal meaning that had been forcefully sucked out of his existence but no alternative presented itself in the space that exists behind the closed eyes. He desperately needed to relocate his sense of self.

Mechanical movements of broom and mop marked the passing of the hours, days and weeks. Rick barely even noticed the four Latino women who labored garrulously in the packing section of Warehouse A. They had however, observed him with interest. Two of them were young and moderately striking with full breasts and curvaceous figures. "That janitor is a strange one," remarked Maria to her companions. "Keeps to himself all the time. It's a shame really when he's so good looking." Condoleezza, a fat lady in her forties, laughed. "He's probably some kind of criminal on the lam, or worse some sort of spy or terrorist." Vanessa, barely nineteen, cut Condoleezza short. "He appears sad and completely absorbed in himself. Maybe he's just experienced a failed love affair or else has terrible financial difficulties." A passing foreman stifled the women's conjecture and forced them back into the pretense of enthusiastic work.

An embarrassingly small number of trees, of the kind reluctantly placed by developers when they bulldoze forests to make way for industry and housing, demonstrated their fondness for spring and actually appeared healthy by the time Rick had saved a few hundred dollars and had been at Brown Bros. long enough to request ten days off. Since annual vacation means just that and Mr. Daly, the maintenance engineer had been with them for only six months, he was granted ten days leave without pay.

Availing himself of the cheapest possible transport Rick boarded a Greyhound bus bound for that famous city whose sons included the likes of Al Capone. It was 8 am on a Monday when the wheels turned and the coach sped from the terminal. An amorphous mass, reflecting the greyness of modern city life sped by. Pockets of slums were interspersed with more generous suburbs whose grandiose dwellings declared to the world the success and moral superiority of their inhabitants. The sights of the inner-city homeless sleeping rough with their pathetic moth worn blankets and piles of dirty newspapers were replaced with the specters of Porsches and BMWs.

The duality of the American Dream never crossed Rick's consciousness. The Greyhound passenger's thoughts were preoccupied with more personal matters. Would he find Rebecca and George? If he did how could he help them or more importantly, how could they help him? What if he couldn't locate them? How would he be able to reclaim his identity? The ten-hour journey took in green fields, junctions of interstate highways and comfortable towns that boasted, "We are the real America and the rest of the country or indeed the world can go whistle."

"You got a problem? Mac?" A surly waitress with the physique of Anna Nicole Smith demanded his attention. The rest of the passengers had dutifully ordered a meal at Bleachers' Highway Diner but Rick had merely taken a seat in silence. "What? I'm sorry. I'll have a white coffee please." Mollified the Anna Nicole look-alike scurried away only to return minutes later with the beverage.

The rest of the trip was uneventful save for an independent Japanese tourist, a girl in her mid-twenties who was seated next to Rick, throwing up. "I so sorry," she murmured in broken English. "It must been the food in that diner. It simply awful." Rick helped the young woman clean up and then began to doze. Fearful imaginings gripped him and he awoke screaming. "Are you all right?" asked Akiko, the Japanese girl, just as several rows of faces turned towards the pair. It was Rick's turn to apologize. "Bad dreams accompany a good life, so they say," he laughed.

As the coach swung into a numbered bay at the windy city's central terminal and ground to a halt alongside dozens of siblings that had arrived from all corners of the nation, it occurred to Rick that he didn't even have a photograph of Rebecca or George. Darkness had fallen an hour earlier and the obvious immediate action was to find lodgings for the night. A porter had suggested Gray's Motel as it was cheap, clean and nearby. A few minutes later and Rick had parted with thirty dollars. The sparsely furnished room was indeed clean. Across the street from Gray's and down a number of paces stood Jacob's Diner. This particular eatery stood on a corner like a giant spider's web, waiting for its victims to enter. Despite its demeanor the bacon and eggs Rick ordered along with his coffee were, in fact, quite tasty.

His hunger sated, he retreated back to his room and turned in for an early night.

The sound of morning traffic awoke him at 6:30 am. Considering the enormity of his task an early start was not unwelcome. School children were in evidence by the time he alighted from the train in Elgin. A short taxi ride took him to the last known address of the other remaining Dalys. A none-too-happy young man who appeared to be a night worker, from the manner in which he flinched from the daylight and rubbed his eyes, answered the doorbell.

To Rick's enquiry he replied, "I have no idea where the previous occupants went. All I know is that this house was repossessed by some bank and then rented out. There were other tenants before me but I have no idea where they got to, either." Rick apologized for disturbing the man and, armed with the address of the Real Estate agent, departed. To his dismay the agent wasn't any more informative. "Sorry I can't help you," a largish woman with glasses replied, "and I doubt the bank in question would have any ideas either."

Having drawn a blank, Rick paced the streets for a while, past fast-food outlets, a car yard and an adult toy store. "George would be the easier one of the pair to locate because of his prison record," he decided. An hour and half later and the searcher was back in downtown Chicago. The Department of Corrections kept a modest office in conjunction with the Parole Board and having discovered the address from the phone book, Rick decided on a personal visit. "Yes, we know of the person you have asked about but unfortunately the privacy laws prevent us from assisting your enquiry." The bespectacled young lady was polite but adamant.

It was well past noon when the next idea struck. His neurones firing with the pizzazz of an aurora Rick decided to switch track. Rebecca would probably have a driving license whereas George well may not. The closest office of the Department of Motor Vehicles was another cab ride away. Rick wasn't quite expecting such a crowd in this establishment. Teenagers applying for licenses, car owners renewing their registration plates and all manner of humanity revisiting a basic connection to officialdom thronged the room. It was an hour after he'd taken a number that Rick's turn for service arrived. "I'm looking for some relatives of mine..." The young woman he was facing cut him short. "We are not allowed to give out any information of that nature under any circumstances!" she almost shouted. Perhaps such requests were by no means rare. "I'm sorry but I really have no other way of finding my cousins, George and Rebecca Daly," Rick apologized.

"Did you say Rebecca Daly?" The girl's eyes were staring wide and her mouth was agape. "Yes, I did," was the reply.

"That's me!" Her shoulder-length hair appeared to frizz. "I'm your cousin, Rick. When do you get off work?" Rebecca still appeared stunned. "Come back just before five," was all she could manage and Rick walked away.

Taking his place in a nearby café he glanced at his watch. The hands declared two thirty in that particularly neutral tone that is the province of machines. Three coffees and one soggy doughnut later he looked again. Two forty-five. His mind raced through the past and several possible futures. By the time three o'clock arrived he was endeavoring to count numerous tiny cockroaches that were scurrying along the walls. The coming two hours were an almost immovable object that seemed to have come adrift from the mantle of time and space. Thoughts of Marilyn, his years in custody and the intrinsic unfairness of collective humanity flooded his consciousness. Such mental deliberations can block out the here and now and even lay a mist over steadfastness of purpose. "Another coffee buddy?" called the waitress. "I...er." The delirium of introspection ended with the same rapidity that it had begun. It was ten minutes before five. "I'm sorry. I'm late. Bye."

Rick sprang from his seat and set off towards Rebecca's place of employment at the double. He burst through its front doors some ninety seconds before closing time. "Rick, I'll be with you in a few minutes," his much younger cousin called from behind her counter.

The longest afternoon drew to a close as the pair left the building. "We have so much to talk about," Rebecca declared, "I don't know where to start. Where are you staying?" Rick hurriedly described his temporary abode and suggested an early dinner. "There's a good Mexican restaurant two blocks away. Let's go there," suggested the girl.

"We knew of your misfortunes in the Philippines and Australia but after your incarceration down under we heard nothing more," Rebecca blurted.

"What about George? Is he all right?" her elder relative responded. "More or less. He took Dad's death pretty hard on top of his other troubles."

They were seated in Montezuma's Glory and sipping a couple of Millers when Rick summoned the courage to ask about Christopher's demise. "The repossession notice on our house must have been the last straw. His health had been on the decline for some time and he simply collapsed. He never regained consciousness. If anybody ever deserved to have a happy old age it was Dad. The natural injustice of life makes me so mad! And you, Rick! What happened to you in this last couple of years?"

A voice of suddenly-induced age struggled to reply. "Some kind of black star has been shining on me. I never believed in all my born days that ideas of truth and justice were only pretty words to brighten a much darker and more ubiquitous reality. Now, however, I find it impossible to believe in anything, even myself." Rebecca appeared shocked. "I'm so sorry, Rick, to hear that but what actually happened to you?"

"After that trumped up sex charge was finally disposed of in Australia I was unceremoniously given a free flight back here. No 'sorry,' no recompense just the boot! I thought I'd reached the bottom but of course there isn't one. After that September 11 thing I was mysteriously arrested just out of New York and kept in a nameless prison for almost a year without charge. Apparently I was considered some kind of Al Quaeda sleeper."

"My God!" interjected Rebecca. "You! How could they think you could be some kind of Islamic terrorist?" Rick loosed a sardonic smile and continued. "You obviously don't listen to our glorious president on the news, Rebecca. The world is divided into two clear camps of good and evil, black and white. Anybody who, however accidentally, has ever landed on a black square in his life is tainted and forfeits any rights. I briefly met some members of the Abu Sayef group in the Philippines, long before it embarked on its career of kidnappings and crime. That was enough for the geniuses protecting this country. I was clearly a Muslim convert and an Al Quaeda sleeper. Suffice it to say, a year later and they realized that their instant wisdom was incorrect. Again I was shunted out on the street but at least I am sort of free and here I am."

"Your account of Life's chess board is certainly a depressing one Rick. Our president is a reformed drunkard and his experience of landing on a black square hasn't stopped him." The wryest of grins appeared on Rick's face just as a plate of burritos and a bowl of guacamole arrived. "It's not what you are or even what you do that counts in this world; it's who you are and how much power you can draw. Besides didn't anyone ever tell you not to trust a man who doesn't drink? Anyway, enough of the darkness; how are you getting on?"

"I get by. People live in a permanent state of low-level depression in any case. Anything else is a form of delusion. I never had the chance of an education or anything fancy like that. I don't even have a boyfriend but I get by." Rick nodded. "And George? The last I heard of him was quite some years ago. He was out of jail and had found the Lord."

The girl's eyes darkened a shade and almost imperceptibly lowered their gaze a notch. "That phase didn't last long. It was just after Dad died and the bank threw us out of our home. I had just enough money to rent a small apartment for the two of us. We'd been there less than a week when George returned from an evening's evangelizing and appeared shattered. He'd just kept mumbling that they were all fakes. When I tried to comfort him and asked why, he just returned a line about the born agains simply wanting a free pass in life. He abandoned that calling as quickly as he'd found it. Needless to say, he couldn't find any sort of job. At first, he hung around the apartment and we started to argue. Then one day he just left. 'Said he had money and would be all right. He took up with some of his old gang members and these days has plenty of money. No more trouble with the police though. I guess he's become more cluey and wiser. He offers me money from time to time but I won't take it as I can guess where it comes from."

"You know where he's living then?" Rick responded.

"Of course. We can go and visit him tomorrow evening if you like." After the tortillas and coffee it was all decided. Rick would move to Rebecca's apartment on the morrow, for the remainder of his stay and they'd visit George. The pair parted and Rick returned to Gray's. His sleep that night produced no dreams.

A stiff breeze was blowing as Rick alighted from the cab at 1237 Sunshine Drive. Handing over the fare plus a modest tip he couldn't help thinking how much more pleasurable a cab ride was, being the passenger rather than the driver. A cantilevered apartment block opened into a modest lobby boasting little apart from a single elevator. After ascending to the fourteenth-floor, a short stroll to the right revealed Rebecca's abode, apartment 1432. He'd barely rung the bell when the door swung back.

"Come in, Rick. Put your stuff in Sarah's room. She's my share mate but is away for a few days." Traversing the hall and across a compact lounge area Rick's eyes had few seconds to take in the scene. A tidy but sparsely furnished household announced itself. Perched on the wall facing the hallway was a tapestry simply framed in driftwood. A slender silver dagger emerged from a somber background of red and white. "Where did you get that?" Rick innocently inquired. "It was a present from George. He gave it to me a couple of months ago," replied his cousin. Saying nothing further Rick took his bags into the assigned room and quickly emerged. "I'm ready," he announced. "Would you like a coffee or perhaps a beer?" asked Rebecca. "No thank you. Let's just make our visit."

George dwelt just far enough away to make walking impossible but not on any train or bus route. Another ten dollars waltzed its way from Rick's wallet to a deserving taxi driver. The visiting cousin had anticipated a grotty, decaying tenement of an amorphously grey brick surrounded by garbage. Instead he was faced with a suburb of verdant and luxurious greenery whose upmarket façade couldn't even be hidden by the present darkness. George's building in the Gold Coast district was a stunning edifice of glass and steel, four-storeys high. Rebecca noted the expression on her cousin's face with a wry grin but said nothing.

Rebecca pressed the button for Unit 17 and the security door released its grip. As the pair entered the plant-studded lobby the girl took the lead. "George's apartment is on the second floor so we can take the stairs." A few seconds later and a mahogany door swung back and they were admitted.

Despite the fact that Rick had never previously laid eyes on his cousin, any more than he'd done with Rebecca before that fateful day in the Department of Motor Vehicles that first glance announced to each that they were in the presence of like minds. "Come in, Sis and Cousin Rick," announced a confident young man dressed in a casual finery. No sooner than the couple had been admitted and seated a bourbon and Pepsi was presented to Rick and a white wine for Rebecca. "I hope I got it right," mumbled the young man. "That's fine. You've obviously done much better than me in the sewerage swim, George," Rick laughed. The disparity between this abode and his other cousin's home shouted. Situated between tasteful plants stood the latest home theatre system.

Rebecca appeared embarrassed at her cousin's state of shock. "George's current work is very highly paid."

George laughed. "I hear you've been in the wars somewhat more than me, Cousin Rick, hard to believe though it is." Having nothing more than the wisdom born of experience to show for his misfortunes Rick could only offer the weakest of smiles. A few minutes of small talk followed until George offered a drink refill. "A gin and tonic, please," requested the elder cousin. George stood and reached high to the top shelf of the bar. As he did so his shirtsleeves rode up. A short distance from his left shoulder a tattoo of a golden dagger backed by red and white squares was visible.

When George produced the beverages and sat down Rick couldn't contain himself. "I'm sorry but what is the meaning behind the tattoo? I've seen it before." Since trust wasn't an issue in this case George told the truth. "It's a company logo, an umbrella company that provides well paid work to anybody willing to make an effort."

"It doesn't sound very law abiding not that I have much respect left for the law," remarked the guest. "Rick, the world isn't about laws; it isn't even about right and wrong. It's about winners and losers, pure and simple." Rebecca squirmed a little in her seat. "Whatever you think is a fair thing," laughed Rick. "I don't suppose the company has anything to do with that teenage gang that got you into all that trouble?"

"Not a chance, Rick. After escaping from those religious fakes and loonies I did run into a couple of the old homeboys. However, the crowd they put me in touch with are much more sophisticated than those teenage posers. Some people even say that the company is connected to Halliburton. All I know is that I do the work and I get well paid."

"You haven't had any trouble with the law since joining the company?" Rick queried. "During the Clinton years there were some feeble investigations involving the FBI and various police forces but they came to nothing. The incumbent Bush administration has been entirely focused on Iraq and the Islamic thing and, unless we behave stupidly, we are left pretty much alone. From what Rebecca has said you are only scraping together an existence as a janitor in New York. Maybe you could have talents to offer to our company."

Rick raised his jaw. "You're right about my miserable situation George. I spent years in jail without even doing anything wrong. The entire system sucks. However, I don't want to take risks that might send me back into that living death." George sipped his drink. "Fear not, Rick, this company is a corporation of great power. Unless you are really stupid there is no chance you will face the wrath of America's justice system." Rick coughed. "You mean America's injustice system that extends to Australia and the Philippines and much of the world, surely."

"You don't need to tell me about the system, Rick. I learned about what is fair and what is not, long ago." Rick just nodded and Rebecca engrossed herself in the latest reality TV program, "Survivor 418." Lowering his voice just a little, George confided to his elder cousin that the company had some difficulties with imports and exports. "Guns, drugs and steel; it's all the same to the system. The law! Think of it this way. Economics must move forward but laws are put in place to regulate the flow so as to keep out the crazies. It's like the traffic laws. It would be impossible to drive out of your garage without breaking some regulation." Rick's mouth cracked into the widest of vicious grins. "You don't need to give me the soft sell. I know that justice died with Socrates if it ever existed in the first place. I just want to survive and maybe get a little patch in the sun."

George leaned forward and whispered. "One word from me and you're in." He purposely revealed his tattoo. "However, it would be ideal if you could assist us with a current problem. Given your previous furniture manufacturing background you may have some ideas."

"I don't …" Rick appeared puzzled. "The entire US economy runs on unkind activities, many that are illegal somewhere or other and others that deal in death." George took on the tone of authority. "The company needs to move arms outwards and drugs inwards. At the moment our biggest problem is the importation of heroin, opium and cocaine. It is absurd that the country runs on these things but sets up policing agencies to intercept them. All that talk about freedom and democracy. It's enough to make you puke. Most of the founding fathers of our illustrious nation hid dark personal secrets. Yet their closets would appear disgustingly bare compared with those of today's leaders. To survive systems seem to need the operation of their own counter systems and the playing out of a deadly game."

The elder cousin moved his mouth in such a way as to produce philosophical lines on his face. "Not having too many choices left, you can count me in." George placed a finger slightly over his lips. "Don't say anything to Rebecca. She likes to pretend." A nod from Rick sufficed. In the lowest of whispers he added, "As a freebie for the organization I can suggest that you make the contraband glaringly obvious, so obvious that the Customs will miss it."

"I don't understand," ventured George. "You could import chess sets," smiled Rick. "Think about it; the white pieces are molded from heroin or cocaine while the black are crafted from opium. The pieces are then encased in a clear plastic that will fool the dogs and the men." The youngest of the cousins leaned forward. "That's good, very good. I think it's safe to say that you have a new job."

"What about my maintenance position back in New York?" Rick appeared ever so slightly confused. "What did they do to you in those prisons?" shouted George loudly enough to disturb his sister. "I hope you two aren't brewing any more trouble," hinted Rebecca before returning to her television program. "I suppose I could telephone my resignation," mumbled Rick. George seemed concerned. "You've got to get a grip on yourself man!"

Having whispered his loyalty and readiness for his new opportunity Rick was on board. By the time he returned with Rebecca to her apartment his future was swimming before his eyes in an orgiastic extravaganza. "I hope George's prattle didn't confuse you," mumbled the girl.

"Not at all. He's done very well for himself under the circumstances." Rebecca glared a little but made no further comment.

"You know, Rebecca, all you can do in this life is play fair with whatever cards you are dealt. More than that is impossible." His cousin didn't answer other than to bid him good night. As he lay on his bed and drifted into sleep Rick's subconscious was having a field day. The dream varied from Marilyn's luscious body to untold tortures in nameless prison cells and back again. The president of the US was about to violate a church secretary when he awoke. Breakfast was scrambled eggs on toast. Rebecca dutifully brewed him a coffee before dashing off to work. "Make yourself at home. I'll be back at six."

"Hi Rebecca," Rick announced to the returnee. "It looks like I'll be around for a while. I've decided to work with George and quit my crumby job in New York. George has found me an apartment near his." Rebecca was shocked but not surprised. "I hope you know what you are doing," was all she could manage.

"You've got to be joking," Rick retorted. "After what I've been through what could be worse?" Admittedly there was no answer to that question.

It was only two days later when Rick left Rebecca's abode. The windy city turned on one of its tricks. Driving rain accompanied Rick's departure. Pools of water challenged his passage from the doorway to the cab. Turning the key on his new front door Rick entered a new apartment and a new life.

Chapter Fifteen

"You're quitting with only a week's notice?" The Human Resources Manager at Brown's was less than amused. "I'm sorry but I've found the Lord and God's work requires me to relocate to Chicago almost immediately." The raised eyebrows said it all.

As Rick departed from Browns and walked along the street he observed a compressed park. In that park was a bench and on that bench sat a homeless man smoking cigarettes and drinking some kind of plonk. Rick stopped and gazed at him from across the road. It seemed as if the man was smoking and drinking as a special kind of activity to mark the passage of time. It was if the act of consumption was designed to protect him in some weird way against time's passing. Undoubtedly, such destructive acts of consumption failed to arrest and indeed accelerated the ravages of that cruel god. The irony wasn't lost on the walker. Is such paradoxical behavior brought about by the very transience of life itself? Rick pondered on these thoughts for a while and then resumed his journey.

A lightning return to New York had been necessary to gather his few belongings and abandon his dingy rented room. By the time Monday had merged into Tuesday, thence Wednesday and finally Friday Rick felt as if he'd aged five years. He'd firmly associated this part of his life with his recurrent status as a perennial victim and wished to move on as rapidly as possible.

In keeping with his fledgling newfound optimism Rick flew back to the windy city. The laborious coach trip with its dismal stops at mundane and greasy diners was also consigned to the personal dustbin of history. Striding from the terminal building he noticed the morning sun bathing otherwise dull surroundings with euphoric color. Earthy scents mingled with the fragrances of a host of daffodils, petunias and roses.

Once again in his new apartment Rick couldn't help but notice its trappings of luxury; paintings hanging on the walls, electronic systems galore and a passable view of the city. Dialing the numbers he quickly reached George on his mobile. "You clear everything up ok down there?" George inquired.

"Sure thing. When can I meet the team?" The survivor of countless miseries was impatient to embark on a new episode and to wreak his revenge.

The following Thursday George brought his elder cousin to lunch at L'Escargot Vert, an eatery on the corner of May and Taylor Streets in Little Italy that dealt in French and Italian cuisine. Waiting for them was a disparate group of humanity; some women, some men and ages ranging between the middle-twenties to late-sixties. None of them were wearing suits. Clad in an array of garmentry traversing the full gamut from denim to twin-sets the ensemble could easily have been mistaken for a family reunion.

George performed the introductions. "Round here I'm called Jack," he whispered to Rick. Only first names were ever used and most of those were bogus. Everything was on a need-to-know basis and the whole affair now resembled a meeting of strangers at a bus stop, hell bent on creating trouble. Even the waitresses made certain to signal their arrival before venturing close. Only Spanish and English voices could be heard from the dining room to the brick-surrounded courtyard. French had been consigned to the menus.

"We liked your suggestion of chess set importation, Richard," boomed Alfonso, a middle-aged guy who belonged on a Harley. "Any more bright ideas?"

"I'm Rick...Richard and I have a couple of other thoughts." Nervously eying the gathering he spoke in a muted tone. "We could use crates marked 'US military hardware – for authorized personnel only.' For sensitive and urgent shipments we could employ frogmen." Gladys, a matron whose father had been in the navy, interrupted, "Frogmen! What do you mean?"

Rick, alias Richard, outlined his scheme. "Ships ply their way to and from our ports and are duly violated by Customs officers. Meanwhile, on many of our beaches, scuba divers come and go. My suggestion is a simple one. A ship with legal merchandise passes within a few miles of the coast carrying a diver. Our cargo is then packed onto an underwater scooter and, just before dawn, the diver, scooter and cargo slip over the side. A mile or so out from the shore the diver dumps the scooter and swims with the cargo covered in marine specimens such as kelp, to the beach. A parked auto then collects him. To avoid immigration-control problems that diver would previously have left that beach or another, collected the scooter from its predetermined position and rendezvoused with that vessel or another on its outbound journey."

It was not only Gladys who was impressed. "Amazingly I've never heard of this method," remarked a thirty-something computer type. "Certainly no arrests have ever been made involving such a scenario." Jemima, a stylish brunette in her late twenties and with generous breasts, cut in. "You were in furniture Richard and yet none of your ideas utilize that medium. Why is that?"

"Maam," Rick whispered, "furniture is simply a commodity like people's votes or anything else. What works on one occasion will dive on another, no pun intended." Jemima shifted her bosoms under her tank top. "Speak up Richard. There are no bugs here." Rick repeated his comment about the expiration date of furniture to a mutter of approval from the entire assembly.

After being formally accepted by the organization Rick was put to work, initially at a relatively low level. He was assigned the most penny ante of operations. Regardless of introductions trust in such enterprises is only built with the speed of the layered rise of termite mounds. Periodically, imports of dubious quality would arrive and have to be assayed. Outsourcing was cheaper in addition to placing a further level of operation between the organization and prying eyes.

A particularly shabby corner grocery was Rick's first port of call. Shimael's Exotic Foodstuffs was the front for a much more scientific endeavor. Powders of various descriptions were whisked into a hidden laboratory at the rear of the establishment and rapidly analyzed. The proprietor was known only as the Squeaker, in reference to his high-pitched voice and the slight odor of mouse and rat droppings that lingered around the shop. In addition to testing products the Squeaker bought and sold those of the smaller operators. His younger brother was a senior officer with the municipal police and Shimael's Exotic Foodstuffs had never even suffered a raid by the health authorities although ample cause certainly existed.

On his first visit Rick experienced the emotions of a newspaper tycoon reduced to selling papers. Colored juveniles as young as twelve, along with a handful of legitimate customers made their way in and out of the premises. "Talk about starting at the bottom," he muttered to himself. A fortnight passed with little variation in the routine. On one occasion he'd accompanied a cash collection detail visiting a small-time dealer. He'd been required to carry a gun and felt ambivalent about the extra weight. Otherwise it was daily visits to the Squeaker. At four in the afternoon one Friday he was exiting the establishment when a pretty brown face entered. It was Cecilia. Their eyes met with the fire of shared experience but no words were exchanged.

How she had turned up in Chicago Rick could not fathom. In any case he hoped that the matter of her unsatisfactory employment in his house in the Philippines had long ago been forgotten. He made an instant decision not to mention the chance encounter or the story behind it to the organization.

◇ ◇ ◇ ◇ ◇ ◇ ◇ ◇ ◇

Some years earlier and half a world away Dolores was hosting a party to celebrate her younger daughter's successful employment with an overseas hospital. The year before, when Cecilia had graduated her nursing course and begun work in Cebu City Doctors' Hospital, no merriment marked the event. Now that her daughter would be a dollar earner at Chicago General the largest celebration possible would be in order.

"Cecilia topped her class you know and has had excellent work reports ever since," Dolores remarked to a neighbor who questioned the justice of her offspring's good fortune. The San Miguel flowed along with the Tanduay Rum and every conceivable variety of edible Filipino culinary produce was laid out. In fact the mother had even purchased a color TV on the strength of Cecilia's new job. The guests, primarily relatives reinforced by neighbors and friends, hoed into the offerings. Chicken adobo, Chicken Ariscaldo soup and Lechon Baboy; it was all there. French champagne was, however, lacking but that would also be on the menu in a year or two, Dolores contemplated. The star of the evening, the about-to-be dollar earner, appeared in a low cut green gown that revealed her alluring cleavage, shocking some of the more elderly family members.

"With our precious Cecilia off to the historic home of gangsters, it's a good thing that Al Capone and his boys are no longer around," declared one thoroughly drunken uncle. A chorus of laughter from the back of the crowd may have been directed at the stupidity of the remark or else been recognition of the fact of Cecilia's questionable innocence.

The new green card holder's send off on the Saturday saw the whole neighborhood abuzz. Not one of the male relatives and precious few of the fair sex made it to church the next day. The final gathering at Mactan Airport was vociferous enough to cause serious pause to the vendors of endangered-turtle shell guitars and other useless wares. Like some Joan of Arc Cecilia was cheered to the plane that would carry her to Manila, the first leg of her journey to America from whence the dreams and the dollars would return.

The party went well enough, Cecilia reflected. Mind you I didn't really appreciate some of the comments or the sniggers about my virtue. I've had to support so many relatives all these years and most of the male ones spend their hours and my money in an attempt to have a good time. At least I never became a prostitute or sold my body. I always studied hard and worked. Sure, there were times when opportunity required favors in return but if I hadn't done it what would have become of the family? "Cecilia, would you like a gin and tonic?" The dirtiest of all the old uncles in my family was probably trying it on again. There were persistent whispers about him and girls as young as eight. Thankfully there were no rumors about him and boys. "No thank you," I replied and excused myself on the pretense of needing to find my sister.

If I say so myself, I deserve all this send off and more. Once out of their clutches it could be time for me to look after Number One. You never know, in America, I might find a man with money who's good in the sack. It'll certainly be a damn sight better than here. I hated having to sleep with the ugliest doctor in the hospital to ensure that my appointment would be confirmed. At least I didn't ever have sex with that foreigner asshole Rick Daly. I think I would've killed myself if I had.

"Don't forget us dear now that you're successful," Mum intoned. "Of course not, Mama," I reassured her whilst primarily thinking about myself. They call Chicago the windy city and they also say that it's an ill wind that blows nobody any good. Just maybe, a fortunate breeze will blow my way and allow me to escape my circumstances and my past. I'm feeling lucky in any case.

A few of my colleagues also gained posts abroad. Two received appointments in Dubai, one in Saudia Arabia and three in Belfast. When I told them of my posting I was unable to stop myself from gloating. "Belfast won't make your fortune, what with that age-old misery, and as for Dubai, if you think you'll have a life there, forget it. Marissa, I hear you're off to Saudi. I suggest you fill your vagina with super glue." I shouldn't have said it. Marissa howled for hours and the others gave me the cold shoulder for the rest of that celebration. That occurred a week before my send-off party.

As the night reached its zenith, I thanked everybody for their support and puked inside. I also promised to share my good fortune but who knows what my new life in the U.S. will bring? I'll just do what I've always done and take opportunities where I find them. The send-off at Mactan was thoroughly disgusting; a giant throng, including relatives and friends that I didn't know I possessed, imploring me not to forget them. When the plane lifted from the tarmac, for the first time in my entire life, I felt sort of weightless.

◇ ◇ ◇ ◇ ◇ ◇ ◇ ◇

The position at Chicago General was not exactly to the Filipina heroine's liking. Rotten shifts, involving much bum scrubbing and little serious nursing, left her angry. "It's because I'm Filipina that I'm treated like an aid rather than a qualified nurse," she confided to a Mexican co-worker. "They drag us here because they need workers and then treat us like little brown turds."

The Mexican girl laughed. "Welcome to the real world."

Needless to say, Cecilia's family were not satisfied with her monthly remittances. Six months had passed and the farewell party was still a 5/6 debt, which meant that Dolores had to repay the local moneylender twenty-percent interest per month, not to mention the TV. "The streets aren't exactly paved with gold," one of her letters to her mother had begun.

It was only after sleeping with a hospital security man that Cecilia discovered a loophole in the accounting system for morphine, general narcotics and other dangerous drugs. It was apparently very easy to falsify the dosage records of terminal patients in their final days. Once they'd died no one ever bothered to check them.

Cecilia felt sheepish pretending to be a hooker as she combed the streets. On only the second night she had learned of the Squeaker's operation. Henceforth between five and ten grams of morphine disappeared from the hospital along with other drugs every week. This newfound enterprise probably had more to do with her innate talents as an entrepreneur than any desire to please her family back home. Nonetheless the remittances doubled and Dolores stopped attempting to call her daughter collect.

By the time she ran into Rick Cecilia had acquired a comfortable apartment and a cherry-red Cobra sports car. She envisaged herself as a cross between Jackie Kennedy/Onassis and Imelda Marcos. Her support to her mother increased further. Having just finished dusting a shiny new stereo in Cebu one Tuesday afternoon Dolores was disturbed by a minor commotion at her door. An ensemble of four beggars stood there. "What! Do you think I'm made of money?" she shrieked. "Lias Ka! (Piss Off!)"

That chance encounter in the doorway of the Squeaker's convinced Cecilia that her old enemy was also engaged in the drug trade. She had never forgotten how he'd wronged her and shamed her family. His misfortunes, as far as she knew them, following Alma's allegations were not enough. The asshole had to be seriously taken down. Betraying the Squeaker's business was out of the question for obvious reasons.

"You think your husband is being unfaithful and also siphoning off joint assets?" Todo Alvarez leaned back in his plush leather chair. "Yes, that's right," confirmed Cecilia, clad in full nursing regalia. "I think we can get to the bottom of any such shenanigans," replied Mr. Alvarez. "We charge two hundred per day plus expenses." Satisfied with the proposal of the Alvarez Inquiry Service the girl handed over seven hundred dollars and described Shimael's Fine Foodstuffs as a place Rick regularly visited before heading off on a clandestine rendezvous.

"I've found your answer, Mrs. Johnson," Todo boomed into the mouthpiece. "It's a strange meeting place for a liaison with a mistress but he always goes to a warehouse on Grosvenor Street. After twenty minutes or so he catches a cab to an apartment at 198 Valediction Road. I didn't see any women coming or going. Your husband just may be innocent."

"Thank you so much, Mr. Alvarez," declared Cecilia. "I shouldn't be so suspicious." Todo appeared a little surprised at the response. "You don't want me to investigate a little deeper to be sure?" he asked.

"No, no. That's fine and you may keep any change from the advance as a tip." The entrepreneurial nurse replaced the receiver and smiled. Mr. Rick Daly would be fixed for once and for all.

"Hello, Municipal Police," Cecilia's voice quavered. "Yes, may I help you Madam?" Taking a deep breath she continued. "I've learned that some kind of drug disbursement center is operating at 55 Grosvenor Street. For reasons of personal safety I'd like to remain anonymous." Exiting the pay-phone booth Cecilia strode off chuckling.

Thirty minutes' warning had been cutting it a little fine but by the time the police raid descended on the warehouse in question they were confronted only with dozens of pallets containing cases of escargot bound for the city's more cultured restaurants. Twenty less-than-amused of the city's finest in full combat gear departed the scene. Not laughing either was the organization. Both George and Rick were summoned before it.

"Our surveillance has revealed that you were followed on at least one occasion, Richard. Since George is your cousin and initially vouched for you your fates are somewhat intertwined." It was Gladys who had spoken. The expression on George's face could have signaled the onset of a reconversion. "What the…?" Before he could finish his sentence Rick decided that it might be opportune to mention Cecilia. "On one of my visits to the Squeaker's I chanced upon this Filipino girl arriving as I left. She worked for me as a maid in the Philippines years ago before I fired her for dishonesty. I didn't mention it before as I thought she was an ordinary customer and a chance encounter was simply that." George appeared decidedly uncomfortable.

"Good that you cared to tell us this finally, Richard. Trust is the be-all-and-end-all you know." Gladys smiled weakly. At that the pair were dismissed.

It didn't take the organization long to trace Todo and Cecilia. Nothing was ever said to Todo. A break-in occurred one night but nothing was stolen. The aging private eye put down the event to the fact that a pharmacy had operated from the premises before and some addled druggie must have come by. The Filipina heroine of a tiny section of Cebu City wasn't quite so lucky. Direct challenges to the structure of a business are never treated lightly.

"That was a particularly long and disgusting shift," Cecilia remarked to the night guard as she exited the hospital. "That Mr. Somerton just took so long to die. You'd think people of that age could exhibit some grace about their exit." The guard smirked. "He was probably trying to summon up the courage to ask for a last naughty – with you my darling!"

Cecilia glared. "It's not funny, David. Just you trade jobs with me any time!"

Methodically the girl's footsteps departed the lighted circle surrounding the entrance and headed in the direction of the car park. Before she had reached her Cobra Roadster she was knocked to the ground, her stunned body prone to further attack. Her malefactors wore full balaclavas and were armed with knives. One held a blade to her throat in complete silence while the other pulled down his trousers and rolled a condom onto his erect member. Her skirt lifted, Cecilia's panties were ripped from her thighs exposing the sparsely covered target. A heavy hand covered the girl's mouth while her booty was plundered. Throughout the ordeal Cecilia's eyes flashed in the darkness. To come so far and be raped by American thugs! To her surprise the second attacker did not join in the invasion. Barely had the first pulled out of her when his accomplice flicked the shiny blade. The slash of silver across her throat against a backdrop of twinkling stars was the last sight Cecilia's eyes ever witnessed.

In the early dawn the entire car park had been taped off. Plain clothes and uniformed officers swarmed like flies around a carcass. Sergeant Everton gazed at the half-naked body. "Bit of a waste," he muttered to his colleague.

"You can't make jokes like that these days, Dean. It could cost you your job." His partner wasn't smiling.

"All right! Let's get serious then," asserted Everton. "This girl's been raped and murdered but there is no apparent evidence of any kind and from the look of the scene Forensics won't be able to come up with much either. The perp is obviously a practiced serial rapist. It's my bet he has a uniform fetish; nurse this time, private schoolgirl the next."

The forensic team confirmed the detectives' suspicions. No DNA of any kind belonging to the attackers was found. "It doesn't look good for us," remarked Everton's more junior partner. "The city stats reflect an alarming rise in rape cases with many ending in murder."

Everton frowned. "That ain't the half of it Mike. These rapists and killers are out there and in this case we have zero clues as to where to start the search."

Cecilia's demise was never even alluded to by the organization. The first Rick learned of it was when he picked up a newspaper. On seeing the photograph of the near naked corpse he momentarily imagined himself as the offender. Everybody's got some good points, he considered, and Cecilia's were definitely of a physical persuasion.

By the time the unfortunate news had travelled across the Pacific, Dolores had spent more and been attempting to lord it over her neighbors. The death of the dollar earner was a bitter blow to the family. If the sniggers of previously jealous folk weren't enough, the sudden re-emergence of poverty was the final straw. Barely had the coffin been lowered into the soil, after an expensive flight from the U.S., when Dolores turned to her elder daughter. "Lorida, you don't have much of an education or any special skills but you do have a good body. You will have to use it." Lorida glared at her mother. "Amateur mama san," she muttered beneath her breath.

Following the family's misfortune, the neighbors began to look Dolores and her brood down. Her elderly husband, long since separated from the avaricious harpy, lived in honorable poverty and exile in a far-flung province. Without any personal honor the matriarch's only claim to notice, was material wealth. Now that the gold vein had been prematurely extinguished, her clan was left to depend on its own virtue. The very friends and neighbors who'd fare welled Cecilia were now distant or even hostile. Before being dispatched to Manila to work as a whore Lorida had remarked on the sudden disappearance of most of their friends. "You don't need friends if you have money," her mother coldly replied.

◇◇◇◇◇◇◇◇◇

A doorbell rang in Chicago. George entered his cousin's abode. "That was a close call Bro'. Don't keep secrets like that from the organization again. That body is a bit like Greenpeace but with a different mantra. You are with them for life or death." Rick apologized again, explaining that he couldn't possibly have foreseen the danger that the deceased girl had presented. A few Budweisers later and the episode was forgotten. Their progress within the ranks of the company had soon resumed. Both now wore suits and were charged with higher-level appointments. The organization was doing well. Globalization effectively brought within their reach partners from as far afield as Russia and Colombia.

To think that criminals never discuss politics would be palpably naive. Rick was facing an associate over morning tea on an August Saturday. Known as Henry, a thickset man with sparse ginger hair and a ruddy complexion spoke in a critical tone. "George, I mean Bush not your cousin Jack, has been wonderful for our business along with countless others at the top end of town. The opium crop in Afghanistan is the best it's ever been and the Drug Enforcement Agency's funding has all but been extinguished in the wake of 9/11. The money is now being poured into the Bush Administration's global crusade to bring their brand of God and democracy to the Middle East. It's absolutely great for us that such an idiot could ever be elected to such a position of power."

Rick laughed. "I've never heard anyone complaining about how good business is before."

Henry seemed despondent. "God talks to him apparently or is it schizophrenia and in any case is there any difference? It's only a matter of time. Mark my words; he'll catch a bullet. The CIA'll get rid of him in the same way they got rid of Kennedy. Despite the advantages to us it is simply too dangerous to allow unstable drug addicts or simple-minded morons alone with that much power."

Rick lowered his eyes. "Why would they do that?" Henry continued but now sounded like a professor. "It is simply too dangerous for the world!

Democratic processes along with their media mogul masters simply cannot be relied upon to remove such ticking bombs quickly and effectively."

"What's your point then?" inquired Rick on behalf of the organization as much as his own. "We will soon have to face a business environment again where there is sane government and a properly funded DEA. To prepare future plans against the likelihood of the continuance of the present regime would be sheer folly."

"Bush is a great guy. Fox News says so!" Rick chortled.

"I suppose his daughters aren't vain strumpets then?" Henry challenged. Rick couldn't help but notice three portraits on the wall behind his companion. The first was that of Robert E. Lee, the second that of Jefferson Davis and the third was of Adolph Hitler. "Don't tell me you're an admirer of the Führer," grinned Rick.

Without smiling, Henry replied. "Bush is a much more dangerous fanatic than Hitler was. The difference between them is that Hitler possessed a considerably greater number of sensible ideas. I also couldn't imagine George Bush dying for his vision of the world as Hitler did." Lowering his spectacles the well-covered man kept on. "The media can be owned and the media controls democracy. So what is all this new democracy really worth? Should we spend all these billions, ignore the environment and destroy the fabric of the earth to export this kind of democracy all around the world? George Orwell would turn over in his grave!"

Rick appeared confused. "I don't understand. Bush Jnr. is good for our business and you're worried."

Henry looked decidedly contemptuous. "To start with," he implored, "it can't last long and we have to make business decisions on that basis. Secondly it would be very nice to leave some sort of habitable world for our children and grandchildren. Two people who should never have been born rich, or better born at all are Osama Bin Laden and George Bush. Not only is it a waste of resources but also power in the hands of such individuals further destroys the well-being of the planet. The price, as always, is paid by the poor and honest. Christianity and Islam aren't the most spiritually rich religions in the first place. The narrow, simple-minded expressions of faith often announced on their behalf are a denial of any intrinsic value that life may possess. The very stars twinkling in the blackness mock the folly of such foolish and intolerant men. Their piety is nothing more than a colorless shade of insanity. It's a sign of disastrous times when the American public considers a little stray lipstick a greater evil in its leader than a lunatic view of the world coupled with fundamental incompetence." Henry added a further remark. "Apparently our illustrious president once said while defending his privileged life, 'Money is like a magnifying glass. It'll make you nicer if you're good to begin with. However if you're a selfish, nasty sod it'll only make you worse.' Can you believe that? It's about as intelligent a remark as that line of Forrest Gump in the movie."

Rick sniggered. "Sure thing, Henry, if you say so." Henry hadn't experienced the years of unjustified imprisonment that clung to his associate. Two coffees later and it was time for Rick to depart. "I say Henry, where's your computer? Don't tell me you conduct business by hand?"

It was Henry's turn to purse his lips. "The more technology advances the more trouble we face and the further removed we are from life. Viruses and the like simply make computers too dangerous!" After Rick had accused him of being a Luddite Henry's voice raised itself a couple of notches. "Technology has produced excess population, pollution and climate change. Hell will have frozen over before our species makes any sacrifices to save the planet. The only likely solution to global warming will be a technological one; such as some way of extracting excess heat, along with carbon dioxide and other pollutants, from the atmosphere and converting them to energy, if any solution at all is to be found, which I doubt. In my opinion technology has merely complicated the basic human conditions – fear and greed."

Rick tossed off a parting remark. "If you're not at all greedy why are you working with the organization?" The answer was swift and sure. "Same as you. I want to survive and don't have too many options." Bidding his colleague a good day Rick exited the apartment and the building.

Chapter Sixteen

The odor of cordite mingled with the sickly scent of slowly evaporating blood. Four bodies lay at various points along the alley. Two were black, one white and the other Hispanic. Before the echo of the last gunshot petered out Rick had scampered along the stones and deftly removed three automatics, one 9-mm machine pistol and any wallets and Ids he could find. Only one of the prone figures belonged to the organization. Rick was thorough in his inspection of Eduardo.

The morning collection run had begun smoothly enough. Rick had been met at a designated northern suburban point by four of the company's soldiers. The run that day included, along with numerous small-time dealers, a medium-level operator known as the king. An old Harlem boy, barely out of his teens, he was the principal distributor for numerous gangs on the south side around Harvey. Bedecked in disgustingly opulent jewelry he lit his apartment in the manner of a Christmas tree. The collection itself transpired without incident. The trouble erupted as Rick and his boys departed. Barely had they entered the alley when they were fired upon. The ensuing gun battle lasted less than three minutes.

Sirens were sounding as the overseer mustered his remaining three comrades. "Time to go!" Rick shouted. "We've done all we can." The white Nissan X Terra cleared the scene twenty seconds or so before the first blue-and-white pulled up. Small furry figures scurried amongst the smoke, pools of vermilion and strobed shadows.

"We lost Eduardo," Rick exclaimed as the survivors entered the aged factory complex that had replaced the warehouse on Grosvenor Street. Charlie the Receptor yelled, "What the f... happened?"

"We were ambushed as we left the king's place. Of the five gang members involved three are dead in the alley along with Eduardo." Rick was genuinely upset. "Did you have time to clean up?" Charlie asked. Rick responded in the affirmative. The Receptor then added, "Better contact Gladys immediately."

The moment his backside hit the couch in his lounge room Rick phoned Gladys on a pre-assigned number. Somehow that lady could remain calm in the eye of a hurricane. "It's a shame about Eduardo's wife and two kids," she purred, "but death is a part of life and we have to keep going. Unfortunately, there will be fallout from this misadventure. The culprits will need to be tracked and dealt with and we always have to watch our backs. I would like you to visit one of our senior members whose acquaintance you haven't yet made. The details will be faxed to you in exactly two minutes. By the way, you did good." Evidently Gladys knew of Rick's phone call to her even before he did.

The shades of evening competed with the incessant gusts of wind for attention. Glancing at the wall clock Rick noticed that it was already half past nine. In line with policy he walked over a mile before reaching a main road. Five minutes had passed, by the time a vacant taxi chanced along. Climbing in Rick spouted, "1119 Greenway Drive, Barrington please." The vehicle sped off making its way through thinning traffic. Fifty-five minutes later the cab ground to a halt. "That'll be seventy-five dollars and fifty cents," announced the driver. Rick handed over eighty-five and walked off.

In actual fact 1119 Greenway Drive was a modest bungalow rented by a car salesman. Neither Rick nor the organization was privy to that information however. Any street numbers in the approximate range of 905-1250 were to be used as cab directions. As the yellow auto disappeared from sight Rick walked for at least ten minutes before reaching the smallest of intersections. In the faintest of moonlight a tiny street sign bore the words, 'Lincoln Lane.' Rick paced up the narrow road for what seemed an eternity. Nothing was visible from the thoroughfare save rows of magnificent hedges. Not exactly the small end of town, the man on-a-mission thought. Finally the road ended. At that exact juncture stood the grandest mansion he'd ever laid eyes on. It boasted its existence even in the darkness. The structure would have put many famous architects to shame. A Cape Cod-meets Eiffel Tower edifice challenged Rick's arrival above an exceedingly plush hedge. Pressing a dimly lit button on the gate Rick waited for a response. "Yes," a voice vibrated, "How may I help you?"

Taking a breath, Rick spoke at the button since there was no visible microphone. "4137," he declared, following Gladys's instructions to the letter. "Welcome Sir. Please proceed." At that the massive steel gates parted and the baying of hounds, previously audible, subsided. It was a considerable walk to the house. The spires of this particular Camelot, visible from the street, belied its true distance. At the completion of his lonely passage a dimly-lit doorway beckoned. There was no bell but the massive oak door swung open before he could knock.

A butler in full livery but holding an AK47 invited the visitor in. "Follow me Sir." Trying his best not to notice expanses of Italian marble, gargoyles that performed when you looked at them and a menagerie of exotic creatures that knew their place, Rick trailed along behind the armed butler. As he finished ascending a flight of stairs a young girl blocked his way. "I'm sorry. I didn't know Uncle was expecting visitors. I was about to water the potted plants. I'm Hannah." The butler scowled and Rick continued on. The third floor was the apparent destination. At that point Rick noticed the elevator but said nothing. After the longest entrance he'd ever seen Rick reached the study of Rodney Meier. Quickly departing the butler pushed him inside.

"It's a shame to have to meet like this!" Rodney extended his arm and Rick shook the appendage at the end of it. "Gladys informed me you were coming of course." Rick smiled weakly. "Since it is my task to clean the messes left behind by others Gladys decided that I should hear the full story from you in person." Rick wasn't so sure that his liberation was complete. The feeling that there is always someone looking over your shoulder dwarfed his aspirations.

"Sir," he began.

"Rod'll do," his superior countered.

"A gang attacked us during a routine collection and a shoot-out erupted. As you know, we lost Eduardo and they lost three of their members." Rodney smiled and offered his guest a drink. "You can have a girl as well if it'll jog your memory." Rick's subconscious kicked into overdrive. Slowly, deliberately he recounted every detail of the awful scene right down to the smells of aftershave lingering above the victims. The debriefing finished, Rodney tempted his visitor with some lobster medallions and wine. Too good to resist Rick enjoyed the hospitality for another hour before taking his leave.

As he passed the second level and before the armed butler would take charge of his exit he noticed the girl again. Her blonde hair framed an exquisite face and her night robe could not deny the fullness of her breasts any more than the allure of her slender figure. Once again blocking his path Hannah spoke. "I didn't catch your name."

"Rick, I mean Richard," the visitor responded with a mixture of lust and fear. The blue eyes stared endlessly. "Quick, give me your contact details." Stunned, he handed over a card and resumed his journey down the stairs. "It went well I trust Sir," the butler remarked as he showed the visitor the door. "No complaints," Rick responded as he entered the darkness.

His head was occupied with thoughts of the mysterious blonde as he trod the lengthy path to the gate. The moment he reached it the structure swung open and he faced the street once more. As the metal closed behind him the baying of hounds could again be heard. It was a very long walk before Rick reached another arterial road and waited for a taxi.

"What do you think?" the butler asked of Rodney. "All right for now but we'll probably need to have him liquidated within a year or two." The butler smiled. "Quality hired help is so very hard to obtain these days Sir." Brushing aside his lengthy silvery locks Rodney's eyes narrowed. "It does appear that Gladys and the whole organization have let standards slip."

The continual ringing of the telephone gave Rick no peace. He tried to ignore it but it wouldn't give up. Reluctantly he grabbed the offending machine. "Hello," he yelled, miffed at being awoken.

"It's Hannah. We met last night at my uncle's place." Rick perked up and felt a stirring beneath his pajamas. "Does the organization know you are calling me?" he stammered. "What organization?" Hannah asked. "I mean your uncle and his business," Rick rapidly answered. "I am a sovereign person and my uncle knows that," Hannah declared. "If you don't like me then that's another matter."

"No...wait," interjected Rick, "but we have to be careful."

"When can we meet again?" the girl intoned.

"Next Wednesday evening should be fine," answered the man, a shiver of fear descending down his backbone. "We could meet at Kevin's on W. Hubbard Street in the city, say at 8 p.m." A few seconds of silence followed. "See you then," a sultry voice murmured. Spasms of desire and anxiety alternated throughout Rick's being.

Wednesday arrived as it has a habit of doing. By four o'clock that afternoon Rick's nerves were getting the better of him. He felt that he should call the whole thing off but a sense of destiny intermingled with a massive case of the hots kept him from it. The morning's labors had been routine, collections and a little enforcement. The first throws of the coming winter lent an icy chill to the air. Glancing at his watch he noticed that it was already six-twenty-five. It was definitely too late to back out now. The thing was madness. Who was he trying to kid? What made him seek an early grave? The questions flew faster in his mind than the second hand on his watch. Yet the girl's beguiling smile and her forthright approach intrigued him. Unable to resist he resigned himself to his fate.

An understated entrance led customers from a moderately amorphous street into the halls of plenty. Kevin's was one of the most exclusive and upmarket culinary establishments in the city. Discretion, along with nouvelle-French, Asian and modern American cuisine, was served with the utmost aplomb. Rick, decked out in a white tuxedo, had arrived ten minutes before the appointed hour. Better to stride to one's fate than be hastily dragged into it. Eight o'clock came, then ten past and finally eight fifteen.

The solitary occupant of a table for two began to feel embarrassed as well as worried. What was happening? Was this some sort of test or joke? He was just about expecting the entrance of gunmen when his date arrived. Circling from behind the indoor greenery a waiter led Hannah to the table without ceremony.

"I'm sorry I'm late," the girl crooned. "It's a real hassle trying to hail a cab." Rick appeared puzzled. "You didn't come from home but from downtown?" Hannah shook her blonde locks. "I came from home all right but uncle forbids anyone in his house from ever ringing a taxi." Rick's appearance of confusion continued. It was obvious the girl didn't work for the organization so why did these rules apply to her? "May I ask why you are forbidden from simply phoning a cab?" he purred.

Looking as serious as this girl could manage, she whispered. "Since you are connected with Uncle you must know the reasons behind his excessive carefulness." Rick's mind felt itself a tabla erasa. Hannah continued. "I never discuss Uncle's business but as you are seriously involved with it I can't see any harm. As I'm sure you're aware, we're a Jewish family. Although we were all born here my uncle makes several trips to Israel a year." Her companion leaned forward. "His industrial maintenance-business is really a front." Rick felt his eyes were about to burst from their sockets. "We've experienced a few visits from Israeli and Arab people. Although Uncle never discusses his business with me, I'm not stupid. Uncle works for Mossad or Shin Bet and is doing his best to assist Israel in its quest for security and prosperity."

Changing the subject and chewing a morsel of seasoned, poached salmon Rick innocently inquired, "How did you come to live with your uncle in the first place?"

"Both of my parents died when I was really small. Apparently they were killed in a boating accident off Florida. Uncle said that they were trying to help some Jews who were being persecuted in Castro's Cuba. Uncle is my mother's elder brother."

"What is your last name then? I assumed it was Meier."

"It's Chibber, Hannah Chibber," the blonde answered as she touched Rick's hand.

Her companion couldn't help but notice the fact that her breasts somehow hardened beneath her evening gown whenever she said anything that she considered serious or important. The solitary candle flickered causing a cascade of soft shadows. By the time the dessert, chocolate mousse with white chocolate sails à la the Sydney Opera House, had arrived Rick had confessed to being an American asset of Mossad. The touch of Hannah's velvety fingers on his thigh reassured him. It was already eleven-thirty as the couple departed from Kevin's. Some ten minutes before, Rick had taken the plunge and kissed Hannah in an inappropriately passionate manner. The potted ferns at Kevin's blocked the view of one table from another.

Hannah's lips had fought back, almost aggressively and the chemistry had seemed to take control. His arm squeezing her waist Rick whispered, "It's not late. Would you like to come to my place for a couple of hours?"

Hannah disengaged herself from his grasp. "Not so fast. Let's not rush things. I want to know you better and I very much desire to see you again." Rick accepted her reply as a rain-check and offered to take her home. "You know the rules. I'll have to say goodnight here. Don't call the house. I'll phone you." By the time Rick hit the sheets in his apartment his main muscle was about to burst. A rapid dose of self-abuse was necessary before any possibility of sleep could occur.

True to her word, Hannah called Rick the following day. It was agreed. They would go to a disco. That date came and went with the same 'nearly but not quite' approach as the first. More clandestine meetings followed and Rick's level of frustration was growing by the day. It was almost a full month before the would-be pole-vaulter was able to lure his date to his apartment with the exaggerated promise that he was a master cook. Everything was perfect. His abode was neater than a pin. Soft lighting and candles beckoned the visitor. On time and on heat the shapely figure rang the doorbell. Rick forced a vodka and orange on her and returned to the kitchen. Oyster cocktails that suggested the main ingredient had died of old age were followed with trout à la Dresden. They were almost burnt beyond recognition. Still the girl ate them and the wine, at least was good.

The repast concluded, the couple adjourned to the lounge where soft music was ever so subtly enticing. They embraced passionately and the fever was consuming Rick when the girl again pulled away. "What's wrong?" he stammered. "Are you a virgin?" Hannah lowered her eyes. "Almost but not quite. When I was fifteen, I went to a party and this guy and I half did the deed before I pushed him off. He wasn't Jewish so it doesn't count."

"Neither am I," remarked Rick, "and I wouldn't like to think that I didn't count."

"My love can make you Jewish," a stone-faced Hannah replied. "I want to marry you. How about it?"

The girl was experiencing the flushes of love while Rick was at least feeling the methadone equivalent. Before the clock was able to count five seconds

Rick's past and future flashed before his eyes. Hot babe; secure future if I do, certain death if I don't, the thoughts rumbled. Breaking into a half-smile he exclaimed loudly, "You must know that I love you. Of course I'd be happy to marry you but I'm not Jewish." Hannah's eyes brightened. "You'll have to convert. That's all."

Before Rick was even aware of it Hannah had informed her uncle of the relationship. That magnate of capitalist prosperity did his utmost to talk her out of such a foolish enterprise but to no avail. Rick's life expectancy had increased and the wedding was arranged. Two months of compulsory lessons on Judaism led up to the big event. The wedding itself was surprisingly low-key, although very refined. From the organization only Gladys was present. She could pass for a Mossad agent, Rick mused even as he greeted other guests. After the last glass of Champagne was drained and the last guest had departed the happy couple were shown their bridal suite. It may have been just another room in Uncle's house but it was somewhat lavish. "That Rembrandt almost looks like an original," Rick remarked. "What do you mean almost?" replied his glowing bride. "It is an original!"

The honeymoon was sweet and short. The couple were dispatched to one of the organization's resorts in Puerto Rico for seven days. Then it was back to work. They would of course live in Uncle's house; he had plenty of room and it was much better for security. The groom's workload changed overnight. There were no more collections, no more enforcements and no more dangerous assignments on the street. Rick was now an administrator, only a level and a half below Gladys herself. Endless paper shuffling and computer-screen staring were punctuated by the demands of real business decisions. Rick almost felt important. Adjusting his little blue skullcap he reached a conclusion. The chosen people are indeed the winners.

The seasons came and vanished and Rick had apparently all that he could desire, wealth, power, sexy wife and endless opportunity. He didn't quite understand when Hannah and her uncle would join other relatives for particular religious ceremonies without insisting on his presence. They were just too kind to spare him those duties. However the demands of his employment kept him engaged. Hannah and he didn't go out too much. Mostly of an evening they'd watch television. The news was Rick's favorite program. In fact it was the only reality television that he could bear. When a CNN bulletin about Israeli settlers appeared on the screen Hannah remarked, "God promised our people those lands and the Palestinians are good-for-nothing layabouts when they're not actively engaged in some terrorist activity or other." Her husband stirred a little. "Don't you think that by stealing other people's land the Israelis are letting themselves in for endless violence?" Hannah looked as serious as he'd ever seen her. "Not at all. Eventually the industrious and hard-working people will secure the entire planet and everything will function properly. It's God's will in any case."

"You don't really believe that stuff, do you?" Rick hesitantly ventured. "It's not stuff. It's true and it's the only way the world can go," was the sullen reply.

Life at the top occupied Rick to some extent if it did not exactly keep him overly busy. Although his hours of toil were much fewer than in the past the increased responsibility took its own toll. Social occasions in this new station were largely displays of wealth only contained by the deep edginess born of saturated caution and intrinsic fear. Rick was puzzled by the non-attendance of any of the organization's leaders at any of the gatherings other than the occasional appearance of Gladys. The advent of some twisted insight caused him to empathize with the isolation that cloistered medieval monks and nuns must have experienced.

On the domestic front Rick had spent the first couple of months following the wedding performing an in-depth exploration of his wife's body. Initially he was far from disappointed. Temporarily devoid of lust sleep often took him peacefully as they lay on the bed. Their daytime exchanges were somewhat less satisfactory. Hannah had no job to speak of other than the care of the indoor plants and a little light dusting. Her not-infrequent excursions downtown for shopping and heaven-knew-what-else formed the basis of her personal entertainment.

"What have you bought this time?" Rick simply stared at his partner as she strode up the stairs in front of the armed butler who was struggling with several cardboard boxes. "It's a networked, digital entertainment system," was the casual answer.

"We already have everything electronic we could possibly need," Rick frowned.

"We don't have one of these. Anyway, its silver-grey components will look really cute in our bedroom." Her husband appeared singularly unimpressed. "We certainly aren't short of money but rather than simply buying junk you could make donations to charity if you want to spend."

Hannah sneered at him. "Charities are a con. They waste the donations they receive in administration or perks for the chiefs. In any case, they attempt to assist people who simply don't deserve to be helped." Rick said nothing but returned to his office. Unbeknownst to him, his wife got a real kick out of buying items and not using them. The joy of acquisition entirely lay in the storage of such things knowing that they were ready to use if needed. If Hannah was compelled to use one of these stored treasures for the first time, the experience resembled that of the loss of her own virginity. The frequency of their evening lovemaking fell from daily to three times a week and then twice. Hannah appeared to offer little imagination into the process. By the time four months had passed from the nuptials Rick had decided that, body or not, she had no mind.

Summer had bathed the entire city in optimistic hues and all seemed well with the world. Throughout Chicago land, people walked their dogs, cyclists traversed the tracks and joggers eagerly sprinted through the parks. Yet shadows from within can darken the brightest sunshine. On a Friday the late news sported one of the less attractive Israeli spokesmen, one Benjamin Gold, defending the killing of a group of Palestinian children. "Disgusting," mumbled Rick. His blonde paramour attempted to agree. "Those Palestinians are worse than disgusting. They are simply a waste of space, space that is badly needed by more-productive others."

Rick looked her hard in the eyes. "You think that Benjamin character is a sincere person who wants to promote peace and harmony in the world? He looks to be simply one of the grossest-possible, capitalist assholes."

"Just because he is successful doesn't mean he doesn't have a heart. You're simply a loser!" This was the first time Rick had heard that epithet directed his way from his bride. "Loser!" The very word evokes the suggestion of a lack of imagination and a talent for being one of the crowd who follows any particular fashion.

By the time summer had descended into fall Hannah had arrived at the idea that she shouldn't surrender her body to her husband more than once a week. The routine shopping expeditions continued unabated. One morning as he was about to enter his office Rick noticed some unopened acquisitions. Next to the label on one package was a hastily-scrawled phone number in scratchy, blue ink. At his desk he immediately dialed the digits. A male voice with a foreign accent answered. Rick replaced the receiver.

"Where are you going?" Rick asked as Hannah had announced on leaving the dinner table that she had an appointment. "For drinks with some of my girlfriends," she replied. "I didn't know you had any girlfriends. I haven't met any of them." Rick failed to suppress a telltale frown. "They're all Jewish. Anyway I've got to go. Don't wait up. I'll probably be quite late."

Unable to stop himself, Rick cast his mind back to the days in Cebu with Marilyn. On more than a couple of occasions the phone had rung and when he'd answered, it simply rang off. Had Marilyn been taking him for a ride all that time? She'd certainly replaced him quickly enough after his drastic misfortune with the law. He seemed to remember catching her talking earnestly with a handsome young man outside the factory one day. Marilyn's face had assumed a strange, embarrassed expression when he'd joined her. "A distant relative asking for money," was all she'd said.

Hannah was late. "I'm so sorry to have kept you," she mumbled as she took her place at the table. Every year, seven members of a teenage secret society from the Jewish girls' school she had attended held a social reunion at one of the city's top restaurants or nightclubs.

"Since you got married you seem to have lost the plot," remarked Ruth, a sallow lass with long, mousy hair and definite scowl lines on her face. Hannah denied any change in her loyalties and the evening progressed. It was indeed very late by the time her shapely form slid next to the sleeping Rick.

Hannah's once a fortnight or so demonstrations of passion began to impress her husband less and less. In his gilded prison he felt that he was a bee in the wrong colony. Sooner or later they are going to kill you, one way or another, he decided to himself before falling asleep. When he awoke, his nocturnal suspicions were reinforced. He was brushing his teeth when

Hannah raised her voice. "Your pajamas aren't folded. You're not only a loser but you're a slob."

"Get real," he tossed off as he continued brushing.

Precisely two weeks after Hannah confided to Rick that she was pregnant he vanished. Saying that he had an urgent business meeting to attend, he'd left the house at 10 am and didn't return. By 2 am on the following day Uncle had contacted Gladys and put in motion all the tracers that he could muster. Nothing. His son-in-law had completely disappeared. Hannah wasn't crying but she was worried. What might have happened to him that could put them all in danger?

The birds were singing the preceding morning as Rick left the house. All he carried was a fawn leather briefcase. His chosen course of action carried enormous risks. He knew that. Yet the American dream had become unbearable. Money, power and all its handmaidens had made their way into his life with all the force of a raging sewer. It was ironic that Hannah had called him a loser. He had never felt like a winner in all his time with the organization and never less so than after his marriage. Even when delving into his darkest memories of false imprisonment and lost love he didn't feel that he'd exacted any sort of revenge on the world's establishment. He now meekly acknowledged that he had become part of it.

Striding down the lane towards a suitable taxi hailing point he heard the flutter of wings as a starling took to the heavens. Oh to be free like that, he yearned. Why was he always a perpetual outsider in a shitty world? From the second the bird had taken to the sky he knew that his choice, however dangerous, was the right one.

"December the sixth" his watch declared as he hailed a passing cab. It was almost four months to the day since he'd consolidated and hidden much of his accumulated wealth from his time with the organization. Scrupulously, he'd never taken a penny that hadn't belonged to him yet had managed to squirrel away nearly $300,000. Still, such principles would not save him from their wrath. The cab dropped its passenger in the most average of suburban neighborhoods and sped off.

Briefcase in hand Rick looked for a quiet street. Finding one, he strolled as nonchalantly as possible along a row of parked cars. From his case he extracted a wire as he reached a silver Mercedes. The door popped and he slid inside. One minute later and the wires behind the dash had been connected and the motor roared into life. Rick felt pleased that all those unjustified years in various prisons hadn't been entirely wasted. Apprehension concerning the reaction of his late employers easily overcame any fear he may have had of the law. The Mercedes traversed the length of the street, turned the corner and was gone. On the two-hundred-and-fifty-mile journey north, to a railroad station just shy of Milwaukee, Rick had only encountered one police vehicle and it had simply passed by.

Dumping the Merc at his chosen point he walked a mile and a half until this area's rail junction came into view. During the journey he'd extracted a razor from his brief case and shaved his entire head of hair. Resembling a resurrected Yul Brynner, he purchased a train ticket under a false name and boarded the three-fifteen express for Salt Lake City. It was as good a destination as any and, as far as he knew, the organization had no presence in that particular town. A two-day journey afforded him more time for thought than he had desired. How far would the organization go to track him down and what would be the likely consequences if they were successful. He was doubtful that being the father of Hannah's pregnancy would save him. Hannah, herself, probably wouldn't overly mourn his loss. The thought of what may have been in store for his cousin George hadn't crossed his mind.

Alighting at Central Pointe Station Rick nonchalantly swung his brown leather case as he strode for the nearest exit. The snow-capped Utah Mountains stared down on him from their safe distance. Knowing what he'd left behind and its concomitant perils was one thing. Even the most immediate future was quite another. Having failed to form any particular plan during the journey the escapee decided to rent a car and drive round the city until he found suitable accommodation and some modicum of a plan. The lass at the Thrifty counter was a little surprised when, after showing the requisite credit card and driver's license, Rick paid cash for a three-day rental. "I'm sure you'll find this model Audi a pleasure to drive Mr. Davidson."

For the first hour Rick drove around the city center but its muted facades simply matched his own mental processes. In ever-expanding circles, the gunmetal-blue Audi aimlessly progressed into the suburbs while its driver waited for a miracle of inspiration born of kinetic energy. He really required a quiet place where he could think. The years in jail had never really afforded him that luxury nor had his time since.

As the rows of houses gave way to areas of meadows and forested thickets and more-sparsely-situated dwellings Rick felt the clean odor of powdered snow blowing in the wind. As he sped past a country lane lined with hedgerows, he caught the briefest glimpse of a sign. For a reason of which he was entirely oblivious Rick stopped his vehicle and reversed back to the green wooden slat with large blue letters. "Yolander Ashram" it announced to any potential audience. The words meant nothing but an inexplicable curiosity caused him to enter the lane. Some five miles or so later a clearing presented itself from amongst the surrounding woodlands. A compact cluster of simple yellow-brick buildings occupied the center. The most prominent was of two stories and sported a strange symbol above the doorway. Another figure off to the left was much more easily recognizable. It was a large black swastika on a background of golden marble.

He parked the Audi and hesitantly approached the door. Having heard the vehicle pull up a woman in her thirties and wearing robes of plain white cotton emerged. "May I help you Sir?" she inquired brushing wisps of dark hair from a serene face. "Pardon my intrusion," Rick responded, "but I was driving by and saw your sign. Curiosity got the better of me I'm afraid. What is this place?"

"It's an ashram," smiled the girl. "We are a community who practice Yoga. It is a path to enlightenment, inner peace and understanding." Rick appeared confused and remarked that he thought Yoga was simply an exercise system. This establishment was definitely not some Neo-Nazi training camp and it occurred to him that it might be an excellent location to lie low. He graciously accepted Janie's invitation to look around. As the pair passed various rooms and the visitor spied groups of oddly assorted members of humanity meditating, chanting or exercising he couldn't help but notice the contrast with the Abu Sayef camp he'd seen in Mindanao all those years before. There were just as many attractive females in attendance but there was no aura of urgency and the swastikas belied any semblance of militarism or violence. Between the various buildings a number of individuals were industriously toiling, some tending the next spring's gardens while others were performing more mundane chores.

"Yoga is one of the most ancient belief systems," Janie remarked. "While not being a religion in any traditional sense it is certainly a lot more profound than a gym routine. Its essential philosophy is that all enlightenment is ultimately to be found in the self rather than in the world." Rick couldn't help himself. "I observed some swastikas around the entrance to the office. I don't suppose Hitler was some kind of misguided Yoga practitioner?"

"Not at all," was the calm but definite reply. "The swastika is an ancient Sanskrit symbol that represents auspiciousness. The Nazis borrowed and reversed it for a while but now we've got it back. It is also often to be seen on both Hindu and Buddhist temples. Those two religions share many common sources with Yoga." Rick bowed his forehead ever so slightly. "I, myself, freely admit to being somewhat confused about the nature of existence. If you had a single wish what would it be?" The glow on Janie's face seemed to add to the inanity of her guest's question. Humoring him Janie laughed and answered, "I suppose it would be to discover a medicine that could cure human greed and selfishness and then have it placed in all the world's water supplies." Rick laughed until Janie added; "If we can't understand ourselves any god won't do it for us."

The end of his impromptu tour left Rick with more questions than answers. "Is your community a sort of monastery where you shun all things physical?" His guide smiled in a way that revealed her inner beauty. "We don't shun the physical or the world in general but we place a spiritual knowledge at our center. Only with a peaceful but active spirit centering our existence can the physical world have any real meaning or purpose. The spiritual and physical worlds can, and should, live in harmony." Rick loosed one last question. "For someone who decides to join your community how much does it cost?"

Janie appeared shocked. "Nothing, although donations are always welcome. Members earn their keep through work. It is a part of Karma Yoga that we should be able to perform even the most mundane and arduous tasks without the slightest sense of misery or any meaningful discomfort." Rick's mind shot back to Werttenburger's defense of 'Arbeit Macht Frei.' Just perhaps there was a grain of truth in it. Marx's theory of the alienation of labor, the Nazis glorification of work and Karma Yoga's emphasis on right action all buzzed around in his head like flies in a bottle. "Would it be possible for me to live here?" he found himself whispering. "I'd like to give it a try for a while."

"Certainly, if you wish." The visitor promised to return on the morrow and departed.

At precisely 11 am the next day, a Sunday, Rick and his meagre possessions arrived by taxi. The simple life and low calorie food took some getting used to as did the hours of often back-breaking toil in the fields. Aside from periods of meditation and other related practices no enforced code of silence existed in the community. The tranquility and quiet that festooned the halls and the walls were simply born of two things; the fact that the people there accepted themselves and their existence was one and a lack of idle chatter was the other. Individuals tended to only speak when they had something to say or a genuine question to ask.

It was while threading mantra beads that Rick made the acquaintance of Sarah, the runaway daughter of a publishing millionaire. Twenty-nine years old and a graduate of sales and marketing she possessed an inner surety that highlighted her hazel eyes and curvy chestnut hair. That otherworldly serenity was complemented by a somewhat earthy curve of the lips when she smiled. Almost the first communication of import she had directed Rick's way was a challenge. "In essence belief is a reflection of what you do. Right action is more important than any mere belief," she asserted as if to forestall any possible mistakes on Rick's part. A bond nevertheless formed between them and it was only a matter of days before each knew all the salient facts about the other with the exception of Rick's life with the organization. Personal enlightenment may help to deal with the world but it can't entirely stop it in its tracks.

One Saturday afternoon following lunch Rick was walking through what, in the spring, would be a flower garden when he spotted Sarah reading on a bench. He strode over and sat down beside her. "As well as being a lovely person," he announced, "I find you physically alluring but I suppose all bodily relationships are forbidden here?" Expecting a speedy rejection and a confirmation of his fear he half turned his head. The girl leaned forward and kissed him ever so chastely on the cheek. "Physical relationships and sexual love are neither encouraged nor discouraged," she whispered. "If the flesh follows the spirit rather than leading or misleading it, all is in harmony.

Although selfishness and greed are more ephemeral than the real values of life, their effects on the world often outlive their origins. The intertwining of bodies or souls must be completely unselfish."

Rick gently touched her hand. "Everything starts and ends within us I suppose," he murmured in reply. "The trappings of life are but a sideshow."

"Quite," said Sarah as she simply gazed into his eyes, "and I feel the same about you." However long he would stay in the community and whatever would come, Rick finally knew that he was on the right road, the road back to himself. He was never to lay eyes on George or Rebecca again. By the time the spring had arrived with its explosions of color George had also mysteriously vanished. Resigned to her loss Rebecca had been able to cope and continued in her employment. Some years later she married an electrical engineer and produced three children.

If the wish of death had lain over the Philippines in the eighties and nineties, it had now spread to the U.S. and thence the whole planet. The Organization continued to prosper and the Neo-Cons in the White House, along with their allies on the Religious Right, continued to shake the Earth as if it were a rag doll, choking the life out of it. In that opaque cloud, which is the future, lay a financial meltdown, the like of which hadn't been seen since the Great Depression, the election of a black man as U.S. president and countless, spectacular natural disasters, followed by the next president, an elderly and unpredictable narcissist. Back on this side of that unknown mist, events marched inexorably onward.

Across the Pacific, priests preached brotherly love, countless unwanted babies made their way into the world and armies of bargirls and beggars fought for every piso. In Cebu, Marilyn was working late at the factory in an attempt to close the books on an overdue order. The computer whined its way to a halt. "Shit!" the woman cursed, perspiration flowing down her brown cheeks. Then the lights went out. Nay